COME TO
ME QUIETLY

PRAISE FOR THE NOVELS
OF A. L. JACKSON

Lost to You

"I was completely hooked from the second I opened *Lost to You*... a beautiful and powerful love story."   —Flirty and Dirty Book Blog

"*happy sigh* I loved this! Absolutely fantastic! A. L. Jackson is one of the most talented authors I've ever read. Her words have a way of reaching deep into your heart and not letting go."

—Aestas Book Blog

"Can A. L. Jackson write anything but excellence? Not in my eyes! Somehow, she always finds a way to get my insides twisted into so many emotions that I feel like it is all happening to me.... 5-star perfection!"   —Madison Says

"A beautiful, heart-stopping love story with a bit of heartbreak thrown in the mix.... You will sigh happily, swoon, smile, cry, and get pissed off. What a great range of emotions to keep your face glued to your screen."   —The Book Enthusiast

"This is an amazing story of two people and their wonderful beginning, how a friendship can grow and develop into so much more, the trials and tribulations that are soon to follow."

—Guilty Pleasures Book Reviews

continued...

When We Collide

"A great read.... The intensity in the novel is extraordinary and I look forward to reading other books by A. L. Jackson."

—Reviewing Romance

"Reading *When We Collide* was like a slow, agonizing torture, but in the best way.... I felt so much love and hope for these characters. It was an amazing read."

—The Book List Reviews

"Books like this remind me why I absolutely ADORE reading. Books like this that grab me, hold me captive, envelop me in the story, and leave a mark on my heart."

—Aestas Book Blog

"A. L. Jackson delivered another emotionally driven love story. I was captivated from the first page until the last. This book evoked empathy, tears, anger, and hope in me. This is another book that will stay with me for a while."

—Romance Lovers Book Blog

Take This Regret

"An incredible touching love story that will have you on the edge of your seat needing to know what happens next; will there be a HEA?!?!... *Take This Regret* is one read I won't soon forget; it still haunts my thoughts ... a truly amazing, beautiful read."

—Flirty and Dirty Book Blog

"WOW!! This is an achingly beautiful, heart-wrenching book about a second chance at love and with a wonderfully sweet HEA that tugged at ALL my heartstrings!! ... I cried. I laughed. This book touched my heart, and I will never forget this story <3. It was an absolutely beautiful read that is definitely going on my favorites shelf!"

—Aestas Book Blog

"Oh this book was amazing. I know I gush like a schoolgirl, but I cannot contain myself when I find a story that leaves me clutching its pages to my heart . . . or in this case my Nook to my heart. . . . My heart broke with this story, I cried for this story, and I fell in love with all the characters from beginning to end."   —Tina's Book Reviews

Pulled

"A novel that will pull at your heartstrings . . . [and] leave you convinced that the power of true love can conquer anything."
                                        —Jersey Girl Book Reviews

"If you want a story that fills your heart, *Pulled* is one you should read."   —Flirty and Dirty Book Blog

"What an emotionally intense roller coaster of a book! I read the whole book with my heart in my throat, either holding my breath, choked up, or in tears. My heart was literally pounding for most of the story. I read the whole book in one sitting—couldn't put it down!"
                                        —Aestas Book Blog

"This story ripped my heart right out more than once, and convinced me that I should buy stock in Kleenex. It also warmed me from the inside out! . . . After being swept away by *Pulled*, I'd read an instructional manual that had A. L. Jackson's name on it!"   —Book Snobs

"I need everyone to prepare for a gushy review. Because I will not be able to control myself with this one. I won't even try. I usually try not to fangirl but yeah, I'm fangirling, and it's not even in an attractive way. I LOVED this book. I am all about the angst and heartfail . . . and this is full of it."   —Books Like Breathing

COME TO ME QUIETLY

The Closer to You Series

A. L. JACKSON

 NEW AMERICAN LIBRARY

New American Library
Published by the Penguin Group
Penguin Group (USA) LLC, 375 Hudson Street,
New York, New York 10014

USA | Canada | UK | Ireland | Australia | New Zealand | India | South Africa | China
penguin.com
A Penguin Random House Company

First published by New American Library,
a division of Penguin Group (USA) LLC

First Printing, January 2014

 REGISTERED TRADEMARK—MARCA REGISTRADA

LIBRARY OF CONGRESS CATALOGING-IN-PUBLICATION DATA:
Jackson, A. L.
Come to me quietly: the closer to you series/A. L. Jackson.
p. cm.
ISBN 978-0-451-46796-6
I. Title.
PS3610.A25C66 2014
813'.6—dc23   2013031497

Printed in the United States of America
1   3   5   7   9   10   8   6   4   2

Set in Bell MT
Designed by Spring Hoteling

For my family. Nothing is worth doing if I don't do it for you.

Acknowledgments

I have a few very special people who I would like to thank:

My momma . . . who always supports me . . . no matter what.

Katie, because you know I couldn't do this without you.

Molly, Kristen, and Rebecca for sprinting with me every morning and listening to me whine that you all write way faster than I do ☺

Kevan Lyon for working with me through a brand-new experience, for your patience in answering all of my questions, and for the advice you give. I'm so thankful for you.

Claire Zion of New American Library for helping *Come to Me Quietly* become what it is today. Thank you for taking a chance on me.

I would also like to say a special thank-you to Robyn Rosenberg. Robyn participated in a fund-raiser hosted by My Secret Romance for Vicki Rose Stewart, who was undergoing treatment for cancer. Robyn won the opportunity to name a character in one of my books. As you all meet Augustyn Moore in the pages of *Come to Me Quietly*, know Robyn picked a very special name for her in honor of this awesome fund-raiser.

COME TO
ME QUIETLY

Prologue

Dashed lines blur until they become a solid line. My bones vibrate from the thousands of miles I've spent straddling this leather seat, the muscles in my right arm screaming from the hours my hand has been locked on the throttle.

But I don't stop. I can't, and I don't know why. Something in my gut spurs me forward. I plow ahead.

Hot air blasts my face and my hair thrashes in uncontrolled chaos. I bite back a bitter laugh.

Uncontrolled chaos. That's exactly how they described me.

The desert sky goes on forever, an ocean of the deepest blue. The city rises like a beacon in the distance. Because I am drawn.

What am I doing?

There is nothing here for me. I know it. I've already destroyed it all. I destroy everything I touch.

Still I can do nothing but press on.

ONE

Aleena

I was propped up on my bed with my sketch pad balanced on my bent knees. Megan was doing her best not to laugh from where she sat cross-legged at the end of my bed, bouncing.

"Hold still," I commanded, biting my bottom lip as I attempted to get her mouth just right. The shading was difficult, and I wanted it perfect. Megan had the most genuine smile of any person I'd ever met. I refused to mess it up.

"But I have to pee," she whined. She bounced a little harder. She couldn't hold it in any longer, and she released this hysterical laugh as she rolled off the edge of my bed. "I'll be right back."

With a groan, I tossed my sketch pad to the bed. "You're such a pain in my ass, Megan," I called after her as she ran out my door and across the hall to the bathroom. She'd gotten up to pee at least three times in the last hour. The girl could not sit still to save her life.

"That's why you love me so much," she yelled back.

The bathroom door slammed behind her, and I picked the pad back up to study it.

Megan's striking face stared back at me, smiling, her normally long blond hair traced in shades of charcoal, her normally blue eyes wide and black.

She'd been my best friend since she'd moved here from Rhode Island during our sophomore year of high school almost five years ago. I loved drawing her because she was so different than the typical model who offered herself up. She was short, just shy of the five-two mark, wore her curves well, and had a unique face. It was somehow both sweet and curious, this constant expression that made me think of innocence trying to work itself out.

She still lived with her parents in the same neighborhood where I'd grown up, just two streets over from my old house where my parents and younger brother still lived. She hung out here a lot at the apartment that I'd shared with my older brother, Christopher, since I'd graduated from high school two years ago. Christopher and I both went to ASU, and our apartment was near the campus. I was going to school to be a nurse, but God, sometimes I wished I could do something with my art. I knew it was absurd, that there was little chance that anything would come of it. That didn't mean I didn't want it.

She was grinning when she came back less than two minutes later.

"Feel better?"

"Oh yeah." Climbing back onto the bed, she crawled forward to steal a peek.

I hid the pad against my chest.

"Let me see." She reached out and tried to grab it.

I shook my head and held it closer. "You know the rules."

"I know, I know." She sat back. No one ever got to see. No one except for me.

From the floor, Megan's phone rang in her purse. She leaned over to dig it out. When she rose back up, excitement had transformed her expression. "It's him," she mouthed to me as she accepted the call and brought it to her ear. "Hello?"

Turning back to my sketch, I tried not to smile while I listened to her talk to Sam. She'd been chasing that guy for the last month, ever since she'd hung out with him at a party our friend Calista had thrown in May to celebrate the end of last semester. One kiss and she was hooked. I wasn't so sure he felt the same.

"Yeah . . . we can come . . . okay, see you there."

She dropped her phone to the bed and squealed.

Oh God. Megan didn't squeal. She was in trouble.

"Sounds like you have a date tonight," I muttered, my attention trained on the motion of my hand.

"Not me, we," she countered. "Sam is having a party tonight, and he wants us to come. I can't believe he actually called," she said, obviously talking to herself. "Two weeks and no word from him. I was beginning to think he was going to ditch me."

Beginning to?

So maybe I was a little protective of my best friend.

I hopped off the bed and went to my closet, dug through until I found the little black skirt I'd tucked in the back. I yanked it from the hanger and tossed it to her. "Here . . . wear this. It'll look a lot better on you than it does on me. You know it was those legs that tripped Sam up in the first place. I think the guy literally stumbled." I pointed at her. "And you better make him work for it."

"Oh, he's definitely going to have to work for it. You know me better than that." Megan held up the skirt to inspect it. "This is really cute." She looked up with a grin. "Maybe you should wear it. You know Gabe's gonna be there." The last she said in that singsong voice that she only used because she knew it annoyed the hell out of me.

"Pssh," I huffed under my breath, and she laughed because she of all people knew Gabe wasn't really that much of a draw. Gabe was my kind-of boyfriend. By kind of, I meant he was a guy who wouldn't leave me alone or take no for an answer. But he was unbearably cute and sweet in a boy-next-door kind of way and I didn't really know how to cut him loose without hurting his feelings.

And he was safe.

She lowered the skirt to her lap. "You should really quit stringing that guy along. It's kind of sad." Her tease turned serious, her blue eyes sober as she looked up at me from the bed.

I tossed a pair of shorts to change into on my bed. "I'm not stringing him along, Megan. He's the one who's strung himself to me."

"Whatever, Aly. You just keep telling yourself that. You always do."

I could see the concern pass over her eyes, could almost hear the argument pass through her lips, *the lecture.*

"Just don't, okay?" I said.

She blinked a couple of times, as if doing that would clear whatever picture she saw in her mind. "I just don't get you sometimes, Aly."

The party was mellow, just a few people hanging out on a Thursday at the house Sam shared with a couple of other guys.

Most of us were out back, sitting around the pool drinking beer. The yard lights were off, the area cast in a muted glow from the lights shining through the bank of windows inside Sam's house. Megan was curled up with him on a lounger at the far end of the pool, their voices hushed and relaxed. Behind me flames rose and crackled from an in-ground fire pit, and a few people sat around in the chairs that circled it.

Leaning back on my hands, I dipped my feet into the pool. Water rippled out over the surface, the ridges illuminated above the shadows as they lapped across the pool. Even at eleven o'clock at night, it was still hot. Summer in Phoenix was my favorite. It always had been. Heat saturated everything, radiated from the concrete and pavement, pressed down from the sky. Bugs trilled and birds rustled through the trees. I loved that I could be in the middle of the sprawling city and still feel like I was out in the wilderness. Peaceful. There was no other way to describe it.

I wasn't surprised when Gabe settled down beside me. We'd chatted a little throughout the evening, but for the most part, I'd avoided him. He was shirtless and only wore a pair of white swim trunks. "You want to join me?" he asked, inclining his head toward the pool in invitation.

"Nah. I'm good," I said, even though the thought of the cool water was incredibly appealing.

Tilting his head back to get a better view of me, he almost smiled. Strands of his light brown hair flopped to the side, and his dark brown eyes swam with something I wished I didn't see. "You're missing out," he said.

I laughed quietly and shook my head. He was so obvious.

"I am, huh?"

One side of his mouth twitched. "Yeah, you are."

"Fine," I said.

What can it hurt?

Or I guessed the more appropriate question would be, why did it hurt? It was stupid. Childish. But I didn't know how to let it go.

Forcing myself to my feet, I pulled off my tank top and slipped out of the little shorts I'd worn over my green bikini.

Gabe's expression lifted with slow appreciation.

Embarrassed, I turned away and jumped in. My body sank to the bottom of the pool. I floated, weightless, the length of my black hair spreading out and drifting away. It was cool, invigorating. The water blocked out the voices and the noise of everyone else, and for a few seconds, I reveled in the solitude. When my lungs grew tight, I propelled myself up to the surface. I sucked in a huge breath of air as I flung my hair back from my face.

Gabe was already waist deep in the pool, smiling at me. "You have to be the most gorgeous girl I've ever seen, Aly," he murmured as he edged forward.

Lights from inside cast his face in shadows, but I could see the beauty in his silhouette. And I wanted to want him, wanted to somehow get back the part of me that I'd given away that night so long ago.

I didn't say anything, just stared at Gabe as he inched forward. I didn't stop him when his hands found my hips and didn't stop his kiss.

It felt nice.

But there would always be something missing.

TWO

Jared

Everything had changed even while everything seemed to remain the same. I rode the streets, searching. For what, I didn't know. In the six years I'd been gone, the city had crawled out past its boundaries, but the old neighborhood appeared as if it'd been frozen in time, like a snapshot I looked at from afar. A picture I'd been erased from.

I pulled onto the dirt off the main street, directly across the street from where I'd grown up. Every memory that ever mattered I'd experienced here. They were only that. Memories. I propped my booted foot on the ground to hold my bike up while I just stared. Cars flew by, my vision blurred in the flashes of metal.

What the fuck was I thinking? That this was a good idea? Because it was most assuredly not a fucking good idea.

I'd been back in town for almost a week. It'd taken me that

long to even build up the nerve to get this close to the old neighborhood. Maybe I just wanted to torture myself, to make myself
pay a little more, although no amends could ever be made. I'd
already tried to pay the price, but fate wouldn't even allow me
that.

As if I were anchored to the past, I couldn't force myself to
leave. I could almost see us playing in the middle of the quiet
street, hiding, chasing, laughing, running through the vacant
land that backed the neighborhood. If I strained hard enough, I
could hear my mom's voice as she leaned out the front door and
called me to dinner, could see my father pulling in to the driveway at the end of the workday, could picture my little sister's
face pressed against the window as she waited for me to return
home.

All of it was an echo of what I had destroyed.

My chest tightened, and I fisted the grips on the handlebars
as the anger raged. Aggression curled and coiled my muscles
and I squeezed my eyes closed. A twisted snarl rose in my
throat, and I bit it back and held it in. My eyes flew open as I
gunned the throttle and shot down the street. I wound through
cars and pushed myself forward. I had no idea where I'd end up
because there was no place I belonged.

I just rode.

Hours later, I sat with my elbows propped up on the bar, my
boots hooked over the footrest on the stool. I took a long drag
from my bottle of beer, eyeing Lily from where she watched me
with a coy smile from behind the bar. The girl'd had the nerve
to card me, and we'd been fast friends since.

At least I hoped we were. A mild grin lifted just one side of
her mouth before she shook her head and turned away to lean

over and restock some beers, giving me the perfect view of her tight little ass.

Ice-cold liquid slid down my throat, and I breathed out a satisfied sigh. I'd forgotten how fucking hot the summers were in Phoenix.

When it felt as if I traveled every street in the city, I'd pulled in to the parking lot of this little bar. I was starving and in dire need of a beer. The place was pretty packed, filled with guys who appeared to be looking for a reprieve after a long day at work, there to unwind and catch the game, mixed in with some groups who were probably college students, dotted with a few like me.

Lily disappeared into the kitchen and reemerged with my burger. She set it down in front of me. She leaned across the bar on her forearms. Pieces of her chunky blond hair fell to one side as she tipped her head. "So, are you going to ask me for my number or just stare at me all night?"

I raised my brow as I took another drink of beer. "I figured I'd just wait here until you get off." I wasn't one to go through the motions or humor girls with pretenses.

She laughed with a hint of disbelief. "Pretty sure of yourself there, huh?"

I shrugged as I polished off my beer. I wasn't, really. I just didn't care. If she asked me back to her place, cool. But I wasn't going to be all torn up if she didn't. I'd find someone else. I always did.

Lines dented her forehead as she turned her attention to my hands, and she reached out in an attempt to trace my knuckles.

My heart sped, my hands fisting as I drew them back, my jaw tightening in warning as I lifted my chin.

She frowned when she looked up and found the expression on my face. She rocked back before she appeared to shake off the jolt of confusion she felt at my reaction. "You want another beer?"

"That'd be good," I said, my tone hard. It was always the same. They always fucking wanted to touch, to know, to dig. I didn't go there. Ever.

She nodded and turned away.

With an elbow on either side of my plate, I wrapped my hands around the huge burger and leaned in to take a bite. It tasted like heaven. I suppressed a groan. It'd been way too many hours since I'd had something to eat. I popped a fry in my mouth and went in to take another bite when in my periphery I sensed someone come to a standstill. He started to pass, but hesitated again before he stopped. Out of the corner of my eye, I kept a watch on him. All I could see were his hands clenching and unclenching at his sides, like he was trying to make a decision about something. I didn't acknowledge him, just focused on this fucking delicious burger and hoped the dude got some common sense and walked away before he got his ass beat.

He came in closer to the bar and cocked his head around to look at me. "Jared?"

My head snapped up to take in this guy who was really fucking tall, and even though he was lankier than shit, it was pretty clear he could go a round or two. His black hair was wild and sticking up all over the place, and his dark green eyes were wide with shock. He dropped onto the barstool next to me, staring at me like I was some sort of apparition.

I was pretty sure we were each having about the exact same effect on the other. For a minute every muscle in my body froze, my mouth gaping, before the shock wore off. Then I laughed and grabbed a napkin and wiped it across my mouth as I spun my stool toward him. "Well, shit, if it isn't Christopher Moore. How the hell are you, man?"

A thousand memories pushed to the forefront of my mind. I could see them all there, too, flickering across his face.

Christopher and I had been thicker than blood. He'd been both my best friend and the brother I never had.

A smile erupted on his face and he shook his head. "I'm good . . . really good." He blinked as if he still couldn't believe I was there. "How have you been?" His tone shifted, grew heavy as he leaned with one elbow on the bar, facing me. His attention shot from my face to my hands fidgeting on my lap and back up to my face again. He sat back, his brow pinching together. "Where have you been, Jared? I mean . . . I haven't heard from you in years. Why . . ." He wrenched his hand through his hair, unable to complete the question, his voice trailing off.

What the hell was I supposed to say? Christopher had written me all these bullshit letters saying none of it was my fault, that everything would be okay, that he *got* it, but he got *nothing*. How could he? I was the one who lay in my cell at night with the pictures of what I'd done burned in my mind. When I closed my eyes, they were the only thing I saw. And it was most definitely *my fault*. I never returned any of his letters, never called, never let any of them know where I went once I was released. I didn't need Christopher or anyone else to feed me lies, to try to convince me one day I'd heal or some fucking garbage like that. Maybe my heart beat on, but I died the day *she* did.

I trained my voice, acted casual. "I've been working up in New Jersey the last few years. I was able to save up some money, so it's been good."

He pressed his lips together. "And when did you get back?" he asked, although I heard the question. *Why are you back?* I was glad he didn't ask because I didn't fucking know.

"About a week ago."

Lily showed up in front of us with a fresh beer and began

wiping down the counter. Her gaze landed on Christopher. "Can I get you anything?"

"No, thanks, I'm good." He waved her off and turned back to me. "Where are you staying?"

I sipped at my beer. "I've been staying at this shitty motel while I look for an apartment . . . across town."

For a second he worked his mouth in consideration. He released a breath and cocked his head to the side. "Why don't you come stay with me while you look? It'd be cool to catch up. It has to suck to be living in a motel."

"Nah, man, I couldn't impose like that."

"It's not imposing. You're like family."

Internally I cringed at his assertion. Yeah, maybe I'd been like family once. Not anymore.

Christopher reached over, grabbed my beer, and drained half of it. I stifled a laugh. The guy hadn't changed at all. Christopher was notorious for *borrowing* stuff. If I was ever missing anything, I knew where to find it.

"Help yourself," I muttered as I waved my hand at my beer, and he just smirked.

"Anyway . . ." He tipped the bottle in my direction as if in thought, working something out. "I have a place I share with Aly. It's just a few miles away. You'll have to sleep on the couch, but it's got to be better than living out of a motel. This is really cool. . . ." He nodded as if he were trying to convince himself this wasn't a really bad idea. "I'm glad you're back. It will be good to catch up . . . ," he rambled on before he slowed. He must have read the surprise on my face.

Aly is his roommate?

"Our parents and Augustyn still live in the old neighborhood, but when Aly decided to go to ASU, we figured it'd be

COME TO ME QUIETLY

cool if she lived with me since we're going to the same school. She moved in a couple of years ago . . . right after she graduated from high school," he added as if to clear up my confusion.

If anything, it grew.

He just laughed. "Jared . . . she's twenty years old."

I tried to work it out in my head, the little black-haired girl who'd followed us around like we were the greatest things in the world while we teased her relentlessly. Still I would've killed for her. A grin fought for release when I thought of her knobby knees and buckteeth. By the time she was twelve, she was so tall and gangly she could barely stand on her two awkward feet. The last time I saw Christopher's sister, she must've been about fourteen, but that year was just a blur. I couldn't even picture her at that age.

I smiled lightly and shook my head. "No shit?"

"Man, you've been gone for six years. What'd you expect? To come back here and everything would be the same?"

I didn't know what I expected.

Christopher let me off the hook with an easy grin. "It's really good to have you back, Jared." He stood and tossed a twenty on the bar, then clapped me on the back. "Thanks for the beer. Now go grab your shit. You're coming back to my place."

Christopher gave me his address, and I rode across town to the motel to get the few things I had, then headed back. It had to be getting close to midnight. Traffic was light, and the trip took me less than ten minutes. Their apartment was in Tempe right near ASU. I turned right into their driveway and up to the gate, then entered the code Christopher had given me. It swung open, allowing me entry into the huge complex. Large three-story buildings were situated around the property, and sidewalks sur-

rounded by trimmed grass and small shrubs lined the walk-
ways. I didn't get impressed by material shit, and it wasn't like
this was the foothills or anything, but it was a thousand times
better than the hole I'd been staying in since I got into town a
week ago.

Why I let Christopher talk me into coming here I wasn't
sure. I'd come to Phoenix without intentions, without expecta-
tions, only with the few meager belongings I could strap to my
back and this foreign need in the pit of my stomach.

I no longer understood joy, but I had to admit, it was good
to see his face.

I had some money saved up from the construction job I'd
somehow landed back in New Jersey. I'd been a supervisor and
made good money. No one knew me from Adam there, and my
records were sealed since I'd been a minor when everything
went down. The day I turned eighteen, I was released, and I'd
hitchhiked my way across the country, putting as much distance
between this place and myself as I possibly could.

Funny how I ended up right back here again after running
so far.

I was going to have to find a job soon. I wouldn't run short
of money for a while, but I'd need some kind of employment to
put on my application if I wanted to get my own place. I couldn't
stay with Christopher forever.

Really, agreeing to come here at all was a train wreck waiting to happen.

He'd hate me before I was gone.

I'd bet on it.

Winding around to the back of the complex, I parked my
bike in one of the visitor spots in front of his building. I hiked
my bag farther up my back and tucked my hands in my jean

pockets as I ambled up the stairs to the second-floor landing. There were only two doors. Apartment 2602 was on the left. I rapped on the metal door.

Two seconds later, Christopher opened it. Cold air blasted across my face from the air conditioner, and I welcomed it as Christopher widened the door to let me in. "Come on in."

"This is seriously cool of you," I said as I stepped inside and took in my surroundings. It was a big, open room, the living area off to the left and the kitchen with a small, round table to the right. The two were separated by a low bar with three barstools sitting in front of it. The couch was in the middle of the living room. Behind it, a large sliding glass door led out to a small balcony.

Christopher gestured toward the couch. "Make yourself at home. Aly and I are pretty casual around here. I'm not doing much of anything this summer but sitting on my ass because I figure my senior year is going to be brutal, and Aly's working at a little restaurant while classes are out for the summer."

"Oh yeah? What are you studying?" I asked. Christopher had never been much of the studious type. I felt bad for even thinking I was surprised he'd made it that far in school.

He shrugged. "Just getting a bachelor's in business administration. I have no clue what I want to do with it, but shit, my parents saved all that money for me to go to college. I figured I'd better make good on it."

"That's cool. I'm sure you'll figure it out."

"Thanks, man. I hope so." It seemed like he wasn't so confident. He ran a hand through his messy hair and heaved the air from his lungs. "Listen, let me grab you a blanket and pillow."

He headed down the hall, tapped his index finger on the first door on the right. "This is Aly's room. Off-limits, obviously." He craned his head back. "She's kind of private and pretty much keeps to herself. You two probably won't run into each other all that much since she's working a lot while classes are out for the summer."

He touched the door on the left. "And this is Aly's bathroom. I don't think she'll mind if you use it." He said it as if it didn't really matter that much, but I couldn't imagine a girl wanting to share her bathroom with a guy she didn't really know.

"My room's at the end of the hall. There's a bathroom in there, too, if you need it."

"Thanks, man." I dropped my bag on the floor next to the huge black leather couch. It faced a large black TV stand with a flat-screen sitting on top of it. Controllers for a game console were stuffed inside a drawer with the wires sticking out.

I inclined my head toward it. "You still play?"

I kinda wanted to laugh because I used to have to drag his lazy ass outside to play or ride bikes or whatever the hell I wanted to do because Christopher always had his nose in a video game. He'd been the scrawny kid. When we were growing up, I'd kicked an ass or two in his name. Nobody had messed with him after that.

I hated fighting then, hated even the sight of the tiniest amount of blood. But I did it for him.

After everything went down, fighting was pretty much all I did. When the pressure built, *the anger*, it had to be released. Fighting served as the perfect outlet—the way the adrenaline spiked, the way it rose until it cracked me open, then flooded through my muscles and wept free from my veins, draining everything until I felt nothing.

Those were the only nights I could sleep. They probably would've let me out earlier if they weren't constantly pulling me off some kid who got in my way. Of course assholes to beat on in juvie were in no short supply. The population there was just a constant string of punks who deserved to get their asses kicked anyway.

Christopher laughed as he opened a closet in the hall. "Nah, I don't play all that much, but it's cool to unwind every once in a while." He tossed me a blanket and pillow. "You're welcome to stay as long as you want. I set a spare key for you on the coffee table." He pointed to the silver key before his hand fluttered in the direction of the kitchen. "Aly and I share food. Just be sure to chip in or whatever when she goes to the store."

"Yeah, for sure." I dropped the blanket and pillow on the couch, sat down, and unlaced my boots to pull them off. Midnight approached, and I felt wasted, worn, but I doubted I'd catch much sleep tonight. Anxiety was my constant companion, and it'd grown since I'd gotten back into town. A disquiet rumbled somewhere deep inside me, the same feeling that had urged me onto my bike and out onto the street little more than a week ago. I hadn't even made a conscious decision to come.

The last four years since I'd been out of juvie I'd been focused, but without a goal. I showed up at the job site every day, worked hard, fought a little, and fucked a lot. A pathetic substitution for life, but it was all I had. And I'd had no intention of ever changing it.

Then nine days ago I got up in the morning and got on my bike and just rode.

Christopher pulled his cell phone from his pocket. "I'm going to give Aly a heads-up that you're here. I don't want her coming in and freaking out that there's a strange guy sleeping on the couch."

Nodding, I kneeled down and unzipped my bag. "Thanks again. I'm going to grab a shower and call it a night."

"Sounds good. Clean towels are in the hall closet." Christopher hesitated at the end of the hall, then finally said, "I'm glad you're back, Jared."

My jaw tightened, but I lifted it in his direction. "Yeah, me, too."

The shower felt awesome. I kind of felt bad to have my naked ass surrounded by all of Aly's girlie shit, like I was some kind of unwilling voyeur, but there was nothing I could do about it. I grabbed a bottle of body wash and squirted a mound into my palm. Coconut. I lathered it over my body with my hands and rushed it over my face. Damn, it smelled good.

Shaking my head, I resisted the urge to laugh because this whole thing was insane.

I toweled off, pulled on some boxer briefs and a clean pair of jeans.

Wandering out into the main room, I rubbed the towel through my damp hair and glanced over at the microwave. Already twelve forty.

Okay, so not really all that late, but was it weird Aly was still out? If I were Christopher, I wasn't sure how I'd deal with it, a sister out at all hours of the night. If I thought I couldn't sleep now . . .

My little sister's face hit me before I could stop it. *God.* I hadn't seen Courtney since she was nine. Not since the day she'd gone to live with my grandparents three weeks after I'd destroyed our family.

In the months that followed, my grandparents had wanted me to go with them, too, like maybe if they took me out of the house where my father drank away his days, they could save me from the downward spiral I was on. But I'd refused. There was nothing they could do to help me.

I was so much older than Courtney that I really hadn't ever known her all that well. I wondered what she looked like now— what she was like—if she was happy or if I'd ruined her life, too.

I flipped all the lights off except for the one that glowed beneath the microwave, spread the thin blanket out over the couch, and sank down onto it.

It was as comfortable as it looked.

Tucking the pillow under my head, I stared up at the darkened ceiling. Cold air pumped continuously from the vents, keeping out the suffocating heat outside. Everything felt incredibly still and silent. I could barely hear the muted passing of cars out on the main road and the quiet hum of insects in the shrubs outside.

Minutes ticked by as I lay alone with my thoughts. Nighttime was the worst, when the memories were so vivid, the images so graphic I was sure if I could just reach out far enough, I could stop it. Change it.

Fix it.

I'd do anything to be given that chance.

When I could stand it no longer, I let my eyes drift closed. They started as flickers, small blips in time. My heart sped as the sickness I kept down all day clawed through my veins and pounded in my ears. Nausea surged and I draped my arm over my eyes, squeezed them tight, wished for anything that would blot it out. Heat seared me from the inside out, and sweat broke out across my forehead and down the back of my neck.

Pain slammed me as everything closed in.

And all I wanted was to die.

THREE

Aleena

Cool water lapped around my waist as I waded toward the steps. I climbed out, the heat of the night a blanket of comfort as I emerged from the pool. Gabe trailed close behind me.

I grabbed a towel from the pile sitting at the edge of the pool. My hair was soaked, plastered against the sides of my face and clinging to my back. I rubbed the towel over my face and through my hair.

On the lounger, Megan was lost in Sam, a tangle of limbs and whispers.

A soft snort escaped my nose. She was making him work for it, all right. I couldn't blame her, though. I'd never seen her look at someone the way she'd been looking at him tonight. I just hoped he didn't turn out to be a complete asshole.

I glanced back at Gabe. I hoped Sam and Gabe were alike because I was sure he wasn't anything close to an asshole. Gabe offered a tiny grin as he grabbed a towel for himself, a silent affirmation of my perception.

I realized tonight had been nice, that I felt good, and maybe spending time with Gabe didn't really hurt all that bad. I smiled back at him.

I turned away, laughing at a few of our friends who decided it was late enough and they'd had enough to drink to peel all their clothes off and jump in the pool.

Glad I climbed out before I ended up a party to that.

Megan rose like a shadow in the darkness, her voice hoarse. "Hey, Aly, I think someone keeps trying to call you. Your phone is lighting up like every five seconds." She reached for it from the small table where I'd left it, held it up while the backlight glowed, the ringer silenced. "Oh, looks like it's Christopher calling," she said, turning it toward me.

Barefoot, I tiptoed to where Megan still lay curled up with Sam. The backlight faded as I took my phone from her. I ran my finger over it and saw I missed three calls from him. "Weird," I mumbled as my nerves spiked.

"Everything okay?" Megan asked.

I lifted one shoulder as I redialed. "I don't know. He tried to call me three times." Christopher never checked up on me.

Over the years, things had changed so much between us. When we were younger, Christopher had done his best to ditch me while I did my best to keep up with him and his friends. Funny, it was his idea that I move in with him once I graduated from high school. Since then, we'd grown really close. We looked so much alike, his green eyes just as bright as mine, though his hair was a shade darker—so black it was almost blue. He was tall, built in all the right places, and thin everywhere else. It made me laugh at how many heads he turned. When I moved in, I'd needed some time to get used to the constant string of girls he had parading in and out of his room. In the end, it came down to respecting each other's privacy. We'd worked it out. He did his thing while I did mine.

I wandered out into a quiet corner of the yard. A slow dread seeped over me as I dialed the phone. I held the towel close to my body as if it were a cloak of protection. The call rang twice before Christopher answered.

"Hey," I rushed out, "is everything all right?"

"Yeah . . . ," he said, his voice doused with distinct relief when he spoke. "I just needed to catch you before you got home."

The small panic that had built up in my chest subsided, curiosity taking its place. "Oh . . . okay. What's up?"

He hesitated, then practically begged as he whispered, "And please don't get mad, okay? Because I really need you to be okay with this."

I felt a frown form between my eyes. I could almost see him shifting uncomfortably as he sat on the edge of his bed. The vibe of this conversation was completely out of character for my typically carefree brother. "What's going on, Christopher?"

He blew out a gush of air. "Do you remember Jared Holt?"

The name was enough to knock the breath from my lungs.

Did I remember him?

When I looked back now, I wondered how it was possible for a heart to be broken at fourteen. But my heart had, because it'd broken for him. Still it was something my young mind could never fully comprehend. My feelings for Jared had haunted me, left this hollowed-out place deep inside me. I'd held on to that remnant of pain for so long, until it faded and transformed and became this mystery that inhabited the deepest recesses of my mind. A shadow of a memory.

The mention of his name ignited it, basking it in light and bringing it to life again.

I swallowed the lump lodged in my throat, though I still choked over the words. "Of course I remember him. Why?"

"He's back, Aly." As if he didn't notice my shocked silence, he continued. "Cash and I were at The Vine having a couple of beers, and he was there, just sitting at the bar like he'd been there all this time." I could hear the sadness wrap through Christopher's voice.

And I could picture the boy, his hair so blond it was almost white, his ice blue eyes somehow warm, dancing with joy and ease and mischief, his red lips stretched in a teasing smile.

Then all I saw was his pain.

"Is he okay?" I whispered.

"I don't know, Aly. How could he be?" Christopher released a defeated sigh. "He's . . . *different*. But he's here, and that's all that matters right now. I mean . . . he's *here*, at our apartment. He's been staying at some old motel, and I told him he could stay here until he found a place." Christopher paused, hesitating. "And God, Aly, I hope I didn't make a mistake inviting him here. He's been in so much trouble and I don't want to go asking for more of it, but seeing him tonight . . . all I could think about was all the good times we spent together as kids. He's my *best friend*. It doesn't matter what he did—nothing's ever going to change that. I couldn't just let him disappear again. I already told him you need your space and not to go bothering you. I really am sorry I didn't ask you first." With that, he stopped talking, an expectant silence hovering in the space between us as he asked me for permission, for this to be okay.

I didn't know if it was. A thousand what-ifs and fears and butterflies took flight in my stomach.

But even if it wasn't okay, there was no possible way I could say no.

"Yeah . . . okay. I don't mind him staying with us for a while." I bit my lip and blinked as I said it, trying to hold in the hysteria bubbling up in my chest.

In distinct contrast to my panic, the anxiety in my brother's voice lifted. "Thanks, Aly. I owe you."

"Don't worry about it."

Of course Christopher had no idea what it meant to me.

"Can we not mention this to Mom and Dad? I know it's our place and all, but I don't need Dad riding my ass about it. You know how he felt about everything."

"Sure," I said.

"Okay, I'll talk to you later, then."

"Talk to you later," I mumbled before the call went dead.

I turned back to the party. Megan lifted her head from the lounger, her eyebrows drawn. "What's going on?"

I shook my head. "Nothing. Christopher just wanted to let me know an old friend is back in town." I shrugged like it had no effect on me. "He's going to be staying with us for a while."

Megan shot up. "Really? Who?"

"Just an old friend who grew up with us. Jared Holt," I said with forced nonchalance.

She frowned. In all these years, it was a name that had never once been uttered from my mouth. "He left before you moved here," I added because I already saw the questions building in her eyes.

Her frown deepened, but for now, she let it go. I knew I'd be hearing about it later.

Gabe reached for me, but I subtly pulled away. "I think I'd better head home." I slipped my shorts and T-shirt over my damp suit.

"Are you about ready to go, Megan?" I asked as I gathered my things and shoved them in my bag. My hands were shaking. *Damn it.* I slung my bag over my shoulder as I stood.

Megan glanced over at Sam, who was running lazy circles along her arm.

"You want me to take you home later?" he asked as he looked up at her.

She turned her attention back to me, apologetic. "I think I'll hang out here for a little while, if that's okay?" She bit at her bottom lip. I knew that expression well, and heard her silent *please.*

I returned a look of my own, my eyes soft, but pointed. *Be careful.*

The nod of her head was almost imperceptible. "I'll call you tomorrow," she promised.

It was crazy that we knew each other so well, could read each other without saying a word, yet she knew absolutely nothing about the one thing that affected me most.

"Okay, see you later."

Gabe's hand found my elbow. Everything about his touch was gentle. "I'll walk you out."

I didn't say anything, just walked silently at his side, through the house, and out into the stillness of the sleeping neighborhood. I clicked the lock to my white Toyota Corolla. The yellow running lights flashed and I opened the door. Gabe dipped down to kiss me, and I turned my cheek.

His breath washed over my face in a frustrated huff as he edged back a fraction. "What's up with you, Aly? One second we're good and the next you won't let me touch you." He leaned in closer. "You're always so fucking hot and cold. Didn't you feel that back there? How good we could be together?"

I inclined my head to look up at him towering over me. "I'm sorry, Gabe," I whispered as I shook my head. I didn't want to hurt his feelings, but maybe Megan was right. I was just leading him on.

His hand was warm when he brought it to my cheek. "I'm not giving up on you." His touch was tender, sweet.

He dropped his hand down to take mine, and he ran his thumb along the raised ridges that disfigured the outside of my left thumb. I squeezed my eyes shut and forced myself to keep from yanking it away. I hated when he did that.

"I'll talk to you later, okay?" I muttered.

I jumped into the driver's seat and started the engine, leaving Gabe standing in the middle of the street staring at me. I sped the short distance back to my apartment. My heart thundered so hard I felt it in my ears.

How many times had I imagined this? Seeing him again? Just to know he was really okay. So many of my years had secretly been given to him. Nights spent in worry, plagued by questions I didn't understand. Seeing him would put it all at peace.

I would finally be able to let it go.

I drove around to the back of the apartment complex and pulled into my covered parking space. I sat there for the longest time, trying to calm my racing nerves.

Sucking in a deep breath, I climbed out of my car and grabbed my bag from the passenger's seat. Heat rushed over my skin, constricted my chest. With each step across the parking lot, my apprehension rose higher, this overpowering need to see him wound up with acute fear.

Finally I found the courage to slip my key into the lock. Quietly, I edged the door open to the darkened room. Muted light bled from the kitchen. The air inside tasted thick with the unknown. My heart rate increased as I chanced a step deeper inside and shut the door. I could hear him, the shallow breaths he exhaled, this tension that radiated through the enclosed space. For a moment I stilled. Pictures of us playing as kids ran through my mind, the way he'd wait for me to catch up, then tug at my hair when I finally did. *"Hurry up, slowpoke, before your brother makes you go home."* The memories of that boy drew me forward.

My eyes slowly adjusted to the faint light. His outline came into view, this unrecognizable man stretched out across the length of the couch, lost in sleep. His bare chest rose and fell, the motion almost labored, as if he struggled to get his lungs to work. One arm was flung over his face. He slept in his jeans, his feet extended over the end of the couch.

The entirety of his exposed body was marked, covered in lines and colors and indistinct designs. I edged forward. An unknown fascination drew me on, my fingers twitching as I fought the need to feel something familiar in this man who was so entirely unfamiliar. I held my breath as I closed in on the couch, inched forward, and allowed my gaze to travel along his body.

His eyes popped open, and I gasped as I stumbled back.

He jerked upright, his eyes wild as they worked to focus on me. They softened minimally as he took me in, roaming as they searched. Even then, they pinned my back to the wall.

I just stood there, breathless.

When he whispered, his voice pierced something inside me. "Aly?"

I was a fool if I ever thought I could let it go.

I blinked and tried to orient myself, forcing myself to speak. "I'm sorry for waking you."

He said nothing, just watched me with fiery eyes. I fidgeted and dropped my face under the intensity of his gaze. Flattening myself against the wall, I slid farther down the hall and fumbled behind me to find my doorknob. I pushed it open and escaped inside because I had no idea what to do with all the thoughts that tumbled through my mind.

I stood in the middle of my room, staring at the back of my closed door. A faint glow of light crept in from underneath.

Shedding my clothes and damp suit, I pulled on a new pair of panties, some sleep shorts, and a matching tank. I crawled onto my bed, flopped on my back, and stared at the ceiling.

My pulse accelerated as I thought of him on the other side of my door.

Jared Holt was here.

A whisper of a smile curled my lips. He was real, no longer a veiled mystery that I'd hidden away in my heart. He lived. He breathed.

And God, if he wasn't the most beautiful thing I'd ever seen.

When I woke up the next morning, diffused morning light slipped into my room through my blinds. Blinking, I stretched, extending my toes and lifting my arms over my head as I yawned. *Jared.* He was the first thing on my mind, and just the name made me smile. This morning, there was no need to coax myself out of bed. A flicker of excitement sparked in my chest when I thought of seeing Jared in broad daylight, hearing him speak, learning what he was like now. I crept across the floor. Cracking the door open, I peeked out. A blanket lay rumpled in a pile on the couch, and I could hear water running from a faucet in the bathroom.

I tiptoed into the kitchen and rummaged through the refrigerator to find the container of orange juice. I stood on my toes to get a glass from the top shelf of the cabinet, filled it halfway, and took a sip. It was cold as it slid down my dry throat, and I closed my eyes as I swallowed, listening acutely as the faucet turned off and the door creaked open. A fever of nerves raced through me, my senses keening when I felt him emerge behind me.

I was still trying to reconcile the memories of my brother's childhood friend, the one I'd fancied as my own even if I had only been a delusional little girl, with the man I'd caught a glimmer of as I stared at him in the dark last night. I tried to make it all add up, the real man who was here with the fantasies I'd played out in my mind over the last six years, the images I'd conjured of Jared as he'd grown and I'd wondered and prayed that one day our paths would cross again. With just the glimpse I'd caught, I knew my imagination hadn't even begun to come close.

His movements were slow as he inched around the bar and into the kitchen. For a moment, we stood in awkward silence, tension radiating between us. He finally mumbled a low "Good morning." His voice was thick, hoarse. My stomach knotted in anticipation as the sound slipped across my skin.

"Good morning," I whispered back. I took another sip of orange juice as I steeled myself. Then I finally gathered the nerve to look over my shoulder.

And I froze when I was able to finally really see him.

God.

Flickers of memories flashed through my vision, pictures of an almost white-haired boy who had spent so much time at my house when we were growing up that he might as well have lived there. The way he was always laughing and the constant tease poised on the tip of his tongue. But above all that, he'd had the biggest heart of anyone I'd ever met. I could never forget the way his sharp ice blue eyes still managed to appear gentle when he spoke to me, or the way he was so interested in everything happening around him, his curiosity extending to the leaves on the trees and even the bugs that crawled along the ground.

Now . . .

His hair had darkened a shade or two, the blond touched by the slightest of browns. It was short on the sides, and the top was just barely long enough that he managed to run his fingers anxiously through it as he stared back at me, while I stared in shock up at him. He wasn't as tall as Christopher, but tall enough to tower over me.

My hand clenched around my glass as my eyes widened. Then wandered.

Stubble coated his jaw, which was clenched tight as he worked one side of his mouth, nervously grinding his teeth. He smelled of peppermint and the faintest hint of cigarettes, this combination that was intoxicating and not the least bit unappealing. I couldn't stop myself from studying him, from taking in every inch of this man who held me in the palm of his hand without the slightest awareness that he did.

He stood in my kitchen in only his jeans. His waist was narrow, his shoulders wide. Sinewy muscle flexed down his arms. Strength rippled with even the slightest movement, and his jeans clung to hip bones that jutted out just above his waistband. My attention drifted down his legs to where he stood barefoot on the tile floor of the kitchen. Even his feet were sexy.

I blinked away the stupor. No. The images my mind had conjured had definitely not done him justice.

But none of those things were what I really saw. Instead my

attention went to what I hadn't fully made out last night. Almost every exposed inch of skin was covered in ink, these intricate designs that bled and wept, wound together to create an allusion to death. They all blended so none were distinct, just sweeps of color and innuendo that blurred from one horror to the next. Flames licked up along his entire right arm, a pair of bright blue eyes staring out from their depths, seeming to beg as if they were eternally damned to this raging fire. My attention was drawn to his hands, where the designs dripped down over his wrists and leaked onto his fingers. The knuckles on one hand had numbers that read 1990. The knuckles on the other were marked 2006.

Sickness coiled in my stomach as I realized the significance of the statement he made.

This boy was painted in his pain.

Tentatively, I dragged my gaze back to his face. Those gentle eyes were no longer gentle, but harsh as they pinned me with a completely different kind of intensity than had shattered me last night. This intensity raved with anger and hinted at disappointment.

He lifted his arms out to the side with his palms up, as if he were some kind of offering, although a sneer transformed his gorgeous face. "Go for it, Aly. You want to get inside me, too? Let's hear it."

I spun the rest of the way around so I was facing him. In the same motion, I floundered back. The sharp edge of the counter bit into the back of my hips as I instinctively moved away from the agitation curling through his body. "I didn't say anything," I said, the words chaotically tumbling from my mouth.

A shot of disbelieving laughter escaped him, and he shook his head as he turned away, his hands laced on the back of his head as he seemed to struggle with what to say. He whipped back around. "Yeah, well, you didn't have to. I get it. I don't need your fucking pity, so do us both a favor and pretend like I'm not here, all right?"

He shocked me by closing the space between us. His head cocked to the side as he nailed me with narrowed eyes. I could feel the rise and fall of his chest as he sucked in frantic breaths. My back bowed over the counter as he hissed in my face, "I don't need your shit, and I promise you, you don't need mine."

He released a bitter grunt as he leaned back, then stalked away.

I stood there trying to stop my head from spinning while he disappeared around the other side of the bar and out into the living room. He left me with a pounding heart and a cutting sense of disillusionment.

I heard him shuffling and digging through his things. I only caught a glimpse of him as he rushed out the door pulling a shirt over his head. He slammed the door shut behind him.

Oh my God. What the hell just happened?

I turned and pressed my palms into the counter for support. Dropping my head, I tried to work through the aftermath of the storm that was Jared Holt. How had we gone from a mumbled *good morning* to all-out war in three seconds flat? My pulse sped, and I pulled in even breaths, trying to calm myself and the panic that had built up in my nerves.

Guilt tugged at my consciousness because I knew part of it was my fault, the way I'd devoured every inch of his body as if he were some sort of exhibit on display. My thoughts had shot between blatant desire and heartbreak, mixed and merged into this thick emotion that had filled every crevice in my chest.

But what did he expect? That I wouldn't look? That he

could stand before me in nothing but jeans and my eyes wouldn't wander and seek him out?

"Shit," I whispered, trying to calm my reaction to him. But I couldn't help the way he'd made me feel. Part of me wanted to lash out at him for treating me like I was *nothing*, while the stronger part of me wanted to reach out and trace the lines that were etched across his body, to feel them because I knew in every single one there was a memory, that each projected a feeling, symbolized a moment in time that meant something to him. He was right. I wanted to get inside him.

Tears welled up in my eyes. They fell, and I wiped them away. Was it pity I felt? Was it pity that had created this emotion that had been born in me that night, pity that had woven itself through my heart and left it aching for him all these years?

I had to believe it was more than that.

Shaking it off, I found my strength and my footing. I went into the bathroom and turned the showerhead to the hottest setting, letting the steam fill the room as I tried to make sense of someone I didn't know.

But underneath all his armor, I did know him.

Beneath the anger, I recognized the boy I'd known so long ago.

I was pretty sure it was Jared who didn't know himself.

FOUR

Summer 1997

"Come on, Christopher, just let her come. She's not hurtin' anyone."

Jared stood facing away from her at the end of the sidewalk. Aly hung back by the front doorstep, wondering why Christopher hated her so much. She was always nice and she never told when he did something bad. It wasn't her fault that she was only five.

Christopher dragged a fat stick along the pavement where he walked in the middle of the street in front of their house. It clattered along the pebbles. "Fine," he said with an annoyed sigh. "But if she acts like a baby, I'm gonna make her go home."

Jared looked back at her with a smile. "Come on, Aly," he said before he turned away.

Ahead of her, Jared darted up behind Christopher and flicked him in the back of the head. Jared laughed and took off running. Christopher chased him. "You're gonna pay for that one, Jared."

"Only if you can catch me."

Aly didn't worry too much. Christopher wasn't really mad. They always acted like this.

She trailed them, pushing her little legs as fast as they could go to keep up. Christopher and Jared ducked through the hole in the wooden fence that blocked the neighborhood from the empty land behind it.

"Wait for me," Aly called, feeling a little stab of fear that she would find herself alone.

Jared peeked back through the hole. "Don't worry, Aly Cat, I won't leave you behind."

FIVE

Jared

I gripped my head in my hands, kicking at nothing while I stormed in small circles in the middle of the parking lot, trying to make sense of what the hell had just happened upstairs.

Aleena Moore was like a fucking trigger.

I hadn't been prepared for her. I rasped a snort as I yanked at my hair. As if I could have done anything to prepare myself for her.

In what felt like a small miracle, I'd dozed off last night, drifting along the fringes of sleep as my mind swam through a dreamlike state. The pain had come, but it'd ebbed as I floated, this calm coming over me before my eyes had popped open in awareness.

And the girl standing over me was some sort of goddamned vision.

Waves of long almost-black hair fell down around her face,

so close I imagined them brushing along my chest. Her chin was sharp and her cheeks high, although a distinct softness pulled at her full lips.

But it was those penetrating green eyes that had shot through me, bolting me straight up to sitting.

Once my sight adjusted, my eyes had raked over the perfect curves of her slender body. She wore shorts and a little red tank top, and the straps of a bathing suit peeked out to wrap around her neck. Her smooth olive skin glowed golden in the dim light. The girl was all legs and undeniably the sexiest thing I'd ever seen. Yet there was something about her that appeared delicate and soft.

It'd taken a few seconds for the awe to wear off, for me to come to my senses and realize it was Aly. I found myself whispering my confusion. *"Aly?"*

Then she'd mumbled some kind of apology as if she was intruding on me when I was the one camped out on her couch. She stumbled into her room, the sharp click of her door shutting me out, leaving me completely unable to comprehend that the gorgeous girl who'd just stood in front of me was the same one who'd clung to my shirttails for the better part of my life.

I palmed the back of my neck and lifted my face to the sun. Even at nine in the morning, the heat was scorching, searing my skin. My lids dropped closed to shield my eyes from the blinding light, and I harshly shook my head.

Motherfucking trigger.

She'd triggered memories, ones I didn't want to remember. Memories of when I was happy and free. Memories that taunted me with what I could no longer have.

But worse than that was what she'd triggered in my body. I could blame it on leaving Lily behind at the bar after I'd planned on spending the night burying my aggression in her, but I'd be a liar. No one had ever caused a reaction in me like Aly had.

Last night, I'd lain awake for hours, fighting it, berating myself that I'd even for a second allowed my brain to trip into those types of thoughts. She was Christopher's little sister, for God's sake. And she'd been like a little sister to me. I'd dug out my journal, intent on hashing out my disgust on its pages, but ended up writing some fucking cheesy shit about a Siren's call.

When dawn had finally crept up to the windows early this morning, I had stepped out onto the balcony for a smoke and watched the sun slowly rise. By then, I'd gotten it under control, had chalked it up to my surprise at how the passing years had changed her, at the fact that Aly was no longer a child.

Then that trigger hit me just as hard when I slipped up behind her in the kitchen. Messy waves of black hair flowed down her back, and she wore a pair of tiny sleep shorts that exposed her long legs, and all I could think about was propping her ass up on the edge of the counter, my hands on her knees as I pressed them apart, my palms on her thighs.

A wave of guilt had flooded me just as soon as that fantasy had popped into my head. I'd whispered a regretful "Good morning," knowing I had to get my shit together because there was not one single thing kosher about the way I was looking at her.

But then she'd looked at me. No. Not looked. *Gawked.*

Judged.

Stared at me as if I were some kind of freak show.

That was the trigger to a different gun. It provoked the roiling anger that was always smoldering at the ready in every cell of my body. Hate had slipped through my gritted teeth as I unleashed it on the girl, although really, it wasn't directed at her at all.

The only person I hated was myself.

Still she had no right to look at me like that. I didn't come here for her pity, for her eyes to wash over me as if she understood. As if she *cared*. No one cared. People just liked to make themselves feel better with their meager shows of compassion.

And I sure as hell did not care.

My fists clenched at my sides.

Shit.

But I couldn't elude the nagging that tugged at me somewhere deep inside. I hated seeing her that way, shaking and nearing tears. Hated knowing I'd caused it. I'd scared her.

But it was for the best. I wasn't lying when I told her she didn't need my shit. And after the reaction she managed to work up in me, I most definitely did not need hers.

I hunched over the desk, filling out what felt like the hundredth application I'd worked on today. Most of my day had been eaten up racing from one construction company to another, chasing jobs that didn't exist in this suck-ass economy. Next to no one was hiring, and I'd spent half the day questioning my sanity. Who the fuck just left their home and a decent job without any plans? Dumb-asses like me, that's who.

I finished the application and stood.

"You done?" The owner, Kenny Harrison, sat behind a large desk on the other end of the room, rocking back in a grungy fabric office chair.

"Yes, sir," I answered as I crossed the room, passing the application to him. Of course I hoped for a position similar to the one I'd left in New Jersey, but I would take just about anything.

He scanned my information, suddenly turning his face up to me. "You originally from around here?"

I just nodded, couldn't speak.

"Hmm," he continued, "your application looks good. We don't have a lot going on right now, but I could maybe fit you in somewhere. You're not going to be close to making what you were at your last job, though."

Disappointment hit me, but I shook it off. "That's fine."

Kenny laughed. "Desperate, huh?"

I shifted my feet, feeling uncomfortable and on display. I forced myself to stand still. "You could say that."

"All right, then. Why don't you come back here Monday morning and you can fill out some paperwork to get you started?"

"Thank you, Mr. Harrison."

"Call me Kenny."

I shook his hand and began to back away, mumbling my thanks once again before I headed out his door.

I knew I should feel relieved, grateful, but the only thing I felt was the anxiety that had ramped up during the day. I felt it buzzing under the surface of my skin. I jumped on my bike, slipped onto the freeway, pegged the throttle, and hoped to out-run it. Hot air blasted my face and whipped through my hair, stirring the aggression higher. I darted in and out of cars. Ran.

Today the adrenaline from the speed didn't do. It only wound the anxiety tighter through my chest, made it hard to breathe as I pushed harder and faster. As the late-evening sun began to set, I cut across rush hour traffic and took the exit not that far from Christopher and Aly's apartment. I found I couldn't go back, but I was incapable of going far.

I ended up behind a deserted building with a bottle of Jack. I figured if I couldn't run from it, I'd drown it. I tipped the bot-tle to my lips, welcomed the burn as it slid down my throat and coated my stomach. I brought it to my mouth again and again, rested my head back on the coarse stucco of the old building, and listened as the night began to crawl through the streets of the city.

I never understood why sounds became more distinct at night, why I could hear the churn of an engine from miles away, the rustle of birds as they settled in the trees, the echo of an argument happening behind closed doors down the street. It all penetrated and seeped, bled into my consciousness as if each sound belonged to me. What some would consider peaceful felt entirely overwhelming. Tonight, those old cravings hit me hard, the intense desire for complete numbness, a moment's reprieve. I just wished that for one goddamned night I could block it all out. I drained the rest of the bottle. My head spun, and I squeezed my eyes shut tight.

But I could never outrun it. Could never drown it.

I would never forget.

My hand tightened on the neck of the bottle, and I staggered to my feet. I roared as I chucked the bottle across the lot. It shattered. Glass burst and pinged as it scattered across the ground. The sound stoked the memories, and all I could hear was glass breaking as it rained down all around me.

I spun and my fist connected with the building. Skin tore from my knuckles as it met the jagged, pitted wall. The tissue whitened and blanched before blood seeped to the surface. I welcomed the frenzy it created inside me.

I slammed my fists into the wall again and again and again until I was panting and the blood dripped free, wept from my skin in the way it should have instead of hers. Rage curled in my chest and erupted from my mouth.

It should have been me.

It should have been me.

Exhausted, I dropped my forehead, pressed my palms to the wall as I gulped for air. Heat rushed down my throat and expanded like fire in my lungs. My head rocked and my body shook as the aggression finally spiked, broke, and the effects of the alcohol brought me to my knees.

"Fuck," I groaned, slumping onto my stomach with my cheek pressed into the hard ground.

I never should have come here. It was all too much, this place that echoed my past and thrummed with familiarity. I refused to take comfort in it. Most of all, I fought against the desire to *stay.*

SIX

Aleena

I drove toward the old neighborhood. I had an hour before I had to be at work, and after Jared left this morning, I had an urge to go home. It wasn't as if I never visited or spent long spans of time without seeing my parents and my younger brother, Augustyn. I saw them often. But right now I felt the need to be back in the old neighborhood where I'd spent so much time with Jared when we were young.

I turned left onto the street where I'd grown up. It was an older neighborhood with a lot of families. I smiled, thinking of how quiet it always had been unless Christopher and Jared had been causing some kind of upheaval in the middle of the street.

Pulling into the driveway, I parked in front of the closed garage that fronted the modest house. Mature trees grew tall in the front yard. My mom, Karen, had planted them when Christopher was just a baby to remind her of her home in Idaho. Mom had met Dad when she was just nineteen, married him when she was twenty, and was expecting Christopher by the time she was twenty-one. She said she never thought twice about leaving her home behind to be with Dad, but that didn't mean she didn't miss it.

They bought this house when Christopher was nine months old. They met Helene, Jared's mother, the first day they moved in. Mom said she'd never forget the blue eyes on the six-month-old baby Helene had held on her hip when she rang the doorbell to welcome them to the neighborhood. Mom and Helene had latched on to each other, those kinds of fast friends who felt as if they'd known each other their whole lives, and all of us kids had literally grown up together.

I trailed up the sidewalk and rang the doorbell once before I let myself in. The door creaked open. "Mom?" I called.

"Aly?"

I followed her voice, stepping into the foyer and through the living room. I walked through the arch leading into the kitchen just as she yelled, "I'm in the kitchen." Her attention was all wrapped up in the cookie dough she was spooning in small mounds onto a cookie sheet.

I slinked up behind her and poked her in the side.

She jumped and I laughed when she spun around. "Oh God, Aly. Do you have to do that every time?"

"Um, yes, because you fall for it every time."

I think I startled her nine times out of ten, even after I gave her a warning I was there. She was such a jumpy thing.

She laughed and pulled me into a hug. "This is a nice surprise. I wasn't expecting to see you today."

I shrugged. "I had a little extra time, so I thought I'd stop by before my shift starts."

She turned away to slide the cookie sheet into the oven and

punched a few buttons to set the timer. I leaned back against the counter. She turned back with a gentle smile. "Well, that was really nice of you to take the time to come all the way over here. I've been thinking we need to have a mother-daughter shopping day. Maybe grab some lunch?"

Mom and I didn't resemble each other all that much. Christopher and I both took after our father—all except for the height that we'd inherited from Mom, who was just two inches shorter than my dad. She'd been a knockout when she was younger, and the years had been good to her. She'd always dyed her hair every color you could imagine and was the first to try a new product or new look. My shopping partner in crime, she knew every fashion that was coming before it hit. She also knew when to save something because it was going to come back around again. And I loved her with all my heart.

"Yeah, I'd like a shopping day." Then I frowned as I finally focused on the mess that had exploded in the kitchen. "And you're baking? Why?"

She rolled her warm brown eyes, although it was as good-natured as an eye roll could get. "Ugh . . . Aug's football team is having a bake sale, and he signed me up for ten dozen cookies." She kind of smiled and inclined her head in the direction of the hall. "They already started tryouts for his senior year . . . Looks like he has a pretty good chance at making first-string quarter-back this year."

"Is he home?"

"Yeah."

"I'm going to say hi really quick."

"Sure."

I pushed off the counter and headed down the hall. I knocked at his door.

"Come in."

I cracked the door open just as Aug sat up in his bed. He pulled the headphones from his ears and tossed his magazine aside. "Aly, hey." He was all smiles and dimples. Of us all, he favored our mother most. "What are you doing here?"

"Just was missing you and thought I'd stop by to say hi."

He pushed his large frame to standing, his dark brown hair falling over his eyes. His hug was warm, and I buried my face in his chest. "It's good to see you," he said.

"Well, if you weren't practicing all the time, maybe you'd have time for your big sister."

"Yeah, yeah, yeah." He pulled back with a grin. "So, what's going on? Anything new and exciting in the world of Aly and Christopher?"

I hesitated for only a second before I said, "Nah. Just working and hanging out with Megan a bit."

Aug's brow rose just as high as his interest. "Megan, huh?"

I slugged him in the shoulder. "You're so gross, Aug. I already told you, Megan is totally off-limits."

He laughed as he turned away and flopped back down on his bed. "Well, that's a shame because I'm bored with all the girls I know."

"You think because you've run through all the girls at school I'm going to set my best friend up with my little brother? Did you hit your head during practice?"

He turned so he could see me, his eyes playful. "What? She's hot."

I picked a football up off the floor and chucked it at him. "Gross," I mouthed as I ducked out the door. He was laughing when I shut it.

I paused when the latch clicked, standing out in the silent hall, my hand still gripping Aug's knob as my nerves escalated.

I glanced down the hall toward the kitchen. A whisk clanking against a metal bowl assured me Mom's attention was occupied. Why I felt as if I was on some sort of secret mission, I didn't know. But I did. I slipped inside my old room, quietly shutting the door behind me.

Mom had left it mostly the same, except for the stack of boxes she had stashed up against one wall. A dark paisley bedspread covered the daybed that was tucked up under the window, and my walls were tacked with pictures of my friends from high school, my tickets from the prom, and little keepsakes I thought I'd always cherish. Funnily enough, I didn't cherish them enough to drag them to my new apartment.

I ran my fingers along them, thinking of those years when Jared had been away. So much of my time had been spent in here alone, imagining the day he would walk back into my life.

I bit my lip, remembering the bitterness that had lined his face this morning. Turned out his return was something I couldn't fathom, something like thunder and chaos.

I climbed down onto my knees and dug my arm deep between the mattress and the box spring of my bed. My fingertips grazed the book, and I maneuvered my hand around to pull it free. Sinking onto my butt, I rested my back against the bed. It took me a couple of seconds to get the courage to open it. My grandmother had given it to me when I was young, right before she passed. She'd told me to save it for something that meant the most to my heart. The old hardbound pad creaked when I lifted the cover.

His face was on every page. All except for what I'd drawn that night.

I traced my fingers along the lines, studying what I had seen then. Though the years had hardened him, his eyes were not so different now than they'd been during those days.

Sighing, I tucked the book into my bag and walked back out to the kitchen. I came up behind my mom and wrapped my arms around her waist. "Love you, Mom."

Her expression was tender when she glanced at me over her shoulder. "Love you, Aly." Then she frowned. "Is everything okay?"

"Yeah." I shook my head as I twisted up my mouth. "I've just been tired."

She nodded, but it was more in appraisal than real acceptance. I could tell she didn't believe what I'd said. Mom knew me well enough to see when I was lying. "You know I'm here, whenever you need me."

"I know, Mom." I squeezed her again before I stepped away. "I've got to run."

She blew out a breath of disappointment. "Fine, then, leave your old mom here all alone with your stinky brother."

I laughed because Mom never seemed old.

I opened the door. Mom's voice called after me, "And let me know when you're off from work next so we can go shopping."

"I will," I promised before I shut the door behind me.

The sun stood proud at the center of the sky, its heat soaking me through in a matter of seconds. I walked back toward my car, but I passed it by. My attention drifted two houses away and across the street to the one that had been Jared's.

Making a quick decision, I turned and strode down the sidewalk, to its end where the rickety fence still stood. I'd be late for work, but today, they were just going to have to wait. Sweat pebbled up on the nape of my neck, and I pulled in a breath as I ducked down and wedged myself through the small hole in the fence that had once seemed like the center of my universe. Wood splinters tugged at my shirt, and I twisted so I could fit through.

On the other side, I straightened as a slow chill crept up my spine. Weeds grew high across the vast expanse of the vacant lot. In the distance, a fence rose to enclose another neighborhood to the south of ours, but in between were six acres of uninhabited land where we'd spent so many hours as children. The trails our play had tracked were no longer visible. The trees that had once housed our fairy tales now seemed out of place, tall and full in the backdrop of this barren desert. Stickers pricked at my legs as I trudged across to our tree. I hadn't been out here in so many years.

I stood beneath the rotting wood, the small pieces of two-by-four that had been nailed to the trunk still offering their escape. I found my footing on the lowest one and gripped a branch as I hoisted myself up. Tentatively I took the next step, and the lower level of our fort came into view.

I yelped when the third step gave, but I managed to hold myself up on a solid branch, pulling myself up the rest of the way.

I settled onto the stretch of plywood that we had so carefully hammered into the safety of the tree. This little fort had seemed so massive when we'd built it. I drew my knees to my chest and rested my head back against one of the large branches that grew up from where the trunk had segmented into four.

And I closed my eyes.

SEVEN

Summer 1999

Aly dragged the heavy piece of wood as best she could. Jared called it plywood, and it was her job to get it from the fence to the tree. Earlier her dad had said they could use whatever they wanted as long as they didn't make a mess and they brought his tools back.

"And watch your little sister, Christopher," he'd said as he and their mom left to run some errands.

Aly turned around, walking backward as she struggled with the flat piece of wood. It was so big she could barely wrap her hands around it. It dug into her palms. She wanted to cry because it hurt, but she wasn't a baby anymore. She was seven and she knew she needed to act like it. She tugged it harder, and it scraped along the ground. She huffed out a proud breath when she dropped it at the base of the trunk. "All done," she said as she dusted off her hands.

"About time," Christopher yelled from somewhere up in the tree, the sharp strike of a hammer echoing in her ears.

She jumped back when Jared suddenly dropped from the tree, landing on his feet.

"Good job, Aly Cat." He leaned down and hefted the plywood over his head, balancing it on one shoulder as he climbed back up the tree. "This is going to be the coolest fort in history," she heard him say.

"Can I be in the club, too?" she called as she attempted to climb up the same way Jared had gone.

"No," Christopher immediately retorted, while Jared said, "Depends. You gotta pass the initiation first."

Her stomach hurt a little. She didn't think she'd be good enough.

She climbed up toward the sounds happening above her, the ground slowly disappearing below. She wrapped her hand around a branch and pulled. It snapped and her foot slipped. She screamed as she fell.

She hit the ground hard. She struggled to find her breath, but it was gone. Her heart hurt and it made her head hurt and she tried to scream again. Finally something gave and she wheezed air into her lungs. She slowly sat up, her attention going to the pain in her elbow. Blood oozed from a big cut. It hurt so bad, and she squeezed her eyes shut because she didn't want to cry.

"Aly, are you okay?" Jared's voice was frantic as he shook her shoulders.

She slowly opened her eyes to find Christopher gaping at her from behind Jared, his eyes wide with fear. Jared shook her again. "You okay?"

"My arm." She couldn't keep herself from crying any longer. Tears fell in hot streaks down her dirty face.

Jared looked down and then squeezed his own eyes. "Christopher, she's bleeding really bad."

"Oh man, oh man, I told you we shouldn't bring her. Now we're gonna get in trouble."

Jared stayed focused on Aly. "Can you walk home?"

Aly vehemently shook her head. Her whole body hurt.

Jared scooped her up in his arms, kind of like he'd done with the wood, but a lot gentler. "Come on, Aly. Let's get you fixed up."

She clung to him while he carried her home. He was breathing all funny and hard by the time he closed the toilet seat and set her down on it. He wet a washcloth under water and kneeled in front of her. It was cold when he pressed it to her arm. She jerked a little because it stung.

"I hate blood," he mumbled as he cleaned her arm.

Christopher rummaged through the medicine cabinet. "Here." He shoved a box of bandages at Jared.

Jared carefully peeled back the wrapper and placed it on her cut.

He let out a breath, then smiled up at her as he ruffled a hand through her hair. "All better?"

She sniffled and wiped her eyes with the back of her hand. "All better."

EIGHT

Aleena

That night, I lay in bed, staring at the shadows as they climbed along my ceiling, listening to the peace outside my window. It was late. I'd gotten off work after eleven o'clock tonight, my pockets filled with tips from the busy evening. Apprehension had fluttered in my stomach when I returned to the apartment. The night had been still, the trees seeming frozen in time as I stepped from my car. Fear had clamored through my chest when I thought perhaps Jared had run, come back to the apartment in the middle of the day while I was gone and packed up his belongings, and turned his back on the things he didn't want to face.

But when I opened the door to the silence of the apartment, I'd found Jared's bag still shoved in the corner of the room, and I was struck with a deep relief that eclipsed the flickers of anger I'd felt throughout the day.

I couldn't stand to leave things between us the way they'd been this morning.

After a shower to wash away the grime from the greasy kitchen, I'd crawled in bed with my sketch pad and allowed my thoughts to drift. I'd captured images, each time feeling I was close to touching on something beautiful, but in every stroke I saw my own imperfection. I'd drawn until my eyes had sagged with exhaustion and I'd finally set the pad aside.

But I couldn't find sleep.

Hours passed, and now I stared.

Waited.

I rose to my elbows when I heard the apartment door whine open. Craning my ear, I listened, trying to discern the footsteps. They were subdued, but even then, I could tell they were too heavy to be Christopher's.

Muted sounds leaked into my room. I rolled from bed, quieting my feet as I crossed the room. I slowly turned the knob, cringing with the slight creak it gave, and carefully pulled it open. Tiptoeing, I edged along the hall.

"Fuck," he muttered, the sound so quiet I wouldn't have heard it at all had I not had my back pressed to the wall, straining to listen.

Desperation filled the air, a tension that slipped along the floor, beckoning me forward.

He came into view as I peeked into the kitchen. Everything was dark except for the bright light coming from the freezer where he stood with his back to me. He was fumbling for something inside. His movements seemed sluggish, although he kept shaking his head with these harsh motions, disgust pouring from him. He wrestled with a cheap blue ice cube tray, twisting it over the sink. Ice cubes shot out in a flurry. Half clattered into the sink and the rest hit the floor. His shoulders slumped as pressed his hands onto the counter to hold himself up, his head hanging low. "Shit," he mumbled under his breath.

Tentatively, I found my way around the bar. I sidled up to him, nudging him back a step. "Here, let me help you."

He jerked with surprise before he twisted his head farther away and moved aside, standing there like a scolded child. He wouldn't even look at me.

My gaze swept over the counter. He had a towel out, and ice cubes littered the bottom of the sink.

"Are you hurt?" I asked quietly, keeping my voice even, training my attention on piling ice cubes in the towel to make a compress. I glanced over my shoulder to catch the horrified expression on his face when he looked up.

I froze, wide-eyed.

That beautiful face was filthy, and his eyes were achingly sad. Pain twisted me in its fingers, wringing me from the inside. He looked like absolute death. His white printed tee was in tatters, smeared with dirt and oil, hanging from his body at odd angles from where it had been stretched and deformed. I stifled a gasp when I saw his bloodied hands. Gashes were opened on each knuckle, the torn skin filled with rocks and rimmed in dirt.

His hands were a complete mess.

I squeezed my eyes shut as realization hit me hard.

It wasn't just his hands. It was Jared Holt who was the mess.

"Come here," I whispered, reaching out to take his hand.

He backed away. "I can take care of myself, Aly. Just go back to bed." This time, there was no anger in his words, just defeat.

I shook my head. "Are you sure, Jared? Because it doesn't look that way to me."

He blinked as if he was trying to make sense of what I'd just said.

"Now come here and let me help you." I offered him my hand. He seemed reluctant, wavering in indecision, before he finally placed his palm against mine. A thrill slithered along my skin. For a second, I remained still, relishing the slight connection. I lifted my gaze to him, and he was looking at me as if maybe the feel of my skin caused him pain.

"Come on." I led him out into the living room to the couch. "Sit."

Reluctantly he obeyed, and he sank to the edge of the couch. A heavy groan rumbled in his chest when he did. He dropped his head, his injured fingers gripping at the back of his neck.

"I'll be right back." I rushed into the kitchen, gathered the pieces of ice melting on the floor, and tossed them into the sink. I got a fresh towel and ran it under some cool water, wringing it out before I made my way back to him. He glanced up at me. All the belligerent hostility from this morning had vanished. Shame had taken its place.

This was the boy I'd found in the pages of the sketchbook I'd retrieved this morning.

I lowered myself onto my knees in front of him, my movements slow and calculated as I reached out to lightly tug at one of his forearms, never looking away from the haunted blue eyes that stared down at me. Again he flinched at my touch, a sharp gush of air rushing from his nose, before he relaxed and allowed me to bring his hand down onto his lap.

A little blood still oozed from the wounds, but it had mostly dried. I placed the towel on his hands. "Here, hold this and try to stop the bleeding. We need to get this cleaned up so it doesn't get infected."

I was a little surprised when he agreed with a quiet "Okay."

I hurried to the bathroom, where I dug through the cabinet under the sink for the first-aid kit. Taking a second for myself in the sanctuary of the bathroom, I focused on quieting the rush of feelings igniting my senses in a way they should not. I was smart enough to recognize when I was on dangerous ground.

Everything about him was dangerous. Just as dangerous as he was beautiful.

I'd witnessed firsthand the destruction that was Jared Holt.

But there was no chance I could stay away.

I headed back out and set the kit beside me on the floor.

"Let me help you." I took the towel and began to dab at this knuckles, hoping to remove some of the dirt. "You should probably run this under some water and wash it with soap."

"It's not that big a deal, Aly." His expression was soft, but filled with confession. Like this happened all the time.

"I hope there wasn't someone on the receiving end of this."

Jared laughed mildly, a warm sound that contradicted his hard exterior.

It made me smile.

"No . . . not this time, unless a grungy wall counts."

"I suppose not," I said, sitting up on my knees to get a better look. I scrunched up my nose. "God, you smell like a Dumpster." He might as well have taken a bath in booze.

"Well, I've got to smell better than I feel. Pretty sure my head might explode."

"And whose fault is that?" I challenged, eyeing him.

I thought maybe he'd lash out at me. Instead he sighed. "Mine, Aly. It's always mine."

His answer stung, and I immediately wished I could take

the accusation back. I knew the root of the issues he bore, the blame he laid on himself, the constant burden he carried.

I fought the urge to hug him, pictured myself inching forward, whispering in his ear that I'd share it with him if he'd let me.

Biting my lip, I focused on cleaning one hand with the towel as best I could, avoiding looking at his face. But I could feel him staring at me, could feel the power of his eyes as they watched me. My heart beat a little faster.

"Almost done with this one," I said, giving in and glancing at him. A soft smile touched just one side of his mouth. Quickly, I looked away. I poured some peroxide onto a cotton ball and gently ran it over his wounds.

He hissed. "Shit . . . that stings."

I cringed. "Sorry."

Placing a piece of square gauze over the knuckles of his hand, I lifted it to wrap medical tape around it to keep the bandage in place.

He sighed as I worked. "Aly, listen . . ." His voice was quiet and took on an undertone of regret. The short flare of softness he'd watched me with last night again transformed his eyes. "I'm really sorry about the way I acted this morning."

I knew his apology was genuine, and maybe I should have let him get away with it. But I didn't want to. What he'd done hurt me. I twisted my jaw as I looked up at him, blindly dabbing at his other hand as I called him out on it. "Are you always an asshole?"

This time his quiet laughter was hard. "What did you expect me to be, Aly?"

"Different," I said, fully pinning him with my eyes.

"But I'm not." His voice was gentle, and I was sure I didn't believe him. "I wasn't lying to you this morning. You don't need my shit and I *can't* handle yours."

I struggled to make sense of how he'd changed the words and the hint of desperation he'd injected in them.

"We were friends once," I said, picking up his other hand to begin cleaning it. "At least I thought we were."

His lids dropped closed for the longest moment. When he opened them, he reached out to gently trace his fingertips along the whitened scar barely visible along the outside of my forearm from when I'd fallen out of the tree. His fingers were rough. Perfect.

My lips parted as goose bumps rose on my skin. I shivered, and he pulled away. He pressed his lips together, his head cocked to the side as he sat back. "Yeah, I guess we were."

"Are you not allowed to have one now?"

He laughed softly, an incredulous sound as he shook his head. It appeared as if he was shaking it at himself. "Aly, you're killing me."

I frowned. "I don't get you, Jared. Did you think you could stay here and I'd just ignore you? I care about you."

"Don't say that," he whispered, something like grief flashing in his eyes.

"But I do. I always have."

He attempted to pull away, but I held tight. "Friends," I emphasized. At the very least, he owed me that.

With his free hand, he scratched at the side of his head, and a teasing smile slowly worked its way onto his mouth. "Fine, Aly, we can be *friends*. Do you have a note you need me to X the box on, too?" He gave me an exaggerated eye roll.

I thought maybe he deserved a punch in the arm, exactly like I'd given him when he made fun of me for the letter he found that I was going to give to Zachary Braggs in the fourth grade. I laughed a little. "You're such a jerk."

Everything about him softened when he tugged at a lock of my hair. "But don't say I didn't warn you. Pretty sure you're going to regret being a friend of mine."

"You're completely full of shit, you know. You don't scare me for a second." It was a lie, of course. Pretty much all my fears were wrapped up in him.

His face darkened. "I'm not trying to scare you, Aly."

"Then don't."

NINE

Jared

What the hell was I doing?

Everything about this situation was wrong. Aly kneeling in front of me. Touching me. She was close, too close. I could taste her breath, and I kept catching hints of that fucking delicious coconut body wash I'd used last night. Somehow it smelled a thousand times better on her.

These urges constantly hit me, and I couldn't help imagining what it'd be like to bury my nose in the haven behind her ear, to press my mouth to her jaw, to tangle my hands in her hair. Against my better judgment, which could so easily be called into question, anyway, I gave in. Took a little.

I was always so good at taking.

The strand of hair I tugged between my fingers was soft, like silk against my callused skin. The action should've been innocent enough. I remembered doing it often when we were children, just a small act of affection to let her know it was okay she was there. There was never anything more to it than that.

But I knew better now, knew it would stir the need I'd felt in the pit of my stomach since I found her backed against that wall last night, since she'd driven me half-mad in her kitchen this morning, since I'd stumbled into her apartment like the piece of trash I was tonight. Somehow she still found me worthy, kneeling in front of me as if I deserved even a scrap of the attention she gave me now.

With her head down, she attended to the wounds on my other hand. I allowed my gaze to fall, to trace the face I wanted to trace with my hands.

I didn't think I'd ever felt intrigued by a girl before the way I was now, had never wanted to crawl inside someone's mind to dig through her thoughts, to find out who she was. Why she was. Aly's green eyes were both fierce and soft, her touch both intent and gentle. She was kind, yet she didn't hesitate to call me out on my shit. She made me itch and squirm, made me want to run and want to stay.

She began taping up my second hand, forging this little truce between us, steadily sucking me deeper into a place I knew I shouldn't go.

But I couldn't stop it.

There was something about being alone with her in the seclusion of this apartment that I liked, like maybe we were sharing some kind of secret that no one else could touch.

A distorted sense of security.

For just a little while, I wanted to drift in the delusion.

I watched her as she worked. Every couple of seconds, she glanced up at me with those eyes that seemed to know more than they should.

Aly shifted closer. I attempted to scoot back without her noticing, but she tugged on my hand. "Would you hold still? You're worse than a two-year-old," she said.

Was she completely oblivious to what she was doing to me? Every time she moved, her chest brushed against my knees, and damn, if it wasn't the greatest temptation I'd ever had to endure. Did she know how badly I wanted to touch her? To take a little more? Maybe take it all? My thoughts raced ahead, and I wondered what she'd do if I edged off the couch and laid her back on the floor. Would she stop me? Or would she allow me to feed off her compassion and goodness? Would she let me wreck her? Destroy her? Because that was the only thing I knew how to do.

I sucked in a breath and held it. No fucking way was I going there. Not with her, even if she was the only girl who'd ever made me feel like I had to have her. The first who'd ever made me *want*. That in itself was a pretty damned good reason to stay away from her.

That and the fact that she was Aly.

My Aly.

She sat back on her haunches. Her smile was soft when she looked up at me. "See? That wasn't so bad, was it?"

"Thank you," I said honestly, because it'd been a long time since anyone had taken care of me. It hurt to think of the last time someone had.

"You're welcome." Her voice was quiet, and she sat there, just staring at me, a lot like we had last night, although now things seemed completely different.

"You'd better get some rest. It's really late," I said. I'd lain flat out on the hard ground for hours while I let myself sober up to the point where I could at least get myself back to the apartment, and I hadn't come crawling up the stairs until three in the morning.

"Yeah, you'd better, too." She sounded a little disappointed.

Her delicate hands pressed into the couch on the outside of my legs as she helped herself to stand. This time her hair did brush against my chest. We both froze at the contact, and she looked down at me, her face three inches from mine. She hovered there, her eyes searching.

Motherfucking trigger.

I wet my lips and found my voice, although it was heavy with strain. "Please go to your room, Aly."

Blinking, she nodded before she pushed herself the rest of the way up. She paused at her door, whispered, "Good night," and then disappeared inside her bedroom.

The next Friday night I sat at the round kitchen table across from Christopher, drinking a beer while I got my ass kicked at poker.

I folded and Christopher leaned over the table. With his forearm, he swept the pile of coins and one-dollar bills to his side. "Easy money," he drawled, taunting me.

"Yeah, 'cause you're a fucking cheater." I laughed as I tipped my beer to my mouth.

"Nah, man, you just suck . . . or have really bad luck, one of the two."

Now, bad luck was something I'd definitely feel comfortable putting money on.

"You want to go another round?" he asked as he began shuffling the cards.

"Sure. Why not?" I tossed my ante into the center of the table. It wasn't as if I had all that much to lose. "You know if you win too much of my money, you're never going to get my ass off your couch." Of course, I was joking. I'd just been too lazy to start looking for my own place in the last week. Or maybe it was just that I liked being here, which I really didn't want to admit to myself because getting too comfortable here was really fucking foolish.

Christopher started dealing the cards. "Nah, man, don't feel like you have to rush right out and get a place of your own. I like having you around. This summer sucked until you got here."

"You could get a job or something." I raised a sarcastic eyebrow, figured I'd mess with him a little since he'd been giving me shit for all my losing hands for the last hour.

"Now, why would I go and do something like that? You know I don't get out of bed before noon."

I shook my head. "Dude, you're so lazy."

He laughed it off. "No, I did have a job lined up at the beginning of the summer, but it fell through. After that, I figured with all the classes I have to finish up next year to graduate, I might as well go ahead and take a couple of months off for myself." He shrugged a shoulder. "I had a little extra money saved up, so it wasn't that big a deal."

"Like I said . . . lazy."

"You're such a dick," he said through his laughter while he picked up his hand and organized his cards. "Seriously, though, like I told you last week, you're welcome to stay here as long as you want."

I took a swig of my beer, studied my cards. "What about Aly? You don't think it bothers her that I'm staying here?"

Maybe I was digging, looking for some clues into this girl I couldn't get off my mind.

An uncertain sigh pushed out of Christopher's lungs.

"Aly's . . ." He hesitated as he seemed to struggle to find the words. ". . . cool. And I think she's fine with you being here. But she's different. You get that, right? I trust you that you won't mess with her, but you should know she's not like the girls you and I go looking for. Just be careful around her, okay?" he added. "She's a good girl." His voice took on a tone of deep respect.

And I got what he was saying, the warning to stay away from his sister, that I wasn't good enough for her. I mean, fuck, I already knew that. He didn't need to tell me twice.

The lock on the front door rattled, and Christopher and I looked up at the same time as the door swung open, our conversation coming to an abrupt halt when Aly fumbled her way in. She smiled. "Hey, guys." She kicked the door shut behind her as she balanced a stack of take-out boxes in her hands. "Brought you some dinner."

"Oh, nice," Christopher said.

She was always so cute when she got off work, all disheveled and exhausted and a little red-cheeked from the exertion of being on her feet running around a hot kitchen all day.

It'd been a week since the night she took care of me. In that time, a sort of understanding had arisen between us. We'd settled into the feigned comfort of casual smiles and pleasantries. She'd ask me how my day was and I'd ask her about hers, but we'd keep it light. But under the surface remained a tension that stretched us tight, pushed us apart at the same time as it worked to suck us together. I knew it. I saw it in her eyes and felt it in my bones. I knew how easy it'd be to sink my fingers into her skin and into her mind. I knew how willingly she'd let me *take*.

And God, I wanted to.

I kept thinking it'd pass, that the newness would wear off, and I'd just see *Aly*. After work a couple of nights ago, I'd gone back to the little bar where I'd met Christopher. Only this time I stayed, went home with Lily, thought maybe I'd be able to erase a little of what I was feeling.

When I saw Aly the next morning, I felt guilty or some shit, an emotion I was all too familiar with, but this . . . this was different. It was fucked up and wrong and misplaced, and I wanted to rip it from my consciousness. I owed Aly nothing, and she sure as hell didn't owe me anything. But no matter how hard I tried to convince myself of that fact, I couldn't shake the feeling that I'd done something wrong.

Christopher got to his feet. "Let me help you with that." He planted a quick kiss on her forehead. "You're the best. I've worked up a ravenous appetite taking all of someone's money over here." He jerked his head in my direction as he took the boxes from Aly's hands.

Her eyes grew wide with feigned worry. "Oh, Jared, please tell me you aren't falling for Christopher's games. You know he never outgrew the whole cheating thing."

I laughed hard as I slammed my palm down on the table. "I knew it, you asshole!" I stretched my entire body over the table to retrieve *his* winnings, opening my arms wide to drag the pile of money back in front of me. "You've been cheating me this whole time, haven't you?"

"Hey, now, hey, now, let's not get hasty. Aly has her own tricks, Jared. Don't let her fool you."

His smile was all warm with the easy affection that swam between the two of them. It was odd, seeing how different they were and still so very much the same.

She smacked him on the back of the head. "Watch yourself."

A short chuckle wobbled up my throat and I brought my

bottle to my mouth, but I outright laughed when Christopher pointed at me. "Don't you two start ganging up on me. It was always the two of you against me."

"What are you talking about?" Aly asked, her brow lifting in defense.

"*Pah.* Are you kidding me? I couldn't get you out of my hair for five minutes when we were kids. And you want to know why?" He lifted his chin in my direction. "Because this ass insisted you go everywhere with us."

"And was I all that bad?" Aly attempted a pout, which looked absolutely ridiculous on her because it was so obviously faked. The girl was too nice, too sweet. I kind of wanted to reach over and smooth it out.

"Hell yeah, you were, just because you breathed." He offered her this mocking smile that earned him another smack to the back of the head.

"Whatever, you loved me, and you know it."

Aly laughed as she disappeared down the hall and into the bathroom. He turned around in his chair, shouting down the hall. "Hey, Aly, you want to join us for the next hand?"

"Sure," she called back from what sounded like her room. "Let's eat first, though. I'm starving."

A few minutes later she returned. She'd changed out of her work clothes and into the same sleep shorts she chose to constantly taunt me with night after night.

God, the girl had the best legs I'd ever seen.

She was twisting her long hair up into a high ponytail as she walked barefoot into the kitchen. The mixture of her skin and the food she'd brought smelled like heaven.

She cracked open the fridge. "Either of you want another beer?" she asked as she bent down to dig through the fridge.

In my head I was screaming at myself to close my eyes or to look up or to look down or to just look the fuck away.

I didn't.

Instead I watched.

A curl of lust twisted my stomach into the tightest knot, so tight I had to struggle to get a breath of air into my lungs.

Christopher's voice broke my trance. "Yeah, I'll take one."

I cut my attention in his direction, and eyes so much like Aly's stared back at me.

I dropped my gaze and mumbled, "Sure, I could use another."

Aly stood and knocked the door closed with her hip. She had three beers woven between her fingers, their caps pressed together. Maybe there was something inherently wrong with me, but I thought it had to be one of the sexiest moves I'd ever seen.

She set them down on the table. "One for you." She passed one to Christopher and grinned as she slid one across the table to me. "And one for you."

"Thanks," I said.

She twisted the cap off the third and plopped heavily into the chair as she tipped it to her mouth.

"Long day?" Christopher asked as he arched an eyebrow at her.

"Oh yeah." She released a long breath. "It was superbusy." A little shrug lifted her shoulders. "Made good tips, but I couldn't wait for my shift to end." She began opening the take-out box lids. My mouth watered when I was hit with the heavy aroma of thick red meat sauce and pasta.

I stood. "Here, let me grab some plates and forks."

She threw a soft smile up at me as I passed. "Thanks, Jared."

"Yeah, no problem."

Even though it was only three feet away, I stumbled into the kitchen as if it were some kind of oasis in the desert. For a second, I dropped my head as I pressed my hands into the counter and filled my lungs with the deepest breath of air I could find.

Get a grip, Jared.

I gathered myself while I gathered the plates and forks. I walked back out with everything, sat down across from Christopher and Aly, the only true friends I'd ever had, and forced myself to relax.

We all ate together, like we did it all the time—like we'd done so many times before. Our conversation was light, and the food was awesome. We drank a few more beers and played some cards. I couldn't remember ever feeling so good.

But I did. I felt too damned good.

From across the table, I tried to suppress my amusement. Aly was obviously a lightweight. After three beers, her speech was beginning to hint at a slur. "I need another beer," she announced, draining the last few drops in her bottle, wobbling a little as she stood. She kind of staggered into the kitchen.

God, she was cute.

"Grab me one, too, would you?" Christopher called.

She emerged with two. "Nah, but Jared can have one." She winked at me as she slid it across the table to me.

I couldn't help but smirk.

"Oh, uncool, Aly, uncool," Christopher mocked, pressing his hand to his chest. "You always liked him better than me, didn't you, Aly Cat?"

Aly's mouth puckered in defense. "Oh my God, don't you dare, Christopher. You two just about gave me a complex when I was little. I can't tell you how much time I sat in front of the mirror, worrying I looked like some mangy cat. One day Mom found me crying, curled up in a ball in my room. It took her, like, two hours to convince me it was about my name and not what I looked like."

Aly Cat.

A smile pulled at my mouth, at my thoughts, and a wave of nostalgia slammed me, threatening to knock me off my feet. It washed over me with warmth, and things I didn't want to remember. Fear tightened my throat. I pushed it down. I'd leave soon, before I could fuck it all up and leave them hating me.

I stood and drained my beer. "I'm going to grab a smoke."

I was hit by a wall of stifling night air when I escaped outside through the sliding glass door. I closed my eyes and sank to the balcony floor, resting my back against the wall. The concrete floor was still hot as I pulled my bare feet up and bent my knees. I dipped my head to the side to light a cigarette. I drew it in, felt it expand in my lungs, welcomed the mild calm it pulsed through my agitated veins. I rushed my free hand through my hair.

Careless.

Coming back here. Staying here. All of it.

Taking another drag, I looked up as the sliding glass door slowly opened. Aly's silhouette emerged in the darkness, her movements somehow softer than they'd been inside.

Just to the side and across from me, she slid down onto the floor. Slowly her face came into focus. She drew one leg to her chest, exposing the skin on the underside of her thigh. She tilted her head to the side, and the length of her black hair fell down around one shoulder, all soft and innocent and a little bit infuriating. This girl was either the biggest tease I'd ever met or was completely oblivious of how perfect she was.

For a while we said nothing, just listened to the sounds of

the night, and allowed a distinct pressure to build up around us. I rested my forearms on my knees and let my hands dangle down between them. I wasn't looking at her, but I could *feel* her looking at me. With the intensity of it, I thought she might as well go ahead and climb inside my head, because she was definitely getting under my skin.

My nerves flared in a way I didn't quite understand. I didn't think I'd ever felt so comfortably uncomfortable, like I wanted to bolt and sink into it all at once. Maybe I was finally slipping over the edge of sanity. God knew I'd been heading there for a long time.

I rocked my head back and lifted my face to the starry night sky as I brought the cigarette to my mouth again. I held it in for a long moment and then slowly blew it into the air. Smoke curled over my head, these wisps of nothingness that I studied as they slowly evaporated.

Finally she spoke. "Are you okay?"

Confusion rumbled through me and I let out a slow sound of exasperation. "I don't know what I am, Aly. Being here is just . . . I don't know . . . It's hard."

"It doesn't have to be." Studying me, she frowned. "I mean, why did you come back?"

I shrugged as if it made no difference in the world. "I don't really know." And I sure as fuck wasn't going to talk to her about it, even if I did.

Her voice came low, earnest and sincere. "I know you probably think of me as the little girl you used to know, but you can talk to me, Jared."

My attention dropped to her thigh, rested there for a beat too long. She believed I still thought of her as that little girl, huh? Incredulous laughter slipped out. I took another drag as I shook my head. I chewed at my lip as my eyes found her face. "That's not how I think of you, Aly." Not even close.

In the dimness I watched as her green eyes softened, filled with something that appeared too much like affection.

I looked down, away, stubbed out the cigarette.

"You *can* trust me," she whispered.

I let my eyes fall closed as I loosely wove my fingers together. I said nothing because I was pretty sure I could trust her. It was me who couldn't be trusted.

We settled back into the silence, and again I took comfort in the distinct discomfort. I thought maybe she took some, too.

There was something about the summer air in Phoenix. Even though it was hot at night, it was almost refreshing. How many times had we been out in it, playing hide-and-seek in the dark? How much had we laughed?

I'd been comfortable then.

In the far distance, at the lowest point on the horizon, a flicker of lightning edged the sky, this faint warning that the monsoon approached. The storms always seemed to loom in the distance before they engulfed the city, teasing us with the promise of a reprieve. On the few days it did actually rain, it was like a torrent of relief pounding heavily into the ground. The thick scent of rain would rise as it met the dry dirt and hot pavement as the heavens opened up and washed the world anew.

I hadn't allowed myself to miss many things while I was away, but this . . . this was one of them.

I had to admit now that I'd missed Christopher, too.

And I'd missed her.

I stood and dusted off my pants, reaching a hand down to her. "Come on, Aly."

She didn't hesitate to accept my hand. Her shy smile told me everything. She liked touching me every bit as much as I liked touching her.

Fuck.

This was so very bad.

My muscles flexed along my arm as I pulled her to standing, and her feet came to hold her weight, although for a few seconds I didn't let go. Finally I forced a casual smile and dropped her hand. Pretending to be the gentleman my mom had always hoped I would be, I slid the door open for her. "After you, Aly Cat." Of course, I couldn't keep out a little tease.

She slugged me on the arm as she passed. "See? You are a jerk."

The next night I sat on the opposite end of the couch from Aly, who was curled up on her side. Those long legs were bent, her knees tucked up close to her chest with her head propped on a pillow that she'd taken three minutes to situate on the armrest. The lights were off, and the television flickered in front of us.

Aly'd gotten off work about an hour before. She'd walked through the door looking exhausted, which she'd confirmed when she dropped the huge-ass bag she always carried on the floor with an exaggerated sigh and followed it up with "I'm exhausted."

Apparently I was perceptive.

Probably too perceptive because I couldn't help watching her now. My side was pressed up against the opposite armrest, as far as it would go, while my eyes were constantly drawn toward her. She was relaxed, and looked engrossed in the TV show, although she was probably close to slipping into sleep. She kept shifting her legs, burrowing deeper into the couch, sinking farther into comfort.

How messed up was it that I really wanted to burrow into her comfort, too?

I shook my head and forced myself to look back at the TV.

About half an hour later, the door opened behind us, and I could hear mumbled voices right outside the door. It was easy to make out Christopher when he whispered, "It's fine. You can come in."

Christopher slipped in the door, leading this dark brunette toward the hall by the hand. Her eyes widened as she stole a glance in our direction; then she ducked her head and studied the floor. Christopher didn't even bother with introductions.

In the last week, the guy'd had more girls in this apartment than I could count, and he kicked them out just as fast as he dragged them in. I mean, I had a pretty bad record, or a pretty good one, depending on how you looked at it. But there was something about this that was different. Something that made me feel sympathy for the girls. For him, it seemed a game, kind of like the poker he'd slung last night. Deceitful.

When Christopher's door snapped closed, Aly lifted her head to look at me. "You've got to be kidding me."

I lifted an eyebrow her direction. "Dude is kind of a slut, isn't he?"

She quieted a dubious laugh. "Tell me about it. I had no idea I was going to have to deal with this every night when I first moved in here."

I had the urge to ask her about it, to find out if she was worried and if Christopher was happy or what the fuck his problem was. Instead I kept my mouth shut, figured I was hardly in a position to judge Christopher's behavior.

The movie played on, but it did nothing to drown out the giggles emanating from Christopher's room. I turned up the volume, but still they were distinct, probably because as much as we didn't want to, Aly and I couldn't stop straining to listen.

Finally Aly blew a frustrated breath toward the ceiling. "Do you want to watch the rest of this in my room? It's always quieter in there."

"Sounds good to me."

Aly clicked off the TV, hugged her pillow against her chest, and headed into her room. She left the door open behind her, a clear invitation.

I stepped inside. As curious as I'd been, I'd never been in here before. It was dark, though moonlight bled in from her opened blinds. A fairly large bed was pushed into the corner of one wall below the window, and directly across the room, a smaller TV sat on top of a horizontal six-drawer dresser. A large mirror and dressing table with a regular kitchen chair were set up to the right of it. Filling the space between her bed and closet was a tall bookcase. Spines and spines of books were lined up. A row of large, unmarked books filled up the bottom shelf, reminding me a lot of the journal I had tucked in my bag back out in the other room.

I resisted a smile. These had to be Aly's sketch pads.

The bed was framed in mahogany wood, the base and carved headboard one large piece. It was unmade, the maroon comforter bunched and twisted with black sheets. Nothing really seemed to match all that well, but it all flowed, this eclectic feel of peacefulness coming over me the moment my feet sank into the soft cushion of her carpet.

Aly gestured toward her bed. "Feel free."

I eyed it. I knew a trap when I saw one. Not one Aly had set, but one that my fingers would fall into. Lying next to her would be a very bad idea.

I dropped to the comfort of the carpeted floor. "I'm good on the floor. I need to stretch out a bit."

"Suit yourself."

She hopped onto her bed and turned the movie back on, the flick popping back to life in the same place we'd abandoned it. Luckily the shit going down in the next room was completely drowned out, and it was just me and Aly and this dumb comedy that really had nothing to offer other than a distraction from the racing that normally happened in my mind.

That and the annoying chime that kept going off on Aly's cell phone every ten seconds.

The screen would light up, she'd tap out a message, tuck it back at her side, and then the whole thing would repeat again.

"You know that's really fucking annoying, right?"

She sat up on her elbow, looking down at me in confusion. "What?"

"You having a conversation with someone when you're supposed to be watching a movie with me."

She rolled her eyes. "I am watching a movie with you." Her phone chimed again. Those green eyes widened, and she laughed.

"And who is so important that you'd rather be talking to them than giving your full attention to me?" I didn't really understand why I was feeling petulant and moody and a little bit pissed off, but shit . . . she was the one who'd suggested we watch a movie, saying she just wanted to relax and unwind. She was supposed to be mine for the night.

"Giving you my full attention, huh? I thought we were watching a movie."

I didn't miss the fact that she didn't answer my question. It was a guy. Motherfucker. I couldn't tell if I was feeling protec-

tive or possessive, because I was seeing flashes of both the innocent little girl I'd always taken care of and a gorgeous one lying
on her bed. And I had no fucking idea if the one on the bed was
innocent or not.

God. I couldn't even stomach the thought.

But shit, she was twenty years old, and I wasn't delusional.

It chimed again, and before I realized what I was doing, I
flipped over onto my hands and knees. Crawling the few feet
across the floor to her bed, I climbed up onto it. I grabbed the
stupid white thing she had buried in the covers. The red light
flashed its annoyance.

"What the hell are you doing?" She was caught off guard and
her voice was shocked and raspy. I'd somehow managed to end
up caging her, my legs on both sides of hers, one hand planted on
the bed above her shoulder and the other gripping her phone.
Her mouth dropped open, her eyes wide with surprise. I was so
close to her I could feel her heart pounding, the beat steady and
hard. Something inside me screamed to back away because I
knew without a doubt I shouldn't be near her this way, that I
shouldn't allow my blood to burn, race, thrum as I listened to her
heart rate escalate. I shouldn't like her reaction to me.

But I did.

"Who is it?" I demanded.

"It's just Gabe."

"And who the fuck is Gabe?"

She seemed to shake herself out of whatever stupor she'd
been in, and she emitted a disbelieving snort. "What are you,
twelve, Jared? Come on. And who the fuck are you to ask?" she
challenged as she plucked her phone from my hand.

I wanted to tell her to watch her mouth and kiss it all at the
same time. "Your *friend*, remember? And friends don't let friends
text dickheads." Or date them.

"Oh, really?"

"Really."

Her breasts jostled as she laughed, and I was sure she meant the sweet little sound to be intimidating and defiant. She pushed up to sitting, squaring her shoulders.

God, I really did want to kiss her.

"And just what makes you think Gabe is a dick? You don't know anything about him."

I inclined my head toward the clock beside her bed that indicated the time was way past appropriate. "Then what does he want?"

"He asked me to come over and hang out with him."

"At one in the morning? That's exactly what I'm talking about. What does Christopher think about this guy?"

"Oh, please. Christopher? Really? And if you hadn't noticed, I'm not a little girl anymore."

Yeah, I fucking noticed.

"Well, I don't like it." Obviously her brother wasn't watching out for her. He never had. That was always my job.

"You don't like it, huh?"

"Nope." My eyes flitted over her face, searching for something. What, I wasn't sure. I didn't own her. I didn't really even know her. But I wanted to.

She blinked a few times, shaking her head as she tilted a small smile up at me. "You're kind of ridiculous, Jared. And I wasn't planning on going. I was telling him I was busy."

Relief tugged at my chest while I reached out and again tugged at a strand of her hair, like it was a little connection between us, something tethering us together. This time I wound it through my fingers, watching her face as I did.

Suddenly everything felt thick and slow, like honey—my mouth, her eyes, the tension that suddenly filled the air. For a minute, I wanted to pretend that nothing had ever happened, that the years had passed and I was still good and that maybe Aly would see me that way. Pretend that maybe I'd be worth taking a chance on. Right then, pretending seemed like a pretty good place to be.

I watched the lump in her throat as she swallowed. "Why don't we finish the movie?" she whispered.

"Yeah, that's probably a good idea."

Against my better judgment, which apparently was lacking in every capacity tonight, I settled down beside her on the bed.

She rolled to her side, tucked her pillow under her head, and angled herself so she could see the TV. I lay behind her, my head propped in my hand. I did my best at trying to pay attention to what was happening on the television. Instead all my focus was directed at her.

"So I guess I probably need to know who this Gabe is?" I finally asked because somehow I knew not knowing would eat me alive.

I sensed her shrug, and heard a soft breath of air pass through her mouth on a sigh. "I don't know, Jared. We've kind of been seeing each other for the last couple months. I like him okay, I guess."

My jaw clenched. This time there was no doubt it was jealousy.

I said nothing, turned my attention back to the TV. For the first time since I'd returned, I truly regretted the decision to come. It was easier not knowing what I'd been missing.

Something inside me twisted. The soft spot I'd always held for her now felt raw. I hated her *I guess*, hated she would even for a second settle for less than what would truly give her joy. I hadn't been back all that long, but I already knew she deserved joy. And here I was, the sick fuck who wished I was good enough to give it to her.

Internally I scoffed.

I could wish all I wanted, but it'd never change who I was.

It only took about fifteen minutes for Aly to fall asleep. Her soft breaths evened out. She stirred and rolled to her back. One arm found its way up to drape over her head, her body bowed as she stretched her long legs out, one tweaked to the side.

I knew I should go and find my spot on the couch where I belonged.

But for a moment, I took. Took in her peace. Took in her beauty.

When I couldn't stand lying beside her any longer, I climbed to the end of her bed, flipped off her TV, and slipped out her door.

Tonight, I refused to sleep. I couldn't go there. Just for one fucking night, I didn't want to see. I dug through my bag and pulled out my journal, sat on the couch in the dead silence. I wrote about things I didn't know but wished I could have.

TEN

Aleena

The next night, moonlight soaked into my otherwise darkened room. Tonight the moon was high, bright, full. I'd gotten home from work to an empty apartment. There was something about a quiet night like this that fueled my imagination and gave me inspiration, even though the product on my page reflected nothing that shone in the sky. My hand swished in quick strokes. The paper felt thick under my skin. I wet my bottom lip, chewed at it a little, then lifted my face to look out my bedroom window again. I didn't have the best view in the world, just a portion of the parking lot below that was lit by streetlamps, although at least they were dim enough that I could still see a whisper of clouds stretched thin across the sky. I contemplated the sight for a bit, before I turned my consideration back to the sketch pad I had balanced on my lap.

I still didn't know what to make of it, what to make of him.

The last week had left my head swimming. It was like Jared and I were in this constant tug-of-war that neither of us knew how to play, pushing and pulling, attracting and repelling.

Reading him seemed impossible. Sometimes I thought I saw it—him looking at me the way I looked at him—like maybe he wanted to touch me, to experience what I'd feel like under his skin. Because God, there was no way to describe how much I wanted to feel him under mine.

But every time I thought we were making progress, he'd grow cold.

I frowned as I tilted the pad. Realization set in as I shaded in the lines that constantly tugged at the edge of his perfect mouth.

No. It wasn't coldness in his expression.

It was fear.

At the faint tapping at my door, my head snapped up. The shift in my heart rate was immediate. Blood pumped hard, forcing the acceleration of my pulse.

Steadying my voice, I called softly, "Come in."

Slowly, the doorknob turned, and the door cracked open a fraction. The face I couldn't get off my mind peeked through, a halo of light from the hall silhouetting him. The apprehension that had pounded my pulse two seconds before was set at ease with just the hint of his presence.

"Hey," Jared murmured, blinking as he seemed to adjust to the dim light.

"Hi. What are you up to?" I shifted so I could see him better.

His eyes narrowed as if trying to make out the scene playing out in my room, his attention zeroing in on me sitting cross-legged on my bed with the large sketch pad in my lap.

He dropped his head to the side, and I could see the flicker of a smile twisting at one corner of his lips, this hint of uncertainty holding him back. "I couldn't sleep . . . and . . . I don't know. I thought maybe you were still awake."

Flipping my sketch pad closed, I set it aside, cocking my head at him. "And what if I wasn't? You were just going to wake me up? It is after midnight, you know."

It was all tease. As if his interruption could ever be one I didn't welcome. By now that had to be obvious.

I wanted him here.

A self-conscious chuckle rumbled in his throat, and he covered his mouth with his palm, dragging it over the length of his jaw and down his chin. When he dropped his hand, a less than remorseful grin had emerged on his face, and even in the muted light, I could see the mischief in his eyes. "So maybe I was passing down the hall and just happened to hear a little rustling in your room when I put my ear to your door."

"Really?" I said with all the offended disbelief I could project into my voice. "You were listening at my door?"

He slipped inside and silently shut the door behind him. "What? I'm fucking bored," he said just over his breath, completely shameless. "Sue me."

I shook my head. "You've got a lot of nerve, Jared Holt," I whispered so he could barely hear. My brow lifted as I sucked in my bottom lip, raking my teeth on it before I set it free, feigned disappointment in the tsk of my tongue. "In some circles, that admission might earn you a reputation."

He laughed as he started across my room. I didn't miss the hardness in the sound. "I already have a reputation, Aly."

My gaze locked on him as he moved toward me. I didn't even attempt to force myself to look away as he crossed the room.

Any attempt would be in vain.

He'd showered, and his blond hair had darkened to a near brown and was pushed back from his face. Sleep pants sat low on his waist, the strength of his chest covered by a tight black V-neck tee. His story peeked above its neckline, the vestige of a distorted rose rising up at the center of his chest. Under his shirt I knew that rose was in full bloom, the red petals beginning to fall like wilted teardrops. Green and blue tendrils of smoke and vines stretched out in a twisted bough around it, crawling along the exposed portion of his collarbones. My gaze traced the ink down his arms to hands that were fisted as he advanced toward me.

My stomach tightened.

God, part of me wished he weren't so beautiful. Maybe then I'd have a chance to look away, to guard my heart, to save myself from the need he had built up in me. But with every step he took, it only increased.

I still couldn't make sense of what had happened last night while I was texting Gabe. Jared's reaction had come at me so quickly it'd left me blindsided and in a bumbling stupor that had taken a few seconds to pass. I couldn't tell if he was playing the asshole overprotective brother or the asshole possessive boyfriend.

Either way, it'd been an asshole move.

But just as quickly as his outburst had come, he'd softened, and I had felt a sadness saturate him, so strong it was tangible. It had wrapped us tight, thickening the air. Nothing had ever been harder than that moment when I'd forced myself to lie still and pretend I was interested in the movie when all I wanted to do was roll over so I could see his face, to find something written there that might help me understand what he was feeling.

My palms had burned with the need to be pressed to his chest or maybe to his face, and my body had itched to see if maybe he'd hold me the way I longed for him to.

Most of all, I had wanted to *tell* him. So bad it hurt.

But instead I'd forced myself to pretend to be asleep.

Now I scooted farther back against the headboard to make room for him.

He sat down on the edge of my bed.

"So you couldn't sleep?" I asked.

Those bare feet were flat on my carpet, his forearms resting on his knees. He cocked his head up, this pensive twist to his full lips as he drew his eyes into tight slits, studying me. I got the distinct feeling a decision was being made. Finally he spoke, honesty laced in his words. "No, I can sleep, Aly. I'd just rather not."

As simple as it was, somehow I knew he was sharing a sliver of the secrets he kept. This was Jared's way of opening up to me.

I brought my sketch pad back to my lap as some sort of security blanket, and tucked my knees up higher to my chest so I could open it to my last drawing and still keep it hidden. Keeping my eyes on the page, I took a chance. "Why?"

My attention flicked to his face, shot back to the pad just as fast. Instinctively my hands went to work, and the sound of my soft strokes covered the mild discomfort between us.

Jared sighed, shifted, threaded his fingers together between his knees. He stared at the floor. "Because when I close my eyes, I see things I don't want to see." Low, humorless laughter escaped his mouth. "They are always there, Aly, but when I close my eyes"—he released a ragged breath—"the images I see are, like . . . vivid." He frowned deeply, as if shielding himself from them now. "Real. So fucking *real* . . . like it's happening right then and there's nothing I can do to stop it."

My spirit thrashed as if I was somehow sharing in his pain. I swallowed, refusing to allow myself to speak because I knew right then what Jared really needed was someone to listen.

Lifting his chin in my direction, Jared seemed to contemplate my pencil, his head gently bobbing as if absorbing the movement of the strokes of my hand. I licked my lips and carried on as if I weren't nailed to the bed by his penetrating gaze.

"I bet what I see is just as real to me as whatever the pictures you keep hidden in the pages of those books are to you."

Shock stilled my hand, and my eyes snapped up to him.

Pain wrapped around his features and deepened the lines that seemed to be permanently etched between his eyebrows. I was caught in it, and couldn't look away.

My voice was soft. "I draw and you wish you could erase."

His lids dropped closed, stayed that way for a moment, his jaw clenching and unclenching, before he opened them to me. "You create and I destroy."

I slowly shook my head, my words hoarse. "That's not what I meant."

Sighing, he turned his attention back to his feet. "It doesn't mean it's not the truth."

Silence settled over us for a few minutes, and I could feel the shift, the way he'd tucked our words somewhere inside himself, as if maybe I'd earned a token of his trust.

Then he looked at me with an amused smile, gesturing to my sketch pad with his chin. "Can I see?"

Shaking my head, I buried a smile by biting my lip. "You should know better than that, Jared."

A throaty chuckle filled my room, and he lay back on my bed. My toes were pressed into the covers just at his side. And I loved it, loved that he wanted to be here with me, loved that what I saw in him was kind.

Even if he couldn't see it himself.

He wove his fingers together and rested them on his chest, the incongruous numbers tattooed across his knuckles meshed. He sat very still, and seemed to drift away in his thoughts.

I kept my attention on my page, until I felt the gravity of his stare burning into my forehead, like I could sense a pull. Drawn to him. I always had been.

When I turned to him, the grin on his face was something I almost didn't recognize because it'd been so long since I'd seen it. But I had, so many times before. I'd witnessed it in the carefree boy who had meant everything to me.

His blue eyes danced as they flitted from my sketch pad to my face. "It used to drive me fucking crazy that you wouldn't let me see what you kept hidden inside those books."

I gasped when he suddenly moved. He twisted onto his knees in almost a crouch, his chin tucked and his gaze peeking at me from just above the top margin of my book. Predatory. As if at any second he was going to pounce and wrestle it from me. My breath caught. Tingles sped under the surface of my skin, and he hadn't even touched me.

My hands tightened around the edges of my sketch pad like a vise.

"And you know what, Aly?" His eyes darted everywhere, absorbing, taking in the lines of my face, my mouth, my hands, the pad I clutched to my chest, before they fixed firmly on my own. "It still drives me fucking crazy."

Strength bunched in the muscles rippling along his shoulders, but in his movements there was this playfulness, so much like I remembered. An echo of our childhood sounded in my ear, the way he'd pestered and begged me to let him see, but never forced me into anything I didn't want to do.

At that time it was because I was embarrassed and afraid he might make fun of me. I didn't want him to see the inexperience in my drawings. Now it was because it'd be like slicing my heart open and exposing everything I wasn't ready for him to see.

It'd scare him as much as it scared me.

Shock stunned me when he abruptly grabbed me by the ankles and dragged me down, forcing me flat on the bed. The sketch pad slid off my lap, facedown on the sheets.

Suddenly I was staring up at Jared's gorgeous face as he hovered over me. He straddled my waist, and I couldn't think, couldn't breathe, could only feel the blood coursing through my veins and pounding in my ears.

His nose was an inch from mine, his hands resting on both sides of my head, but he was everywhere—everywhere—sinking into my consciousness and my spirit.

Then he smirked, all cute and smug, and my eyes went wide when the realization hit me. "Oh my God, Jared Holt, don't you even think about it. Don't you dare," I begged in a whisper, my voice strained with need and a little bit of old childhood fear.

He knew exactly how to get me.

"What?" he asked with feigned innocence, before his fingers began to tap at the center of my chest on my breastbone with his index fingers. His legs cinched around my sides to keep my arms pinned to the bed. This had been Christopher and Jared's favorite form of torture.

I bucked up, trying to throw him from my body, or maybe I was trying to bring him closer; I couldn't tell. "Jared . . . stop . . . Oh my God, you're such an ass."

I made an attempt at flailing my arms. His thighs held them down. Held me down.

Oh my God.

He laughed, quiet and low. "You've tortured me for years. Don't you think it's only fair I pay you back a little?"

The taps came harder, faster, his touch no longer that of a boy's fingers, but now heavy and strong. But somehow it felt the same.

How intensely had I missed this?

The push and pull. The tease and the taunt.

I'd missed my friend.

Furiously, I squirmed. Tears gathered, streaking down the sides of my face, and dripping into my hair before I knew it. A low whine rose from deep within my throat and mixed with the quiet laughter I couldn't hold back.

A hushed chuckle tumbled from Jared's mouth, so thick it was almost a pant, his expression so soft, like just maybe he was seeing the exact same thing as I was.

And I could feel this change in the air. As if every cell in his body shifted, Jared slowed, then stilled. Mesmerized, I watched as his tongue flicked out to wet his full lips. I was hyperaware of every inch of his body that touched mine, the fire that lit under my skin, how our chests rose and fell in sync. He raised a cautious hand, his attention pitching between my eyes and his intent. A dense hesitation weighted his movements before he seemed to give in and gently ran the back of his fingers along the trail of tears that had slipped down my temple.

A fragmented sigh stuttered from my lips as they parted. Never had I felt anything better than what I found in Jared's touch.

His gaze captured mine before his fingertips traced down

my cheek, swept along my jaw, and barely glanced over my lips. "You grew up on me, Aly," he murmured, the words rough, almost in awe.

"You were gone for a long time," I whispered against the fingers he fluttered along my bottom lip.

"For too long." He seemed to blink away the thought, as if he didn't want to believe the truth that had just fallen from his mouth. He rolled to his side. Intuition made me follow, and I turned to lie face-to-face with him. In silence, I stared at the boy who had held me hostage in my heart and mind for so long. My secret.

Could anything be more surreal than the fact that he now lay in my bed?

Thankfulness swept through me in a torrent of joy.

Smiling softly, he reached out and pressed the pad of his thumb to my chin. The notion was sweet, but it did things to me that I didn't quite understand. I mean, I did. I understood desire, the overwhelming need that built in the pit of my stomach and longed for more. But this was so much greater than that.

"I bet whatever you keep hidden in the pages of those books is absolutely beautiful, Aly." He swallowed, diverting his gaze to the far wall before he dropped it to meet mine. A tender palm came to rest on the side of my face. He caressed his thumb over the apple of my cheek. "How could it not be? Look at you . . . you have to be the most beautiful creature I've ever seen."

Pain reverberated in his words. Still they wrapped around me like the warmest embrace.

My fingers ventured to his chest, twisting in his shirt. The strong throb of his pulse thundered under them. "Everything I love is in the pages of those books, Jared."

The admission sounded like a confession of my heart. I realized that was exactly what it was. On some level I wanted him to know what he wasn't ready to hear.

Stark sunlight blinded my eyes. I squinted and adjusted my sunglasses as I settled back in my chair and lifted my face to the intensity of the summer sun. Stretching my legs out in front of me, I bathed in the comfort seeping into my skin.

Megan slurped from her iced coffee beside me. "I'm sweating like a dog over here, Aly."

I tossed her a grin. Her blond hair was all mussed and piled in a mess on the top of her head as she fanned at the back of her neck. "You are such a wimp." I lifted my face back to the sky. "Are you ever going to get used to the heat or am I destined to hear you complain about it for the rest of our lives?"

"Um, yeah, you're probably going to hear me complain about it for the rest of our lives. There will be no shaking Rhode Island from my bones just like there's no shaking Phoenix from yours."

"Touché." I smirked, and she laughed before she leaned her elbows on the small bistro table between us.

"I feel like I haven't hung out with you in forever. I miss you," she said. She took another sip from her straw, and I went for mine. We sat outside a little coffee shop on Mill, watching people as they ambled down the busy street. This was the first day we'd had to ourselves since the night when my life had been tilted on its axis.

Thrown, really. I no longer knew where I stood.

Megan and I had shared a few texts, but our work schedules seemed to always conflict, and we hadn't really connected in the three weeks that had passed.

"I know. It's ridiculous I haven't talked to you in so long." My brow piqued in question as I turned in her direction. "So, how are things with Sam?"

She shrugged and busied herself with her straw. Sadness wove through her sigh. "I always promised myself I'd never be that girl . . . the needy one who'd do anything to win that little bit of attention that some guy is willing to give her." She released a bitter laugh. It was a little angry and a lot disappointed. She offered me a telling smile. "I didn't make him work for it, Aly." She blew out a breath. "I should have listened to you. Now it's like I'm sitting around waiting for . . . something . . . *anything*. Sometimes it seems like he's totally into me, and the next it's like he couldn't care less that I exist." She shook her head at herself. "So stupid."

I swiveled toward her and leaned on the table. I couldn't stand this coming from her. Guilt twisted in me, because I should have realized something was going on when I received her texts. I should have been there for her.

She chewed at her lip. "You know that's not me, right?"

"Megan." I frowned and edged in closer. "I'm not going to judge you. You know me better than that. We never know how things are going to turn out, and more important than that, we can't help how we feel."

She nodded, but the small jerks of her head resonated with shame. "But you've always been so strong. You've never allowed yourself to become vulnerable like that. I mean, sometimes it makes me worry about you and I get scared you're never going to find someone to love because you won't put yourself out there to be loved. But mostly, I've just admired you."

Another stab of guilt. I'd always been vulnerable. I'd just never been honest enough to allow her to see it. "I guess I've been holding out for the right guy, Megan. We all find them at different times and in different ways."

Only I found mine when I was fourteen. A flutter swam through my being, Jared's youthful smile forever etched in my mind. Really, I'd known him my entire life. I *found* him in almost every memory I had.

Confusion creased Megan's brow. "How will we ever know when it's right?"

Pursing my lips, I took a chance at what I knew as my own truth. "I think we'll just know."

She groaned and dropped her forehead to the table. "But this feels so right . . . and so completely wrong."

Quiet laughter spilled from my mouth. "You have it bad, Megan."

She grinned up at me from her resting place on the table. "Pathetic, aren't I?"

"Nah." I shook my head. "It isn't worth it if it doesn't hurt a little."

She rose, nodding as if those were the most important words I'd ever said.

Or perhaps the most foolish.

"So, what about you? Have you been hanging out with Gabe?"

Pausing, I searched for what to say before I finally answered. "No. I've been busy at work and at home."

Speculation lifted her brow, and I knew the questions were coming. "Busy at home, huh? Does this have anything to do with this mysterious visitor who showed up a couple of weeks ago? One I've never even heard of before? Hmm?" She drew this out in a suggestive prod. She struggled for a look of offense. I thought she might be too innocently beautiful for it ever to work.

"He's just an old friend, Megan," I said with the least amount of defensiveness I could inject in it. No need to raise more suspicion than I already had.

"And not important enough that you ever thought to mention him to me?"

No. It was completely the opposite. He'd been so important it seemed impossible to utter his name.

"It's not that, Megan," I admitted. "We were all really good friends when we were younger . . . We grew up together. Even though Christopher was his best friend, he was *my* best friend. You know?"

I searched her face, wondering if she could understand. Her expression told me maybe she did. Sadness clouded my tone. "In one day, he lost it all, Megan."

"What happened?"

"There was this accident . . ." I shook my head. "He could never see past what happened and he started making some really bad choices. We all watched him fall apart and we couldn't do anything about it. He ended up getting arrested and sent away." I lifted one shoulder in resignation. "That was the last time I saw him."

"So he's the one," she mused.

"What are you talking about?"

"Just because you keep secrets, Aly, doesn't mean I don't know you have them."

I couldn't say anything. My throat was suddenly dry.

"You care about him a lot, yeah?"

"Yeah," I admitted. "I have no idea how long he's staying, so I've been spending as much time with him as I can." I didn't mention that I would be devastated when he left.

Since we'd watched that movie in an attempt to drown out

another of Christopher's conquests, Jared had snuck into my room every night. Two weeks had passed since the night after when he'd first touched me, the hand on my face rocking something loose deep inside me. Every night he'd come to me, his knuckles lightly rapping against my door before he would silently enter into the dimness of my room. He always came when it was late, an hour or two after I'd told him and Christopher I was going to bed. I'd say good night, then lie awake in my room listening as the apartment slowly fell into silence. It was as if I could anticipate him in the moment before he knocked on my door from, a subtle tension filling the space as I waited. Why he felt the need to sneak into my room, I didn't really know. But it was like he got it, too. The time we spent together felt like something that was our own, a secret shared between friends as the trust between us grew. I'd come to expect him just as much as he seemed to expect me, and a slow trust had begun to build between us.

We'd talk for hours about nothing and everything. I'd glide along the banks of his sadness, dipping my toes to test the water but without ever diving into the torrent where I knew Jared continued to drown. My mouth was continually dry, begging to be opened, to ask the questions I so desperately wanted to know.

But I was scared, didn't want to douse this weak flame that had been lit. If I pushed him beyond the place he seemed comfortable taking me to, I was sure he'd stamp the fire out just as quickly as he'd struck it.

The worst of it was how badly I ached, and each night it only grew. I *wanted* him, more than anything I'd ever wanted in my life. It didn't help that he was constantly brushing his fingers along my face, weaving them through my hair as he wound my confusion higher.

But it never went past that.

Megan tilted her head as she dug a little, a whisper of a grin threatening at her mouth. "Is he hot?"

"Megan," I scolded, before I laughed and shook my head. Slanting my eyes in her direction, I gave in. "Incredibly."

It felt really good to admit it. To hell with raising suspicions.

She snorted and sat back in her chair. "I don't think I've ever seen you blush before, Aly Moore."

"I'm not blushing," I insisted, even though I could feel the heat on my cheeks. Damn it. "It's just hot out here."

"Sure it is." Her smirk deepened before she gentled it into a smile. "I'm glad your best friend is back, Aly . . . even if he is encroaching on my best friend territory," she teased, although there was nothing that even suggested jealousy in her words.

It wasn't hard to see why she'd so easily become mine.

Megan and I parted with a huge hug in front of our cars. "See you soon," I said before I dropped into the driver's seat of my car and headed home. Anticipation spurred me forward. Going home had become what I looked forward to most.

Was it ridiculous I could hardly wait to see Jared again?

Maybe.

But like I'd told Megan, I had no idea how long he would stay, how much time I'd be granted.

I wanted every second I could get.

Pulling through the apartment gates, I wove through the complex and parked in my space. My steps were light as I crossed the pavement. The sun hung low on the horizon, the evening's promise of the coming darkness. Pink rays stretched far across the sky, painted the clouds every color of pink and blue and orange. The edges of the clouds lit like a burning rim of fire before they were swallowed by the approaching night.

Gorgeous.

I hurried up the steps and let myself into the apartment. Christopher was in the kitchen. Making dinner. I fumbled to a standstill, taken aback. A slow smile slid across my face. What was going on here?

Jared sat at the bar, the heels of his boots hooked on the barstool, sipping from a beer. God, was he beautiful.

He looked up as I entered, this welcoming smile crossing his face that touched me from across the room. "Hey," he said.

Christopher peeked at me from over his shoulder. "Aly! Where have you been? I thought you were off today."

I dropped my purse to the floor and tossed my keys on top of it. "I was. I was just hanging out with Megan this afternoon."

"I was getting worried. I'm making you dinner."

I shot Jared a worried glance, then turned back to Christopher. "You're making dinner, huh? Should I be concerned?"

He laughed. "Nope. No reason for concern. I just feel bad you're feeding us all the time. Figured it was my turn." Christopher leaned in to smell the pot. "And this is going to be fucking delicious. Just wait." He grinned at me. "See, no need to worry, little sister."

Wandering into the kitchen, I grabbed a soda from the fridge. I closed the door with my hip and leaned back against the cool metal. Jared sat directly opposite me, something playing around the edges of his mouth. He shook his head before he lifted his bottle to drain the rest of his beer, exposing the underside of his muscular neck. I wanted nothing more than to press my mouth to it.

I wondered what he'd think if he knew my thoughts, if he saw what I continually played out in my mind. Did he want it as much as I did? Did he think of me when he left my room to take his place on the couch while I lay on my bed, wishing he were sharing it with me instead?

He lowered his bottle, eyeing me over the top.

I hoped he did.

When I sensed Christopher watching me, I dropped my attention to the floor. Whatever he was thinking, he shook off, and he grabbed some plates from the cupboard. "Okay, this is ready, you two."

I walked up behind Christopher and wrapped my arms around his waist. "Thank you. This was really sweet of you."

He handed me a plate, smirking. "Don't get used to it."

I covered my heart with my hand. "I wouldn't dare."

We all moved to the table and ate the stew Christopher had made together like the family we had once been. Satisfaction churned in my depths. I peeked up at Jared as I took a bite, and that same place deep inside me clenched.

How badly my heart wanted him to stay.

My gut warned me he would not.

When we finished, I gathered our plates to do the dishes. Christopher grabbed them a couple of beers. I passed. The two of them moved to the couch, and Christopher flipped on the TV and turned it to a game.

Once I finished the dishes, I went into my room, picked out a book, and retreated outside to the balcony. I settled onto a chair. The small lamp mounted to the wall shed muted light on the words splayed across the pages. Tonight it seemed impossible to focus on them. Instead I watched the lightning touching down in the distance, the gathering of cumulus clouds as they rose high and ominous in the night sky, illuminated in the bright flashes of light. Nothing could compare in beauty to a desert storm.

I got lost in it.

I jumped when the balcony door slid open. My face flashed up to meet Jared's smiling one.

"What are you doing out here all by yourself?" he asked as he stepped out onto the balcony.

"Just relaxing." I drew my feet up onto the chair and hugged my knees to my chest. "It's so beautiful out here."

Jared slid down against the wall the way he always did, his knees bent and his feet flat on the concrete. He dipped his head to the side as he lit a cigarette. Smoke curled up around his face, casting him in a veiled halo. He inhaled deeply as all the weight seemed to drop from his shoulders. He exhaled toward the sky, spoke quietly. "This was always my favorite time of year."

"It's always been mine, too." I hugged myself a little tighter. "I love that I can feel the monsoon coming . . . building up."

A comfortable silence coiled us together, as if we both were lost in the memories of the summers we'd shared long ago. They'd been so easy and good.

"Do you remember that lightning storm we got stuck in?" he asked before he took another drag, leaning forward to rest his forearms on his knees. "When we were at the tree fort and the storm came really close?"

Mild embarrassment tugged one side of my mouth into a smile. "Yeah."

Jared's laughter was warm, a low rumble from the deepest part of his being. "God, you were the cutest fucking kid I ever met. Always trying to act so tough so you could hang out with us. But the second that bolt of lightning struck out in the field, you froze." He chuckled and smoke filtered from his open mouth as he lifted his face to the night sky.

And I could see it, the bright flash of energy that sizzled through the air when the lightning struck just a hundred or so yards away.

Quietly, Jared continued. "Christopher hightailed it out of there, but no matter what I said, there was no getting you down from that tree fort. God, that was probably the worst place to be in a lightning storm."

My voice softened as I floated through the ripples of his memory. "You sat with me in that tree for an hour while it poured rain down on us." Even then, his arms had been warm as he sheltered me from the cold. A comfort. And he'd promised me he'd never leave me behind.

Warmth swam in the pools of his blue eyes. "We were in so much trouble when we finally got home. Your mom was so pissed off at me. Said I should have known better than to keep you out in that weather. Mom busted my ass when your mom sent me home. . . . I must've been grounded for a week . . ." He trailed off, and he dropped his head, his fingers twitching in agitation.

I raised my face to meet his when he finally looked back up at me. "And you never told it was me who'd begged you to stay." I hesitated, drew in a breath, before I said, "You were my best friend, Jared."

A wistful smile ridged his perfect mouth. Then he shook it off and stamped out his cigarette. "It's hot out here. I'm going to head inside."

I nodded away his excuse. Guess that time I'd dipped my toes in too deep.

"Okay," I mumbled, turning my attention back to the horizon, as Jared climbed to his feet and slipped back inside without a parting word.

An hour passed before I finally gathered my things to go inside. I pulled the slider open to find Jared and Christopher on the couch, watching a game. The room was dark save for the images playing out on the screen. Christopher seemed absorbed while Jared seemed detached.

And I didn't know what it was, but a surge of bravery flooded me. I took a chance. I passed close by the back of the couch and wove my shaky fingers through Jared's hair. It was soft. So soft. He trembled beneath my touch. I suppressed the overwhelming need I felt to bury my face in the haven of it, maybe to press my nose to his neck and inhale. To breathe him in. Instead I edged around the couch and said, "I'm going to bed. See you two in the morning."

Christopher seemed to barely notice me and tossed me an offhanded "Night," oblivious of whatever was building between Jared and me.

"Good night," Jared whispered, his eyes trailing my steps, locking on mine when I paused to look back at him from my door. His expression made it clear he was the furthest from oblivious.

It took him an hour, but finally I heard the light tapping that tickled my ears and escalated my pulse before the door cracked open. A sliver of light from the hallway bled inside as Jared stole into my darkened room.

I lay on my bed, waiting.

Chuckling, Jared crossed the room. "Christopher just left. Said he has some girl he promised he'd go see. Don't think I'm quite interesting enough for him."

Jared climbed onto the bed beside me. He didn't hesitate to

twist his finger through a lock of my hair as if it belonged there, didn't hide the heave of contented air he pushed from his lungs. He settled so close to me I was sure he could count the thundering beats of my heart.

"Haven't you figured that out by now?" Still I whispered. I wasn't sure why.

Throaty laughter ricocheted against my walls. "Yeah . . . I might have noticed. What is up with him, anyway? Is he happy?" Jared turned a fraction, blinking toward the ceiling. "It's like he's chasing after something and can't seem to find it."

"Aren't we all chasing after something?"

Lines deepened on Jared's brow, a frown marring his face. "I don't know, Aly."

I inched forward. In the small space separating us, I relished the warmth I felt radiating from his body. My hands went to their safe spot, to his T-shirt-clad chest. I was still too fearful to touch the skin I wanted to disappear into.

"I think he's happy, Jared, but he changed when you were sent away."

Jared stiffened under me, because for the first time, I *jumped*. I was ready to submerge myself in the dangerous waters that held Jared under. I'd been treading them for too long.

With honesty, I opened my mouth. "I think it was fear . . . fear of losing someone who was so important to him." I'd never forget Christopher's eyes that night, when we'd found ourselves face-to-face in our hall, listening to our mother sobbing in her room. The vibrant green had waned from his eyes as Christopher had lost the last bit of his childhood, his innocence replaced with pain. Haunted. There was no other way to describe it. When I thought of what I saw in his eyes that day, I sometimes wondered what he had seen in mine.

"He ended up breaking up with Samantha about a week later." Christopher had dated her for a year. I was pretty sure they'd been each other's firsts. She was devastated, but Christopher had just seemed numb to her pain like he was to everything else. "He started going out all the time," I slowly continued, knowing I was traversing dangerous ground, "hanging out with random girls. Now I can't really tell if it's a habit or a game or if he's subconsciously guarding himself from something he doesn't want to feel."

Jared's lips spread into a thin line, as if something that had nagged at him had been confirmed.

"It's all so meaningless to him," I said quietly, self-consciously fidgeting with Jared's shirt. "I hate that those girls mean so little to him . . . that sex means so little to him." I tipped my face up and captured his gaze. My mouth opened and closed as I struggled with what to say. As much as I didn't want to know, I couldn't keep myself from asking. "What about you? Have you ever been in love with anyone?"

Jared tilted his face away as if he didn't want me to see his confessions waiting there. He wavered before he spoke. "Sex is like fighting for me, Aly. It's a release, nothing more. I use girls just as shamelessly as Christopher does. Maybe in a different way. I don't know, but in the end, it's the same . . . It means *nothing.*"

I winced. Jealousy was not a pretty emotion. But it hit me hard. I'd grown so accustomed to this place that was ours that it'd become easy to imagine that this was all either of us had ever known . . . just the quiet of my room and the steady beat of our hearts.

In it, nothing else existed.

But Jared had known so much, so much pain, so much loss.

He'd known girls and what it felt like to be touched.

Was it wrong that I wanted that, too?

Pushing past our boundaries, I let my fingers climb up his chest and over one of his shoulders. Sinewy muscle jumped under my hands, beckoned me forward just as assuredly as they fought to resist my exploration.

I held my breath when I reached the bare skin of his neck. Every inch of my body lit, flames licking through my veins and blazing in my stomach. Shivers coursed over the surface of my skin.

How was it possible that one person could affect me this way?

I glanced up at his face. Turbulent blue eyes stared down at me. In them I felt a range of emotions, a warning, an appeal. Anger and affection. Most of all, I saw fear.

Tentatively, I dropped my gaze and watched as my fingers trailed down over his shoulder and traced the ink on his left arm. This arm was covered in blacks and grays, twisted shapes and faces that screamed his horrors. On the inside of his wrist was scripted *Lest I forget*.

Jared shuddered as if the contact caused him physical pain. But he didn't pull away, and he released a stuttered breath across my face.

"Were you scared when they sent you away?" The question came so softly I thought perhaps I'd only uttered it in my head.

Still it sucked all the air from the room.

Frozen, Jared remained still, a million emotions spilling from his silence, before he finally spoke. "I was pissed, Aly." He grunted through the words. "It wasn't supposed to turn out like that. I thought I'd finally found a way to pay for what I'd done, and I managed to fuck that up, too."

Chills crawled along the surface of my skin. Jared had just confirmed my greatest fear. All these years I'd tried to convince myself otherwise, that there was no chance Jared would have tried to take his own life. Asked myself, *How could he?* Convinced myself I'd just misunderstood because it seemed impossible to believe.

And to know he'd been angry that he'd failed?

Confusion and hurt and fear saturated my spirit because I couldn't help worrying he'd try again.

I tried to swallow the lump wedged in the middle of my throat. "Maybe it turned out the way it was really supposed to be."

Hard laughter rocked from his chest. "Nothing turns out the way it's supposed to, Aly. And even if it did, I would only ruin it. You need to remember that. I warned you that you'd regret doing this. . . ." His fingers twisted deeper in my hair and he shifted to palm my neck with the other hand. He squeezed to emphasize our *friendship*, so hard it almost hurt. But it was my heart that hurt.

"How could I regret you?" I brought my hands to his face, held them there, gave in to the smolder singeing my skin. "I missed you, Jared. So much. They sent you away, and I thought I'd never see you again. Do you know how much that hurt?"

But I knew he really could have no idea.

How could he?

"I thought about you every day," I admitted, burrowing my head farther into the bed, farther into his warmth. We skirted along the edges of an embrace, his hands on my face, mine on his, the expanse between us so great I wasn't sure we'd ever be able to cross it. "What was it like?" I asked, lifting my face to his.

He paused, his breath palpable in the room. "I don't know, Aly. It sucked, I guess. People were always telling us what we could and couldn't do, all the while they were calling it a reha-bilitation center. There were some really good guys there, ones who just did some stupid stuff. I always hoped that maybe it did them some good. Most of us there were hopeless, though. It wouldn't matter what punishment we had, there was no chance of coming up with a different result."

Hopeless. I blinked, trying to understand, to make sense of the tone in his voice. "You felt you were like that?"

Sadness swelled in the room, a thickness that made my skin crawl with goose bumps.

"They let me out when I turned eighteen, Aly. *Eighteen.*" His voice cracked. "How fucking ridiculous is that? As if I'd paid my dues? As if spending two years of my pathetic existence behind bars would make up for what I'd done?"

Anger rushed from him, these waves of rage that pounded and fought against my spirit. Jared's body jerked, and I could feel him trying to hold it back, to hold it in. His face contorted as if he were trying to block it all out. "What kind of bullshit is that? She was worth so much more than that."

"Jared—"

In a blink, he shot off my bed and onto his feet.

Shocked, I twisted around and scrambled onto my hands and knees as I faced the man standing in the middle of my room. Agitation spun through him, twitching his muscles. My breaths came heavy and strong, mixed with the hostility seeping from Jared's pores.

Jerking both hands through his hair, he glared down at me, his eyes frantic. "Just don't, Aly." He touched his chest with a fisted hand, then dropped it. "Please don't say something that means *nothing*." He squeezed his eyes shut. "Please. Not you, too."

When he opened his eyes, the walls were down, everything bared to me.

Devastation.

It was the only thing I saw.

My heart twisted, this pain slicing me through to the core, cutting to the place where Jared had been a fantasy in my mind. There I'd imagined he had somehow still been whole and not what I saw now, a mess of the few mangled pieces of himself that now remained in the wake of his ruin.

"Jared," I whispered, my hand fluttering out in his direction, silently begging him to take it. Seeing him this way killed me. It reminded me too much of those months when I could do nothing but watch him fade away. Some part of me had held on to the hope that time had healed some of those pieces.

Now I was certain it had not.

He stumbled back to the door, recognition flashing in his eyes. "You can't fix me, Aly."

I winced and dropped my chin as if I could conceal the place where he attempted to extract my thoughts. "I know that," I whispered.

"Then don't try."

ELEVEN

Jared

Fuck.

I stood with my back to her door and tried to reel the evening in. My hands fisted in my hair, and a scream locked in my throat.

I couldn't breathe.

Because I didn't fucking know how.

Being in Aly's presence had proven that.

How had I allowed this to completely spin out of control?

Aly.

Damn it. Motherfucking trigger.

She was slowly driving me mad. Insane. Constantly pushing me up against a wall there was no chance of breaking through, needling her way into my thoughts and mind, invading places I couldn't allow her to go.

Still she managed to sink her fingers under my skin.

Urges slammed me harder than they had in years.

Addiction was a bitch like that. No matter how many years passed, it never let me forget the temporary escape it gave. The moment's euphoria. The only place where I could forget. Well, maybe not forget. It just numbed me to the place that I couldn't feel.

Crossing the room, I fumbled out of my sleep pants and pulled on the jeans I'd worn earlier. I shoved my feet in my boots, grabbed my keys from the coffee table, and bounded down the stairs. I turned my bike over, the loud roar of the engine coming to life. Power vibrated under my hands and feet. I kicked it free of its stand, rolled back, put it into gear. Slowly, I wound around the complex and slipped out one of the side gates.

As soon as I hit the street, I flew. Heat blasted my face. Lashes of hot, angry air tore at my shirt and whipped through my hair. I had no idea where I was going, no destination.

Motherfucking story of my life.

But I couldn't stay there with her sweet eyes and tender hands. Couldn't allow myself to slip into her false comfort, to settle into her warmth.

God, I wanted it.

Craved it.

Craved her.

She was doing things to me I couldn't allow. Fuck, I'd even let her *touch* me, her fingers like fire as they sketched along the lines that marked my skin with my sins. She'd traced those lines as if she'd drawn them in the pages of one of her books. I'd opened my mouth and let things pour free that I'd never once uttered out loud before.

I let her take a little of what I wasn't willing to give.

I pinned the throttle as far as it would go. The street blurred below me, and I shook with the speed, shook with the anger.

Stupid.

She admitted that she'd thought about me. Missed me.

On some level, I'd missed her, too. Too much to admit.

But it was on a level that no longer truly existed, just a hollowed-out place that echoed the joy I once had and what might have been. The fucked-up thing was she inhabited that space like she was made for it.

There was no need denying it. I cared about her. But I couldn't care about her the way she'd want me to. Couldn't love her the way she deserved to be.

I refused to ever love anyone again.

I was done destroying the things that were important to me. It hurt too much when they were gone.

Resentful laughter tumbled from my twisted mouth when I noticed where I'd ended up.

Of course. Directly across from the old neighborhood.

Shocking.

I was drawn here just as strongly as I'd been drawn back to Phoenix. Just an empty ache that called to me. Taunted me. I came to a rolling standstill, easing my bike off the side of the street just opposite to the spot that had been my everything and where I'd tried to end it all.

The field used to be open. There had only been a wooden fence that separated it from the old neighborhood that bordered it to the right. The expanse of vacant land had once seemed to go on forever, even though there was another neighborhood off to the far left. But to us, this empty field had been our refuge. We'd play here for hours as if it were the only place in the world that existed.

Now a new fence rose at the front of the street, blocking off the area. No TRESPASSING was boldly stamped on a black sign. Undoubtedly, that sign had been placed there because of me.

I just stared, pinned to my bike, my hands kneading on the handlebars. Memories hit me like the worst beating I'd ever gotten in my life, pummeled me as they fell. And it fucking hurt because so many of them were good.

My lips twitching with an unshed smile, I was barely able to make out our tree in the distance. I wanted to go to it, but I couldn't bring myself to. It'd once seemed so tall, building it an incredible feat we'd achieved with the brute strength of our hands and the imagination in our minds.

So much time was spent there.

That place inside me expanded, pushed as it struggled for freedom against its confines.

Shit.

I pressed the heels of my hands into my eyes as if doing that would somehow blot out the pictures that spun through my head. For a second, I just wanted to forget. But this was my life.

I'd take death over it, any day.

But I would live it as a penance for what I had done.

TWELVE

Aleena

The next morning when I crept out of my room before dawn, his space on the couch was empty. But I already knew that. I'd heard him leave right after he'd fled my room, and I hadn't heard him return.

Sleep had eluded me the entire night. All I could do was wonder where he had gone and worry if he was okay.

I'd pushed him too hard. Too fast.

Work passed in a dazed blur. My vision seemed to bleed in and out, and I mumbled as I approached each table, moving through the day in a stupor.

It killed me to think I might not ever see Jared again. That he was gone. Stabbing pain sliced through my middle at the thought. I reached to the wall for support and squeezed my eyes to shut it all out.

Karina lightly touched me on the back, and I turned and

opened my eyes to my boss. She was older, and the top of her head only came to my shoulders. Worry creased her kind face. "You don't look so good today, Miss Aly. Are you feeling okay?"

I shook my head. "I'm kind of sick to my stomach." It wasn't a lie.

She glanced around the dining room. The small round bistro tables filling the space were dotted with customers, but it wasn't extremely busy. It was late evening, and the customers sat along the curved bank of windows that overlooked the street, sipping from coffees or enjoying a sweet dessert. "I think we can manage without you for the rest of the night. Why don't you go on home and get some rest?"

She patted my shoulder, and I smiled down at her in appreciation. She had always been a great boss. She'd opened the restaurant years before and made it successful with her own hands. She always treated her staff like family. "Thanks, Karina. I think I'll be past all this tomorrow."

By past, I meant I'd be either devastated or out of my misery. But whichever I faced, I knew I had to get home.

It was relief that washed over me when I pulled around to the front of our building and saw Jared's bike sitting at the far end of the lot.

Easing my car into my spot, I sat for a moment to gather my thoughts. When I got out of the car, I crossed the lot, my legs sluggish as I took the stairs up to our apartment. I could feel it, this unease that had accumulated in the air, built up, and bound itself to my heart.

It was confirmed when I opened the door to an even denser sense of tension inside. Jared was here, but instinctively I knew things were not the same. He sat on the couch watching TV by himself, but he barely looked in my direction while I stood awkwardly in the middle of the room. I heard Christopher shuffling around in his room. A few seconds later, he came out of his room and rushed down the hall.

"Hey, Jared, you feel like going out tonight?" he asked as he ran his hands through the messy locks of his black hair.

Jared looked up at him with something akin to a grimace. "Nah, man, I had a long day at work today. Think I'm just going to hang out here and relax."

"Ah, that's too bad."

Christopher grabbed his keys and tucked his wallet in his back pocket. "Did you have a good day at work, Aly?" he asked with a casual smile as he gathered his things. He didn't seem to notice the well of emotion that had broken between Jared and me, or how our movements had slowed to match the weight in our chests.

"Yeah, it was fine," I said.

"Cool. Well, I'm going to get out of here. Give me a call if you need me." Then he shut the door behind him without a second thought.

Jared barely acknowledged me when I said I was going to grab a shower, just obliged me with a small nod as he turned back to the television in the same motion.

I turned the shower as hot as it would go. Steam filled the small room, streams of scalding water assailing my skin. Redness seeped to the surface, and I wished the hot shower could somehow burn the questions from my mind the same way it burned the fatigue from my body. But those questions remained locked tight in the boy sitting out on the couch.

Wrapped in a towel, I unlatched the bathroom door and looked down to the end of the short hall into the darkened living room. Flashes from the TV lit the end of the couch, and I could feel him there just as I knew he could feel me. Yet I sensed no movement, no shift in his presence.

Out of respect, I left him there because I didn't really know what to say. How could I take back last night? Because it was my heart. He was my heart. I didn't regret the fact that I'd invited him to open up to me. I only regretted the reaction he'd had to it.

In my room, I dropped my towel to the floor and pulled on a pair of sleep shorts and a tank, then curled up on my side on my bed to stare out the open window. Even though it had waned, the moon still shone bright enough to light up my room. My sketch pad lay on the floor next to my bed, but tonight I didn't feel like drawing. It had always been my therapy, the way to work out my thoughts, fears, and desires. A way to show my love.

But tonight I clung to those thoughts, let them tumble around in my head while I rested on my side in the soft glow of the moon. With my back to the door, I stared out the window. In the dull light of the city, I could only make out the few brightest stars. Time passed too slow and too fast because I longed for him and was entirely terrified of what hid inside him at the same time. I'd fallen a long time ago, had held tight to the remnants of his memory that he'd left in his wake. It'd been foolish then, but safe, because it was only an illusion. I'd given myself to him when he'd never even had me at all.

Now my bones trembled with reality.

I didn't know if he would come, and many hours passed before he finally did.

Tonight Jared didn't knock. I tensed when the door creaked open, listened as it quietly snapped shut behind him. He said nothing as he inched up behind me. I sensed the hesitation in his steps, the heavy breaths he pushed in and out of his lungs.

For a second he just stood there at my side, and I could feel his eyes burning into my body. Then the bed dipped behind me.

I stilled myself as he settled, and his weight spread out over the surface of my bed. Tension radiated and poured out of him, so thick my mouth went dry.

He exhaled toward the ceiling, his arm pressed up against the length of my spine. I could picture him lying there, flat on his back, staring into nothing. Waiting. Waiting for what, I wasn't sure. I didn't know what he wanted. All I knew was I wanted him to want me.

I couldn't take it any longer.

Slowly, I turned. His arm dug into my ribs as I rolled over it, before I settled into the safety of his side. Tonight I erased the physical space that had always been left between us, but somehow I knew the distance to what I wanted—to what I needed—had never been greater. I buried my nose at the juncture of his shoulder and chest, breathed him in the second he gave in and pulled me into his arms. My hand twisted in the collar of his T-shirt, and the other burrowed beneath his back.

Every nerve in my body fired, my muscles straining as I clung to him, as I did everything I could to bring him closer.

Nothing had ever felt better than being in Jared's arms.

Nothing.

Under my arm his heart beat fast, and I slowly uncurled my fingers from his shirt and slid my flattened palm down to feel it pound beneath my skin. My stomach flipped and turned, pooled with desire and need and the affection I'd held for him for so very long.

And I wanted to tell him how much he really meant to me, but I knew saying it would only force him further away.

Jared held his breath, then brought his right hand up to

settle on top of mine. He pressed my palm harder against his chest, as if he, too, couldn't stand the thought of letting me go. His voice was raspy, low, and so incredibly sad. "What are we doing, Aly?"

"I don't know," I answered with my mouth hidden in the fabric of his shirt. I loved the way he smelled, his shirt thick with the crisp scent of fresh laundry, mixing with the essence that always surrounded him—peppermint and cigarettes. It was the aura of the man that each second sucked my spirit deeper into him.

The fingers on my back found their way into my hair. Gently he tugged, like he'd done so many times before, only this time it was a fistful. "Christopher is right, you know. You were always my favorite." The words came out in a murmur, his face focused on the ceiling, though his fingers soothed into my scalp.

Tingles spread along my neck, then rocketed down my spine.

"I don't know what it was," he continued with a soft reverence. "I guess I liked the way you followed us around. I liked that you couldn't keep up and that I had to take care of you. I liked standing up for you. Protecting you. I liked the way you looked at me like I really mattered. I liked that when I thought back about you and Christopher after I was gone, I was thinking about the good times I had in my life." He squeezed me closer to him and pressed his mouth to the top of my head.

"But I don't get to have this, Aly."

I shifted to lay my cheek on his chest. Sadness crashed over me in a breaking wave. I knew there was nothing I could say that would sway him, that there was no convincing him otherwise. He'd already promised me that last night. Instead I just held on to him, told him through my touch how much he meant to me and that he deserved happiness, too, whether he found that with me or someone else.

"I ruin every fucking thing I touch, Aly, and I refuse to ruin you." His hold increased. "Fuck," he groaned under his breath, tipping his face down toward mine, grief striking like a match in his eyes. "I shouldn't even be in here with you." He squeezed my back in emphasis. "Hanging out with you like this has absolutely been the most selfish thing I've done in a long time." A short breath filtered from his nose. "I can't do this with you anymore . . . this whole friend thing. I can feel it coming, Aly, that something bad is gonna happen and I'm going to hurt you, and I refuse to do it."

"You'd never hurt me," I said. This time I couldn't keep myself from refuting his words.

Dry laughter filled my room. "You're right . . . because I won't ever let it get that far."

Pain fisted in my chest. I was wrong. He could hurt me. He already was—hurting me and hurting himself.

But I guessed hurting himself was what he knew how to do best.

I laced my fingers through his right hand, lifted them so our hands shone in the dim light. My skin looked so pale woven with his, his skin darkened with the sun and his fingers marked with the year of his birth: *1990. Life.*

I squeezed his hand, willing him to hang on to it.

He pulled our twined hands to his mouth and pressed gentle kisses to my fingers. He ran his lips along the back of my hand, brushed them over the puckered scars on the outside of my thumb. My throat constricted, and I was struggling to hold back tears.

"I need to go, Aly."

Panic rose in me, and I struggled to hold him tighter. "Please," I begged, trying to tug him down, "just lie with me. Just for tonight."

His sigh was heavy and filled with sadness. But in it was his surrender. His arms tightened around me, and he pressed his lips to my forehead. His warm breath filtered all around me, wrapped around and cocooned me, and I shuddered as I fell completely into his embrace.

Maybe if I lay here and never closed my eyes, I'd be able to hang on to him forever.

And I tried. But inevitably they drooped and fell because there was not a safer, more comfortable place than resting in the security of Jared's arms.

In the morning, I woke to an empty bed.

I hadn't expected anything different. It didn't mean it didn't hurt. For a few seconds, I held my eyes closed because I didn't want to face the wedge Jared had driven between us last night.

Rolling to my side, I pulled the sheets with me as I sought some form of comfort. Something crinkled on my pillow as I moved.

I lifted my head. A small piece of parchment paper sat folded on my pillow. My throat constricted, and I turned onto my stomach, eyeing the washed-out tan piece of paper, one side tattered from where it had been torn from some sort of journal. My fingers trembled as I reached out to take it in my hand. Slowly I unfolded it.

Tears welled in my eyes when I saw the simple statement written in a strong-handed scroll.

When beauty sleeps.

Turning onto my back, I held it against my chest, cherishing the words that Jared otherwise didn't know how to say.

———

Two weeks had passed since the last time Jared left my room. He'd become distant. Withdrawn. Rarely was he at the apartment. I'd hear him creeping in at ungodly hours of the night and he was usually gone before I got up, as if he could hardly stand to be anywhere in my space.

And I missed him.

The hardest part was in those moments when he was in the apartment and I'd catch him looking at me.

Looking at me as if he missed me as much as I missed him.

Just as quickly, he'd look away, drop his gaze, and pretend all those nights he'd spent lying with me in the sanctuary of my room had only been figments of my imagination.

As if they didn't matter.

As if they hadn't changed who we were.

But I didn't push him. The last time it had backfired. He'd panicked and had driven this unbearable space between us.

Somehow I knew if I pushed him any further, I'd never see him again.

Sighing, I forced myself from bed. Exhaustion dragged my feet. Restful sleep had been scarce for the last two weeks. There was always that hope, this little flicker of anticipation that he might come back, slip inside my room, wrap me up in his arms, and whisper that he'd made a mistake.

But he never did.

It didn't mean I didn't spend most nights awake trying to will it to happen.

Now I crept out into the hall. Stunned, I stilled when I found Jared sitting silently at the bar, sipping from a mug of coffee.

Motionless, I indulged, appreciated his beauty in a moment when he had no idea he was being watched. He wore a pair of jeans and a thin white V-neck tee. His bare feet were propped on the footrest, his elbows heavy on the marble bar. He seemed consumed in his thoughts, a million miles and a hundred years away. His hair was all unruly, and it appeared as if he hadn't shaved in at least three days, this coarse stubble shadowing his strong jaw.

My fingers twitched.

I wanted to reach out and run them down the side of his face. To whisper his beauty against his ear. To tell him I saw the good, that it was alive, so transparent in his words and in his eyes.

Instead I slinked by and murmured, "Good morning," as I passed.

I could barely discern the subtle flinch in his muscles, but it was there. I'd taken him by surprise.

He mumbled, "Morning," into his coffee cup.

I went to the fridge, grabbed the orange juice, and poured a glass. With my back to him I spoke. It was hard to do, but I didn't want this unease to eat at us forever. "So, no work today?"

He grunted. "It's the Fourth . . . boss closed up shop today."

The Fourth of July.

Right.

I didn't even realize the date.

Guess I'd been fixated on something else.

I leaned up against the counter that Jared had backed me into all those weeks ago when he'd first confronted me, and thought about the day. It was funny, how much I used to look forward to this holiday, the days dense with summer's heat, our revelry shared out in our field as we played the sunlight away. How the excitement would build as the sun began to set, and our families would gather to turn our faces to the night sky to witness the beauty of the fireworks.

It had always struck me with an overwhelming awe.

I remembered how deeply it always struck Jared, too.

I stared at the floor. Off to my right, his presence tugged at my spirit as if mine were chained to his, a tension that wound through my consciousness and congealed in the air between us.

I doubted now we'd ever escape it.

Christopher suddenly shattered the strain wrapping up the room by barreling down the hall.

"Morning," he said as he clapped Jared on the back and came around the bar and into the kitchen. He dropped a swift kiss to my cheek. "And good morning to you, little sister."

"Morning," I returned, confused by the overeager man-child almost dancing in the kitchen.

"Is there milk?" he asked.

I kind of laughed as Christopher dug into the fridge. It was about three hours too early for my brother to show his face.

"Should be," I said, grinning at his back.

He stood and flashed me a huge one.

"What has you in such a good mood this morning?" I frowned in question.

"It's the Fourth. Why wouldn't I be in a good mood?" Christopher tipped his chin in Jared's direction. "We haven't all spent it together in years, and Timothy has his annual Fourth of July party planned." He shrugged one shoulder. "Just think it's going to be really cool to spend the night with everyone."

Christopher had mentioned the party at Timothy's house several weeks ago. I'd been to a few parties at his place. They were always packed, crawling with so many bodies that I usually ended up in the backyard, trying to catch a breath of fresh air.

From the corner of my eye, I caught Jared shaking his head. "Nah, I think I'll just hang out here tonight or maybe go for a ride on my bike or something," he said.

"What the hell are you talking about? Not a chance. I've been looking forward to this party all week. And it's been so long since we all were together." Christopher turned to me. "You're still coming, right?"

It wasn't really a question. I knew he'd force me into it if I even thought about backing out. "Yeah, I'll be there. Do you mind if I invite Megan? I haven't gotten to hang out with her that much lately."

"Sure, Timothy's not going to mind."

I nodded before Christopher returned his attention to Jared, leveling him with a glare that vowed he wouldn't take no for an answer.

Jared casually sipped from his cup. "I don't really do the party thing."

"Really?" Christopher asked, completely incredulous. "You do remember I picked you up at a bar?"

Jared smirked and dropped his cup to the counter, that old playfulness filling his eyes when he taunted my brother. "You picked me up at a bar, huh?" he asked, the question packed with innuendo.

There was my friend.

I laughed, and Christopher did, too. "Fuck you, dude." Christopher pointed at him. "You're coming."

Jared chuckled mildly, then sobered as he stole a glance my direction. I knew he was feeling me out, wondering if I wanted him there or if he'd already hurt me enough that I didn't want to be anywhere around him.

I offered him an easy smile, one that promised I still would take whatever it was that he would give. And I would. I could be his friend. I could shove all these feelings aside, lock them in that place that had always been reserved for him. Could pretend that I didn't crave his touch on my face, pretend he hadn't spoken things that I knew he'd only ever spoken to me, pretend this bond we shared was just an invention of my imagination.

I'd been successful at hiding my feelings for so many years. What had changed?

I resisted the urge to roll my eyes at myself.

The change currently sat at the bar in my apartment, his expression guarded but achingly tender at the same time. Could either of us ever forget the connection we'd shaped, one carved out in those perfect hours spent alone in my room?

No. Not me.

But I could pretend.

Resigned, Jared turned back at Christopher. "Fine. I'll go."

Warily, he chanced a glance back at me again, his eyes wavering as they fluttered over my face. Then he dropped his gaze back to his half-empty cup.

Was it foolish that I was excited for him to be coming? Foolish that this was the first Fourth I'd looked forward to in all the years he'd been gone because this was the holiday that had always been ours?

I risked lifting my face to find his eyes downcast, his hair flopping down to cover his gorgeous face.

Yeah, I guessed it probably was.

THIRTEEN

July 4, 2002

It was hot. The sun shone down, scorching everything in its path, the sky so bright it hurt to look up. Sweat beaded on Aly's neck, and she pushed back the bangs stuck to her forehead. For what felt like the millionth time, she jammed the shovel into the hardened dirt, barely making a dent.

"If we're going to make any jumps, we're going to need a whole lot more dirt than that, Aly," Christopher said, frowning at her progress.

"But it's hard." Both the work and the ground. Aly felt out of breath, and a blister threatened on the palm of her right hand. She'd been helping Jared and Christopher build their stupid bike track all day and she didn't think she could work any longer. But if she didn't work, she knew Christopher would still try to make her go home. Even though she was ten, he was still always trying to boss her around. The only difference was now that she'd gotten older, she didn't listen to him all the time.

"Christopher, Aly, Jared!" Her mom's blond head peeped over the top of their backyard fence as she called for them. "Come on home! We're getting ready to leave."

Thank God.

Christopher dropped his tools, jumped on Jared's bike, and shot across the lot over the tracks they'd just made, laughing at them over his shoulder as he left them behind.

"Do ya always have to be such a jerk, Christopher?" Jared yelled after him, throwing his pick onto the ground. "Damn it," he swore, kicking at the dirt. Then his attention flashed to her. "Sometimes I want to pound your brother's face in."

Aly bit at her lip and felt her cheeks flush red. Jared was gonna get grounded if his mom heard him talking like that. But Aly was too damned tired herself to remind him of it. She dropped her hands to her knees, leaning over as she tried to catch her breath.

"You tired, Aly Cat?" Jared asked, his anger over the plundering of his favorite bike all but vanished. Christopher and Jared never fought for long. Her mom said they should've been brothers, the way they were fighting one second and best friends the next.

She heaved hot air from her lungs. "I think I'm going to pass out." She didn't really think so, but she liked what Jared's face looked like when he thought something was wrong with her.

"Come on, Aly. Hop on my back." He bent down so she could climb on.

She didn't hesitate. She jumped on his back, wrapping her legs around his waist and her arms around his neck.

Jostling her around, Jared hoisted her higher; then he

laughed and darted across the field, holding her by the legs as she fiercely clung to his neck. She bounced against his back as he ran.

"Hold on tight, Aly Cat." Jared dipped and twisted, and he laughed loudly as they soared.

To Aly, there was no better sound.

"Don't you dare drop me, Jared Holt," Aly shouted near his ear as he raced across the lot, ducking down to miss a tree branch as they passed.

"I won't drop you, silly girl."

But really, she already knew that. Jared would never hurt her.

He hiked her up higher, and Aly held on tighter. When it was just the two of them like this, her stomach felt funny—light and excited and a little bit scared—and she knew it must be a real secret because she instinctively knew no one else should know. Least of all, Jared.

She didn't want him to laugh at her.

He dropped her to her feet at the hole in the fence. "Beat you to your house," Jared challenged before he took off running.

Aly almost kept up, her exhaustion from before all but forgotten. Her legs had grown long. She was almost as tall as Christopher. Her mom said it wouldn't last, that boys got their growth spurt later, and she'd told Christopher not to worry that his little sister would pass him up.

Aly and Jared burst into the house, each clambering to get in front of the other. The front door slammed against the wall with a loud bang.

"Hey, you two," Aly's mom shouted from the kitchen, "settle down before you break something."

Jared's mom, Helene, called out even louder, "Jared! What

have I told you about playing rough in the house? That's for outside."

But Helene was smiling when they came into the kitchen. Affectionately she ruffled Jared's hair as he passed, and then she turned back to piling the containers of food into a basket for their picnic.

Chaos ruled the kitchen. Aly's dad, Dave, lugged folding chairs from the backyard while their moms put everything they needed in paper sacks, yelling at the boys to get their things together. Jared and Christopher and Aug stuffed firecrackers and sparklers in their pockets.

Aly loved the buzz of excitement in the air.

The Fourth of July was one of her very favorite days.

"Jared, do you think you could help me out?" Helene asked as she maneuvered the basket from the counter and held it out for him to take.

"Sure, Mom." He came to her side, grinned up at her as he took the handles in his hands.

"You got it?" she asked, her hands poised to help him get a better grip if needed.

"Yep."

"Thanks, bear," she said with a gentle smile. She turned back to take Jared's little sister, Courtney, by the hand and grabbed a paper sack with the other.

Jared's dad, Neil, hefted an ice chest from the floor and balanced it against his stomach. "Everyone ready? We need to get a move on if we're going to get a good spot."

"Ready," everyone said in near unison.

They all filtered out the front door and piled into the old station wagon Aly's mom drove. The kids were all cramped in the far backseat, Jared's arm pressed up tight against Aly's.

"You excited?" he asked as he looked down at her.

She bounced a little, unable to contain just how excited she really was. "Fireworks are my favorite."

Jared's smile was soft. "Mine, too, Aly Cat. They're mine, too."

FOURTEEN

Jared

Twilight spread its fingers across the yard. Oranges and reds and golds rose up and shot from the brink of the distant horizon, bright rays streaking through the sky to clash with the waning blue as all the light was sucked from the sky. A few of the brightest stars had begun to make their mark on the inky canopy above.

And it was hot. Really fucking unbearably hot.

I tugged at the neck of my T-shirt, hoping to find some sort of relief. I pressed a cold beer bottle to my cheek in search of reprieve.

Voices were too loud and too carefree, the crowd laughing and chatting. A steady stream of people had slowly but surely filled Timothy's backyard far past capacity.

I'd hidden myself in the farthest recesses of the yard, concealed my discomfort in a bottle of beer while doing my best to ignore the constant urges that poked and prodded at me, alerting me that it'd be a really good time to run. I'd developed this perfect radar, a warning system that told me when to grab my shit and get out.

It was blaring now.

With a harsh shake of my head, I rushed a hand through my hair and rubbed at the tense muscles coiled at the base of my neck. If there was any possible place on this earth where I could feel comfortable, this definitely wasn't it. Holed up at some party with the people Aly and Christopher had come to know, with their friends. Everyone seemed to know each other and they laughed without restraint and talked as if they'd known each other for years. These were all people they'd met after I'd gone and had been erased from their lives.

But how the hell could I say no? I mean, I'd tried to refuse, to come up with an acceptable excuse to convince Christopher that this was a bad idea. But he was insistent.

And the truth was, I fucking *missed* her. So much it'd become this crushing weight on my chest and an overbearing burden on my shoulders.

Nothing was ever right. But being without her just felt wrong.

The two weeks I'd spent hidden away behind her door had been the best two of my life. I'd almost felt as if I belonged.

Almost.

That was the problem, really. I'd gotten too comfortable, had felt too at ease, had allowed too many unwise words to pass from my mouth.

Worse was I'd gotten too used to how unbelievably good she felt lying next to me.

I'd come to want it. Need it. And it was wrong. It was insanity and stupidity all wrapped into one, selfishness in the extreme. But I wanted her. God, I wanted her. So badly that I'd ignored my conscience and snuck into her room night after night, dipped into her comfort, and taken from the girl who was so good and kind. Aly had welcomed me into her bed as if that was exactly where I was supposed to be.

Like she trusted me.

I wondered what she'd think if she could crawl inside the darkened corners of my mind, if she could witness the fantasies of her that I kept hidden there. If she could see how depraved I really was. How could I lie there beside her and pretend I was just her friend, while I listened to the throaty lilt of her thick laughter and imagined what it'd be like to have her laid out, taking it all? Burying myself in her—her flesh and sweat and sweet and every ounce of pleasure I knew I'd find in the tenderness of her touch. I'd gone so far as to imagine the exact way her lips would part and the expression that would hood her intense green eyes.

I shook my head to chase off the visions invading my mind.

I will destroy her.

My eyes traveled the yard, washing over the groups of friends swarming the space. Water sloshed up from the pool, swelled, and spilled over the side from the movement of the bodies that sought a retreat from the heat. Everyone wore bathing suits or shorts and flip-flops, and here I sat in my jeans and boots.

Not that I cared what anyone thought about me. Christopher had introduced me to most everyone, toting me around the yard as he sang my praises. The guy was cool, that much was for sure. He might have his own issues, but he definitely had my back. Most of the people there looked at me with indifference or mild interest. A few girls had approached me in the last hour I'd been sitting here by myself. But none of them were the reason I was subjecting myself to this abuse.

I found her under the shade of a tree. She was in the same clothes she'd been in the night I'd first seen her, a red tank top with the green straps of her bikini peeking out and wrapping around her neck, the bottoms covered in little white shorts. The girl was perfection personified. Every inch. Every curve. She was laughing and talking with Megan, one of the friends she'd introduced me to earlier.

I searched Aly's face. A casual easiness had taken her over as she enjoyed the setting sun. Maybe that's what attracted me to her most, the fact that she was genuine, lacking all the superficial bullshit so many of the girls crawling the backyard seemed to have. But she was also fun, easy to smile. Not to mention she was undoubtedly the sexiest girl I'd ever seen.

She tipped her head back as she laughed, exposing her creamy neck. Dark hair toppled over one luscious bare shoulder and rolled down her back.

Lust curled through my stomach and tightened in the pits of my consciousness.

God.

I dropped my eyes to the dirt under my booted feet.

She had gotten so far under my skin I couldn't think straight anymore. At least I'd had the strength to put to a stop those tortured nights because they were heading nowhere good—and fast. What I should do was end it all, pack up my things, and leave before I left behind inevitable ruin. It was like I could feel it building. *Destruction.* I'd never outrun it. It followed me wherever I went. But the last two weeks of existing through the days, avoiding her as much as I possibly could while wishing for nothing other than to be near her, had made it impossible for me to leave.

So I'd taken from afar.

Watched her in the moments she didn't know I was there, traced her face with my eyes instead of my fingers, hated myself a little bit more.

I was the worst kind of coward because I stayed when I knew I should go.

Throaty laughter floated through the yard, a distinct reminder of her presence. With my elbows on my knees, I barely lifted my head and stole another look in her direction. From under the hedge of my hair, I watched her chat with the group that had grown around her.

My attention shifted as some guy I'd never seen before came through the large sliding door. There was no looking away when the asshole snuck up behind her and lifted her off her feet.

Releasing a little surprised squeal, she flailed her bare feet in the air. He laughed and said something in her ear. The dickhead had barely set her back down when he spun her around and was smothering her in his fucking arms.

Uncontrolled, my hands flexed and fisted, the grinding of my teeth grating in my ears. Something knocked loose in my chest, and it was about the most fucking unpleasant feeling I'd ever experienced.

Who the hell is this guy?

For my sake . . . or his . . . she extracted herself, because I was damned close to losing it.

Fucking Christopher, goading me into this shit. I should've known better, known that Aly had a life outside the hours we spent closed behind her door.

Needing a reprieve, I turned away and tried to focus on

something less excruciating than the scene unfolding with Aly. Across the yard, I found Christopher scoping out his next target, this little brunette with huge tits and a round ass. A subtle chuckle rolled from my tongue. He was relentless. I watched as he flirted with her, ran his finger under her jaw, made her smile. I had to admit, the guy was good.

But a distraction could only last for so long. Fidgeting with the rough edges of my beer cap, I finally gave in and turned my attention back to Aly. Dickhead had sidled up to her, attaching himself to her being like some tacked-on afterthought. His fingers slipped around her back. Even from a distance, I knew they were kneading into her side.

I drained the rest of my beer. That internal warning system roared. Looked like a really good time for me to make an exit. I wasn't sticking around to witness this shit.

Standing, I tossed my bottle into an overflowing garbage can and turned to leave. I froze midstride when I saw Aly weaving her way through the crowd, making her way over to me. There was something in her expression, something wholly sad and earnest and entirely too sexy that had me all itchy and irritated. My jaw ticked as she approached, and I kind of wanted to lash out at her for having the ability to make me this uncomfortable.

"Hey," she said, stopping a foot away from me, her chin tilted up, her face searching mine. A light from the porch reflected the emerald of her eyes. Discomfort mingled with the warmth, and she shifted on her feet. She knew I'd been watching her. "What are you doing hiding over here by yourself?"

I struggled to appear detached and lifted a shoulder in indifference. "Nothing. Just was going to take off."

Disappointment flashed in her eyes. "What?" She inched forward, invading my senses with her soft scent, coconut and fresh and overwhelmingly girl—everything I'd tried to rid my brain of over the last two weeks. "You can't leave now," she argued. "The fireworks are going to start in like ten minutes. Jared," she said, her voice quieting, "I was really looking forward to watching them with you." A gentle hand fluttered out and grazed against the side of mine, and she almost whispered, her full lips moving slowly as she spoke, as if it were our greatest secret, "They're our favorite. Remember?"

Damn it.

I wrenched an agitated hand through my hair, looked over her shoulder at her group of friends, eyed Dickhead, who was eyeing her ass.

She must have seen the excuse I was trying to work in my head because she suddenly squeezed my hand. "Please, Jared. I know things have been weird between us, but I really wanted to spend tonight with you. Even if it's only for old times' sake." Redness colored her cheeks, as if her admission caused her some kind of embarrassment. But still she forged ahead. "It would mean a lot to me."

"Aly . . . ," I said quietly, just under my breath.

"Please," she whispered. Then she smiled and took a single step back. "Let me get you another beer."

She didn't wait for my response, for my agreement that I would stay, because she already knew I would.

Had she always held this kind of power over me? A glimmer of a smile and a brush of her hand and the girl would get her way? Memories swirled through my mind like the whirlwind she was, the little girl who'd barely had to look at me and I already knew what she wanted or needed. Mom once told me Aly had me wrapped around her little finger. She'd been wrong. Aly had held me in the palm of her hand.

"Fine," I mumbled as she edged away. She crossed the yard to a cooler sitting under the patio. Lifting the lid, she leaned down and disappeared behind it. She dropped it closed. Something inside me fluttered when she smiled across the yard at me as her face came back into view. Popping the cap and tossing it to the trash, she beckoned me to join her with a tic of her head.

Sighing, I gave in because I had no fucking idea how to tell this girl no.

Slowly, I crossed the space, never dropping my gaze as I approached, and accepted the proffered beer that she held out toward me. "Thank you," I said.

"You're welcome." She twisted off her cab and tapped her bottle neck with mine. "To old times."

Under my breath, I laughed and said, "To old times," even though there was a huge part of me that didn't share the sentiment. Old times hadn't made me feel like this, as if I wanted to wrap her up and hide her away. They didn't cause my blood to pound in my ears or make me want to knock that smug smile off Dickhead's face when he glanced her way.

Okay, maybe that wasn't entirely true.

Protecting her had always been my job.

But now it clearly was for different reasons.

He had started talking to someone else, but still he managed to keep her in his line of sight, a subtle trailing of her movements, each motion counted and calculated, as if he was assessing when he was going to make his move.

Possessiveness rose in a wave and crashed over my being.

Yeah, maybe Aly was right. I didn't need to go anywhere. Right here was exactly where I was supposed to be.

"Come here, I want you to meet some of my other friends."

Aly took me by the hand and led me to the group of people she'd been standing with before.

A thrill shot through me with just that touch.

Dickhead's brow rose to his hairline when he saw us walking toward them, hand in hand. Aly introduced me to a couple of new friends who'd arrived, a couple of girls who were obviously too flirty and some dude named Sam. I barely acknowledged them because I couldn't stand the feel of Dickhead's eyes roving over me as he sized me up. I could feel him considering, adding me up in the same breath he put me down, judging.

Nothing pissed me off more than people making assumptions they didn't have a right to make.

Aly turned to him and gestured between us. "Gabe, this is Jared. He was one of my very best friends growing up." Hesitantly, she looked at me. "Jared, Gabe."

Gabe. Of course, Dickhead was Gabe. The same guy who tried to get her to come over to "hang" out with him in the middle of the night. How fitting.

I shoved my hand out in front of me. "Nice to meet you, Gabe."

He shook it, squeezing it hard. A warning. "Likewise," he said, his voice tight.

I wanted to laugh. He had to be fucking kidding me. He was warning me?

Staring him down, I crushed his hand in my hold, silently promising him I would do anything to keep Aly safe. Safe from him. Safe from me. Safe from anyone who even for a minute thought of messing with her. Clearly, this douche bag didn't deserve her any more than I did. I could see it there, written all over his self-righteous face and in his eyes, the *nice* guy act well played. Perfected.

Unbidden, my hand clamped down on his as thoughts of him with Aly swam through my vision like some fucking horror flick that you really didn't want to see but can't look away from, the slasher kind where there is blood and guts and gore and nobody comes out alive. When I was a kid, they always gave me nightmares until the cause of my nightmares became real and utterly unbearable.

Thinking of her with him felt pretty much the same.

I pulled away from him, and Aly took my hand again. "Come on, let's find a good spot to watch the fireworks."

With her voice, I shoved off the images, turned, and gently smiled at her, ignoring the guy whose gaze burned into the back of my head with outright hate.

Instead I focused on her words, which sounded so damned cute, like they used to when we'd run ahead of ourselves to find the best spot at the park. We used to get so close that we'd feel the fireworks rumble through our bodies, and we had to dodge the little pieces of paper ashes that flitted down from the sky.

She led me to a lounger that sat out in the open on the grass. She pushed at my side and grinned. "Take a seat."

Quirking an eyebrow, I smirked at her but did as I was told. I sat sideways on it with my feet on the ground. Aly settled to the grass, and instinctively my knees parted to make room for her. Nestling between my legs, she shifted a bit to rest her head on the inside of my thigh. Then she released a breathy sigh as if this was the only place she wanted to be, murmuring, "I'm so glad you're here, Jared."

Desire coursed over every inch of my skin and pooled in my stomach. There was nothing I could do to stop it, the way I hardened at her slightest touch, at the soft sound that fell from her mouth, at the smell of her hair that had become permanently ingrained in my mind.

Night fell further, collected across the sky, and the darkness deepened the silence of the cocoon Aly and I found ourselves in. The heat had ebbed the slightest bit, the warmth of the day beginning to dissipate into the inky dome overhead.

Most in the yard had quieted and taken their spots to watch the sky, anticipating the show that was about to begin. Everyone else bled into obscurity, and in that instant it was just the two of us.

Aly jumped with the first boom. It rumbled along the surface of the ground, vibrating below us, and a long whistle cracked before color exploded in the sky just in the distance.

Quietly she gasped, the way she'd done what seemed like a million times before. A perfect memory of her as a child suddenly overtook my mind. The tips of her delicate fingers fluttered up to her mouth as she watched in awe.

I was powerless to do anything but thread my fingers through her hair, to anchor myself to her, even if it was only for this moment. Even though I'd been the one to cut myself from her, right then it felt impossible to let go.

Reds and blues and whites streamed from the sky, lit up the darkness above, increased in intensity, then fell before the next wave erupted in an electrifying thrill.

Blood thundered through my veins. It'd been so long since I'd felt this close to someone. Part of me fought it, knew I should push her away. The dominant part of me just wanted to stay, even if it was for a little while. I'd been alone for so long. Was it wrong to take away these memories, something to hold on to when I seeped back into nothingness?

Shifting her weight, Aly sank deeper into me. Her body burned into mine; her head pressed into my thigh. She tilted her head back and looked up at me with wistful eyes, watched me with kindness, with a yearning for the way things had been in the past, with ideas of what could never be.

I stared down at her.

And I knew it was wrong, that I was only making things worse, prolonging the inevitable, but right then I just didn't care.

A pensive smile kissed her mouth, before she turned back to the show above. She snuggled closer, her shoulder dipping down under my leg so her neck was nestled against my thigh. Her hand skimmed over my knee and down my leg before she firmly wrapped her arm around my calf. Her hand tightened there, and my fingers found their way to the nape of her neck, twisting in the fine hairs and tickling her skin. A small whimper escaped her mouth as I massaged my fingers over the base of her scalp, ran them up to the back of her ears and down again.

As if this wasn't agonizing, having what I wanted most in my hands and knowing she was completely out of reach.

Untouchable.

But right then she was mine. So I gave in, took a little more, leaned forward, and buried my nose in the fucking delicious coconut in her hair. Breathed in the life and the goodness and everything that was Aly.

I wanted to remember.

Her fingers curled into my leg, begging just as desperately as my body begged for hers, and I felt strung up, strung out. I ached and needed and felt as if I was going to lose my mind.

Fireworks filled the sky, this constant barrage that illumi-nated the night. I felt them more than saw them as they knit with the shocking intensity radiating from Aly, a feeling that sped through my veins faster than any high I'd ever experienced. Overhead the finale came to life, pounded through my system, set my skin on fire.

I tightened my hold on her, my nose behind her ear, wanted to take it all.

"Aly," whispered from my mouth.

Chills rolled down her spine in a palpable wave.

Fireworks popped and cracked, a rapid succession of booms and streams of fire, and an outburst of cheers rose up from the crowded yard.

Someone beside us whistled and clapped, and for one second, I held Aly a little tighter.

The last of the fireworks blinked out above as darkness again fell across the sky. The patio lights were flipped on. People climbed to their feet and began to disperse as conversations rose all around us.

That was all it took to break the spell Aly had me under. I sat back as she released her fingers. She straightened, stared ahead as if she'd been affected just as much as I'd been, while I struggled to regain some semblance of composure.

Because inside I was shattered.

I had to keep myself from jumping when I looked up to find Megan standing in front of us, holding her hand out for Aly. Questions ran across the girl's face, her eyes darting between Aly and me. She seemed to waver before she spoke. "Do you want to come for a swim with me?"

Confusion rolled from Aly in billows, a heavy hesitation in her movements before she finally accepted her friend's hand. "Sure."

Megan tugged at Aly as she helped her to stand, though the girl managed to keep one eye firmly rooted on me.

Aly dusted off her shorts, her expression guarded when she glanced back at me. I could see the question she silently asked me in her eyes.

What was that?

I just blinked into the dim light, because I didn't know, either. All I knew was that I felt as if something was being ripped from me when she walked away.

Aly followed Megan to the edge of the pool. Her friend tore the sundress she wore over her head, laughing as she jumped in the pool. She bobbed to the top of the water. "Are you getting in, or what?" she called to Aly.

"Yeah, yeah . . ." Unease trickled from Aly's mouth in a small giggle. "You know I need a little time to work up to it."

Megan laughed. "You're such a baby. Get in here."

I felt like an asshole because I couldn't look away when Aly's fingers fluttered down to the hem of her tank top and she slowly raised it over her head to expose the creamy skin of her back, watched as she unbuttoned her shorts and let them slip to the ground. She stepped out of them and toed them aside.

Fuck.

Aly was . . . *indescribable*. Curved and slender and supple, both strong and delicate, like this painting that shouldn't be possible, one that took your breath away as you stared at it in awe.

She dipped her toes in the water, her long legs slowly submerging as she waded down the steps and into the pool. The water looked black, shimmers of light reflecting off the ripples. Aly's long hair appeared just as black as she slipped into the water's depths. Her voice was soft as she spoke with her friend, and Megan splashed her a little. Aly splashed her back.

It was really cute, too, the way the two of them seemed to

get each other. Aly had talked about her several times, and it was cool to finally meet the girl who Aly seemed to be so fond of.

That was when Dickhead made his move. He jumped in and dunked Aly under the surface. A second later, she shot up from under the water, flinging the hair from her face.

"Gabe!" she shouted. She punched him in the shoulder and he laughed. "You're such an asshole."

He shoved her, then tugged at the mass of wet hair stuck to her back, and I could sense him laying his claim, moving in. She shoved him back.

Hostility wound through me, every muscle in my body stretched thin.

Fucker was about ten seconds from getting his ass torn limb from limb if he didn't stop touching her.

The worst part was the playfulness in her actions, this casualness she shared with him. *"We've kind of been seeing each other for the last couple months. I like him okay, I guess."* This was what she was settling for? Her *okay?*

She splashed around with him and Megan, laughed while I sat there fuming. My hands fisted. As badly as I wanted to gouge my eyes out, I couldn't look away.

Did she have any clue what she was doing to me?

I knew I was the one who'd set this into play, had told her whatever was happening between us had to come to an end, even though whatever it was we labeled a friendship. Fools fell into those kinds of traps. We both knew it went so much deeper than friendship, even though that was why its foundation was so solid.

Under my breath, mocking laughter climbed from my throat. Who was the fool now? Me, sitting here feeling like I might lose my mind because after whatever the hell had just happened between us during the fireworks, watching her with him now felt like I'd been sucker punched in the gut.

But what did she owe me?

Fuck. I raked my hands through my hair, wanted to scream, to claim that she did owe me because no one knew me the way she did. She was the only one who knew how to get inside me. She had accomplished it so easily. Right then I hated her for it.

Gabe ducked under the water and came up right in front of her. He'd shifted, the teasing set aside as he approached her as if he *knew* her.

Anger pushed at my insides, and I was twitching, aching to unleash this aggression on Dickhead's face, because I couldn't stand to watch him closing in on her. Fighting had always been a release. But this was different. This was a need.

Jealousy roiled and my feet came up under me before I knew how to stop them. But I paused on the fringes of the yard when I saw Aly mumble something to him and disappear underwater. She emerged at the steps and took them one by one. Water dripped down the length of her body. She grabbed her things from the ground and wrapped herself in a towel. Warily she glanced over at me with sad eyes before she headed inside, like maybe there was some way she knew she'd just spent the last ten minutes torturing me.

It was fucking cruel, even though there wasn't a chance she had any clue about how much she affected me.

I watched her retreat through the sliding door.

What was I thinking? Doing this? Allowing my feet to move? But they were, my footfalls heavy as I crossed the small thatch of lawn and twisted through the groups of people huddling in circles on the patio.

From a safe distance, I trailed her inside. Music blared from the living room, the lights dimmed, the rooms packed wall to wall with people, faces and bodies and movement that I wanted to play no part in.

I just wanted Aly.

The need was blinding, yet it was all I could see.

Watching her head bob through the crowd, I saw her turn and dart down a hall. She disappeared into a door on the right. I followed her and stopped in front of the closed door. In the darkness I paced, the agitation I felt unlike anything I'd ever experienced before. I knew it was her, that she'd managed to unlock something inside me that should never have been released. Behind the door, water ran and clothing rustled.

All I could think about was Aly on the other side, that body wet and those eyes sad. All I could focus on was the raging in my heart and the madness she'd sent careening through my mind.

The door opened, and Aly straightened with a shock when saw me there. A confused smile lit her mouth, and she whispered, "Jare . . ." before my name died on her lips as she made out the expression on my face. She shifted on her feet, blinking as uncertainty danced in the warmth of her green eyes.

Control eluded me, left me at a complete loss as I stared at the girl.

And it was stupid, so fucking stupid and greedy and selfish, but I took. I lifted her by the waist and spun her around to pin her to the opposite wall with my hips.

Aly gasped.

And like I'd imagined the first time more than a month ago, those perfect legs were wrapped around my waist. With my nose lost in the sweetness under her jaw, I flattened myself against her, groaned aloud because even through our clothes, I'd never felt anything better than Aly's body pressed to mine.

She whimpered and wove her fingers through my hair.

I trailed my palms down the length of her thighs, and my heart was beating so fucking hard I was sure it was going to hammer right through my chest.

My mouth sought hers, hard and demanding. Her lips were soft and yielding. And I took, deepened the kiss because I knew this would be the only taste of Aly I would ever get. Desire surged, flooded, and every inch of my body hardened. I strained against her, edged back for a breath as I whispered her name.

"Jared" fell from her mouth, her eyes wild, before she dove back in and sucked at my bottom lip. Her sweet tongue flicked out to tease at my skin. Returning the kiss, I consumed her mouth with mine.

She tightened her legs around my waist, desperation pouring from her as she struggled to bring me closer, hunger in her eyes and impatience in her touch. "Jared . . . please." Her fingers dug into my shoulders.

My head spun and my pulse sped, and I wanted to devour every inch of her. Overwrought, my senses were on overload—overwhelmed—everything quickened and slowed and amplified.

Reality came crashing back to me.

No.

I tore my mouth from her, panting, my eyes frantic as they roved over her face.

She burrowed her fingers deeper into my skin, pleading.

No.

I edged back, forcing her legs to drop free as I supported her at her waist, her knees weak as she grappled for footing when her feet fell to the floor.

I steadied her before I pressed my hands to her shoulders and forced myself back.

Her fingers fluttered up to touch her lips, so much like they had done when the first of the fireworks had blanketed the sky. "Jared?" It came low, a breathy question whispered into the dimness of the suffocating hall.

"Shit," I mumbled, stumbling back from the girl who held so much power over me, the one who chased away every rational thought.

I didn't deserve her.

I never could, no matter how fucking badly I needed her.

Hurt wrapped her tight, just as tight as she wrapped her arms protectively over her chest.

What had I done?

I shook my head as I backed away. "I am so sorry, Aly."

Turning, I rushed down the hall, pushed through the throng of sweating bodies, and burst out the front door, gasping at the reprieve of the thick night air.

Pain hit me full force, as clearly as if my eyes were closed and I was living it all again, the day I destroyed everything, took my family's joy, the day *she'd* died and taken my soul with her.

I don't get to have this.

At eleven seventeen the next night, I finally put my key in the lock and turned the knob. I hadn't come back to the apartment at all last night. Facing her after what I'd done felt impossible because I knew what I now had to do. There was no other way around it. I'd fucked it all up, ruined it, the way I always did, and now it was time to pay.

A deep ache clamored in my chest when I stepped through

the door and into the low-lit apartment, the only illumination bleeding from the small light under the microwave in the kitchen. This would be the last time I'd enter it.

And honestly, it made me fucking sad because the last month had felt like *something*, like I wasn't just existing, but there was some kind of purpose to it all.

Only I'd been deluding myself because I'd always known it'd come to this.

Most of all, this hurt because I was going to miss *her*.

Latching the door behind me, I took in the silence of the empty room. At the end of the hall, Christopher's door sat wide open, the room vacant. The only sound in the apartment seeped from the thin walls of Aly's bathroom, the dull hum of the shower telling me she stood under a steaming fall of water.

I rubbed at the soreness on my chest. Yeah. It was unbelievable just how much I was going to miss her.

I couldn't help wondering what she was thinking. Was she hurting after what I'd done to her? After I'd left her standing there confused? Used? Because that's what it had been, hadn't it?

Me consumed with the way she made me feel, the way she filled up this fucking void in my chest like she belonged there. Me deceiving myself that for a few seconds it was okay.

But this was Aly. My Aly. And I'd used her because I wanted her so badly and because I'd never known anything that felt so good. Her presence was like this balm I didn't understand, solace in the insufferable night.

So like the asshole I was, I'd taken.

I pressed the heels of my hands into my eyes. *Shit*. I was always fucking taking.

Guilt had eaten at me all night and day. I shouldn't have

touched her, shouldn't have allowed her to touch me. Now it lingered on my mouth and swam in my spirit, the memory of her kiss.

Overpowering. Intoxicating. Too much.

The sickest part was that I wanted more. I had to get out of this apartment, out of this city, before all this shit caved in on us, before we imploded and there was nothing left of either of us.

The shower squealed as it was shut off, and the metal curtain rings screeched as they were pushed aside.

Thank God Christopher was gone. I wasn't sure I could handle sitting on the couch beside him, acting as if everything was normal after everything had gone to shit, after I'd pinned his little sister to the wall, after my hands had been on her. He would fucking kill me if he knew what had gone down last night, and he had every right to. I wished he would. I deserved it.

Now I would give her an apology. Try to explain myself a little.

The hardest part was it seemed as if none of my reasons or explanations fit together because it felt like maybe Aly and I did. I heaved a breath through my pursed lips and shoved that dangerous thinking aside. Without a doubt, that wasn't possible. I wasn't made for anything but ruin.

I'd apologize the best I could and promise her I'd pack my shit; then she'd never have to see my sorry ass again.

Rustling echoed from her bathroom. A drawer opened and closed, and a cabinet door banged shut. I imagined her standing in front of the mirror, drying off, then slipping on those sleep shorts she always wore. How wrong was it that I was hoping so? That I wanted nothing more than to endure living through the sight of Aly dressed like that one more time?

That'd be the last thing I took with me—the memory of her

kind face mixed with that body. The two combined made me dangerous for her to be around, and I was putting an end to it all.

I stopped outside the bathroom door and rested my forehead against the wood, listened to her subtle movements on the other side, and wished things were different than they were.

What I was getting ready to do was going to hurt worse than any conscious decision I'd ever made.

I kind of wanted to laugh because all of a sudden I was thinking about all the phrases they'd used while I was in juvie, during the sessions they'd placed me in because that's where they sent all the junkies. I'd thought all of it bullshit because they knew nothing about me. They'd talked about the withdrawals we'd experience, but how it would be so much easier while we were on the inside and separated from all the temptations on the outside. They'd warned us that once we got out, we'd have to be careful to stay straight, to keep our noses clean and the triggers at bay.

Two weeks ago I'd made the decision to keep my trigger close. Aly was the greatest temptation I'd ever had, and I'd decided to pretend that just extracting myself from her room would be enough. As if seeing her every day wasn't going to wear me down. I should have known I would slip.

I was assaulted by visions of Aly pinned up against the wall by my hips, the feel of her body and the taste of her skin.

I'd slipped, all right.

Fallen.

Heaving the air from my lungs, I turned away, crossed the hall, and let myself into the stillness of her room. I didn't know what the hell I was thinking, just going in without her permission, but I felt like this good-bye had to happen here. In the place where she'd affected me so deeply. The lights were off, but her blinds were drawn, and the lights from the parking lot below spilled onto the floor.

Her bed was all tussled, the sheets twisted and tied, and I pictured her there last night, tossing as she turned, sleep evading her as she longed for me.

And I knew she did. I'd felt it in her touch. She wanted me just as intensely as I wanted her.

Those sheets looked so damned inviting. Like a creep, I had the urge to bundle them up, to press them to my nose, to breathe in all that was Aly before I walked away.

Yeah, it'd be wise to avoid her bed.

I pulled the chair out from under her dressing table and turned it around to face the room. Then I carefully sat on the hard, wooden chair. I fidgeted as I took in her space, tugging at the hem of my T-shirt. Everything here was so distinctly Aly. Comfortable. Right.

One of her sketch pads lay on the floor. God, I wanted to know what she kept inside them so badly, to get a little further inside her head, to catch a glimpse of her soul. I could so easily cross her room and look inside, but I instinctively knew whatever she had there was as personal to her as the words I wrote in my books. I was still shocked by the impulse I'd had to give her a little glimpse into mine, the words I'd left on her pillow. I wanted to show her that even though I could feel no joy, I could still see beauty. That night when I lay awake with her sleeping in my arms, it was all I could see, the beauty in this girl.

I tore my attention from the pad because there was no chance I'd disrespect her privacy like that, and I let my eyes trace her bookshelves, the pictures on her walls, memorized her space.

As if I could ever forget it.

Agitation bounced my knee, each passing second excruciating. I didn't know what I was going to say to her, but I refused to be a coward and disappear without an explanation. Even if telling her good-bye was going to kill me.

I froze when I heard the bathroom door open across the hall.

This was it.

The knob to her room rattled as it turned, and I swallowed hard when Aly came into view. Her hand was on the doorknob as it swung open, her body in motion until she stumbled back when she saw me sitting in the shadows. Her hair was wet, and she'd obviously run a comb through it. The length of it fell in long sheets that had deepened to black, and errant strands curled where they clung to her shoulders. She was wearing those same tiny pink shorts and a matching tank, the softness of her breasts swelling at the top, the long stretch of her legs exposed.

Instantly I was hard.

My knee bounced faster as I struggled with the intense urge to run or maybe give in to a repeat of last night.

Motherfucking trigger.

I raked a shaky hand through my hair while Aly remained rooted in the doorway. I couldn't tell if she was pissed or relieved or confused. Troubled green eyes darted across my face as if they were searching for some sort of clue, and I wondered just how badly I'd injured her when I walked away from her last night.

My jaw ticked, and she just stared.

What the fuck was I supposed to say when she was standing there looking at me like that? When her chest rose and fell in a heavy pant, her eyes wide with surprise, her mouth slack with what looked like relief.

"Jared," she finally said so quietly. She made my name sound like a statement, maybe even an answer.

She'd wondered if I would return and now I was here. And God, I didn't want to leave.

Her eyes softened, though her expression remained intense, and her chin lifted as she stepped forward and latched the door. She reached behind her and blindly turned the lock. The little click sounded deafening in the silence of the room, like this overt warning that there'd be no running tonight.

But running was exactly what I'd be doing.

Aly laid the full force of her eyes on me, their intensity pinning me to the hard wooden chair.

Shifting in discomfort, I searched for words in a situation where I didn't want to speak, because really all I wanted to do was stay. I leaned forward to rest my forearms on my legs, threaded my fingers together, and dropped my head while I gathered my thoughts. Then I lifted my face to meet hers and whispered slowly, "I'm so sorry, Aly."

"You're leaving," she said, the words not so much a question but an accusation.

Straightening, I groaned and scrubbed both palms over my face, dropped my hands back to my lap and looked up at her.

"What else can I do? I'm so sorry, Aly. I'm so fucking sorry. I don't know what came over me last night. . . ." It all began to flood, a rush of words that couldn't be contained in my mouth. I had to get them out so I could *get* out. I couldn't be closed in here with her, with her scent and her smile and everything that was Aly that had become the only thing in this world that I wanted.

"I mean, I did *fucking* know. I was so pissed off because that dickhead wouldn't stop touching you." Harshly, I ran my hand over my head and down to my neck, hoping it would quell that feeling that rose in me again, the possessiveness I felt for her like this poison that I had to somehow expel. "It made me fucking crazy, and I fucking ruined it. I'm sorry I ruined it, Aly, but I warned you that I would." My head tipped to the side, my eyes tightened in emphasis as I tried to make her understand. "I told you I'd make you regret this. I knew this was happen—"

My words died on my tongue when the expression on her face shifted into something I wished I couldn't make out. I wanted her to be pissed, to be angry with me the way she should be, but instead she was looking at me a little like I'd been looking at her for the last month. Her eyes were tender, but her lips were parted, and something like need rose and sucked all the air from the room.

I drew in a ragged breath. "Aly . . ."

Don't.

I barely shook my head.

Slowly she began to approach, and I sank farther back into the chair the closer she came, my knee bouncing harder as she timidly inched up in front of me. Her movements were slow, hypnotizing, and I couldn't stop myself from watching those legs. My eyes darted to her hands. She was rubbing her thumbs over her fingertips as if she were searching for some kind of friction or maybe looking for confidence. My gaze flicked up to meet her face. A color I didn't understand had darkened her eyes. There was no looking away as she crossed the room, and my head continued to tilt back, locked on her, lost in this place where I knew I absolutely shouldn't fucking be.

She stopped just a breath from me.

My hands dropped slack, dangled at my sides.

Everything became heavy. My fingers twitched, and I had to force the air in and out of my lungs.

I swore I could actually hear Aly's heart beating as she hovered in hesitation an inch away. She blinked hard, squirmed before she looked at me with determination. "Jared, I don't want you to leave."

"Aly . . . I . . ." What was I supposed to say? Because I didn't want to leave, either.

I had to.

Erasing the last of the space between us, Aly allowed the front of her legs to touch my knees, and she groaned as if the contact seared her. She wavered, before she reached out to run the back of her hand down my face, testing me. Tempting me.

I stopped breathing altogether when she slowly straddled my lap and murmured close to my ear, "Please . . . don't leave me."

Fuck.

This was bad, really fucking bad. And I knew I should push her away, make her stop because what she was doing was only bringing us a little closer to the edge. She held on to the chair behind me, her warm body pressed into mine. There was no chance she wasn't feeling just how much I wanted her.

"What are you doing, Aly?" My hands went to her slender hips with the intention of edging her off my lap. Instead my fingers dug into the soft skin.

A shudder sped up my spine when she trembled above me.

Wetting my lips, I tried to move her back but only managed to brush up against her farther. Her expression was severe but soft, her movements shaky but sure. She searched my face, her eyes burning a path as she left me utterly exposed. And I could smell her, and the memory of the way she tasted, the way she felt, overwhelmed every last one of my senses. She didn't even have to move, and she was already touching me everywhere.

She swallowed, then spoke. "Did you want to kiss me last night?"

"Last night was a mistake, Aly. I—"

Her hands went to my face, and she held me there, forcing me to look up at her. "I didn't ask you if it was a mistake. I asked if you wanted to."

A frustrated sound worked its way free of my throat, and I shifted again, which only brought her closer. Right then I knew there was not a fucking thing I could do because nothing else mattered in the world except for the way she felt pressed up tight against me. My fingers dug farther into her hips, and we were nose-to-nose, Aly's hands firm on my face. I realized we were moving, our bodies subtly rocking.

I groaned. "I've wanted to kiss you every single second of every single day since the moment I opened my eyes to find you standing over me, Aly. But you know we can't do this." My voice cracked. "I don't get to have this. I already told you . . . you deserve someone who can love you, someone who will be good for you, and you know that's not me."

I hoped maybe she'd listen to reason, but instead she crushed her chest to mine and dipped her head to the side. Her mouth came urgent against my neck, and she kissed at a sensitive spot under my jaw that very nearly made me jump out of my skin because it felt so fucking good. And she was sucking and moving and touching and . . . fuck.

Making her way up my neck, she kissed along my jaw, then lifted her soft lips to mine as she murmured, "Then tell me you don't want me."

Pleasure rocked through my body when she ground herself against me. A growl clanged around in my chest and rumbled up my throat. "Aly . . ."

And she did it again, holding me close as if she were hanging on to life. "I said . . . tell me you don't want me."

"You know that would be a lie." My eyelids closed with the admission, and I knew I shouldn't say it, but I needed her to know. "God, I want you so bad, Aly. So bad."

I could feel the affection in her touch as she slowly slid her hands down my chest and over my stomach. Her deep green eyes never released mine when she sat back a little to take hold of the bottom of her tank. Slowly she drew it up, inch by excruciating inch. And I was frozen, everything except for my eyes that trailed her movements as I took in the lush flesh she exposed.

Aly wasn't wearing a bra, and I thought maybe somewhere in my subconscious I already knew that, but this . . . this was shocking, too much, and I sucked in a fortifying breath because I had no idea how I was ever going to get out of this.

I didn't want to.

Aly's hair fell in a tangled mess around her shoulders as she finally lifted the shirt over her head and dropped it to the floor.

And I was trembling, my body losing all control as my attention shot between her face and her full breasts.

What the hell did she think she was doing to me? This was almost as cruel as making me watch her splash around with Dickhead in that fucking pool last night. Although neither time had there been anything callous in her movements, nothing meant to taunt, and tonight it was clear this was spurred by the same need spinning through her that was spinning through me.

"Touch me," she commanded, her voice low. There was

something in the demand, a hidden shyness that only affirmed the goodness I found in her.

"Aly . . . damn it . . . you need to stop."

"Please," she begged.

My fingers worked deeper into her hips, and Aly sat back, her hands on my shoulders as she bared herself to me. This girl was so unbelievably gorgeous, her skin a creamy color that seemed to glow in the dim light. So soft. Perfect.

My fingers moved, slowly trailing up her sides, dipping into the faint divots between each of her ribs. "Aleena" quietly slipped from my mouth like a prayer.

With my touch, goose bumps pebbled over the expanse of her skin and the rosy buds of her breasts tightened. Her head listed just to the side as she drew in a shaky breath, her dark hair falling all over one shoulder, a silent whimper falling from her trembling lips.

"Aly, I . . ." I looked up at her, unable to understand why someone like her wanted to give herself to someone like me.

"Shh," she begged. "Don't, Jared. I need you . . . want you. I don't care about anything outside my door. Here, it's just the two of us."

Gentle fingers swept down my chest and teased under the hem of my shirt. Warm palms flattened on my bare skin, and she slowly skimmed them up my stomach, dragging my shirt with it, pressing harder as she passed over my ribs. She splayed her fingers wide as her hands moved over my shoulders.

I shook, but I was powerless, so I let her take control. In surrender, I lifted my arms so she could tug the shirt over my head. She tossed it to the floor on top of hers.

Aly sat back to take me in. She'd seen me without my shirt on before. I mean, I'd even let her *touch* me. But never in my life had I felt as exposed as I did right then. Her fingertips softened as they traced along the outline of my sins, as she caressed the markings of every mistake I'd ever made as if this girl somehow found some kind of beauty in them. She explored, caressed down my chest, back up my sides, and over my shoulders.

She should be repulsed because I was every time I looked in the mirror.

But she was gazing at me, touching me like maybe she really did understand, like she wasn't humoring me with some kind of bullshit pity party. She leaned down and kissed the dying rose at the center of my chest.

A tremor coursed through my body.

I knew it wasn't feigned. I could feel it. Aly understood me.

And again I was thinking that maybe she and I did fit because she was fucking perfect and good and every kind of beautiful, and I was corrupted and impure and vile, and just maybe piecing two people together so contrary meant we could somehow create a whole.

That kind of thinking, though, was all just a painful delusion. But right then, I didn't fucking care. I'd be happy to die in this deception.

"You are so beautiful," Aly murmured as she reached out to touch my face with nothing but sincerity in her words, and I knew she would be happy to live in this illusion, too.

I folded my arms around her waist and lifted her up as I stood from the chair. She hooked her legs over my hips, locking herself to me, and I was kissing her as I walked her to the bed. She cupped my face in her hands, smiling against my lips, kissing me hard and soft and everything in between, and then she was pressing these little kisses to my chin and my cheeks and my nose.

Something that almost felt like joy rose up from the inside and pushed against my ribs.

Another delusion, but I'd take it.

Because right then, taking felt right.

One of my knees hit the bed, and I crawled up with her still clinging to me. I untangled her from my neck and waist and gently set her on her twisted sheets. I edged back to standing, looking down on this girl who I should be running from instead of running toward.

She lay there wearing nothing but her sleep shorts, her feet flat on the mattress with her knees parted and bent. Her bare chest heaved as she stared up at me staring down at her. A faint smile curved her lips while her eyes continued to explore every inch of my skin.

For the first time in years, I didn't mind.

"Jared," she said, her hand fluttering up to beckon me forward. "Please."

I leaned down to unlace my boots, watching her while she watched me. I stood and kicked them off. Slowly I began to work through the buttons on my fly.

Part of me was praying she'd stop me, that she'd finally grasp reality and see me for exactly what I was. But the rest of me screamed for her. It was like I could feel her spirit sinking under my skin, slipping through my veins, taking hold.

A blink of fear shot through my heart.

No. I don't get to have this.

I shoved the feeling off.

Pushing my jeans down to the floor, I shrugged them aside and stood at the edge of her bed in my underwear while I took in every inch of the girl who had some kind of insane hold over me.

Light filtered in from the window above her. Her stomach

was flat and her breasts were full, her legs so fucking long and slender and strong. She lay there with her arms draped out to the side, rocking a little side to side as if she were just as impatient for me as I was for her. The muscles in my chest and arms twitched and flexed as I slowly climbed onto her bed. I nudged her knees farther apart. With one hand I supported my weight and hovered a foot over her while I touched her face and ran my fingers through her hair.

"Look at you," I said as I cupped her cheek. My gaze rushed all over her face, along her chin and her delicate neck, down the curves and the lines that I was dying to touch. "Aly, you are so incredibly beautiful. Do you know that? Do you have any idea how perfect you are?"

Redness flushed along her skin. She drew her shoulders up and crushed her chest to mine as she splayed her hands across my back, like an embrace that greeted me body and soul, and I couldn't imagine feeling closer to anyone until the second she covered my mouth with hers. This kiss was slow, just a gentle caress of her lips on mine, a soft breath of air from her nose.

She pulled back. Meaningfully, she gazed up at me. "I'm not perfect, Jared. No one is."

A pensive smile formed on my mouth as she wrapped me in undeserved kindness. I wanted to dispute her claim because to me, that's what she was. This girl who'd shaken me. I wanted to tell her she was wrong because I knew inside that pure heart of hers she believed the two of us were just the same.

Maybe her soul burned so bright she couldn't see the blackness in mine.

Fingertips trailed along my jaw and wound in the hairs at the nape of my neck.

With a harsh shake of my head, I asked her the same question I'd been asking myself for the last month. "What are we doing, Aly?"

She tightened her hold and whispered along my jaw, "Whatever feels right."

I released the air from my lungs and gave in. Devoured her mouth. I sucked her bottom lip between both of mine. Her jaw slackened as she fully succumbed to my kiss. Colors flashed behind my eyes as I let my weight cover her, chest to chest, breath to breath. I caged her, her tiny body pinned below mine as our mouths collided, reckless, hard, and demanding.

Heat blanketed us, flames and fire and need. I'd never wanted anyone like this, had never ached to bury myself in someone this way. I wanted to lose myself there, disappearing forever in this blissful delusion.

Aly was panting when I pulled away. She gasped and clutched my head when I dipped down and took the rosy bud of her breast in my mouth. "Oh my God . . . Jared," she breathed, her words shooting straight through me.

Writhing, she moaned, and I lifted my weight to my knees so I could drag my flattened palms down her sides. Her muscles jumped and ticked, and she arched as I sucked at her. Almost frantic, her hands tugged at my hair.

I eased, gently kissed along the underside of her breast, then ran my nose back up over the sensitive skin. Her hands loosened and she sighed as she massaged her fingers at the back of my scalp. My kiss traveled the valley of her chest, and I took the opposite breast in my mouth.

Her hands fisted in my hair again. This time, Aly begged, "Please."

Shit.

And again I was asking, "What are we doing?" because I

was hard and straining and so was Aly and all of this seemed so fucking crazy. Because I wanted her. I wanted her more than I'd ever wanted anything in my life, this consuming need that made my head spin and heart pound.

Slipping my hands under her back, I ran them all the way down to cup her perfect round ass and pressed her a little harder into me.

Aly whimpered, a frenzy alight in the depths of her green eyes. She rocked against me, purposed and strong. "Please."

That was all the confirmation I needed, and I was pushing those little shorts and the black panties hidden underneath over her hips, revealing every inch of this beautiful girl. My chest felt too full, and my stomach tightened as I lowered them down her thighs.

Jerking back, I rested on my knees and tugged her shorts free from her legs.

Fully exposed, Aly stared up at me. Shadows danced in her eyes, her expression tense, and a little mewl slipped from her mouth as she nervously pressed her knees together. In it, I heard so many things, a whimper, a cry, need, and maybe something that sounded like fear.

Caressing her skin, I slowly spread her knees apart. Under my touch, she trembled, her legs shaking as they fell open and her naked body was completely exposed to me. Never before had I witnessed a more perfect sight.

"Shit . . . Aly . . . you're fucking gorgeous." Maybe it was crass, but damn, she was.

I watched as Aly's tongue darted out to wet her lips, her hair all tangled around her face. Anxious green eyes stared up at me. Her expression was both intense and shy, shifting with desire and apprehension and lust.

A lick of fear lashed at me again. Squeezing my eyes closed,

I swallowed hard and fought for control. This was wrong. So wrong. Yet I just opened my eyes and let my hands wander back down her legs, my palms firm as I ran them up the inside of her thighs. I shifted forward and captured her mouth.

Aly wrapped her legs around my waist.

I rubbed against her, shameless and brash.

"Aly . . ."

"Jared . . . I want you." Aly's touch became urgent, her kiss greedy. Desperate hands rushed down my back to grip my ass. "Love me, Jared. Love me."

My mouth opened in a silent cry that I buried in the haven of her neck. And I wished that I could. Even though I knew that wasn't what she meant, for one fleeting moment, I wished I could love her and that this beautiful girl could love me back.

Unbridled hunger washed over us in waves, sweat slicking our skin as our bodies grasped for each other.

And I felt powerless, consumed, hard.

So fucking hard.

Overwhelmed, I pushed back to my knees and dropped a kiss to her soft belly. Aly sucked in a sharp breath and her hips jerked from the bed. Then she threaded her fingers in my hair and begged my name. My arms wound under her bent legs, and I tucked her close. Shifting, I leaned forward and rested one hand on the bed beside her waist. Her leg was trapped between my arm and side, scorching my skin.

I glanced up at her. Aly watched me with chaotic eyes as I smoothed the opposite hand along her stomach, down her thigh, and then ran the backs of my fingers over the bare skin at her center.

Aly shook.

I held my breath as I slipped two fingers inside her.

She gasped and writhed, and her hands fisted in the sheets at her sides. She was warm . . . so fucking warm . . . and so fucking tight. I searched her, listened to the rapid tumbling of discordant words that whispered from her mouth.

Realization hit me like a flood.

"Why the fuck are you a virgin, Aly?"

Aly just lifted her hips and begged me more. "Please."

I continued to search her, please her, pressed my thumb to her clit as I lurched forward and covered her mouth with mine, demanding through my kiss, "Why are you a virgin?"

Aly's hands flew to my face, her hold firm but her eyes sincere as she looked up at me. "Because I want it to matter."

"Shit . . . Aly."

Crushing my chest to hers, I curled my arm over the top of her head and mashed my cheek to hers.

I quickened my hand, my fingers filling her hard and fast.

Her nails cut into the skin of my shoulders, burrowed deep enough to sink into my blackened soul. Aly tightened, her breath rasping from her lungs and filtering across my face. "Jared . . . I don't . . . so good."

I could feel it hit, her pleasure as she convulsed all around my hand. Affection rushed through my chest.

No.

And still she was begging, "Jared, please," lifting herself to me as she tried to get to my underwear.

I rose on my knees between her thighs, grabbed her hands, and pinned them to the bed. "No way, Aly."

I might be an asshole, I might take and take and take, but there was not a chance in hell I was going to take *that*.

My eyes searched hers, trying to understand, trying to make her understand. "You said you want it to matter."

Sadness clouded her features. "How could it not matter with you?"

Regret twisted through my gut because I knew better than to have allowed this to completely spin out of control. But it was me who lacked control, and it was Aly who held me.

And it would matter. To me. But that wouldn't make a fucking difference in the world because I could never be what she needed. Could never be what she deserved.

I would destroy whatever we created, would ruin her, would wreck this beauty.

I loosened the hold on her hands. The tension that had stretched me tight ebbed, and my body softened as I rested my elbows on the bed, bracketing her shoulders. I swept the hair on her forehead from her face. "You matter, Aly. You've always mattered to me. But this . . ." I twirled a strand of her hair with my finger. "I keep warning you we can't do this, and you just keep pushing me further and further. I don't know what it is you think you want from me . . . what you think I can give you."

Aly frowned. "I just want you to stay."

She made it sound so simple. Easy.

Stay.

Staying here would only be another transgression added to the uncountable others. Another blemish. Another mark. Surrender heaved from my lungs in a heavy sigh.

I'd already fucked it all up anyway. In the end, what would staying a little longer change? No doubt, when I finally left, it was going to hurt.

I spread my palm over the cheek of her trusting face.

Not just me, but it was going to hurt Aly, too.

"Stay," she whispered again, lifting her chin to place a tender kiss on my mouth.

I rolled to the side and took her with me. "This is crazy."

She wiggled closer and plastered herself to my side. "I know ... but I like it."

Quietly I laughed at the simplicity that was unbearably complex, and I smoothed my hand over the top of her head. "You do, huh?"

Her fingers tickled over my sensitive stomach. "Yeah, I do."

I squeezed her and turned my mouth to her ear. "No sex, Aly. You waited this long ... don't waste it." And fuck, if my body wasn't still screaming for her. But I meant it.

"Okay," she whispered seriously, her hand trailing up my torso to flatten on my chest. Then she lifted herself up on her elbow, a new shyness taking her over as she chewed at the inside of her lip. "Will you let me touch you?" she asked as she moved to straddle my legs and sat back on her knees.

She didn't wait for an answer.

A slow moan locked in my throat when she freed me, and vibrations rocked me to my core when she took me in her hand. I shot up to sitting, gripped her head in my hands, and bunched her hair in my fingers, kissed her hard.

This girl. This girl.

"Aleena."

Why would she want someone like me?

"Jared," she breathed. Her soft hand was wrapped around me, her intense green eyes locked on mine as she began to move. Slowly at first, almost tentative. "Is this okay?" she murmured.

Okay? This girl just had no idea what she did to me.

"Fuck, Aly ... that feels so good. You don't even know."

A whisper of a smile edged her mouth, her tongue darting out to wet her lips as she increased her pace. She leaned back a fraction to make herself room, bringing her other hand up to anchor to my neck.

We were nose-to-nose, and the air panted from her mouth

mixed with mine as she heightened me to a pleasure that shouldn't have been possible.

I grunted, my body fucking straining, desperate for more of her touch. "Aly . . . shit." Pleasure shot through every nerve in my body as I came.

And Aly was kissing me, whispering my name as she led me through my release.

I wound her in my arms and buried my face in her chest, clinging to her. Because God, I didn't want to let her go.

Aly slipped off my lap and pulled me down to her side. Warmth swam in her eyes as she stared at me, gentle fingers brushing through my hair. "Thank you . . . for tonight . . . for staying here with me."

I kissed her forehead, unable to understand this girl. "You're beautiful, Aly."

She snuggled into my side and I held her closer, listened to her breaths as they slowed and evened, her heartbeat a steady thrum against my ribs as she drifted off to sleep. I got lost in it, lulled by it. Finally I let go and closed my eyes.

Sleep teased along the edges of my mind, a murky haze taking hold. Colors flashed. In defense, I squeezed my eyes tighter. But the inevitable came. Helplessly I watched as trails of blood made a distorted path down one side of her face. My chest convulsed and I was sure it was fire that pricked and singed my flesh.

"Jared," she mumbled.

So badly I wanted to cry, but no tears would come, like they were locked inside with the fear and the pain.

She looked so sad. So sad and so scared.

But still she managed to smile.

A soft hand came to my face and moved down to cup my

neck. "Shh," Aly whispered. "Wake up, Jared. You're shaking. It's okay. I'm here. It's okay."

My eyes flew open to meet the pitch-black darkness of Aly's room. Sweat drenched my body, and ragged breaths rasped from my lungs.

Aly pulled me closer and placed a kiss just below my ear. "It's okay."

I crushed her to my chest, my frantic heart pounding against hers. It wasn't fucking okay. It never would be. But just for a little while, I wanted to pretend it was.

We lay together, curled up as one, and I fell asleep again and slept like I hadn't for so, so long.

Faint light seeped through the window, and I awoke to find Aly sleeping in my arms. Her hair was spread all around us, the length spilling out behind her and a few wayward pieces crawling across my chest. I pressed my nose to her hair and breathed her in. One of her arms was draped across my chest, her flawless skin a striking contrast against the colors marring mine.

The pure and the impure.

Guilt seeped all the way to my bones.

I kissed her head and untangled myself from her hold. Pausing at her door, I listened to the silence on the other side, before I slipped out into the main room. Christopher's door was closed. Who knew what time he'd come in last night? I sure hadn't heard him.

Guess I'd been otherwise occupied.

I flopped onto the couch. A tangle of emotions surged through me. Mainly it was guilt, but simmering beneath that was something that felt . . . good.

Really good.

I resisted a smile when I thought of Aly falling asleep in my arms. I itched to return to her, to climb into the warmth of her bed and her spirit, to sink in and never let go.

Instead I grabbed my notebook and a pack of cigarettes and headed out the sliding door to the balcony. Morning threatened at the horizon and I slid to the concrete floor. Lighting a cigarette, I took a drag and drew it deep into my lungs, then released it toward the sky.

Shaking my head, I pulled my notebook onto my lap. I thumbed through to the back. The pages were thick, tattered, words scribbled and bleeding together in savage chaos.

Except for the few pages where she lived, where in my words she was more than just a fantasy and I had brought her to life. I turned to them and lost myself there.

Two hours later I sat on the couch beside Christopher. He was playing one of the video games we used to play years before. He'd staggered from his room about thirty minutes ago, looking about as disheveled as I felt. It was early, and I had no idea why he was up since the guy tended to sleep half the day away. He'd grunted a "good morning" as he slumped to the couch and flipped on the TV in the same motion.

After what went down last night, shame was twitching my fingers. I did my best to act normal, but that kind of deception was hard to manage because what happened between Aly and me was anything but normal.

Even if it felt so right.

I rubbed a nervous hand across my tense jaw, listening as the shower in Aly's bathroom sprang to life.

God, the girl was dangerous. A minute ago she had quietly slipped across the hall from her bedroom to the bathroom, shooting me a shy smile as she passed. Crimson colored her face with a ridiculous blush, and her hair was all a mess because my fingers had been tangled in it all night. She wore the same tank and shorts that had been discarded on her floor.

My knee bounced because I was thinking about Aly peeling them from her body before she climbed under the hot sheets of water in the shower.

Closing my eyes, I fought for restraint.

It was Saturday, which meant no work for me, and I had no idea what I was going to do with my sorry ass all day. Aly had to work. How pathetic was it that I didn't want her to go?

The shower shut off, and a few minutes later Aly emerged from the bathroom wrapped in a towel. She rushed to her room and clicked the door shut behind her.

I shot off the couch and sought the isolation of the bathroom. I didn't think I could handle sitting by Christopher any longer, hanging on to this secret that felt like a million tons on my shoulders. So much of me wanted to shout it, to scream out that I had touched beauty, that for a few minutes I had felt more than the nothingness that was my life. Years of isolation did that to a person, and when emotions were freed, it was hard to keep them contained.

But instinctively I knew to keep my mouth shut.

When I left, I wouldn't leave Aly ashamed, couldn't bear to shed light on the sickness I was tainting her with. This would be our secret, our fantasy, and for just a little while, I was giving in to it.

Steam filled the small space, and the mirror was coated, hiding me in the misty haze. I swept my hand across the surface and looked at my reflection in the foggy mirror.

Hate spun through my insides and throbbed down my limbs.

What the hell did she see?

When I heard her bedroom door open, I quickly opened the bathroom door, wanting to catch a glimpse of her before she left for the day. Feigning apathy, I slowed when I stepped out into the hall.

She stood at the bar, gathering her things.

"Have to work today, huh?" I asked. As if I didn't already know.

She dropped her face, looking all shy and innocent and perfect, and then shoved her wallet into her purse. "Yeah. I'm just working the short lunch shift, though, so I'll be off a little after one." Gathering up the mass of dark hair from her neck, Aly twisted it into a ponytail. "It shouldn't be too bad," she said.

She glanced up at me with awareness in her eyes, as if she knew exactly what I was thinking, that I couldn't stand to watch her leave. She knew I was going to be counting the hours before she returned and she even knew how much I absolutely hated the fact that I would be. The thing that twisted me all up was Aly looking as if she felt the same, like she was dying to bury those fingers in my skin.

I fisted my hand. It took everything I had not to push her up against the wall and kiss her senseless.

Considering Christopher was sitting on the couch playing video games, I figured that was a really fucking bad idea. I sat back and played it cool.

"I guess I'll see you later," Aly said as she heaved her ridiculously huge purse onto her shoulder.

I barely lifted my chin, blithe and indifferent. "Sure . . . drive safe."

She turned away, stole a glance back at me, then turned to leave. "See you after work, Christopher."

Furiously he thumbed at his controller. "Bye," he said as if he couldn't be disturbed long enough to notice she was there.

Aly walked away, her dark ponytail swishing along her back. She opened the door and bright sunlight burst around her frame as she stepped out into the day.

I inched forward to the end of the hall. I realized I was standing there like an idiot, watching the space she'd just taken up as she snapped the door shut behind her.

Shit.

"You better watch yourself, man." The warning dripped low and slow through Christopher's lips, hardness coiled tightly in the words.

Taken aback, I blinked hard and turned my attention to where he sat with his focus trained entirely on the TV. I swallowed down the pool of saliva that gathered at the back of my throat. "What are you talking about?"

Incredulous laughter seeped from Christopher, and he slowly shook his head in disbelief. "You think I haven't noticed the way you've been looking at my little sister?" He cut his eyes to me, scrutinizing me in clear disgust, before he tore them back to the TV. "I wasn't joking when I said her room was off-limits. I just didn't think I'd have to spell it out for you."

I tried to rein in the panic that jackhammered in my brain. Guilt hit me hard, but not hard enough to keep me away from Aly. My body still burned with the residue of her touch. Nothing would stop me from going back for more.

Just a little more.

I shook my head and forced a frown that could only speak of my own distaste. "We're just friends, Christopher. We've always been. You know that." The words pushed out with the force of my faked revulsion, blended with the solemn oath. "She's like a sister to me." My tongue burned with the lie, and this time the guilt was consuming.

I was just going to stand here and lie straight-faced to my best friend?

He will hate me before I'm gone.

He turned to face me fully, his green eyes probing.

In discomfort, I fidgeted.

Then he slowly nodded. "Sorry, man . . . I just . . . we already talked about Aly being different than the rest of these girls. I can't stand the thought of someone fucking with her."

My exhale came heavy. "I know that." She was perfect. I hated the thought of someone fucking with her, too. Especially if it was me.

FIFTEEN

Aleena

Joy reverberated through my being.

Intense, consuming joy. It was the kind of joy fraught with apprehension and stifling doubt. I wasn't sure Jared came close to understanding what last night had meant to me, how his touch had become my truth.

Never before had I allowed anyone to touch me that way.

Either physically or emotionally.

Megan was right. I just hadn't been able to fully see it. Every relationship I'd had, one way or another, I'd subconsciously sabotaged. I'd held myself just out of reach, staved off every advance, rejected every wandering hand. Maybe somewhere inside me I'd been saving myself for him because part of me had always believed that one day he would return.

Or maybe it was just that I had been waiting for someone who could possibly make me *feel* the way he had made me feel.

Someone who could fill up the space Jared had left when he was so brutally torn from my life. Someone I cared enough about that it would cover up the sadness I felt for Jared, the ache that seemed to never dissipate. But there had never been anyone like that because it turned out it had been Jared all along. There was no one else who fit.

And it was shocking just how ready I was to give myself to him.

For him to take me.

I'd come so close to losing him again. I'd sensed his intentions the moment I found him sitting alone in my darkened room, and I knew it was all or nothing. And I wanted it all. Kissing him at the party had rocked my foundation. Last night had shattered it. I would never be the same.

Affection expanded in that place deep inside where I'd kept him hidden all these years. I no longer wanted to hide it, even though I knew that was exactly what I had to do. Jared was . . . volatile . . . irrational . . . ashamed. Not of me, but of himself. I knew there wasn't a chance he could see himself the way I saw him. Would I ever be able to convince him he was wrong? I saw it there, dimming the light in his eyes, the idea that what he felt for me was somehow undeserved, impure, something disgraceful, bred for shame.

He couldn't even admit what he felt was real. But I could feel it. I felt it in every brush of his hand. I found it in the words he'd once again left for me, words he didn't have the strength to say. They were written on the same type of worn paper that he had left before.

A still heart quickens as beauty graces the foul.

Last night I'd burned to tell him, to open my mouth and expose it all. To tell him he was the reason I remained untouched because he'd already *touched* me in a way that bonded him to me. Intuition held me back, warning me that I'd already pushed him just about as far as he could go.

No longer was I that delusional little girl. I couldn't fix him, and I knew I could never erase his pain. Honestly, I didn't want to. Trying to would only minimize what he'd suffered. But maybe one day he could let go of some of the guilt. If he could be freed of the blame, he could begin to heal.

I wanted to be a part of that. Even if my only purpose was to give him a flicker of hope.

Work turned out to be just the distraction I needed. The lunch rush had the diner packed with customers, and my hands stayed busy with menial tasks while my mind stayed close to Jared. But I itched to be back in his arms.

Still I found myself driving to my parents' house after I finished my shift. I wasn't quite sure what it was, but I felt like I needed to get my feet back on solid ground, to be granted a sense of certainty, before I offered myself back up to uncertainty.

I knocked once before I opened the door. "Mom?" I called. There was no answer, and I walked through the silent house. "Dad?"

Out the sliding glass door, I caught a glimpse of them. They were curled up together on one of those two-person loungers by the pool. For a second, I remained still, watching. Wearing bathing suits and sunglasses, they had their faces turned to the blistering summer sky. Dad sat up higher, his arm draped casually around the top of Mom's head, his fingers mindlessly toying with her hair.

They'd always been natural together. Comfortable. Even when they fought.

I shook my head and slid open the door.

Mom jumped and shot up in the lounger. Her hand went to cover her heart. "Oh my God, Aly, you scared me."

"I always scare you, Mom." I laughed as I stepped into the backyard. "You just jumped, like, ten feet in the air." No surprise there.

Dad chuckled and tugged at her hair. "See? Even Aly knows what a twitchy little thing you are."

Mom playfully swatted him across the chest. "I'm not jumpy. I'm vigilant. There's a big difference."

Dad pushed himself up to a sitting position. He lifted his sunglasses from his eyes and ran his hand over his face, then turned to me. "So, how are you, sweetheart?"

"Good . . . really good. How have you been?"

"Oh, you know, just the same," he answered absently, never one to call much attention to himself.

I loved my dad. He was the kind who was fiercely protective, one who would willingly stand in front of a moving train if it meant he could spare someone he cared about even an ounce of suffering.

It also meant he would never understand about Jared.

Black and white. Good and bad. Even after everything Jared had gone through, Dad still could only see Jared as a punk kid who had taken his family further down in the midst of all their hurt, rather than realizing he was just a boy who couldn't find his way out of the pain. A week before Jared had been sent away, Dad had actually forbidden Christopher to ever see Jared again. But it wasn't as if Jared had been trying to hang out with Christopher. At that time, he was already gone, mentally, emotionally. Just . . . gone.

No question, Dad would see Jared as a threat now. One to his family. One to me.

"So, what are you doing here?" Mom maneuvered off the lounger and pranced across the hot concrete in her bare feet. She hugged me close, then held me by the upper arms and leaned back to take me in. She squeezed in emphasis. "It feels like I haven't seen you in forever."

"Well, that's why I'm here," I said dryly, shooting her a small smirk promising I was just playing around, affection shining in my eyes. I'd missed her, too.

She grinned, then softened as she touched my chin, asked quietly, "How's my baby girl?"

"I'm good."

Mom smiled and softly inclined her head. "Come on, let's get something to drink." She slid the door open. "Do you want anything, Dave?" she called behind her.

"No . . . I'm fine." Dad lay back on the lounger, folding his hands over his chest.

I ran across to him and kissed him on the cheek. "Love you, Dad."

"Love you, too, sweetheart."

I skipped back across the yard and into the house. Inside, Mom was pouring two glasses of iced tea. She handed me one.

"Thank you."

She sipped at her tea, eyeing me over her glass. I prepared for the inquisition.

"So you just popped by, huh? After I haven't seen you in more than a month *and* after you never called so we could have a shopping day? I think something's up . . . and judging by that smile that keeps creeping to your mouth, I'd guess it's a *boy*." The last she sang as she wiggled her shoulders.

As hard as I tried to hold it in, I let go of a small, self-conscious giggle and felt the flush the second it lit my cheeks.

Even though what Jared and I had shared last night had been incredibly intense, that he'd left this heaviness weighing down the deepest recesses of my heart, there was another piece of me that felt light.

Like maybe I'd just experienced my first kiss.

Mom's eyes widened. I'd never talked boys with her because there'd never been anything to say. None of them had mattered except for the one I'd kept from her. But Mom was all about girl talk. I remembered her and Helene staying up until all hours of the night, sharing a bottle of wine while they just talked and laughed, lost themselves in their secrets and dreams. I wondered now how much she missed those days.

"Am I right?" Mom prodded, the words teasing, although she looked on me with a slow tenderness as she ribbed me. She knew I'd always been private about these things, only because I'd never had enough courage to tell her.

I'd come so close to telling her that night. Terrified and shaking, I'd gotten as far as her bedroom door, ready to confide in her. But I'd frozen, paralyzed, when I heard her crying behind it, the vibration of Dad's harsh, angry voice overriding her tears. After more minutes than I could count, I'd turned to find Christopher staring at me in shocked disbelief, as if all of us were set adrift and had been scattered to deal with things none of us could handle.

Never again had I mentioned his name. That's the way we'd all handled it until the day he returned.

"Aren't you always?" I hopped up onto the counter and swung my legs the way I did when I was a little girl.

Amused lines deepened at the corners of Mom's eyes. "No, not always. Most of the time," she added with a wink, "but not always." She leaned up on the counter next to me. "So, tell me about this boy who makes those green eyes dance."

I squeezed both shoulders in a confused shrug and blew the air from my pursed lips. How could Jared be contained by simple words? I looked at her, and again I could feel the admission trembling on my lips. "He scares me, Mom."

She stilled, her hand clamping down on her glass before she shakily set it down and turned to face me. "What do you mean, he scares you? Aly—"

"No, not like that, Mom." I cut her off, struggling for words. "It's just . . . it hurts to care about him so much." It always had and it felt good to finally admit it aloud.

She searched my face. "Oh my God, Aly . . . you love him?" I didn't answer.

"How long have you been seeing him? I don't . . . Who is he?" Mom seemed to flounder through her thoughts, like maybe it stung that I was just telling her this now.

Guilt swept through me. After all these years, I was still keeping him a secret. "I don't even know what we are, Mom. I just care about him, so much, and when we're together I . . ." I frowned, blinked, then let the truth flow free. "It feels like the best thing that ever happened to me."

She moved in front of me and softly ran a lock of my hair through two of her fingers, this wistful expression on her face. "Love *is* the best thing that will ever happen to you, Aly."

Slowly I nodded as I let her words take hold. My voice was rough. "Thank you, Mom. You don't know how much I needed to hear that."

"You know that's what I'm here for," she whispered. Then she shook herself off and stepped back, her voice returning to normal. "So, when do I get to meet this mystery man? Oh, why don't you bring him over for dinner?" she asked, clearly excited by the proposition.

"I don't think we're quite there yet. But someday." I could only hope.

Doubt chipped a little fissure in my belief. Jared had made me no promises. And it was true, I didn't even know what we were. I only had the promise of his touch, only knew he looked at me the same way I looked at him. That was what buoyed me, what filled me with faith.

Mom frowned and regarded me seriously. "I know you're grown, Aly, but I would really like to meet him."

Just then a key rattled the lock in the front door. Mom reached for her tea glass as we heard the heavy footfalls of someone entering the house.

Was it terrible I was thanking God for the interruption? But I didn't know how much more information I could give Mom now before it all became obvious.

Augustyn walked into the kitchen, tearing a sweaty T-shirt over his head. He wore basketball shorts and tennis shoes, his deeply tanned skin gleaming with moisture. I sometimes wondered how Mom and Dad had raised such a jock when Christopher and I were anything but.

He smiled wide. "Aly! I was excited to see your car out front. How are you?"

"I'm doing really good. I've been missing you, though," I said with all honesty.

He didn't hesitate to envelope me in a hot, sweaty hug. "I know. Me, too." Aug's voice had permanently roughened, thickened like a man's. It made me smile.

"So, guess what I found out today," he said as he drew back, grinning with pride. "You are looking at our first-string quarterback. They announced the selections today."

"Really?" I jumped off the counter and hugged him again. "Congratulations."

Mom nearly tackled him. "You did? Aug, I'm so proud of you."

I was all mixed up in their embrace and it felt really great.

When Augustyn had his fill of pats and hugs and congrats, he pulled back. Mom pointed at him. "And you stink. You need to take a shower."

Laughing, he backed away. "Think I'm just going to take a swim. Dad's out there anyway, and he told me he was supposed to be the first to know." Aug lifted his chin in my direction. "It really was good to see you, Aly." He slid the sliding glass door open and smirked at me from over his shoulder. "And tell Megan I said hi."

My mouth dropped open in feigned disgust, my lips animated in silent embellishment. *Gross.*

He laughed and the door slid shut behind him.

I turned back to Mom. "I think I'm going to head home."

Disappointment flashed across her face and she huffed out a frustrated breath. "Fine, but honestly, Aly. Don't shut me out, okay?"

I nodded, though I wasn't sure I could keep that promise. It wasn't because I didn't want to. God, Christopher had asked me not to even mention that Jared was staying with us, and Jared definitely didn't want Christopher knowing about us. I wasn't sure that I did, either. I was pretty sure Christopher would freak out. No doubt my dad would freak out. And their knowing would undoubtedly throw Jared over the edge.

"Love you, Mom." I hugged her close to me, her touch tender as she rubbed my lower back.

"Love you, too." She pulled back and held my face. "I'm happy for you . . . whoever he is."

I bit at my lip as his name danced on my tongue. I realized how much I wanted her to know. I swallowed. "I'll see you soon."

"Okay," she said.

I headed for the door.

"And be safe," she hollered after me.

Shaking my head I smiled and pulled the door shut behind me.

Outside, it was humid, the sky overhead cast in a shimmering blue. Instantly sweat clung to my skin, and I squinted up into the blinding Arizona sun. Heavy cumulous clouds gathered far to the south, built and piled as they stretched toward the heavens and slowly encroached upon the city.

The monsoon was here.

Starting my car, I made my way across town. I slipped through the gate. Anxious excitement caused a stir of butterflies to take flight in my stomach when I rounded the corner.

Jared rode just ahead of me, and he used his feet to back his sleek bike into the spot he always parked it in. He came to a standstill facing out. His booted feet were stretched out wide, balancing the metal between his legs. He wore his typical dark low-slung jeans and a black tee that exposed the story woven over the strength of his arms. The bold numbers strewn across his knuckles sat prominent where he gripped and flexed at the handlebars. That gorgeous face remained stoic, almost hard, but his hair was wild, untamed from where it had been battered by the wind.

I lost my breath.

Last night I'd spoken the truth when I reached out to touch his face, this coarse beauty that was something utterly terrifying and altogether captivating.

I struggled to smother my reaction to seeing him, gathered my things, and climbed out of the car. Jared swung his leg over his bike and retrieved a couple of grocery bags from the leather pouches hanging on each side of the long seat.

"Hey." I crossed the lot, approaching him. I was seriously doubting my ability to play it cool when he looked like that. Or when he looked *at* me like that.

He turned just as I came up behind him, roughing a hand through his hair, which I was itching to do myself. His smile was slow, and his gaze swept over me, head to toe, then traveled back up again. "Hey," he said with a smirk quirking his mouth.

How the hell were we supposed to manage this? Because all I really wanted to do was crush myself to him, to press my lips to his to find out if it would feel just as good as it did last night.

That place in the deepest part of my stomach fluttered, sure that it definitely would. Memories of his touch slammed into me, tickled along my flesh, and I couldn't help blushing when I thought that I couldn't wait until he did it again.

His smirk grew right along with the redness on my face.

Yeah, the boy could read my mind.

I turned away and started up the steps. He was right behind me, his presence thick—consuming. My heart thudded.

Fingertips grazed up the sensitive skin at the back of my neck. Chills raced down my spine. Just at the door, he pressed his chest to my back, bent over to graze his nose along my jaw before he whispered in my ear, "You were gone longer than you said. Were you trying to make me worry about you?" His voice came out in a slow rasp of accusation and his hand ran up my arm to hold on to the cap of my shoulder. "You already drive me crazy when I'm around you." He edged his fingers down to the neckline of my shirt and teased at the skin. "Do you plan on driving me crazy when you're gone, too?"

I sucked in a shaky breath. "I just stopped by to see my parents."

His palm slipped up to hold me at the neck, the slight pressure lifting my jaw. "I hated not knowing where you were . . . when you would come." His tone was hard, and my pulse stuttered. Jared held me there, his nose skimming along the base of my neck as he breathed me in. "I don't know what the hell we're doing, Aly, but whatever it is, I can hardly stand it."

Abruptly he stepped back, and I stood there gasping for air. Desire crawled along the surface of my skin and sank deep into my bones. God, I didn't know how to handle this, the impulse to turn and lose myself in him.

Wetting my lips, I worked my face into a neutral expression. I unlocked the door and stepped inside. Christopher was there, sitting on the couch in the same spot I'd left him in this morning.

Jared's voice startled me from behind. "Look who I ran into downstairs."

Christopher cut his attention back to us, gestured his hello. "How was work?"

I forced myself to act normal and dropped my bag to the floor just inside the door. "It was pretty good. Stopped by Mom and Dad's to tell everyone hi after I got off. Augustyn made first string. You should give him a call."

"No way," Christopher said, pushing back the hair that had fallen in his eyes. "That is seriously cool. I'll give him a call. Damn, I need to make more time to hang out with him." He'd started to mumble, talking mostly to himself.

I smiled as I walked past him. "I know, I know . . . has to be so tough carving out a couple hours from your tiresome summer schedule of no school or work," I teased.

Christopher rolled his eyes. "Ha-ha."

I headed for the hall. "I'm going to change really quick."

Snapping shut the door behind me, I stood in the refuge of

my room. My attention traveled to the tangled sheets of my bed that had become like a sanctuary, the safest place, where Jared and I were free and our mouths whispered and our hands touched.

And I prayed for darkness because I couldn't wait until he held me there again.

I tugged the tight rubber band free from my hair, let it fall loose, and changed into some shorts and a clean tank top. Contentment spread through my entire body, and I inhaled deeply as I let go of all the stress I'd allowed to slowly build and invade, allowed to encroach and taint my thoughts.

In the end, all that mattered was he was here.

We spent the afternoon relaxing in front of the TV. I loved it, the feeling that things were the way they were supposed to be, just Jared, Christopher, and me. I lay on the floor while the two of them sat on the couch. Often I would catch Jared stealing glances at me, his eyes soft as they caressed my body. It was as if he managed to touch me without ever laying a hand on me. I shivered and hugged myself, longing for time to pass because I couldn't wait to be back in his arms.

Night dimmed the sky, and a dense calm hovered in the room as the day bled away. Jared sank deeper into the couch, his legs extending farther and farther out in front of him. His feet rested on the sides of my head, flanking me, casual, but with a presence that warmed my soul. I yawned and settled into the comfort of it.

Christopher jumped to his feet. "I can't stand to sit around here any longer. Let's go play pool or something."

"Ugh, Christopher, I'm half-asleep over here," I said, rubbing my eyes with the heels of my hands.

He pointed at me as he headed for the hall. "Exactly. That's why we're getting out of here. It's nine o'clock at night, and I've been sitting on my ass all day."

Warily, I tipped my head back to peek up at Jared, and frowned.

He just idly smiled and nudged me in the shoulder with his foot. "Get up, lazy girl. We're going out."

Charlie's was Christopher's favorite dive bar. There were plenty of pool tables, the drinks were cheap, and one band or another was playing almost every night. I pulled into the overflowing parking lot and the three of us climbed out of my car. The draw of this place was easily understood. Most appealing to the city's delinquents had to be the fact that they didn't card at the door. Christopher had been coming here for years and began dragging me along when I moved in with him.

We made our way through the groups of people huddled outside and entered through the large wooden double doors. Inside, it was dingy, dank, the lights cast low. Old neon bar signs glowed from the walls, and hardwood planks covered the grimy floors. Straight back was a large horseshoe bar, surrounded by at least twenty stools. Three or four bartenders contended with the overeager patrons, and waitresses rushed between the high, round tables that claimed the space directly in front of the bar. Music blared from overhead speakers, and to the right was a small stage where a band flitted around preparing for their set. A few couples danced within the boundaries of the smooth dance floor facing the stage. To the left and extending farther down the side were rows and rows of pool tables. Vintage stained glass billiards lights swung from the rafters, illuminating the well-worn felt tables below. Just like the parking lot outside, the place was packed.

Christopher elbowed Jared to get his attention. "I'll go grab us a couple of beers. You want to get us a table?"

"Sure."

Christopher lifted his chin toward me. "You want anything?"

"Um, would you get me a Coke?"

It hadn't taken much for him to convince me to be DD.

He grinned, walking backward. "A Coke it is." He turned and disappeared into the crowd.

Jared's attention trailed him until the second he was out of sight. As soon as he was, Jared reached for my hand, squeezing it as he drew it to his mouth. A subdued groan vibrated against my skin. His blue eyes were all warm when he looked down at me. "I've been dying to touch you for hours. Do you have any idea how much, Aly?" He pressed my palm to his nose. When he pulled back, he was biting at his full lower lip, something like confused wonder slipping through his expression as his eyes roamed over my face. A smile suddenly widened his mouth, and he folded my hand in his and tugged. "Come on, let's find a table."

My grin was uncontrollable as he wove us through the crowd. I loved this feeling, like we were natural and meant to be. We found an open pool table in the far back. He picked a cue and helped me do the same, and I watched as he leaned over to rack the balls. He grinned back at me, all sly and cocky.

This side of Jared was so unexpected, this boy who smiled so effortlessly, as if for the moment his pain had been suspended and he'd been granted a reprieve. I wondered if he noticed the stirring of joy I witnessed in his eyes or if he was so conditioned he could only recognize the bleakness glutting his heart and mind.

I had the overwhelming urge to approach him from behind,

and I thought that was surprising, too. I wanted to run my hand up his back and feel his strength as it rippled and bunched beneath the cover of his shirt, to be intimately reminded of what we had shared last night. I was different with him. Better and worse, too confident and incredibly naive. Jared made me desire things I'd never desired before. It confused me, left me both vacant and filled. Almost complete.

Jared frowned at me as if he'd caught the perplexity of my thoughts. Self-conscious, I dropped my gaze and distracted myself by chalking my cue stick. The band struck up, lifting the din in the bar to deafening levels. Christopher returned with the beers and my soda.

"Here you go, man."

"Thanks." Jared accepted his, flicked off the cap, and tipped it in Christopher's direction before he took a long swig. He wiped his lips with the back of his hand.

"I'll sit out the first game," I offered as I leaned up against the wall, sipping my Coke from a straw, "but I play winner."

Christopher grabbed his cue and grinned. "Well, sounds like you'll be playing me, then, little sister."

Taunting laughter fell from Jared's mouth, his blue eyes gleaming with mirth. "Ah, feeling pretty sure of yourself there, huh, Christopher? I'd say we need to put a little wager on this." He pulled a twenty out of his wallet and slapped it on the table.

"Oh, you're on." Christopher dug out his wallet.

They picked up their play while I hovered near. We laughed and the guys drank. Jared was good, but so was Christopher. The two of them battled in this constant harassment, flippantly slinging low-blow gibes and sordid insults at each other that neither took to heart.

By the end of the game, Christopher was tucking Jared's twenty in his pocket, all too happy to rub it in. "Jared, will you ever learn? You should know I always end up coming out on top."

Jared leaned up against the wall with an easy grin as I stepped in for my game. How good would it feel to claim him openly, this beautiful boy, to stroll up to him, lift up on my toes to brush my lips across his? For a fleeting second I wondered how he'd react, how Christopher would react.

I glanced at Christopher, his black hair unruly and his green eyes sharp. Without a doubt, that would be a really bad idea.

I shook off the thoughts and feigned confidence as I sauntered up to my brother. "You're in so much trouble now," I said, tipping my chin up in mock challenge. I held back laughter that threatened to work its way free. The only time I'd ever beaten Christopher was the one time he let me.

He quirked an amused eyebrow and his green eyes sparkled. "Really?"

"Really," I said with a resolute nod.

It took him about five seconds to annihilate me.

Jared dragged a high barstool over and set it up near the wall for me. "Here, hop up here so you can see better while I kick your brother's ass in this next game." His smile was loose as he gestured for me to sit. He reached out to help me climb onto the chair. And I assumed it was the few beers he'd already consumed that had lowered his walls, because his touch was gentle and lingered a beat too long. His hand gripped at my side and his thumb caressed along one of my ribs.

That simple display of affection quickened my heart. Because with him, I wanted it all. There was no disguising my yearning as I looked up at him, his eyes so soft as they looked down on me. I watched as he swallowed, the heavy bob of his throat; then reluctantly he turned back to Christopher. "All right, my friend, time for me to show you how it's really done."

Another hour passed, and I sat on the stool slowly swinging my legs, watching the two of them. I'd fully bailed out of the good-natured contention three games before, saying I'd been humiliated enough for one night. Christopher won another game while Jared won two. They drank a few more beers, their laugher and jests increasing, their banter so much like it used to be. A hum of satisfaction pulsed into every crevice of my being.

Jared had *stayed* and I thought maybe he was happy.

Christopher was obviously having a really good time. Probably a little too much of a good time, as his jests started verging on the edge of obnoxious. It only made me laugh. With his bottle lifted high, he polished off what had to have been his seventh beer of the night. He slammed the bottle down on the small table before he leaned in to attempt a ridiculous jump shot. He fumbled and knocked the cue ball into the side pocket.

"Ah, shit," he yelled through his raucous laughter as he stumbled back. He knocked into a guy trying to take a shot at the table behind him. Christopher jerked around, stretched out a hand to steady the guy he'd run into. A casual apology rolled naturally from his mouth. "Hey, sorry, man." Christopher's grin was wide.

But the other guy was furious. His hand fisted on his cue stick, aggressive as he sneered. "What the fuck, you little prick?"

He was shorter than Christopher, but wider, older, rougher. His head was shaved or bald, I couldn't tell. I could almost read his thoughts in his too dark eyes, the flame of aggression as he made the decision to mess with my brother. The guy liked it.

Hostility dripped from his body, and he took one antagonistic step forward.

My heart pounded and my hands clenched around the seat of the stool. I hated fighting, hated when nights meant to spend unwinding turned into bad memories because sick people would rather hurt someone than let them be.

Lifting both palms, Christopher took a step back. Realization had sobered his face. This time his smile was obviously forced as he aimed to temper the situation. "Hey, man, I said I was sorry. No harm intended."

Christopher usually got along with everyone. He was one of those people everybody wanted to hang out with. He had this charm about him that drew in the masses. He knew it, too, used it to his advantage to lure in his prey or to calm a charged situation. I'd only seen him fight a couple of times, always out of necessity, when there was no other choice. And Christopher could hold his own, no question about it. But against this guy? I wasn't so sure.

I eased off the stool and found my footing. I slipped up behind Christopher, intent on pulling him away. None of us needed to deal with this tonight, and I just wanted to go home. Where it was safe.

"Christopher," I said quietly as I slowly approached him, hoping to get his attention so we could get out of there.

Jared's mouth was suddenly hot at my cheek, his large hand splayed against the opposite side of my face as he firmly held my head, demanding my attention. He uttered a low warning in my ear. "Get back, Aly. I don't want you anywhere near this asshole."

Then he nudged me behind him, his arm extended back to keep me at bay. He crept forward to take up Christopher's side.

A clear declaration of alliance. Jared rolled his shoulders, this checked energy vibrating through his being. His hands clenched and curled, aggression coiling through the muscles of his arms that rippled and bunched under the colors marking his skin.

Fear turned my stomach. Fear of the guy staring down my brother, staring down Jared, fear at the violence skimming along the surface of Jared's skin, itching to be released. I could feel it, this fierce rage that emanated from Jared's spirit, like something dark had been unleashed and set free.

I turned my concentration from Christopher to Jared, sensing where the real danger lay. I placed an urgent hand on his upper back. "Jared, please, let's just go," I begged, so quietly I wasn't sure either of them could hear, their focus entirely on the guy who cracked a menacing grin.

Jared twitched and shrugged me off, fisting his hands as he cocked his head in clear provocation.

We'd collected attention. A frantic murmur of voices and eyes descended upon the scene, a rustle of morbid interest as people began to draw near.

Panic prodded at my chest and twisted my stomach. We had to get out of here.

I edged in between Christopher and Jared, remaining just behind, determined to assuage the malice that had filled the air. This time I spoke a little louder and pulled at the back of Christopher's shirt. "Jared . . . Christopher . . . come on, let's just go. *Please.*"

The guy's face contorted into a mocking sneer, taunting them. He looked directly at Jared. "Why don't you tell your whore to shut her fucking mouth?"

Hearing those words, Jared snapped. He moved faster than I'd ever seen anyone move, rushing the guy with his arm cocked back. I watched in horror as Jared's fist brutally slammed into the guy's face. The punch connected with a sickening thud that reverberated in my ears. Blood spurted, gushing from the man's nose as it ran profusely down his face and dripped from his chin.

At the sight of blood, Jared seemed to lose it completely. He roared, descended on the guy in a fury of pent-up madness. Fists flew in a constant barrage as Jared's attack drew more blood. Each hit landed more savagely than the last. The guy tried to fight back, but Jared was too agile and dodged every returned blow.

Finally finding his feet, the guy swung his cue stick with a thundering cry. It whipped through the air as he angled it for Jared's head.

Jared ducked. In the same motion, he ripped the stick from the other man. Grabbing it in both his hands, he held the weapon horizontal as he charged. Jared's teeth were bared, clenched, and he rammed into the guy's chest. He bent him backward over the pool table, the stick holding him down by the chest. The guy thrashed, pinned to the green felt with his legs flailing as he fought to find leverage on the ground.

Jared leaned in close and growled in his face, the words hoarse as they ripped from his throat. "What the fuck did you say? Say it again, fucker. I dare you, say it again." Pulling back a fraction, Jared slammed him down again. "Say it again."

The crowd swarmed, vying to get a better view.

"Fuck you," the guy all but moaned. Jared had stripped him of any other form of defense, so the guy spat in his face.

Incensed, Jared roared and raised the cue above his head.

I realized I was screaming, screaming Jared's name. "Jared, stop! Oh my God, please stop!"

Seemingly prompted by the fear in my voice, Christopher

reacted. From behind, he yanked the stick from Jared's hands. Jared whirled around, flinging his fist, his blue eyes wild as he readied for another attacker.

Christopher was quick enough to jump back, and the aimless punch connected with air. "Jared, come on, man, look at me." Christopher came in close to Jared's face, his hands on his shoulders. Jared struggled to break free. "Come on, Jared, snap the fuck out of it. This asshole isn't worth it, and I guarantee the cops are on their way. We have to get Aly out of here."

Bouncers were making their way through the leering crowd just as those wild blue eyes darted to me. Pain crumpled his face, and he raised his bloodied fists in some kind of tortured surrender.

Christopher jumped into action and jerked me by the hand. "Come on. We have to get out of here." Shoving through the throng, Christopher headed toward the back. The crowd seemed to open and swallow us whole. People pressed into us, holding us back, then surging us forward. I grasped at Jared's hand, holding tight as Christopher expertly forged our escape.

We stumbled out the back door. More people were cluttered in groups as they gathered to smoke, standing in the thick night air that was heavy with the growing storm. Thunder rumbled overhead, flashes of lightning illuminating the blackened sky. Wind gusted hard, whipping up dirt and debris as it blew in low. Cringing, I looked to the ominous sky.

"Come on, this way," Christopher commanded. He pointed to the right, then tightened his hold on my hand as he took off at a jog into the darkness that ran behind a strip mall that had long since been closed down for the night.

My hold tightened on Jared's hand as I dragged him behind me. I refused to let him go.

Christopher wound us back around the long way. The approaching storm pressed in from above. Energy crackled through the clouds and sped along the ground. Lightning flashed, and I stole a furtive glance over my shoulder at Jared. He kept his face hidden as he trained his eyes on his feet, his hand almost limp where it burned against mine.

I wanted to stop, to take his face in my hands, to beg him to tell me he was okay. Instead I struggled to keep up with Christopher, who raced ahead. Desperate, I squeezed Jared's hand as I tugged him harder, hoping he would at least understand my worry. His touch remained unresponsive.

We slowed our pace as we rounded the corner and slinked around to the front of the buildings. "Just play it cool, Aly," Christopher warned.

We hit the sidewalk, the dull streetlamps lighting our way as they blinked through the haze of the storm. Jared removed his hand from mine and dropped back two feet, and I walked hand in hand with Christopher, nestled up against his side with my head held low, as we approached the bar parking lot.

We'd come full circle.

Three cop cars sat in the middle of the lot. Red and blue lights flashed. No one even noticed us as we drew near. All attention seemed focused on the mayhem that was undoubtedly still taking place inside.

Silently, we slipped up to my car that sat in near darkness, dim lamps from the front of the bar casting shadows across the lot. I clicked the door locks on my fob, and we slid into our seats, Christopher in the front and Jared directly behind me in the back.

We said nothing, just let the tension stretch between us as I fumbled with the keys to start the ignition. Finally I found the slot and turned over the engine. Shaking, I backed out, put the car in gear, and slowly eased out onto the street.

In silence we waited for something . . . for someone to follow . . . for some consequence to come. Warily, I glanced up in the rearview mirror to the empty street behind us. No one followed. My eyes wandered to find Jared's head hung how, his face buried in his bloodied hands.

Christopher turned fully in his seat and searched the distance. Then he cracked up. "Holy shit, man." His smile was wide and sloppy when he looked at Jared, his buzz making a resurgence as he slapped Jared on the knee. "That was fucking awesome. You beat the shit out of that asshole. The second he said something about Aly, I knew you were going to lose it." He laughed as he rushed a hand through his disheveled hair. "You were always that way . . . sticking up for her. Shit . . . I bet you'd kick my ass if I said something bad about her."

He slanted a grin at me, then turned it on Jared. "You're like some kind of avenging angel, or some shit. Who knows what would have happened if you didn't step in tonight? Either my ass would have ended up in jail or I'd be the one in that asshole's place. Dude was huge." He laughed, glib, making light of whatever had occurred back at the bar. Christopher was oblivious of Jared's misery, to the restlessness that twitched through his muscles, to the anxiety silencing his tongue.

Christopher turned up the radio and sang along to some terrible pop song, his voice raised and completely out of key. Leave it to my brother to completely miss what was really going on.

I turned at the gate to our complex. Again I lifted my face to search Jared's in the mirror. I could feel it, him warring with whatever he'd been stricken by as he sat silently in my backseat. Punishing himself for his actions.

The protecting, I understood. One hundred percent. I would never criticize him for that. And maybe it was just the two of us who recognized it; the two of us that had felt his seething burn, the loss of control.

It scared me, and I knew it scared him, too.

Catching his eye in the mirror, I tried to convey that I understood. Ashamed, he dropped his gaze.

I pulled into my parking spot and cut the engine. Christopher and I climbed out of the car. It felt like an entire minute passed before the back door finally unlatched, resting ajar on the jamb. With his hand on the handle, Jared seemed to hesitate before he finally pushed open the door. When Jared slowly rose from the car, Christopher clapped him on the shoulder before he turned to head toward the apartment. Jared said nothing while the two of us made our way up the stairs. Walking a couple of steps ahead of him, I kept glancing back, searching for something. Jared gave me no response. And again I was silently pleading with him not to go.

All I wanted was for him to stay.

We entered into the sanctuary of the apartment, and I found myself wishing we'd never left it.

Christopher was in the kitchen, loud as he rummaged through the refrigerator on a mission to find something to eat. Just inside the door, I stopped. Exhaustion suddenly weighed down my arms, while adrenaline still knotted my stomach. It left me agitated and unsure.

Jared brushed by me and started toward the hall. Guarded, he paused and looked back on me with something that appeared to be an apology, before he disappeared into the bathroom. The door quietly snapped closed behind him, the click of the lock shutting me out.

I retreated into my room, calling, "Good night," behind me. It was an invitation. *Please come.*

I changed from my jeans and T-shirt into pajama pants and a tank, twisted my hair up into a messy tie. Sitting back on my bed, I leaned over and pulled my sketch pad from the floor and onto my lap. I turned to the last page I'd been working on, let my mind drift as I freed my hand.

Thunder rumbled overhead, shook the walls as the wind barreled and whistled through the trees.

The pencil rushed over the page, shading the perfect planes of his face, darkening his eyes because in them there was so much pain. Every time I thought maybe we were ebbing the pain away, it was only exposed how much deeper it went.

Outside my room, I listened to water running in the bathroom. I pictured him hunched over the sink as he tried to wash the night from his consciousness. Blood dripping from his knuckles, swirling through the water, tinting it pink before it vanished down the drain. But I knew even though he was erasing the physical traces of the fight, Jared would hang on to this as another scar.

I kept stealing glances at my door, willing him to come.

To come to me.

To love me the way he had done last night.

Or maybe just lie with me, hold on to me while I held on to him.

Two hours passed, and still he didn't come.

I wanted to go to him. Comfort him. Finally, when I could take it no longer, I did. I rose from my bed and padded across my floor. As quietly as I could, I pulled open my door. I looked out into the empty hall. Blackness seeped from under the crack in the bathroom door. I stepped out. To my right, Christopher's door was closed. Silence hovered thick in the apartment, and I tiptoed out into the main room. The couch was empty, without evidence of blankets or pillows. My pulse raced in fear, before I noticed Jared's keys left in a pile on the coffee table. I shuffled around the couch and pressed my face to the sliding glass door.

The night sky was turbulent. Sheets of lightning sliced through the heavens, igniting the world in bright bursts of light before it fizzled out. Furies of harsh wind pummeled the thin branches of paloverde trees, slanting them askew. Frantic, I searched the darkened balcony for evidence of the one who'd always set me off-kilter, the one who'd set the standard of my beliefs because he'd been the one who'd managed to touch me so deeply. The sky flashed. It cast the balcony in transient light.

Jared wasn't there.

I took two steps back. I fisted my hands in frustration, my attention darting all over the empty room. For a second, I studied the front door, before I swallowed down the lump in my throat and found the courage to cross the room. Quietly I opened it.

Relief washed over me when I found him sitting by himself on the floor with his back propped up against the wall beside the door. That relief clashed with the pain, this overwhelming surge of feeling that crested and rose.

Like a partner to the storm, Jared rocked in agitation as he brought a nearly spent cigarette to his mouth. His bare chest expanded as he filled his lungs. Smoke swirled above his head. Thick chunks of his blond hair lashed with the wind, beaten and stirred. Aggressively he stamped out the butt. A twisted snarl bled from his lips, and he curled his lacerated knuckles and mashed them against his temples, as if he'd do anything to silence the demons whispering in his ear.

Just for tonight, I wanted to make it go away.

I felt the moment he registered my presence, the way his hands pressed harder to his head, his movements harsh as he severely shook it. His voice was hoarse, barely audible above the howling wind. "Just . . . go back inside."

He knew me better than that. He knew there was no chance I'd turn away, just like I knew him well enough to know he would try to shut me out.

Thunder crashed, and I delved deep to find the same courage I'd uncovered in myself last night. Creeping forward, I kneeled in front of him, my knees scraping on the coarse concrete floor. Slowly I crawled between his legs, my hands resting on his knees.

Jared rocked his head back on the pitted stucco wall. He kept his eyes closed tight, shielding me from the hurt I knew he harbored there. "You shouldn't be out here," he forced through gritted teeth.

"Why not, Jared?" I demanded. "Why do you think you have to go through everything alone?"

Tortured blue eyes opened to me. They skimmed my face, like this painful embrace. "Don't you see it, Aly? This is exactly what I warned you about. I'm a fucking disaster." Reaching out, he touched my face, his head tilting to the side as he dragged his fingertips down my cheek, searching for understanding.

Flames burned beneath his touch, stoked the devotion I'd eternally hold for him.

Did he think he was somehow pushing me away, warning me, when all I wanted was more?

"I never wanted you to see me like I was tonight," he said, "but it was inevitable . . . all of this is . . . *inevitable*. And still I stay because I don't fucking know how to walk away from you.

Last night . . ." He wrenched a trembling hand through his hair. "Fuck, Aly . . . last night was the closest I've come to feeling something real in so long."

With his admission, warmth flooded and pooled, filled me whole. My hands clamped down on his knees, my fingers burrowing in his skin.

Stay.

A fierce squall of wind pushed into the space, rippled with energy, stirring my blood, stirring my heart.

Stay.

Leaning in close to his face, I captured his gaze, spoke above the churning storm. "None of that matters to me, Jared. And it was just a fight. You were sticking up for Christopher. Sticking up for me. What is wrong with that?"

My hair thrashed around my face, and Jared twisted his finger in a wayward lock as if he were anchoring himself to me.

Lightning flashed. Thunder rolled.

I sucked in a breath, losing myself in his simple touch.

"You know it wasn't just a fight." Jared shook his head, his eyes narrowing severely as he opened his mouth in confession. "Christopher was right when he said I lost it. I lost it the second that asshole even looked your way. I wanted to . . ." Hesitating, Jared dropped his gaze to the side, wet his lips, before pinning me with the full force of his stare. "I wanted to *hurt* him . . . I wanted to rip him apart. Just the thought of someone messing with you makes me insane." He blinked, winding his finger tighter in my hair. "You make me fucking crazy, Aly. Dangerous. It's like all I want to do is protect you even though I know I'm going to end up hurting you. And God, it kills me to think of hurting you."

I grasped his face between urgent hands. "Then don't."

His mouth collided with mine, his hands frenzied as he possessively sank them into my hair. He kissed and sucked, mumbled, "Aly . . ." as he gasped for air. He pulled back, my hair threaded in his fingers as he splayed them wide. His eyes grew earnest as he held my head in his hands. "Baby, I don't want to . . . God, I don't want to." He drew me back, his mouth forceful as it overtook mine.

I pressed my chest to his, felt his heart pound. I struggled to meet his kiss, to bear part of this anguish eating him alive. My fingers curled around his jaw before I wrapped my arms around his head. "Jared," I begged.

Pricks of pain bit at my knees as I rose, battling to get closer, desperate as my body sought his.

I just needed to feel. To know his heart in his touch. For him to know mine.

Jared hoisted me up in one swift movement. My back was suddenly nailed to the door, his body covering mine. All the breath left my lungs. I moaned, making a frantic play to bring him closer as I clung to his wide shoulders.

Jared took my face in his hands, pulled back to search my eyes. He wet his lips, the frenzy that had blazed between us abating to a slow smolder. He hesitated, wavering, before he returned to me with a gentle, closemouthed kiss. He rested his forehead on mine. "Aly, can we . . . will you just lie with me? I just want to feel you."

My exhale was shaky, and I sucked my bottom lip into my mouth, nodding against him.

Carefully he lowered me to my feet, fumbled with the knob, and let us into the silence of the darkened apartment. He led me to my room, quietly snapped the door shut, and turned the lock. In front of my bed, he pulled his shirt over his head, before he slowly removed mine.

"Aleena, you're so beautiful," he said as his eyes swept the length of my body.

Aleena.

Last night when he'd spoken my name like that, it had stolen my breath as he'd murmured it again and again. It made me feel beautiful. Made me feel loved, even when he couldn't admit loving me was exactly what he was doing.

Lightning struck the same instant thunder crashed. A sudden torrent of violent rain pelted the window. I shivered, a rush of chills blanketing my skin. Jared reached out to caress them, fingertips light as they tickled along my collarbone.

He left us in only our underwear before he took my hand and guided me to the bed. He drew me near, his arms encircling me, his nose buried in my hair. The storm raged around us, so much like the man who held me in his arms. Violent. Unpredictable.

Beautiful.

Hours later, I listened as rain pattered lightly against the windowpanes, and thunder rolled in the far distance as the storm gave up its hold on the city.

For the longest time, I'd just lain on top of this sweet man who was so utterly hardened. It was difficult to reconcile the two. We'd said little, just held each other in the peace of the passing storm. After tonight, I knew that was really what Jared needed. Just to be held. His heart thrummed steadily beneath my cheek. He had me wrapped in his arms, his fingers playing along the skin of my bare back. He just stared at the ceiling, lost in thought.

I snuggled closer because I didn't think I could ever get close enough. His fingers found their way into my hair, massaging up the back of my scalp. Contentment warmed me as it spread through my veins.

"This feels so good." Jared's hushed voice broke into the silence.

I trailed my fingers up his chest and to his shoulder. "So good."

I didn't want to ruin the peace we found ourselves in, but the question had sat quietly in the back of my head since that first morning when he'd confronted me in the kitchen and then stumbled into the apartment later that night with bloodied knuckles. Seeing him at the bar tonight had pushed my worry back to the forefront of my mind, where it plagued and nagged me. "Can I ask you something without you getting upset?" Timidly, I traced the dying rose that rested over his heart. I kept my head down because I couldn't look him in the eye.

Humorlessly, he chuckled and toyed with my hair, lifting thick chunks and letting them fall in waves down my back. "That sounds like a loaded question, Aly. I think the better question would be if you can ask it without getting upset. Because I won't lie to you, but I'm not sure you'll like the answer."

I swallowed. "It's not like that. It's just something I've been wondering about and you've never mentioned." Okay, worrying about. Jared was right. I wasn't sure exactly how I'd handle his answer.

"All right, then," he prodded.

I paused, searching for some way to frame the question without sounding as if I were accusing him of something I really didn't know all that much about. Because it wasn't an accusation. I just needed to know. "I heard what they found in your locker when you were expelled . . ." *Knew what I had seen.* My heart thudded a little too hard.

Jared sighed with impatience, but he didn't seem all that surprised or angered by the question. "You want to know if I still use? If I'm an addict?"

I cringed at the bluntness of his words.

Jared sighed again, but this time it sounded like an apology. "Hey, look at me." He nudged me. I lifted my head and he placed a warm hand on my face. Sincere blue eyes locked with mine. "Yes, Aly, I'm an addict because I'll never forget how easy it is to slip into oblivion, and I'll never stop wanting to go there. There are days when I think I'll go crazy because I crave it so much and other days when I don't think about it at all. But using is the easy way out. I tried that route, and it didn't take long for me to realize this life wasn't going to be easy. I haven't used since the night they sent me away. I learned then I don't get an escape."

"Jared—"

"Don't, Aly." He ran his thumb over my cheek. "You think I can't feel this? How badly you want the things I can't give you? That's why it makes me sick that I'm doing this, because I already warned you . . . you can't fix me, and you can't say or do something that will change my mind or fill up the void in my soul."

There was no anger in his words. Just sadness.

He increased his hold on my face and I nuzzled closer to him, wishing I could disappear inside him. Wished I could fill that void.

"I know that. I just care about you," I whispered seriously.

A wistful smile quivered around his mouth, his eyes gentle, and I knew he cared about me, too.

"I know you do, Aly," he admitted before his blue eyes dimmed. "Just be careful that you don't care too much."

I pulled his hand from my face, kissed across the numbers tattooed on the ripped and torn knuckles of his left hand: *2006. Death.*

The year he'd lost it all.

I prayed that somehow he could again learn to live again.

The next day, I had to get up early because I was scheduled to work both the breakfast and lunch shifts. Jared had crept from my bed sometime in the very early morning hours, but not without leaving me another glimpse into his thoughts.

The foul spoils the beauty.

His words both touched me and saddened me.

I'd left him with a token of me, a tender kiss I'd placed just below his ear. He'd smiled, his sleepy eyes flickering open to look at me as soft words rasped from his hoarse throat. "Hi, beautiful."

I'd left feeling good. Alive. As if maybe Jared and I had stumbled upon some kind of understanding, as unstable as it was.

I blew the bangs back from my forehead and began to tap an order out on the computer. Sundays were always busy, which I loved because it meant time passed quickly. I peeked at the clock on the wall. Only half an hour until I could go to him.

"How are you holding up, Aly?" Karina asked, popping her head through the swinging door.

I smiled at her. "I'm all caught up. It's finally slowing down out there."

"Looks like the rush is over. Why don't you go ahead and finish up your last table and then you can cut out of here?"

"Thanks, Karina."

"No problem. Let me know if you need anything."

"Sure thing."

The door swung closed behind her, and I turned my attention back to the computer and put in my last order of the day.

Two seconds later, the door swung open again. I glanced to the side to see another waitress, Clara, standing there staring at me, a question framing her set mouth.

I frowned and tucked my order pad back in my apron.

Suspicion tipped her head to the side. She was in her late twenties, bleached blond, wore too much makeup, and was one of the hardest workers at the restaurant. She once told me that being a single mom gave you a whole new work ethic.

I couldn't help but like her.

"What?" I asked, a smile wobbling at the corner of my mouth. I just couldn't help it. Happiness had that way about it.

I grabbed two glasses and began filling them with ice as I glanced over at her.

She shifted her weight back and crossed her arms over her chest, her expression glimmering with smug humor. "So, Aly, my friend," she drew out, "do you care to explain to me why there's a crazy-hot, scary guy asking for you out at the hostess podium?"

My hand tightened on the glass I was filling.

Jared.

Warmth flooded my face, spread down to wind through my heart. He was here.

Laughing, she edged forward and started filling glasses with ice and tea. She knocked me with her hip. "And I'm guessing by the look on your face you know exactly who I'm talking about."

I bit my lip and rocked my head noncommittally. "Maybe."

She chuckled low but lifted her chin to study my face. "Just be careful, okay? There's something unnerving about him."

Defensive needles prickled along the back of my neck, and heat burned the rims of my ears. "You don't know anything about him. And I would have thought better of you than making judgments based on a few tattoos." The words came out harsher than I intended.

She scoffed. "Come on, Aly, you know me better than that. . . . I wasn't talking about his tattoos. I was talking about his eyes." She stepped back and looked at me seriously. "And you're right. I don't know him. I don't know anything about him and I know it's not really any of my business."

Her voice softened. "But I like you, and believe me, I've been there before. There are just some boys who are so broken they can never be tamed, and in the end, they just end up breaking you." Old wounds creased the corners of her eyes. "I don't want to see that happen to you."

Her words hurt because they rang with truth. Doubt fluttered in my consciousness, but I shoved it off. "I know, Clara. I appreciate it. But it's . . ."

She just smiled knowingly and finished the thought I never would have been brave enough to say. "But it's already too late."

Too late had come a long time ago. "Yeah," I admitted softly.

She forced a soft breath from her nose. "Well, then, why don't you let me take your last table and you get out of here?"

"Are you sure?"

She brushed off my worry with a wave of her hand. "Yep. I could use the money, anyway."

Appreciation edged my mouth. "Thank you, Clara."

"Don't worry about it."

I handed her my table's drinks, which she arranged with hers on a tray.

She walked across the kitchen and began to back out the

swinging door. She peered out the small crack she made. She turned her attention back to me, lifting her brow in playful observation. "Good God, Aly. I don't blame you for a second. I'd be lost, too. And did you say a few tattoos? Have fun memorizing those."

Laughing, I threw a wadded-up dish towel at her. "Shut up," I said, unoffended because Clara's intentions were only good.

Of course, memorizing Jared's ink was exactly what I intended to do, but for entirely different reasons than she assumed. I wanted to explore each one, to know the story behind it, and to understand the wound that had inspired it.

She ducked out of the way, grinning as she backed farther out the door. "Be safe," she called out before it swung shut behind her.

Yanking off my apron, I grabbed my purse and headed out into the dining room. Jared stood near the wall just at the entrance, his hands stuffed in his pockets while he shuffled his feet. My heart sped, trying to keep up with the thrill I felt at seeing him here. I loved that he had sought me out. That he was taking a chance of exposing us here and not just keeping us hidden away in my room.

As if he felt me, he lifted his head as I approached. Self-consciously, he smiled and brushed a hand through his hair before he ran it down the back of his neck. He was nervous. And I couldn't help thinking it was the cutest thing I'd ever seen him do.

I was grinning as I walked up to him. "Hey . . . what are you doing here?"

His smile widened, and he waved his hand toward the dining room. "I just hadn't had lunch yet and heard this was a good place to eat."

"Really?" I said, planting my feet on the floor, dubious.

He chuckled sheepishly, then reached for me, his hand at the back of my head as he pressed his cheek to mine, murmuring near my ear, "I fucking missed you, okay?"

We found a table in the back, near the curve of windows that faced the street. Jared and I talked, and he held my hand under table, the circles he traced with his thumb on the back sending these little shots of joy down my spine. There was no urge to pull away when he shifted and ran it along the ridges of the scar on the outside of my left hand.

Because I was his.

"What happened here?" he asked casually as he ran his fingers over the long-healed skin.

I shrugged. "I just burned myself."

Claire appeared at our table, her grin wide and knowing as she asked what we'd like.

Jared and I ordered, and we ate together, Jared's smile easy, his words kind and free. We laughed. And it was natural. Exactly the way we were supposed to be.

SIXTEEN

January 2006

Aly hated the way things had gotten. As they had grown, so had the distance.

It'd been cold out the last couple of weeks, too cold to find escape in their empty field, not that they would be out there, anyway.

Her dad called her a tomboy, teasing that she always wanted to be outside, playing in the dirt and climbing trees.

But really, she just wanted to be near him.

She quieted her feet as she flattened her back to the wall and slid farther down the hall. It was wrong, she knew, eavesdropping on Jared and Christopher as they talked in her brother's bedroom, but she didn't know how to stop herself. Shielding herself from the conversation happening on the other side of the door seemed impossible because she felt drawn. As if she had to hear. As if she had to know.

Still she'd never believed hearing something could cause her so much pain.

For years she'd imagined being thirteen would make her feel mature. Grown-up. She'd studied herself in the mirror as her body had begun to change and thought maybe Jared would begin to notice her in the same way she noticed him.

But now that she was just a few months from turning fourteen, the only thing she felt like was a stupid little girl.

On the carpeted hall floor, she slid her bare feet a little farther down, coming right up to the outside of Christopher's door. Anxiety twisted her stomach into heavy knots that made it hard to breathe. Or maybe it was the pain in her chest that made her feel as if she were suffocating. She couldn't tell.

She only knew it hurt.

She swallowed over the pain that lodged in her throat and tried to still her shaking hands.

Christopher's door was barely cracked open, but she could make out the back of her brother's head from where he sat on the floor in the middle of the room. Loose sheets of homework and a textbook were spread out in front of him. Every few seconds, Aly would catch a glimpse of Jared's face whenever Christopher leaned to the side.

She inclined her ear, keeping herself hidden as she subjected herself to their hushed words.

"Oh man," Christopher said through suppressed, envious laughter. "In her parents' bed? Dude, that is messed up."

Jared chuckled as if the whole conversation was absurd. Aly saw him press his hands to his face, then drop them to his lap with a one-sided shrug. "I don't even know what I was thinking. It was weird, anyway. . . . I don't even like her."

"She's hot, though," Christopher pointed out.

Suggestive laughter fell from Jared's mouth. "That she is."

Those knots tightened in her stomach, and she was sure she was going to be sick.

"What about you and Samantha?" Jared asked, resituating himself as he pulled a textbook to his lap. "That girl is wound up so tight I don't know how you're ever going to undo that."

Christopher shook his head, his shaggy black hair brushing over his shoulders. "Nah . . . Samantha is cool. She wants to wait until she turns sixteen . . . six weeks." He laughed almost as if he were embarrassed and rubbed at the back of his neck. "I like her a lot. I mean, like, a lot."

Christopher lowered his head, and Aly caught sight of Jared's curious expression.

"Yeah?" he asked, completely without ridicule.

"Yeah."

"That's cool, man. I want that someday." Then Jared cracked a smile, wide and cocky. "Just not when I'm sixteen."

Christopher crumpled up a piece of paper and threw it at his head. "Fuck you." He laughed, unrestrained. "You just can't stand it that I have to drive your sorry ass around all the time *and* I have an awesome girlfriend."

"Hey, man, two weeks and I'm free." Jared looked up with a grin.

"Yeah, and I bet the second you get that car your parents are giving you, you'll have Kylie in the backseat."

Aly felt sad, a sadness she didn't know how to deal with. It was as if this disease crawled over her flesh, pressing down, seeping in, taking hold. She wanted to scrape the feeling from her skin, purge it from her mind.

She wasn't one of *those* girls. She'd never been able to understand the packs of girls gathered around one another in the bathroom while one girl cried because the boy she liked didn't like her back. Inevitably, she *liked* a different boy the next week and suddenly the world was right.

It wasn't as if Aly really thought badly of them. Most of them were her friends. She just didn't understand the shift, the distraction from one boy to the next in the matter of seconds, the fleeting attraction that never lasted. Because the only boy she'd ever wanted had been one and the same. She forced out a ragged breath from her lungs and tried to blink away the pounding in her head.

Aly froze when Jared suddenly lifted his face and caught her eye as she stared at him openmouthed through the sliver in the door.

He kicked Christopher on the sole of his shoe to get his attention. "Shh . . . ," he hissed in warning. He announced her presence to Christopher with a gesture of his chin. "Your little sister is right there."

She stepped back, shaking, hating that she'd managed to make herself the fool.

"Aly?" her mom called from the living room.

She hurried to the end of the hall before she allowed herself to speak. "I'm right here."

Her mom both smiled and frowned. "I thought you were running to your room to get the picture? Helene is dying to see your first-place winner."

Jared's mom, Helene, twisted around her seat, smiling at Aly from across the room. "I knew you'd do it, Aly, baby." Her blue eyes shone with warm affection, her long natural blond hair pulled to one side and flowing down her slender shoulder. "I've never seen anyone who can draw like you . . . ever since you were just a tiny thing . . . always drawing." She smiled knowingly at Aly's mom.

"Let's see it, sweetheart," her mom said.

"I couldn't find it," Aly lied, shifting her weight from foot to foot. She'd been too busy spying on Christopher and Jared. "Let me look a little more."

Aly rushed to her room, slammed the door shut behind her, and rested her back against it as she fought against the tears.

Jared'd had sex with some girl and she'd never so much as held a boy's hand.

She'd been waiting for him.

Anger pulled at the knots in her stomach, knitting them tighter. She stomped across her room, knew she was acting like a baby, like one of those stupid girls at school with a stupid crush and even stupider tears, but she couldn't stop them. They flooded down her face. She just wanted to curl up in her bed and die.

Instead she jerked up the hem of her shirt and used it to harshly dry her eyes.

He'd promised her he'd never leave her behind.

But he did.

"Stop it. Just stop it," she scolded herself below her breath, drawing air into her tight lungs. "Stop being dumb, Aly. He's almost sixteen."

What did she expect? That he would actually want her?

She had to pull it together, forget about this, shove it aside.

She dropped to her knees and dragged the portfolio from under her bed, retrieving the large charcoal drawing that had been awarded first prize. She'd felt proud when they gave her the ribbon, proud when they gave her the check to put into her savings account for college.

It was a landscape, the mountains stretching up to kiss the horizon as the sun sagged behind the mountain, distorted, as if the two were melting into each other.

But this art wasn't her treasure.

Her treasures were the faces she kept safe, bound up in sketch pads that she'd never show another person.

Now she knew why. She'd been right.

Jared would have laughed.

She swallowed down the humiliation and rushed back down the hall. At the brink of the living room, she slowed, her movements guarded as she made her way to Helene. Jared's mom was so beautiful . . . as beautiful as her own . . . but different, the woman somehow both exotic and plain. Aly wasn't exactly sure how that could be, but she'd drawn her face so many times she knew it was the truth.

With shaky hands, she gave Helene her offering.

Helene quietly gasped. "This is incredible, Aly. Absolutely beautiful." She smiled up at her, reflective tears simmering in her eyes. "You did good, baby girl. So good."

"Thank you," Aly whispered, feeling heat on her cheeks and warmth in her chest as she took her drawing back into her hands.

"What's that?"

Aly jumped when the voice that haunted her thoughts came from directly behind her. She jerked to look over her shoulder and came face-to-face with the boy who stole her breath. Her stomach ached again, but this time in a different way. Her mouth went dry, her mind completely blank except for the fact that he was standing less than foot from her. "It's nothing," she finally managed to force out.

"Nothing?"

He touched her shoulder, gently prodding her to turn, and took hold of the top of the large image while she held the bottom. For a long moment, he said nothing and just stared at the thick paper separating them, before he lifted his face. "Aly, did you draw this?"

Blue eyes searched her face, and it hurt and stung and soothed, and again, Aly wanted to cry. "It was just a stupid art project I had to do for school."

"That ended up winning the state championship," Helene was quick to add. "It's really beautiful, Jared, isn't it?"

He didn't look away from Aly. "Yeah, it is." Admiration filled his soft smile. "Is this the kind of stuff you keep in your sketch pads?"

Aly swallowed and shook her head. "No," she admitted with her eyes pinched shut tight.

"Can I see one of those drawings?" he asked.

Helene tsked, her smile light. "Jared, that's as bad as asking a girl if you can read her journal. You should know better."

He stumbled through a chuckle and stepped back. "I guess so."

A timer sounded in the kitchen. Aly's mom got up and disappeared through the archway. She popped her head back out a minute later. "All right, time for dinner. You kids get washed up."

Augustyn and Courtney abandoned the cartoon they were watching in the family room and rushed down the hall.

Their families ate together the way they always did, a jumble of people scattered about the room, their parents at the dining table, Jared, Christopher, and Aly at the nook, and the little kids on stools at the bar.

As soon as dinner was over, Jared and Christopher announced their departure.

"You two be careful," Aly's mom ordered, wagging her pointed finger at the two of them.

"Of course, Mom," Christopher promised, jingling his keys at his side.

"I don't want to hear any more excuses about being late for curfew, Jared Zachary," Helene warned. "You be home on time tonight."

Jared just smiled and nodded, quick to head for the door.

"And just because you're getting ready to turn sixteen doesn't mean you're too old to give your mom a kiss good-bye," Helene called out.

Jared laughed and rushed back up to Helene. He dipped down to kiss her on the cheek. "Never. Love you, Mom."

"Be good, bear," she said with nothing but affection.

Aly focused on her plate as Jared passed behind her. She felt a tug on a thick lock of her hair. Her eyes dropped closed because he hadn't done that in so long. Quiet and subdued, his words came from behind her. "I'm really proud of you, Aly Cat."

Aly's heart pressed at her ribs.

Maybe he hadn't forgotten her after all.

SEVENTEEN

Jared

I was in deep. So deep.

She held on to me from behind, that gorgeous body wrapped around me as if it were supposed to be there. As if she were molded for me.

Wind whipped through my hair, hot, hard, the sun blazing down from overhead.

Aly's hands tightened their hold on my stomach, and I increased my grip on the throttle, ticking it back a little more as I eased us onto the freeway. The engine warbled deep as I set a cautious pace.

I couldn't comprehend it was already the beginning of August, these treasured days speeding past faster than I wanted them to. We'd been like this for three weeks now, sneaking in every second we could get with each other. Workdays were brutal because all I wanted was to be back in the confines of her room, to be back in those arms that were all comfort and seduction and torment. My perfect Siren because even though I knew destruction would come, I still stole into her room night after night, where I slept curled up to her after I'd sought sanctuary in her touch. Sometimes we didn't get any further than a few hungry kisses and just lay with our legs intertwined, silent and nose-to-nose, resting together.

But it didn't matter what night it was. I wanted her. Every fucking night I wanted to take her, to finish off what our bodies begged for. Just touching her was never enough.

I wanted it all.

My tormenter snuggled closer as I took the off-ramp and began to wind us up to South Mountain.

The smile that lifted one side of my mouth was unstoppable. I covered her clenched hands with one of mine. "You doing okay back there?" I yelled as I slowed and leaned into a turn.

"Perfect," Aly shouted over the rushing wind.

I took us all the way to the top and pulled into one of the parking lots. Aly climbed off the back, careful to avoid the exhaust pipe. Before I let her get on my bike the first time, I'd drilled it into her head a million times over that it was hotter than all hell and would give her the burn of her life if she even brushed against it.

She unclasped the white helmet from her chin that she looked all kinds of adorable in, grinning at me as she shook her hair free.

Yeah, I'd fucking bought that for her, too.

God, I was in deep.

I pulled her in for a quick kiss and hooked my thumb under her chin. She beamed up at me. That thing that almost felt like joy rose up in me again.

That feeling had to be the most terrifying part of all.

"Come on, let's go find a trail." I took her hand and cautiously began to lead her down a narrow path. The rocky trail wound through thick desert brush, sparse trees, and overgrown cacti. The sky simmered with intense blue, the temperature so high heat waves sagged on the packed ground. We hiked down to a small overhang that looked out over the expanse of city that seemed to go on forever.

I tugged her from behind me and tucked her back to my chest. Slipping my hands around her waist, I secured my chin on her shoulder and pressed my cheek into hers. Held her close as I could get her.

For what seemed like forever, we said nothing, just stared at the beauty laid out in front of us.

"It's gorgeous up here," she finally whispered as she looked out over the horizon.

I nuzzled her neck, because that's exactly what she was.

"Thank you for bringing me up here." She ran her fingers over my knuckles, my hands splayed out over her stomach, locking her to me.

Aly sighed and sank deeper into my hold.

I blinked, trying to make sense of the thoughts that jumbled my mind, the words that fought for release. They sat on my tongue for the longest time, before they finally broke free. "My dad used to always bring me up here." My voice cracked, but I couldn't stop myself from speaking. "One day a month he'd plan some father-and-son day, pack us a lunch, and take me out somewhere cool . . . hunting or hiking or whatever I wanted to do. This was one of my favorite places."

Why the fuck was I telling her this? And why did I feel compelled to bring her here? To share it? But I did.

"I remember that," she said quietly. She released a small, wistful laugh. "I used to hate those days. Christopher and I would run up and pound on your door to ask if you could come out and play, and your mom would tell us you were with your dad." She expelled a delicate snort. "It's funny how we see things so differently when we're kids." She paused, before she admitted quietly, "It makes me really happy to know you cherished those days with him, Jared."

My chest tightened as the wounds flared. I squeezed her closer and tried to stuff them back inside with all the other shit I'd let slip away. With the memories of what I'd ruined.

"Do you ever think of finding him? Finding your sister? Visiting them?" she asked.

With her words, the memories only thrashed and the anger surged.

"I ruined my dad's life, Aly. He doesn't want to see me." Echoes from that last night flooded my mind. The circumstances had been blurred in the haze of drugs and alcohol and pain, warping and skewing his face, but there was no mistaking the disgust that had been written there. "He didn't come to my sentencing . . . didn't come to speak for me." Not that I'd expected him to. "He stood aside and let them send me away, and there's no going back."

She paused, and her hands clamped down on mine. "What if you're wrong, Jared?"

I swallowed the lump wedged deep in my throat. "I'm not." I knew I should push her away because this girl who had managed to sink her fingers into my spirit was going to end up as just another one of them—a fucking perfect memory to torture me through the rest of my worthless life.

Instead I clung to her, crushed her to me because I couldn't stop myself from taking from her until the moment she was taken from me.

The next night I was antsy. I hadn't seen Aly since early in the morning when I'd climbed from her bed to get ready for work. By the time I got back to the apartment, she'd already left for her lunch and dinner shift at the café.

Christopher lounged on the couch next to me watching TV, wearing nothing but an old ratty pair of jeans and with hair to rival any 'eighties rock band, though I doubted very much he'd put any effort into making it look that way. I sat there next to him, pretending to be doing something other than sitting there waiting for his sister to get home.

I knew I needed to start looking for my own apartment. I was beginning to feel like a loser sleeping on their couch, even though I'd been giving Christopher a third of the rent. But I'd only be lying if I chalked it up to the money. Christopher wouldn't care one way or the other. He'd welcomed me, given freely when all I'd done was turn around and take advantage of him and his generosity, deceiving my oldest friend when I'd promised him there was nothing going on between Aly and me. But how could I admit it to him? He'd already made it clear he'd never be okay with it. I mean, fuck, I wasn't okay with it. It wasn't like I could blame the guy for wanting to protect his baby sister.

Guilt over it had been impossible to shake, too. Every morning I'd study him, wondering when he would finally see through all my bullshit. Hiding away with Aly covered my consciousness like a shroud of shame. And like the asshole I was, I still stayed.

"Timothy is having another party tonight. I'm going to head over there in a little while. You wanna come?" Christopher asked, confirming my suspicion that he actually liked having me around.

I glanced over the bar at the clock on the microwave. It was just after nine. Aly would be home soon.

"Nah, man, I have to be up at six for work in the morning. I might walk over to The Vine for a couple beers to unwind, but I can't come stumbling in at three in the morning the way you always do." I smirked at him while guilt wound me tight. It was the same excuse I'd used the first morning he asked me where I'd been when he got home and I wasn't on the couch. Of course, my bike had been sitting like a witness of my guilt in the parking lot downstairs. I'd claimed I couldn't sleep so I walked to The Vine to grab a beer when I'd really been locked in Aly's room.

Aly would be worth any lie if I knew I wasn't slowly destroying her, if there was even a chance that what was happening behind her door wasn't going to end in ruin.

"God, do you always have to be the responsible one all the time? You kill my buzz just looking at you." Christopher smiled, all easygoing and cool.

"Shut up." Shame spiked, but I just laughed.

A key rattled in the front door lock.

That shame evaporated and a thrill of exhilaration took its place. I'd been missing her like crazy today. I didn't know what it was, but I couldn't wait to see her.

I jerked my head around to see her face just as she pushed open the door. She rested her foot against the bottom to prop it open as she jostled her key free from the lock, smiling up at me. Her hair was up in a high ponytail, and the long pieces that had fallen free framed her face, her cheeks tinted with red from a day of work. Welcome shone in her eyes.

Warmth spread just under my skin, and my heart pounded a little harder than I wanted it to. God, no wonder Christopher had noticed the way I'd been looking at her because there was no stopping the smile that pushed to my face.

"Hey, guys," she said a little breathlessly as she stepped inside. She nudged the door to fall shut behind her, then yelped when it was smacked back by a huge hand holding it open at the top.

Aly whirled around just as I scrambled to my feet. Aggression shot through me, fast and hard. I figured the quickest way to get to her was by jumping over the back of the couch because someone was about to get their ass kicked.

"Damn it, Gabe, you scared the shit out of me," she shouted.

Aly's words stopped me in my tracks.

Her hand was pressed to her chest as she heaved her surprise from her lungs, while Dickhead stood in the doorway grinning as if scaring the hell out of Aly had been the highlight of his fucking day.

I wanted to smash him in the face.

"Sorry." He laughed it off. "I didn't mean to startle you like that."

"It's okay." Aly shook herself as if shucking the jolt of fright from her body. "I just didn't hear you come up behind me."

He pressed his lips together, his hands in his pockets as he rocked back on his feet. "So, listen, I thought maybe we talk a little bit?" Warily, he glanced into the room at me and Christopher. Christopher was in about the same position I was, one knee on the couch and both hands on the backrest as if he'd been ready to rocket himself over it, too, before he realized it was this ass standing at the door.

Gabe shifted in clear discomfort.

That's right, fucker, you are not welcome here.

Aly seemed to hesitate, glancing at us over her shoulder, before she spoke. "Yeah, sure, of course," she rambled, lifting her hand to point down the hall. "We can go in my room."

Okay, that sounded like a really fucking *bad* idea.

I looked over at Christopher for backup, but he'd just turned around and plopped his lazy ass back on the couch with a resigned sigh.

Aly headed toward her room. Dickhead kept two steps behind her wearing that same smug smile on his pompous face that I would be all too happy to erase for him.

Neither of them said anything before Aly snapped her door shut behind them.

Shit. I stood in front of the couch, shifting my feet, still on edge. How the fuck was I supposed to just sit here and not do anything while he had Aly behind closed doors?

"I don't know what she sees in that guy. Dude is a complete douche bag," Christopher said as he mindlessly flipped through stations on the TV.

"Maybe we should go in there and check on her or something?"

"They've been in there for five seconds, Jared. I hardly think that warrants checking on."

"I don't like it. That guy's an asshole."

Incredulous, Christopher chuckled. "You think I like it? You know I can't stand the thought of her with some guy, but she's been seeing him for, like, six months or something . . . at least he's been hanging around that long. And it's not like she's fifteen. I can't tell her she's not allowed to have guys over."

So it was fine for Dickhead to be in her room but not me?

I wanted to laugh at myself. As if I didn't know the answer

to that question? I'd been in jail, an addict, and Gabe was the fucking pretty boy college student.

But I hated it, knowing he was in there with her, hated that I didn't know what was being said or what was being done.

Forcing myself to sit, I focused my eyes on the TV and my ear on her room, hoping that I could at least keep myself planted on the couch and not bolt for her door.

I mean, I trusted Aly with everything, even when I had nothing to give. I'd let her touch me, allowed her fingertips to memorize my sins, let her ask and dig and suggest fucking impossible things like reconciling with my dad.

We'd never talked about what *this* meant, these nights that were only temporary. But I'd always imagined they counted. That in them we were *something*. I couldn't begin to imagine being with another girl while I was with Aly. Not a fucking chance. I only wanted her. I guess I'd just assumed the same for her, and she'd have cut this asshole off the second she'd come to me, the moment she had stripped me bare when she'd offered herself to me.

Anxiety gripped me by the throat.

No sound could be heard from her room, something about this apartment that I normally viewed as an asset, but right then detested. Gabe with her in there was enough to drive me mad, enough to chase every rational thought from my already fucked-up mind.

All this time she'd remained innocent. Pure. I couldn't stomach the thought of her with someone else. Of someone taking her, touching her and loving her and giving her everything I couldn't, even though I knew that was exactly what she deserved. Exactly what she should have.

It only got worse as time passed. The unspent aggression

I'd been slammed with earlier flared and surged, and I was fucking bouncing in agitation, trying to sit still on the couch when all I wanted to do was bust down her door and toss his ass out of the apartment.

Christopher dropped the remote to the cushion. "I'm going to get out of here. You sure you don't want to come?"

"No, I'm good."

At this point, he couldn't drag me out of here.

Christopher inclined his head in the direction of Aly's room. "Glad you're here, anyway. You can keep an eye out for her."

"Yeah, of course."

Christopher went to his room to change, and waved over his head as he left.

I bounced a little more. Time had slowed to the most excruciating pace. I kept looking at her door, willing Gabe to emerge.

Thirty minutes later, he did. Her door slowly opened and Dickhead appeared. The good-guy expression I was sure he reserved only for Aly transformed the second he caught my eye. He lifted his chin in a silent insult, tossed me a grin that smacked of arrogance and self-satisfaction as he pulled her door shut.

The intense need to completely take him out engulfed me. I wanted to make him pay for showing up here. For thinking for a second he belonged with her.

For being stupid enough to fuck with me.

I just sat there, leering at the little twit who was obviously so ignorant he believed I'd continue to sit here if he kept looking at me that way.

I was gritting my teeth, itching to loose my aggression on him, when he turned his back and headed out the door. That was all it took before I was at hers.

I didn't knock, just turned the knob and let myself into the muted light of her room. Tonight, the blinds were shut. Thin lines of moonlight bled through the slats, and a small lamp sent a golden glow crawling up the wall behind her dressing table. It cast the rest of her room in shadows.

With her back to me, Aly stood as a silhouette in front of her bed. Her work clothes had been discarded at her feet, and she'd pulled on those same pink sleep shorts she always wore, giving cover to that glorious ass. She was in the middle of pulling a tank over her head. Waves of chunky hair fell down her back, all mussed and sexy. My fingers twitched, because damn it, I *really* wanted to touch, but I stayed rooted because I figured I was in no frame of mind to give in to it.

Over her shoulder, she peeked at me as she adjusted the hem of her shirt. Discomfort lined her face, the green of her eyes subdued. "I was just coming to find you," she whispered.

Swallowing hard, I stared at her from across the room, not sure what to do with the hostility still boiling in my veins. I felt on edge. Unhinged. But *this* felt completely different than the sickness that would forever darken my soul. It felt a little too much like the night I'd lost it at the bar at the mention of her name.

Motherfucking trigger.

I reached back to lock her door before I turned to look at her, rushing an agitated hand through my hair, trying to quell the fucking insanity she spurred in me. "What are you trying to do to me?" My tongue felt thick as I struggled through the admission. "I don't . . . fuck, I don't even recognize myself around you, Aly. I thought I was going to lose my mind out there, thinking about you in here with him."

Aly slowly turned around and took one step forward. With her head angled low and tipped to the side, she squinted, like maybe I'd just pissed her off.

That was okay because I was a little bit pissed off, too.

Lines deepened between her eyes, disbelief laced in the words that spilled from her mouth. "Do you think for one second I'd choose him over you, Jared? He came here to tell me he missed me. That he wanted to be with me and he'd do anything to fix whatever had gone wrong between us. But the entire time, the only thing I could think about was you in the other room. How the only thing in this world I want is you. Don't you understand that?"

All that fucking aggression snapped, like a band that had been stretched too tight, colliding with the need she had so tightly spun up in me. I crossed the room in two long strides. One second later, I had her in my arms, lifting her feet off the floor as my mouth seized hers. I was kissing her, my tongue demanding as I dragged her to her bed.

Her covers were piled in a heaped mess from where we'd slept curled in them last night, where we'd kissed and tempted and left ourselves panting and still in need. Our scent still lingered in them, thick and strong. Unwilling to break our frenzied kiss, I shoved the covers out of the way with one arm, the other supporting her back as I laid her on the bed.

Aly arched up as if she ached.

I grasped her perfect face between firm hands, my hold just as commanding as my mouth. Consumed, I pressed the length of my body into hers, blanketing her as my forearms fell to the bed to support my weight.

I wanted to possess her. Take her.

Fuck.

I wanted it all.

Aly moaned as her fingers threaded in my hair. She murmured assurances at my mouth in between our desperate bid to bring each other closer, our mouths just as frantic as the beating of her heart. "It's you, Jared . . . you . . . only you."

Growling, I pulled back, my fingers spreading out over the back of her head as my thumbs rushed along her delicate jaw. We were nose-to-nose, and I was unable to discern the sharp gasps of air she drew into her lungs from mine. The words scraped from my throat. "Did you tell him that you're mine?" My hands tightened, underscoring the madness she created in me. "Did you tell him that you belong to me?"

Those green eyes darkened, hinted at her fears, spoke of her desires. "Do I?" came as a plea from between her full lips.

My heart skidded, and the frenzy that had racked my body stilled.

Obviously, it was me who belonged to her.

I ran my thumb along her jaw, smiled softly at the girl. Her eyes searched, begged, everything about her perfect and kind.

My chest squeezed.

Fuck. I was in so deep.

"Aleena," I whispered, before I brushed my lips across hers. A statement.

She was the only one who'd *touched* me in years, the only one who'd made me feel.

Tipping her chin up, she met my eye, her fingers gentle as they fluttered across my face. "You," she quietly murmured.

I smoothed the back of my hand down the flush on her cheek. Her mouth dropped open as she leaned into my touch. Joy teased along the fringes of my consciousness, quivered, and rose. This—this was our deception, where I wanted to live until the day I died. Where nothing was real but the secrets we whispered in the night.

I shifted to my hands and knees, bending my elbows as I

dropped my shoulders down to kiss her softly, slowly. Because I never wanted it to end. Our tongues played.

And I reveled in this fantasy.

Aly cupped my face, lightly scratching her nails through the stubble coating my jaw, her smile warm. Tingles spread and coiled, flaring the unending need for her that seemed to never let go.

Gentle hands roamed over my shoulders, down my back, unhurried, just as unhurried as our kiss. I sucked in a ragged breath when she ran both of her index fingers just under the waistband of my jeans, dipping them into the two dimples peeking out just above my hips.

Flames scorched my already heated skin.

God, the girl set me on fire. Innocent and sweet, and still the sexiest thing I'd ever seen.

"Aly, what are you doing?" I warned.

She just nipped at my chin and flirted with the hem of my shirt, before she flattened both palms on the small of my back and slipped them up my skin, taking the shirt with her as she went.

I lowered my weight to my elbows and ducked my head to twist out of the shirt as Aly dragged it over my head. She giggled lightly when she did. There was something so pure about her smile. It set me reeling, and I kissed her again, couldn't stop. I pressed my bare chest against the thin cloth covering her breasts.

My palms wandered down her sides. I pulled at the bottom of her shirt before I edged back enough to slip it up between us. We were a tangle of arms when I tugged it loose, our faces a breath apart.

In the dim light, her hair was the deepest black, her eyes a searing green. For a moment, I just gazed at her, curling a lock of her hair around my index finger. A bond. I didn't get it, why anchoring myself to her this way felt as if I were home . . . even when home was what I'd destroyed so long ago.

Aly just stared, her throat bobbing heavily as she swallowed down whatever doubt flashed across her features. Shaky fingers reached out to caress my bottom lip. "I am yours, Jared. Take me."

Deep inside, I thrashed, a fury of nerves and need and a broken spirit that for the first time felt as if it were almost whole. Fear beat a steady drum and bound itself to my heart. It danced with the guilt, the shame of what I already knew I was about to do.

Because every part of me knew this was fucking wrong.

All except for the part that knew her, wanted her, the part that was drowning in a desire that screamed louder than any lash of fear and hurt worse than any lick of shame.

The part that knew the only thing that mattered was Aly.

My Aly.

I sat up on my knees as I leaned over to work her shorts and panties down her slender legs. I tossed them behind me to the floor.

Aly wet her lips, her chest rising and falling in spastic quakes, her gaze intense. "Jared, please, I need you."

Lust shot through me as I looked down at her fully exposed, lying back on the bed that had become like a reprieve from the storm that ruled my life. With hungry eyes, I traced the slope of her neck, the swell of her breasts, the curve of her hips. Her knees were bent, her feet planted, her arms draped over her head where her hair was fanned out, framing her perfect face.

No doubt, she was the most beautiful thing I'd ever seen.

But tonight, looking at her felt different, felt like maybe I was looking at life. Another lie. One when behind her door, I'd be foolish enough to believe.

I rose from the bed and shed the rest of my clothes.

A small smile whispered at just one side of her mouth as she watched me. Trust I didn't deserve edged out the fear on her face.

Nudging her knees apart, I climbed back onto the bed and settled between her thighs. I kissed her slowly while my body screamed. I pushed up on one hand and held her face in the other, my thumb caressing the apple of her cheek, searching her eyes for any sign that I should stop.

Her jaw was slack, her skin flushed. Aly arched her back, forcing her chest into mine, her neck extended as she begged for my touch. She lifted her chin as if in supplication, offering herself to me. "I am yours," she promised again.

Need tumbled through me, surged, and rushed. I groaned into her neck and kissed along the sensitive skin. My nose ran along the ridge of her jaw as I held her by the back of her head. My fingers got lost in the mass of her hair. I pressed a gentle kiss to the hollow beneath her ear, before I turned to the swells of her breasts, devouring her skin, feasting on the pure, taking the good.

"Please," she begged as she lifted her hips.

Straining, my body begged, warring with the hesitation. I was at her center, rubbing shamelessly against her warmth, our skin bare as I brought us closer than we'd ever been.

My arms caged her, fingers boring into the skin at the base of her scalp, my voice little more than a ragged grunt. "Aly, are you sure? We said we weren't going to do this."

She buried her face in my neck and mumbled, "All I want is you."

It was the thought of being fully lost in her that left me without resolve. We'd spent so many nights as fools, pretending we wouldn't end up in this very place. Those nights had only been a taste of the pleasure that I knew was now to come.

I'd seen those pink packs of pills in her bathroom a thousand times. And I was clean. I'd checked that shit out after I began sleeping in her bed. No chance would I risk spreading her any filth.

My stomach tightened, and I edged back until I was poised at her center. I barely pressed into her, let her warmth send shivers rushing up my spine as I watched her mouth part and her eyes darken exactly the way I imagined they would.

"Jared." Aly swallowed frantically. She seemed to be flailing for solid ground. Fingertips dug into the bunched muscles of my shoulders that were held tight in restraint. The nerves that raced across her skin were palpable, lifted as goose bumps, and spread as heat. Aly quivered a smile and exhaled a shaky breath across my face. "I feel you."

Shit.

I was about to lose all control. I pulled back before I took her deeper. Aly's legs trembled and she tightened them on my hips.

Her face pinched. "Ow."

Fuck, I hated myself so badly for doing this. My knees shook, my elbows digging into the bed as my hands fisted in her hair. She was so tight. Painfully tight. I couldn't fucking breathe as I slowly spread her.

Broke her.

Took what never should have been mine.

"Aleena" wept from my mouth.

Tears gathered in her eyes and streaked down the sides of

her face, trailing along the crease of her ears before they disappeared into her hair.

"Fuck, Aly, baby, I'm so sorry . . . I'm so fucking sorry."

A smile trembled at her mouth. "Don't." Hoarseness coated her voice. "I want this. I want you. It's just . . . all of this . . . it's perfect."

A sheen of sweat glistened across her forehead, and strands of hair clung to her dampened face. I swept it back, looking down at the girl who'd completely shaken me as she stared up at me. Her expressive eyes shone with affection.

We just lay there.

Bonded as one.

If I believed in soul mates or any of that shit, I knew she was mine. I could feel it, this connection with her I couldn't possibly share with anyone else. Like we fit, this fucked-up puzzle that made no sense until we aligned the pieces. But it wasn't possible. I didn't get the happy ending, and even if I did, I'd only ruin it. Just like I knew I was ruining her now.

I held myself rigid, refusing to move while she adjusted, while the shock of what I'd taken from her passed. Her uneven breaths slowed and her legs loosened the grip they had on my hips. My thighs shook with the loose thread I had on my control.

I felt the moment she let go. "I'm yours," she mouthed.

And I took. My body strained, pushed, and pled as hers accepted and gave. I rocked into her again and again. I savored the little pants I forced from the depths of her throat, the way her fingers felt as they cut into my skin. Our bodies burned, heat slicking our stomachs and pooling in the valley between her breasts as I moved with her in a way I'd never moved with anyone before. I mean, how many other girls had I been with? I had no clue. Because they were easily forgotten. But this . . . being with Aly was different, and I knew I'd never forget.

"Fuck, Aly, you feel so good." So good. Perfect. Almost as if she were truly mine.

With my words, she whimpered, and I gave myself over to her. Pleasure knotted at the base of my spine and spread down the back of my thighs. I throbbed and ecstasy hit. Spasms jerked through my body, every nerve alive. With my face buried in the crook of her neck, I cried out, her name on my tongue the only fucking thing that made any sense. Gasping, I searched for air, smelled the delicious coconut and the good and the girl. I gathered her up, my face still hidden in her warmth, hugged her to me closer than I ever had before.

"Aly" whispered from my mouth.

My Aly.

I wound a finger in her hair.

I'd given in, chased after her comfort.

Now there'd be hell to pay.

EIGHTEEN

Aleena

Jared had made love to me. Completed me.

We lay on our sides, face-to-face, his warm hand cradling the side of my face. "You beautiful girl," he murmured, kissing me softly.

Emotion swamped me, filled my heart, and expanded my chest.

"Are you okay?" Jared tilted his head back to read my eyes.

I blinked and whispered, "Yes," because it was the truth. I was perfect, so long as he stayed.

It was a Friday night, and I stood in front of the TV in the living room, playing *DanceStar*. Laughter bubbled up from my gut. Music blared from the speakers set up around the TV. I was in front of it, wondering why I couldn't get my feet to keep up with my brain as I watched the character dancing on the TV and tried to mirror his steps. I held the controller in my left hand. The glowing sensor bulb at the top seemed like the perfect stand-in mic. Without remorse, I screamed Billy Idol's "Dancing with Myself" into the prop.

I couldn't hold a tune. Not to save my life.

But tonight, I just didn't care.

Megan jumped around beside me. Blond hair whipped dangerously close to my face as she swung her head around, completely offbeat.

Christopher sat directly behind her on the couch, and she bounced back to shake her butt in his face. "It's your duty to shake your booty," she sang over my fruitless attempt to win points by keeping in tune with the song, her tiny frame wiggling all over.

Yeah. She and Christopher had been doing shots of tequila in the kitchen.

Christopher covered his face with his hands, laughing so hard he fell to his side on the couch. "Holy hell, you two suck so bad."

I stuck my tongue out at him, then turned and belted the song even louder near Megan's face, held the mic between us so she could sing along. Giving up on the choreographed moves, the two of us busted out in some impromptu dance, uninhibited and free.

Laughter overtook the words I tried to sing. I'd really never known joy like this. I'd always been happy, but I'd never known the intense satisfaction that came with being loved. It was something that seeped down into the marrow of my bones and pervaded every fiber of my being.

Not once had he told me, but I knew he did. I felt it, even when it clearly was something impossible for Jared to see. Something he didn't recognize himself. But I took him for what he was, this beautifully broken boy who deserved every touch I gave while I treasured every single one he returned.

On what had become his side of the couch, he sat nursing a beer, his legs casually stretched out in front of him. Playful blue eyes glinted their amusement as he watched us dance in the middle of the living room.

Almost a month had passed since the first time he made love to me. Every day since had been an exploration of hands and tongues and bodies that couldn't get enough.

The first time had been overwhelming. Painful. Both physically and emotionally. It was as if something had shifted inside me. Captured me. Changed me.

Emotionally, it still remained the same, this intensity that swept through me like wildfire, though now I'd come to crave that feeling.

But physically . . . I'd just never understood that anything could feel so good.

Shimmying up to him, I shook my shoulders and lowered myself to get level with his face. He laughed softly as he turned his head to the side. Clearly, he was too embarrassed to continue watching me make a fool of myself. His hand came up to rub at his chin when he lifted his perfect face back to me, accosting me with this coy grin that made my stomach flip. Something about it was so incredibly sexy I was about five seconds from revealing us to Christopher.

I hated hiding us.

All I wanted to do was take him by the face and kiss him.

Instead I settled for taking him by the hand. "Come dance with me," I shouted over the TV that was turned up much too loud.

Redness colored his face, and that smile tipped up on one side. He shook his head. "Not a chance in hell, Aly. I don't dance."

I tugged a little. "Please."

"Ever," he added, the word emphatic, though his clear eyes still shone.

"What, you expect me and Megan to stand up here and entertain you two all night? Come on. Please," I almost whined, yanking at his arm. I guess I'd probably had too much to drink, too. "Please." This time I squeezed.

He just sat there shaking his head in disbelief, but then he seemed to be shaking his head at himself because he couldn't believe he was giving in. "Fine."

Pulling him to his feet, I flashed a victorious smile. With his beer secured in one hand, he loosely threaded his fingers with mine in the other.

I danced around him. Twisting, laughing, singing. That grin was back on his gorgeous face, and he lifted his hand over my head and led me into a twirl. Unrestrained, Jared laughed and spun me some more.

That intense joy wrapped me tight.

He was happy. I could see it. Feel it. God, I wanted it so badly for him, for this man I cared so deeply for to have a chance to heal. I smiled up at him, couldn't contain what I felt from bursting from my face.

Wiggling in between us, Megan nudged me aside and stole my spot. Jared took a turn twirling her around. She bumped him once with her hip, then dropped his hand and danced toward me.

She knew what was going on between us. A couple of weeks ago, I'd finally confided in her that I slept with him, admitting he came stealing into my room every night. It wasn't as if she was all that surprised. She said after seeing the two of us together on the Fourth, she didn't know how it hadn't happened sooner.

Even though she was drunk, she remained aware, her eyes slanting to me before they quickly shifted to Christopher and back to me.

A warning.

I was being obvious.

Tonight I didn't know how to care. How could what Jared and I had be wrong?

Still I backed off and turned to take Christopher by the hand, my crazy brother who'd had so much to drink he could barely stand. He didn't come quite so reluctantly as Jared had. As if Christopher wouldn't jump at the chance to join in.

Jared wormed his way back to the couch, content to be the spectator to our silliness. The rest of us danced and sang and drank until the night grew deep.

Christopher finally called it quits and staggered back to his room.

I whispered a reluctant "Good night" to Jared before I retreated to my bedroom with Megan. Tonight would be the first night I'd spend without him in so long, but I'd missed my friend. Megan and I used to do this all the time, her hanging out here, staying all night. Christopher had earned a good smack to the back of the head the first time he'd teased us about sleeping together.

She joined me in my room and curled up on her side of the bed with her back pressed to the wall, her cheek resting on her hands.

Sinking onto my side, I smiled at her as I tucked my pillow

under my head. "I'm glad you came over tonight. This was a lot of fun."

"Yeah, it really was." She bit at her lip. Knowing eyes darted to the door, her voice soft. "You love him, Aly?"

I looked at my best friend, unsure why I'd kept this secret for so long. Unsure why I still did.

"So much," I whispered. I knew it sounded as if it hurt because, really, it did.

She blinked as if trying to work it out. "You're different with him."

I glanced away, then back at her. "Is that good or bad?"

She cringed a little, as if she might not want to answer. "Both, I think. Maybe it's just that I've seen you shut off for so long it's weird to see you like this. I guess it worries me some." Her eyes were wide and honest. "I just want you to be happy, that's all."

"I am happy."

She nodded, though worry creased her face. We both fell into silence, lost in thought.

Sleep was quick to overtake her. In no time, her soft snore filled my room.

I stared at the darkened ceiling and tried to find sleep of my own. I should have known my efforts would be fruitless.

Finally I climbed to my feet and tiptoed out into main room. It was pitch-black, the heavy curtains drawn. My eyes adjusted, and I shuffled to the place I knew he would be.

Heavy, burdened breaths filled the room, this anxiety winding through him where he lay just on the cusp of sleep. I knew it because I found him there every night, shaking, twitching, silent in his pain.

I just wanted to take it away.

Slowly, I climbed onto the couch, straddling him at his waist. He jerked up as if in shock, the strong planes of his stomach stretched taut as he lifted his head. Rough hands dug into my hips.

"What are you doing out here?" His voice was all gravelly.

"I missed you," I said.

I felt his palm come to my face. His fingers traveled up to comb through my hair. "You shouldn't be out here like this, Aly."

I leaned down, pressing my hands to the cushions on both sides of his face. "I'm not ashamed of us, Jared," I whispered urgently toward the shadows that blackened his face.

His hand tightened into a fist in my hair. "You should be."

Steam filled the bathroom the next day as I took my shower. Sheets of hot water pounded on my shoulders before they cascaded down my back. Rivulets gathered as thin lines that snaked along my legs before they crawled to the shower floor. I lathered my body wash on my loofah and scrubbed it over my skin, breathing in the freshness as the hot water slowly cleared my head.

Megan had left half an hour before.

We'd all slept in, Megan and me stumbling from bed at close to noon. Jared had still been asleep on the couch, his hair sticking up in every direction when he'd lifted his head to throw a frustrated squint at us when we emerged from my room. His pained expression didn't come close to the one I was sure Megan would be sporting all day. She'd woken with a drawn-out groan, ramming her fists in her eyes to block out the light.

I'd asked her what she expected when she'd consumed half her weight in tequila the night before.

Rinsing the soap from my body, I turned off the shower and blindly fumbled outside the curtain for my towel. I pressed it to my face where it absorbed my contented sigh.

There were few things that felt better than a hot shower.

Redness rushed to the surface of my skin because echoes of Jared's touch suddenly flooded my mind. Sometimes I didn't know what do with the thoughts I had about him, the way he made me feel or the things he made me want.

After I dried off, I lathered lotion on my legs and dressed in shorts and a T-shirt. I wiped the fog from the mirror and slowly pulled a brush through my hair. Today was the first Saturday I didn't have to work in a long time, and I was just looking forward to spending the day with Jared, in whatever capacity that might be.

Someone tapped at the door, and then I heard Christopher. "Hey, Aly, I'm going to run to the grocery store really quick. Do you need anything?"

"Um . . . more orange juice. I just drank the last of it," I hollered back.

"Okay, sure." Then he was gone.

Thirty seconds later, there were two low thuds at the door, the two seconds separating them like a silent plea. That was all it took for my heart to speed. I fumbled with the lock and pulled it open. Jared stood on the other side of the doorway, waiting for me.

He'd seemed irritable this morning, and I thought it was because he had a hangover of his own. But now he seemed edgy. Intently he dragged his gaze down my length, his movements pulsing with uncontained intensity. Hungry. Possessive.

"I didn't think he'd ever leave."

There was something about his tone that made my stomach

lurch and sent my nerves careening. I shook in impatient apprehension as he crossed the threshold and locked the door behind
him.

"I've been dying to get you alone all morning," he said, his
voice deep as he swallowed hard. "I need you, Aly, I need you so
fucking bad."

Butterflies swarmed.

That powerful body flattened against mine, one strong
hand taking me firmly by the back of the head, the other kneading at my thigh, then splaying over my ass as he pulled me
roughly against him.

His mouth owned mine.

Decided and fierce.

Weak-kneed, I emitted a stuttered breath.

Jared pulled back, those blue eyes burning, fire and ice.

His hands encircled my waist. Lifting me up, he propped my
bottom on the edge of the bathroom counter, groaning when he
ground his body into mine.

I writhed, unable to control what he did to me.

His throat bobbed heavily, and he pulled off my shirt. In the
same motion, he took one step back, grabbing the neck of his
own shirt and ripping it off over his head. Strength rippled under the colors that bled, that rose at the center of his chest like
this beacon that called me home.

I desperately gripped at the lip of the counter, my stomach
flexed as I struggled to balance my weight, to balance my senses
that Jared had thrown into overdrive. He brazenly looked me
over. Tingles spread in a slow blaze and redness bloomed.

"You make me crazy," he whispered hoarsely as he inched
forward, ridding me of my bra before his fingers came out to
work the button free on my shorts. Wetting his lips, he tugged

them down and slowly dragged them off my legs. He skimmed his hands back up the inside of my thighs.

"I love your legs, Aly. I could spend my entire life wrapped in them."

And I wanted him to, to spend his life with me, for him to live one he thought himself unworthy of. I wondered if he even realized what he'd said, that his heart spoke of forever just as his mind so clearly promised him this would pass. That this would end.

My spirit thrashed, unsure of which he would hang on to.

I stared up at him, couldn't look away as his eyes flashed in the vanity lights. His beauty was so strong, his body perfection despite every inner flaw.

Those butterflies flitted and spun, tumbled around in the lowest part of my core.

He twisted his fingers in my panties, and he shed them slowly. My pulse stuttered, my body aching, begging. Once again, it'd taken Jared two seconds to strip me of every ounce of control.

"Please," I whimpered.

Jared growled. His face contorted, and hot, aggressive hands grasped my knees, forcing them apart. Then his mouth was on me.

Sensations burst behind my eyes. Desperately, my fingers dove in his hair, curled and held and gripped. Every inch of my body moaned. And I thought maybe I should be embarrassed, that I should try to contain the muffled cries that spilled from my mouth. But there was no place in me where I could find shame.

Not with him.

Again I begged, "Please."

Then he was touching me, sure fingers filling me in the most exquisite way.

I arched. Came undone. Pleasure surged and rushed, spread out to saturate every crevice in my body. Still it was not enough. It was never enough.

I fumbled between us for the fly of his jeans. I freed him of all his barriers, shoving them down his hips. Jared twisted out of them and kicked them aside.

He completed me in one solid thrust.

My mouth dropped open in a soundless gasp, and my nails raked down his back. His hands rushed up the back of my thighs, and he wrapped them under to grip me by the hips, my knees hooked over his forearms.

"Beautiful," he grated from his throat. He took me hard and fast, then torturously slow, never looking away from my face as he tempted and teased, then brought me back to the brink. Our bodies pitched and strained, grasped and clutched.

"Jared, please . . . don't . . . just . . ."

He understood my plea. He quickened as he filled me again and again. "Aly, baby," he grunted.

It hit me in a shocking wave, this blinding rapture that ripped through my core and erupted as an aching cry from my lips.

"Fuck . . . Aly . . ." Ice blue eyes sparked like wildfire when he crushed his chest to mine, his hands leaving my hips to grip the counter. Jared's movements were harsh and rushed, his body jerking, his breaths short and ragged.

I bowed as he came.

In the mirror on the wall behind him, I saw him as he struggled to catch his breath. His back flexed beneath the scars that wept where they bled, a pattern of despair, and I knew he could see me in the vanity mirror behind us. Through the two, our eyes met, almost hesitantly, the reflection like this illusion of us that went on forever.

Infinite.

Something like torment filled his eyes. He buried his nose in my hair behind my ear and whispered his praise. "Aleena."

And I loved him.

I loved him with everything I had.

We stayed that way for the longest time, neither able to move, our bodies locked. My fingertips strayed, traced, and explored. They gentled over the flames on his right arm. Here, under the color, the skin was too smooth, but on the edges it gave rise to rough ridges that felt like hardened seams.

Jared sucked in a jagged breath, then released it in a slow hiss as I trailed down to the tortured eyes that writhed in the fire. I caressed them, my voice soft. "Is this you or her?" It was as if I could sense every nerve in his body fire, his brain only registering pain.

"Me, Aly. It's me." That pain bled from his mouth in bitter agony. "It should have been me." His fingers dug into my sides. "I fucking tried to make it right. I tried." The last fell as a breath of defeat.

I wanted to shake him, scream *no*, tell him how wrong he was.

I wanted to *tell* him.

He took my face in his hands and kissed me, his eyes squeezed tight. When he opened them, he acted as if what had just passed between us hadn't happened. "You need to get dressed. Christopher is going to be back soon." He leaned down and gathered up my clothes, handing them to me with a forced smile. "I'm going to take a quick shower."

I nodded, swallowing down the emotion that constricted my throat. "Okay."

He turned away and I watched as he climbed into the shower, this beautiful man who broke my heart and made it whole.

I quickly re-dressed. Vacillating, I paused, looking back to where he stood veiled behind the shower curtain. There were so many things I needed to say, but I had no idea how to get them out. I didn't know if they would hurt him or heal him, if he'd run or if he'd stay.

I let myself out into the apartment, combing through my damp, tangled hair with my fingers. I barely had time to fill a glass with water before Christopher was unlocking the front door.

God. What was I doing? Keeping this from my brother? From my family? Keeping what I really wanted from myself? But how could I have him any other way?

"Hey," Christopher said as he kicked open the door.

"Do you need some help?" I asked, setting my glass down on the counter and coming around to where he'd dropped the bags at the front door.

"Yeah, that'd be cool. Thanks."

Leaning down, I gathered a few sacks and stood back up. Then froze.

Blood drained from my face and flooded through my chest to squeeze my heart. It swept through me whole, leaving me weak in the knees. My attention locked on the two people mounting the stairs.

"Oh, good, you're both here." Mom was all smiles when she hit the landing. Augustyn trailed her two steps behind.

Tension twitched Christopher's shoulders when he registered her voice, a subtle tic of his muscles as his eyes shot to my face. His panic was just as thick as mine.

Christopher rapidly blinked, then slowly stood up and turned around. "Mom, Aug, hey, what are you doing here?"

"We were running some errands nearby and thought we'd see if we could catch you two. Thought maybe we could go grab some lunch together or something." Mom didn't hesitate to take Christopher into a huge hug. "I've missed you." She rocked them a little as she squeezed, then stepped back to hug me.

Aug and Christopher shook hands and clapped each other on the back. "Hey, man," Christopher said, "how's practice going?"

"Good . . . really good. Can't wait for the season to actually start next week."

Christopher kept glancing at me while he talked, as if asking for help, stalling. I could see him plead with his eyes. *What do we do?*

It was our dad Christopher had wanted to keep this from, the news that Jared was back and staying with us. But I wasn't sure how Mom would react, either.

Part of me knew she needed to know. I just wasn't sure this was the right way for her to find out. I'd imagined Christopher taking her aside, letting her know Jared was staying with us, that she'd ask questions and want to see him and she'd slowly ease Dad into the idea of him being back in town . . . into the idea of him being back in our lives. None of us had spoken about him in so many years I had no idea where my mother's thoughts lie or the way she felt.

It was wrong. We had betrayed him in the silence of our words.

But our mom was kind. I knew that, and now I had to trust that she would understand.

Christopher scratched at the back of his neck and inclined his head. "Listen, Mom, I need to talk to you about something."

Clearly, Christopher understood that, too.

The second he said "I," I realized my brother was going to take responsibility for this, as if he thought he had somehow coerced me into allowing Jared to stay with us. Christopher still thought I was the unwilling partner in this deception, when in truth, he was the one who had unknowingly allowed Jared to become the most important person in my life.

Mom frowned. "What's wrong?" Worried, she flicked her eyes to me, then back to Christopher. Nervous energy instantly wound her tight. She shifted on her feet.

The shower squealed as it was shut off.

Mom paused. She turned her attention inside, her eyebrows drawn tight as she looked down the hall of our apartment toward the bathroom.

Someone using our shower in itself wasn't really such a big deal. But it was like this awareness seeped over her and she suddenly sensed the unease that radiated out from Christopher and me.

"Who's here?" she asked, stepping into our apartment.

"Mom—"

Jared opened the door and came out into the hall wearing only a pair of jeans, rubbing a towel over his wet head, oblivious of what he was stepping into.

The second his eyes met with Mom's, he stopped dead.

Mom just stood there, as if lost, thrown back in time. Then a strangled sob tore from her throat and her hands flew up to cover her mouth. "Jared. Oh my God, Jared, is that you?"

Tears leaked down her face. It took a few seconds to pass before she seemed to snap back. Then she shot across the room,

throwing her arms around him, hugging him, while he remained limp under her touch. She pulled back, frantic, as she
searched his face, her hands pressing into his cheeks as if she
were making sure he was really there. "It's you . . . oh my God . . .
it's you. I didn't think I'd ever see you again."

And Mom was crying, holding on to him as if he might
disappear.

From across the room, I caught the expression on his face.

And I was sure he would.

NINETEEN

Jared

Cold slipped through my veins. Pictures of *her* face slammed me as if she were locked in time. One by one, they struck me, battered and beat my mind, like an everlasting penalty sent to taunt my spirit.

Laughing.

Smiling.

She was always that way—smiling, laughing, loving.

She'd been beautiful.

Good.

And I'd stamped out that light. A rose trampled underfoot.

A shuddered breath burned as I drew it in, my lungs pressing against my ribs. Fire clashed with the cold, and pain pelted my insides as needles prickled along my skin. I was always ruining the good.

Now Aly's mother, Karen Moore, clung to me as if she'd just

witnessed a resurrection of the dead. All I could do was stand there wishing for a way to disappear.

I squeezed my eyes shut, trying to block all of it out.

What it was about Karen Moore that was such a stark reminder of *her*, I didn't know. Maybe it was because they had been such good friends. Maybe because she had been the other mother in my life when I was growing up. Maybe it was because she was in so many of the memories that haunted my nights, laughing and smiling, too.

As if the girl owned me by some force of attraction, my eyes sought out Aly. She still stood near the door, worry creasing every line on her face. She was wearing that expression that said she got me, that she really fucking understood.

The good.

Maybe it was her. Maybe it was the way she'd managed to strip me bare and shred me thin.

Fuck.

Two warm hands pressed into my cheeks. I hated the way they felt, like welcome and forgiveness and all this bullshit that could never be, like maybe she understood, too, and it was about all I could do not to knock them away. I gritted my teeth, doing my best not to lose my shit. I was teetering right on the edge of that fucking cliff, and when I fell, I knew I'd be taking the people I cared about down with me.

"Oh my God, Jared, where have you been? How long have you been here? Why didn't you let me know?" Questions tumbled from Karen's mouth just as quickly as tears streaked down her face. Her attention jumped around the apartment, hunting for clues, before she turned her gentle brown eyes back on me, eyes that reminded me of too many things.

Guilt spun, stoking the agitation that was working its way

free. Anxiety buzzed through my consciousness, clenching my jaw, fisting my hands. My head fucking pounded. That warning system was sounding off louder than it ever had, screaming at me to bolt. This time I was apparently in full agreement because all I wanted to do was grab my shit and go.

Christopher scratched at the back of his head, the same way he always did when he was put on the spot. "Uh, yeah, Mom, that's what I wanted to talk to you about. I ran into Jared a few nights ago and I invited him to hang out here while he's passing through town."

Passing through.

The lie bled so easily from him, quick to cover that I'd actually been staying with them for close to three months. He cautioned me with a glance that said it was okay to correct him, but he was giving me an out. I could take it either way. The guy always had my back while I continually fed him lies night after night.

I almost spat the words. "Yep . . . just passing through."

Aly's face crumpled, like I might as well have kicked her in the stomach when I didn't dispute Christopher's claim. Shame pressed down on me from all sides, sucking every fucking last drop of air from the room.

"Oh?" Karen kind of frowned. "Well, I'm just glad you're here." Smoothing herself out, she took a step back, like maybe she'd just clued in on the fact that I was about to snap. She wiped under her eyes to rid herself of the evidence of her tears. A strained smile pushed to her trembling lips. "It's been far too long. How long are you staying?"

Helpless, I could do nothing but cast a furtive glance in Aly's direction. Of course, I got stuck there. She filled up my line of sight like a buoy bobbing in the water, just out of reach, while I slowly drowned.

I could barely speak through the fucking rock lodged in my throat. "Not long," I said, and somehow I knew it was the truth, because I could feel it building. The destruction.

I don't get to have this.

Because I owed my life.

I sat in the empty lot behind the same deserted building I'd found myself in almost three months ago the night after I'd first confronted Aly in the kitchen. I was slumped back against the coarse stucco wall, my head lolling from side to side. Alcohol soaked my senses, dampened them into a suffocating heaviness, like maybe I was being buried alive. But it did nothing to lessen the images, the pictures that had spun through my mind on an unending reel since the second Karen Moore had stepped foot through the door.

I rammed the heels of my hands to my eyes, desperate to blot it out. Colors flickered, visions streaming in this unbearably vivid light. I roared into the silence.

Motherfucking trigger.

Both of them.

Clutching the back of my head in my hands, I buried my face between my knees as I gasped for breath. "Fuck" scraped from my raw throat.

What had I expected, coming here? This was what I wanted, wasn't it? To punish myself a little bit more? There was no other explanation for the fucking impossible draw I'd had to return to this place.

Unbidden, Aly's face lit up like a flare that struck behind my lids. My lids were mashed together tight, but the image hung on like it didn't want to give way to the ones that destroyed me. The girl was like a second's relief amid the insufferable penance I served.

God, I wanted it to be her. It skirted along the brink of my reality, the idea that maybe there was more, because, damn it . . . maybe I really did want there to be.

I let my head rock against the wall and lifted my face to the haze of the night sky.

But that was just a fantasy—and not the fairy-tale kind.

I didn't get the happily ever after.

Still I didn't want to let the idea go. I needed to feel her. Just for a few more minutes I wanted to let her touch take the pain away.

I stumbled to my feet and made my way back toward the apartment.

It was late. The city slept, the dense silence only broken by the drone of semitrucks echoing from the freeway and the random car speeding down the road.

The hour Karen and Augustyn stayed at the apartment had been complete hell. Aly had suggested we all stay in to catch up instead of going out, so I'd sat down at the kitchen table with them all. I'd done my best at forcing smiles and tossing out bullshit answers to all the inane questions Karen asked. Clearly, she'd been tiptoeing around the questions she really wanted to ask. The entire time, I sat there itching to run. If I'd stayed in the confines of those walls for one more second, no question, I would finally have hit the edge.

It only made me feel worse that the entire time Aly had again offered me that comfort she so freely gave. Though this time, it wasn't in her arms, but in the way her eyes constantly washed over me, and in the one gentle brush of her hand she'd hazarded under the table. Like maybe she was telling me it was okay and she understood the misery her mother brought with her when she walked through the door.

But like the asshole I was, I left the second Karen and Augustyn finally said their good-byes.

I knew Aly was dying to talk to me, but Christopher had been there, and there was little she could do, little she could say, although her plea radiated from every cell in her body.

Stay.

She should already have known I couldn't.

Now, with my shoulders hunched, I stuffed my hands in my pockets and strode toward the apartment that was just a block away. The humid night clung thick to my skin. Lights from the city glowed against the blackened sky, dragging the heavens too close to the surface of my fucked-up world.

Before I'd ended up behind the vacant building, I'd spent the entire afternoon and most of the night at the Vine. Once again, I'd been foolish enough to think there was some way I could drown the past out. But it didn't matter what I did. I could never outrun it. Could never hide from it. I could fight it all I wanted, but it'd never change who I was or what I'd done.

Incredulous laughter rocked from my hoarse throat. All these nights I'd been lying to Christopher, telling him that I'd been unwinding at the Vine, when really I'd been locked away in Aly's room, lost in her comfort and her touch and everything I wished was real. If I just had stayed at the bar that first night, none of this would have happened. If I just had told Christopher no.

I never should have come. Not to this city. Not to their apartment.

And most definitely, I should never have come to her.

Now she was the only thing in this miserable life I wanted. The one thing I could never really have.

No doubt, it was time to leave. For good. But I'd never claimed not to be a fool, and I just wanted to take a little bit more.

Hoisting myself up, I scaled the towering apartment wall, swung my legs over, and jumped to the other side. I grunted when I landed too hard. Nearly the entire complex lay dormant, and I lifted my face to the muggy air and sucked in a rattled breath as I crossed the apartment parking lot.

I could sense it, the disturbance filling the air, a dark energy that covered me, demanding that I bleed back into nothingness where I belonged.

But I didn't fucking want to.

Upstairs, I let myself into the silent apartment. Christopher's bedroom door sat wide open. No question, he was on the hunt, doing what the guy did best.

Quieting my feet, I crept across the room. At her door, I paused and tried to make sense of what I really felt.

When I first came here, anger was all I knew.

Tonight, I just felt fucking sad.

And I knew it was her.

It was her.

I turned the knob and stole inside her room.

Night seeped between the slats at her window, shadows playing their secrets out across her walls. Aly lay sprawled out on top of her bed, her body twisted slightly to the side. She wore these little lace panties and a matching white camisole. The dark mass of her thick hair was bunched up high over her head, the long strands spilling down all around her.

And her face . . .

I rubbed at my chest.

She was so beautiful it hurt to look at her. So fucking sexy and perfect and good. Like this light that shone into the blackness, lit up something in me that had been dead for so long.

Locking the door behind me, I quietly crossed the room, careful not to wake her. I just watched over her as I slowly undressed down to my underwear.

I needed to feel her.

God.

I needed to feel her.

The bed dipped as I eased down beside her and took her in my arms. Relief broke over me in waves, like maybe for a few seconds I could come up for air.

A contented sigh murmured from her lips, and her cheek found its way to my chest. "Jared," she exhaled, the word trickling out in her own relief. Gentle fingers crawled across my rib cage before they affixed to my opposite side.

I inhaled deeply, memorizing it all, the perfection I held in my arms. She consumed me in ways I never should have let her. The last month had been like a fucking dream I somehow had been given the chance to live.

I crushed her to me and buried my nose in her hair.

But it was just that.

A dream.

I don't get to have this.

Aly shifted to her elbow, and sincere green eyes opened to me. "I was worried about you." Her voice was all scratchy as she searched my face in the dimness of her room. "I tried to call you."

I blinked hard, trying to shun it all, this pain I didn't know how to deal with. "I hate that you worry about me." I stared up at her, knowing it was both a lie and God's honest truth.

Aly snuggled back in the crook of my arm. It was impossible

not to find comfort in her warmth. For a few seconds she held me close, soft fingers playing along my bare chest. She seemed to waver before she slowly climbed to her hands and knees, caging me. She just hovered there, looking down at me like maybe I meant too much, like when she looked at me she saw things she shouldn't see.

I mean, fuck, to her, I knew she did. I *knew* it. I knew she saw things that really weren't there.

Her eyes stayed fixed on mine as she gradually leaned down, her lips gentle as she pressed them to the rose at the center of my chest. "You miss her," she whispered.

I wheezed for the air her words knocked from my lungs. My heart squeezed so fucking tight, and I struggled to breathe under the pain crushing my chest. The memories I'd fought to block out all day came flooding through, unrepressed. Aly had destroyed all the barriers I fought so hard to keep in place, leveled them with the touch of her hand.

A trigger I was powerless against.

And I thought maybe I should be pissed off at her, saying something so ridiculously obvious. But I wasn't. Because in her words was everything I kept concealed. It wasn't pity or some fucking lame attempt at sympathy that I didn't even begin to want.

Aly understood.

Locking her to me, I fisted my hands in her hair and drew her face close to mine because I needed to see her.

I needed her. Every fucking second of every fucking day.

Fear lifted in a flurry of nerves. My mouth was so dry, but the words that had festered for years sought release from my tongue. I couldn't stop myself from talking, from telling Aly because I just needed someone to know. "I have no right to, Aly,

but I do. I miss her so much. I would do anything . . . give anything . . . to take it back."

Sadness swept across her features, and I hated that I put it
there. How many times had I warned her that she didn't need
my shit? That I had nothing to give and everything to take? I
fucking took and took and took.

And here I was again, ruining the good.

When would I ever stop?

Emotions rushed, guilt and anger and fear.

Aly dipped down and kissed the rose again. I gritted my
teeth, my hands like vises in her hair as she caressed over the
imprint of my sin, covered it wholly with her nose and her
mouth and her breath, showering me in everything I'd never
deserve.

She rose up, and unshed tears glistened in her eyes. "I'm
here for you, Jared. You know that, don't you? You can talk to
me. You can *tell* me," she murmured almost urgently. "Please
talk to me."

I squeezed my eyes shut. Visions flashed.

Aly took me by the face, forcing me to look at her. "It's
okay . . . You can trust me."

I couldn't look away from the eyes that watched me so ear-
nestly, like she really believed it would be.

Because it wasn't fucking *okay.*

That was the problem with Aly. With her, I was always
pretending it was. Pretending that it was okay to feel this way,
pretending it was okay to care about her so much. Pretending
that maybe someday all of this really might be okay.

And I couldn't fucking stop.

She swept her lips across mine. "Talk to me . . . please,
Jared . . . I'm here."

I clung to her a little harder, my tongue darting out to wet my lips, my voice ragged. "I was so reckless, Aly . . . so fucking reckless. Just a stupid punk kid."

Just like the assholes I constantly beat down in juvie, ungrateful for everything they'd been given.

Mindless.

Shameful.

Unforgivable.

That hatred flared, thrashed as it clamored through my spirit.

Deep inside, that warning system was blaring, a merciless siren that could never be silenced. It was shouting at me to shut my mouth before it was too late. Before I couldn't take it back.

But with Aly, it was already far too late.

My eyes dropped closed, and I grated out the words "I was so excited that morning." My body jerked as I completely freed the memories I'd suppressed for so long. It was kind of shocking how I could still remember exactly the way I felt. But after so many years, it was there, like this glaring reminder that promised I had no chance. "I thought I was on top of the world."

I tucked my chin to take in Aly's expectant eyes. They just watched me, comprehending too much. With a shaky hand, I reached out and fused myself to her, winding a lock of her hair around my finger. I turned my attention to the motion, fixed on it, as if holding Aly this way could somehow keep her from slipping away.

"I remember her coming up behind me while I stood at the mirror getting ready for school that morning. She'd wrapped her arms around my waist and told me it didn't matter how old I got, I would always be her baby. The whole week before I turned sixteen, whenever I walked into the room, she'd stop

what she was doing to take me in. Her gaze would drift over me
like she saw something fading away. She just kept saying she
couldn't believe how quickly time had passed."

And I'd never suspected time was getting ready to end.

My tone hardened. "She picked me up after school in that
fucking car my dad had promised me as long as I got good
grades and stayed out of trouble."

Saliva pooled in the back of my throat. I swallowed hard,
lines denting my brow as I got lost in that day.

"She drove me there, telling me stories the entire way." I
flinched, remembering how soft, how sweet, her voice had always been. "She kept peering out the windshield up at the sky.
She had this look on her face, Aly . . . almost like she was a little
bit sad. She told me that day felt almost exactly the same as the
day I'd been born. That the sky was blue and the air was cool."

I remembered it so clearly.

*"I was so anxious for you to come," she said, her somber eyes
brimming with affection. "I kept thinking you were going to be born
early because I was huge." She laughed, slanting a knowing smile over
at me. "But your grandma told me not to worry, I'd know when it
was time. Your dad and I were sitting outside when I felt you, and I
knew I was going to meet you that day. It feels just like yesterday."*

A ragged breath wheezed into my lungs. Aly's fingers trembled along my jaw, her touch overwhelming amid the sickness
clawing at my spirit, surging up, pressing down.

"She took me to my driver's test. Afterward I walked out of
that building with my license thinking I was the coolest fucking
thing in the world."

Revulsion boiled under the surface of my skin. Searing.
Burning. Blackening.

"She tossed the keys at me, and she said, 'I think these belong to you.'" I almost sneered. I'd never forget the pride that had filled her voice.

Aly exhaled, shaky and hard, her attention jumping all over my face like she had no idea where to look, and still I continued. "When we got in the car, she said she wanted to take me out to eat . . . to celebrate . . . just the two of us. But all I cared about was myself, Aly. All I cared about was the party your brother had planned for me and the fucking girl I was supposed to meet up with there. I *lied* to her . . ." The word cracked, and my finger twisted tighter in her hair.

If I'd just slowed down . . . if I had taken one goddamned hour and given it to her, then I wouldn't have taken it all.

"I told her I had a big project that was due on Monday and I had to go to this girl's house to work on it when I knew I was going to be spending the night partying with my friends."

I could so clearly feel it, the way my chest had felt so full. Like I was in control. Like nothing could touch me. Indestructible.

I'd never thought of myself as a bad kid. I mean, I was no angel, but I'd always hated when I disappointed my mom and dad.

But I'd been wrong. I'd been selfish. The worst kind of fool.

"I was in such a hurry, and she kept telling me to slow down. We were almost home. I knew I should stop . . . that the truck was too close . . . but I just gunned the engine and turned left across the intersection."

A tremor rolled down the length of Aly's body, and silent tears dripped unchecked down her face. Gripping her face between my hands, I forced her to look at me.

"She was screaming, Aly, fucking screaming at me to stop and I went anyway because all I wanted to do was get home so

I could go back out." My throat felt like gravel, and beneath the girl, I shook, the horror of that moment so clear, so vivid. Just like every night, it was like I could reach out and stop it. But I could never change what I'd done.

"That truck hit us so hard," I said, my voice low and rough. "Everything was so loud . . . God, Aly, it was so loud."

I could still hear it—piercing—the sound of metal shearing as my entire world was ripped apart.

"It was like I was weightless or something, but everything was heavy at the same time. Then we were jolted into this suffocating standstill. It was so quiet . . . too quiet." I sucked in a breath through my gritted teeth, reliving the pain of that moment. "I hurt everywhere, and I couldn't even make sense of why. Then I heard her moan." I forced the words out over the panic that bubbled up in my throat. "But it was my name, Aly . . . she was fucking saying my name, fucking crying for me."

My heart thundered, and my hands constricted on Aly's face. Her tears seeped into the webs of my fingers. She placed her hand over one of mine, holding me close. "It's okay," she murmured. Drawing my hand back, she kissed across my knuckles. "It's okay."

And I could feel it, the tears locked up inside that could never be shed, the ball of unspent sorrow that had burdened me for all of this condemned life. Agitation curled with it and sent a rush of anger surging through my veins. "When I looked at her . . ." My voice shook. "She was staring at me with this shocked horror, like she didn't know what'd happened any more than I did." I drew in a faltered breath. "But then I saw the blood. It was running down one side of her head and cutting across her face . . . but her shirt . . . it was soaked. God, I wanted to reach for her so bad, to help her, but I couldn't move my arms.

I could hear the sirens . . . they were coming . . . but she was breathing all funny. I was so scared, Aly . . . and I wanted to cry but I couldn't. . . ."

I could never forget it, could never outrun it, the way she'd struggled to speak, my name ragged on her lips.

"Jared . . ." She shuddered as she tried to smile, her face so sad when she promised me, "It'll be okay."

"It'll be okay," Aly whispered frantically, breaking free to kiss the rose at my chest, her fingers digging into my skin, promising again, "It'll be okay."

I grasped her by the outside of her shoulders. "It's *not* okay, Aly. Don't you get that? It's never gonna be okay. I *killed* my mom. I sat there and watched her die."

"No, Jared—"

Anger raged. I shook her. "Don't."

I knew she'd do this. I knew she'd try to convince me of things that weren't true. "What do you want from me, Aly? I keep telling you I don't have anything for you. I *can't* be what you want me to be."

Aly shook her head. Wetness soaked her face, pieces of her hair sticking to her cheeks, her green eyes desperate. "You are what I want, Jared. You're everything. Don't you understand that?"

My fingers dug into her arms. "No."

She started crying harder, little choked sounds hiccuping from her throat. She clung to me, hot tears dripping onto my chest as she battled to get closer while I pushed her away.

"I love you, Jared."

And there it was.

What I could never give and what I could never receive. The reason I should have fucking run that first night when I'd opened my eyes to find her green ones starting back at me. Because I'd felt it then, the shift in my wasted world.

I took my mom's life and now I owed mine. A penance. My payment.

I don't get to have this.

My hands clenched, fingertips burrowing into her soft flesh. "No, you don't, Aly. You feel something that's not real. You and I have both been hanging on to something that isn't really there."

I knew I'd do this. I knew I'd fucking take and ruin and destroy. I could see it clearly on her face.

"No, Jared, no . . . can't you feel this?" She wrestled to free my hand and pressed it over her heart. Erratic, her heart thundered under my palm. "You feel it. I know you do."

"Just stop, Aly." The words raked from my throat as a plea. "Just stop."

I did it.

I ruined the good.

"Yes . . . I do . . . I love you," Aly choked over the words again, forcing my hand closer to her heart. "I know you can feel it." She stared down at me, begging, "Tell me you love me, too."

"No." I ripped my hand away and grabbed her by both wrists, restraining her. "No, Aly. You're wrong. I *warned* you. I fucking warned you."

Aly thrashed, jerking free. Determined, she forced my arms down, her mouth back at my chest as she begged through her whisper, "You don't understand . . . I love you, Jared. Oh my God, I love you so much . . . Please tell me you love me. Please."

And I let her . . . I let her pin me down as she sobbed. The sound of it constricted every fucking cell in my body, as if each cell were compressed so tight there was nothing they could do but implode. My back arched as Aly covered me whole.

Because I wanted to. I wanted to love her. But that was impossible.

I don't get to have this.

"Stop," I cried, taking her back by the shoulders. I shook her hard. "Just fucking stop," I shouted. The words fell as a vicious plea from my mouth because I couldn't handle one more second of this torture.

The crash at Aly's door came without warning. The entire room shook, the impact vibrating along the walls. It took little for the thin wood to begin to splinter and crack.

Aly gasped, and her eyes widened with fear.

With the second kick, it busted open, flying back where it banged against the wall.

I was still clutching her, pinned under her body with the two of us wearing nothing but our underwear, when Christopher appeared in the doorway, vibrating with hostility. He pointed at me. "You're dead, you sick bastard."

He launched across the room, his face contorted in rage.

Aly screamed, lying over me like shield. "Christopher, don't!"

Her voice didn't penetrate his wrath. He was screaming his insults, maligning my name—as if there'd been anything left to malign. Every word he spoke was the truth. "You really think you'd ever be good enough for her? For my little sister?" I saw it all written there, the disgust lining his face. The hatred that I'd already known he would feel.

I destroyed everything I touched.

And I welcomed it, willed his assault because I deserved whatever beating he could give.

What I wasn't prepared for was Christopher yanking Aly off me and shoving her aside. He threw her back so fucking hard, his attack unwarranted and fierce as he directed some of the hatred I'd earned at her. Like he somehow didn't know how perfect she was, this girl that was the only good thing I knew.

Aly flew off her bed. The crack of her skull against the bookshelf reverberated through the room. She cried out, clutching the back of her head in her hands.

"Are you fucking stupid, Aly?" He spat the words at her like she was garbage while she lay curled on her side, crying. "You're really sleeping with this piece of shit?"

Aly whimpered, "Please, Christopher, you don't understand." Her voice was rough, tortured. Her hand fluttered out toward Christopher, a silent entreaty.

The tips of her fingers were covered with blood.

Fury rose in me like a tempest. Red colored my vision. I was blinded by it. The only thing I could see was what he had done.

He *hurt* her.

Jerking up, I dove for him, ramming him in the stomach with my shoulder. He grunted and stumbled back. Aly's cries rose from where she lay, an unwilling participant in all this shit, her cries taunting my ears.

He hurt her.

Christopher sneered. "Come on, you piece of shit."

My fist collided with soft flesh. The blow resonated around the room as pain exploded in my hand. Blood spurted from his nose and streaked in webbed lines down over his mouth.

The walls closed in and the red glowed.

So much blood . . . so much fucking blood. I couldn't stop it. I couldn't stop it. The girl cried.

My fists landed again and again, ragged breaths ripped

from my lungs, skin tearing under the rage leaking from my hands.

He fucking hurt her.

He hurt her.

I hurt her.

"Jared, oh my God, please stop." She'd jumped on my back, begging, trying to haul me away from her brother, who lay crumpled on the floor, his arms shielding his face while the blows continued to land with incoherent violence against his stomach and arms and sides, any fucking flesh I could find.

"Stop!" she was screaming, and screaming, and finally her pleas broke through. "You're hurting him . . . stop." The last she begged in my ear in a muted whisper. Her breath rushed across my face, invaded my senses, took me over.

In horror, I staggered back with my hands fisted in my hair.

And everything hurt. My hands. My heart. This blackened soul.

Aly slowly slid down my back, never let go as she found footing on the floor and wrapped herself around my waist. She buried her face in the small of my back. Pleading hands locked to my stomach, clinging to me as if I were something other than the piece of shit her brother knew I was. As if I were something more than ruin.

But *this* was the only thing I knew.

I stared down at my oldest friend as he climbed to his hands and knees, his head hanging. Blood dripped steadily from his face onto the floor. He pulled up his shirt and wiped his face, his back heaving as he tried to catch his breath. He cocked his head up.

He no longer appeared angry. He just looked like he felt sorry for me. "Just go, Jared. Get out and don't come back."

I began to back away, raising my hands in surrender. Because I was already gone.

From behind, Aly's arms tightened. "No."

"I'm sorry," I mumbled into the disordered air spinning through the room. I didn't even fucking know who I was apologizing to. I guessed both of them. No doubt, I'd done both of them wrong.

"Nnnnn . . . no. Jared, no. Please stay." Aly fought to hold on to me, but I wrestled away from the desperate hands clinging to my hips. I turned around to face the girl who'd become my refuge. A moment's respite in the life that had become my death sentence. Everything I'd never wanted to see shone up at me . . . love and heartbreak and belief in what could never be.

"I'm sorry," I said again. Because I really fucking was. I bunched her hands together and pressed them tightly between mine because I didn't want to let go. Then I gently nudged her back. "I'm so sorry, Aly, but you know I can't stay here."

Leaving her standing there, I ran out into main room and pulled on a pair of jeans, a tee, and my boots. It both crushed and relieved me that she didn't follow.

It took me all of five seconds to pack my things.

The only things that mattered I was leaving behind.

I slung my bag over my shoulder and hit the door. My feet pounded on the concrete stairs.

I was halfway across the lot when Aly's fractured voice pelted me from behind. "Jared, don't leave. Please . . . don't leave me."

The sound broke against my ears, pain lacerating me deep. I fucking couldn't stand listening to her cry, especially knowing I'd caused it. Tentatively, I chanced glancing behind me to find the girl who'd shaken something loose inside me. I really had been a fool to think she wouldn't follow.

She'd stopped long enough to pull on a pair of pajama pants. Now she ran barefoot down the stairs, that perfect face splotchy and red. Anguished.

Shit.

How was I supposed to deal with this? With her? With what I'd done?

Slowly, I turned, my arms held out at my sides in resignation as Aly closed the space between us. I continued to walk backward, because there was nothing else I could do.

She'd been the only one who managed to move me, a touch of joy in the unbearable dark.

Hot air gusted through the parking lot, and I was pretty sure it was fucking impossible to breathe. I never should have come here. Never should have touched her. Never should have taken what could never be mine.

"Jared." Aly was panting when she threw herself in my arms. Lifting her off the ground, I held her close, took comfort in her warmth one more time. I buried my nose in her hair, in the coconut and the sweet and the good and the girl who had for a few moments injected something more than pain into my shattered world.

Her voice came soft at my ear. *"Stay."*

Pain knocked at my ribs, pressed and pulsed while I held her near. Slowly, I lowered her to the ground. My hands shook as I brought them up to hold her face. My thumbs ran just under her eyes, brushing away her tears. She was staring up at me, her green eyes swimming with light, with affection, with the admission that had struck me like a stone that had been cast from her mouth.

I kissed her softly, savored the last taste of her as I breathed her in. Aly held me at the wrists, kissing me back, a soft groan from her mouth whispering so many things. She inundated all my senses, her comfort only amplifying the pain.

I drew back and swallowed around the ache. My hold tightened to emphasize my words, my voice strained with the promise of them. "I'm going to walk away and I'm going to forget about you, Aly. And you're going to do the same." I squeezed her, my hands pressed into her cheeks soaked with tears. "You're going to forget about me and find happiness. You're going to find someone who can love you exactly the way you deserve to be loved." I lowered myself so I could directly meet her face. "Do you hear me?"

Aly frantically shook her head. "No."

I blinked hard as I stepped back. "You will, Aly. I promise . . . *it'll be okay.*"

"No, Jared, no."

I backed away.

Aly clutched her stomach, bent over at the middle.

I turned around, my hands shoved in my pockets as I headed for my bike.

And I could fucking hear her crying, begging me to stay. "Jared, no. Please don't do this. Don't leave me. I love you."

I hopped on my bike and kicked it over. The engine rumbled loud, covering up her cries, blocking her out. I let my bike roll back from the parking spot, and I turned it around. From across the lot, I met the broken face of the girl who was screaming my name, imploring me through her tears. Christopher was holding her from behind, refusing to let her go.

She kicked her legs, struggling to break free. I could see her screaming it again and again.

Don't leave me. Don't leave me.

I revved the engine to drown her out.

I'd thought it was impossible to hate myself more than I already did. But I realized now, I hadn't even begun.

Nailed to the spot, I got lost in the torment that I'd inflicted on this girl, wishing for some kind of miracle that could erase it. That I could take it back.

Mocking laughter burned on my tongue. I was always wishing I could take it back.

In hesitation, my feet rocked on the ground, my hand gripping the throttle.

Christopher met my gaze, looking at me like he knew exactly what I was thinking, like he was offering some kind of fucked-up trade. He would take care of her if I would just go.

Aly continued to fight and beg and cry. One last time, I let my eyes lock on her. The engine garbled then roared when I teased at the throttle. Aly screamed as she wept, "Jared . . . no!"

And I was going to remember her just like that, fucking broken, the spoil of my ruin.

Because this was what I did.

I ruined everything I touched.

TWENTY

Aleena

"Jared, no!"

As if I were detached, the words echoed in my ears. As if they weren't mine. As if this voice couldn't possibly belong to me.

Because this voice hurt too much.

I watched his taillight disappear as he rounded the corner, the thunder of his bike bleeding into the night.

Devastation crushed me. Every hope I had splintered, fragmenting as they were torn away.

"Jared, no."

This time it was a whimper, an utterance of the heart Jared had taken with him when he turned his back on me.

Once I'd promised that I'd take him any way I could have him. That I would take any piece he offered. Willingly, I'd submitted to the risk. Somewhere inside me, I'd always known I would lose him.

I just wasn't prepared for what that would really feel like.

"Jared . . . ," I whispered again.

Steadfast, Christopher held me from behind.

I gave up my fight and buckled, clutching my stomach as I tried to hold myself up.

But Christopher already was.

His mouth was urgent against the back of my head as he supported all of my weight. "Shh . . . Aly . . . come on, please stop crying," he begged.

But I could do nothing but weep for the man who had just wrecked something so true, for the man who held so much hatred for himself he couldn't see what we really had.

"Come here." Christopher slowly twisted me around in his arms and pulled me against the safety of his chest. My arms were pinned between us, my hands clutching his shirt. "It's okay," he promised.

I cried a little harder.

Christopher went rigid, one arm holding me tight around the back as he pointed somewhere behind me. "Why don't you all go back inside and mind your own damned business? There isn't anything out here for you to see."

Christopher mumbled close to me ear, "Come on, Aly, we need to get you upstairs. I think we woke up the entire complex, and neither of us needs to deal with this shit right now."

I was barely able to force a nod.

Christopher wrapped his arm around my waist and led me toward the staircase. I held on to the railing, listing to the side, trying to stand under the pain forcing me down. My feet dragged as I staggered up the stairs.

Christopher held me a little closer. "It's okay, Aly . . . Come on, you can make it."

Inside, the apartment was too quiet, echoing with what I'd lost.

Every part of me hurt, an ache so deep I felt it in places I didn't know existed.

He was gone.

Nausea turned my stomach. "I think I'm going to be sick." I ran to the bathroom and fell to my knees, purging the riot tearing through my insides.

Ravaging.

Pillaging.

Ruining.

He'd promised me he would.

I dropped my head, crying toward the floor, the hard floor digging into my knees.

I *knew* he would.

Christopher followed me in and latched the door behind him. He dug through the bottom cabinet for a washcloth and turned on the faucet, getting it damp.

Then he kneeled down at my side. "Here." He wiped my mouth and the sweat drenching my forehead. His face was a mess of sympathy and anger and the remnants of Jared's violence. Blood had dried in smeared streaks where he'd wiped it. One side of his mouth had already begun to swell, and a bruise was forming on the outside of his right eye.

He got up and rinsed it and then handed the cool cloth back to me.

"Thank you," I mumbled quietly. On my side, I slumped all the way to the hard floor.

Christopher sank down across the cramped room, slouching up against the closed door with his legs lying limp out in front of him, staring at me, his body just as beaten as my heart.

"I'm sorry," I whispered, clutching the cloth to my mouth, searching for comfort where none could be found.

He dropped his gaze and shook his head, then raised it again, his gaze pinning me with a portion of the anger that had spurred his intrusion into my room fifteen minutes before. "How long was it going on, Aly?"

I swam in my shame. Not of the fact of Jared and me, but for keeping it from my brother. Yeah, I was twenty, and Christopher had no right to tell me I couldn't. But the way we'd gone about it was wrong. "A month . . ."

The answer couldn't even penetrate the thick air because I think both Christopher and I knew it wasn't true.

"Longer, I guess," I finally said, my fingers wringing the washcloth as if it would give me courage to speak. "He started coming to my room a couple of weeks after he got here . . . but at first we would just talk." This slow sadness seeped through my veins. "Over time I think we both became something neither of us could live without."

And I had no idea how I would live without him now.

Christopher drew up his knees, propped his forearms on them. "Why didn't you just tell me? You don't think I would have understood?"

I frowned. "Would you have? Because it didn't seem that way tonight."

Groaning, he released a heavy breath toward the ceiling. "I don't know, Aly . . . Maybe I wouldn't have. Maybe I would have flipped out like I did tonight." He looked straight at me. "Either way, keeping it from me was wrong. I heard the two of you fighting when I was walking down the hall . . . and shit . . . I *knew* something was going on between the two of you. I mean, I fucking point-blank asked him, Aly, and he swore that you were just friends, said he only cared about you and was looking out for you. And here I invite the asshole into our apartment, and he's the one taking advantage of you."

"He wasn't taking advantage of me, Christopher." My voice strengthened as I denied Christopher's assertion. "I love him."

I loved him so much.

And he was gone.

A sharp pain stabbed me in my gut, deep, deeper than any place I'd ever felt before. I shuddered and wheezed.

"Yeah, well, you made that abundantly clear tonight." Sarcasm wound its way through the words, before he blinked, and his expression filled with sympathy. "You always have, haven't you?" It wasn't a question, just a realization that finally latched on to his consciousness. As if disillusioned, Christopher rubbed his battered face, a choked sound forced from his throat. "Shit . . . I'm such an idiot."

Remorse seemed to hit him, and he wrenched both hands through his hair and spoke toward the floor. "God, Aly, I can't believe I hurt you like that. I really am sorry. I had no right to react like I did. I just . . . lost it."

"None of us were thinking straight," I whispered.

There was no justification for anything that had happened tonight, but I knew he'd never purposely harm me, and it hurt too much to be angry with my brother. I'd already been stripped bare, every place in me left raw. I couldn't deal with Christopher now. I was too consumed by this unbearable void suddenly prominent in the middle of me.

He sighed and focused on me. "I know you care about him, and I care about him, too, but he's messed up, Aly. Dangerous. It's best that he's gone." He shook his head. "I heard what you said . . . what he said, and you deserve better than that."

My body shook, recoiled at the words.

I'd known I shouldn't say it, that the love I held for Jared should only be shown and never spoken. But listening to him talk about his mom was one of the hardest things I'd ever done, hearing the hatred that had poured from his mouth, feeling the blame he harbored so close. Worse was knowing how the guilt had destroyed him ever since that day. I wanted to take it away, show him he was worthy of being loved—that I loved him and I always would. I didn't even know how to regret saying it. Even with him gone, I still needed him to know. To take that piece of me with him that I could never give to anyone else, because I would always belong to him.

"He's really gone, isn't he?" I whispered.

Grief gripped me by the heart.

"Yeah, Aly, he's really gone."

TWENTY-ONE

February 3, 2006

Aly crossed her arms over her chest and lifted her face to the cool winter sky. Evening approached. Pinks were strewn across the deepening blue, twilight casting a striking chill in the air. Aly tugged her sweatshirt a little tighter to keep herself warm. After school, she'd gone to Rebecca's house to hang out, one of her best friends who lived in the next neighborhood over. But she was supposed be home before it got dark.

Her backpack bounced on her shoulders as she hurried. Turning right on the street where her family lived, Aly jogged across the street and up the sidewalk to the front door. She opened it, rushing in, the announcement of her arrival poised on her tongue.

Then she stumbled to a stop.

Her hand shot to the wall for support, and a chill so much different than the one she'd felt outside trickled down her spine like a rush of frigid ice. She shook and crept forward, canting her ear to the sounds coming from her mother in the living room.

She was crying.

No.

Not just crying.

Aly had only heard her mother sound like this once before—the day Aly's grandma died.

She was weeping.

The cries slithered along the floor, crawled up the walls, pierced Aly's ears. Fear and panic struck her heart. It pounded hard. She felt along the wall, her back pressed to it and her eyes pinched shut as if it would protect her from whatever had done this to her mother. She stopped at the archway to the living room, holding her breath as she risked peeking inside the room.

Her mom was on the floor, on her knees. Her dad kneeled over her, rubbing her back, trying to calm her. But her mother sobbed toward the floor, completely inconsolable.

"Shh, Karen . . . I'm right here . . . I'm right here."

"Dave . . ." She said his name as if maybe he could take away whatever was hurting her.

In some sort of daze, Aly wandered out into the middle of the room and stood there gaping at her mom falling apart. The ball of dread sitting like a rock in her stomach promised her something was very, very wrong.

Her dad caught sight of her. "Aly, sweetheart," he said, his voice instantly on edge, protective, as if he wanted to shield his daughter from whatever was happening, but was unwilling to leave his wife's side.

With a short gasp, her mom jerked her head up. "Aly, baby."

She struggled to climb to her feet, though her shoulders stayed slumped and her back bowed.

For two seconds they just stared at each other, and then Karen rushed toward Aly and took her in her arms, lapsing back into tears that she expelled in the crook of Aly's neck. "Oh my God, my baby . . . my baby . . ."

"Mom, what's wrong?" Aly begged. Right then, she just needed her mom to tell her that everything was going to be okay, the way she always had done when Aly had been a little girl. In just the assurance of her words, she made everything better.

Karen edged back and took her face in her hands. Her head tilted to the side, her brown eyes so sad.

Aly knew this time whatever her mother was getting ready to say wouldn't be bringing her any comfort. She shuffled her feet, and that rock in her stomach took it all the way to the floor.

"Baby . . . there was an accident . . . Helene . . ." She trailed off, seemingly unable to complete the thought, her expression steeped in sorrow.

Aly shook her head, trying to make sense of the stream of turmoil coming from her mother's mouth.

Karen's lips quivered. "Helene . . . she's gone. Baby, she's gone."

"What?" Confusion flooded through Aly's consciousness. She was unwilling to believe the meaning of her mother's words. "What do you mean?"

Her mom winced and grimly drew together her lips.

Aly shook her head.

No.

Helene was dead?

"Jared was driving them back from getting his license . . . they said he pulled out in front of a truck."

And Aly could feel her mom's heartbreak, could feel it quivering in her touch. But in that moment, Aly was numb with disbelief. It seemed impossible.

"Is Jared okay?" she finally managed to whisper.

Her mother shrank, her lip blanching as she bit it hard. "They don't know if he's going to make it." The words bled from her mouth, slow and unsure, filled with sympathy, but sharp with grief. "He's in bad shape, Aly. Neil just called . . . He's at the hospital. Your dad and I need to go."

"I'm coming with you."

Her dad stepped in. "I want you to stay here with Christopher. He was supposed to spend the night at a friend's. I just called him and told him what happened. He's on his way home."

"No, Dad, I want to come."

"I think it's best if you stay here. I'll call you once we get there to let you know what's happening."

"Dad, please."

He hugged her, smoothing his hand over the back of her head, his tone pleading. "Just stay here, okay, sweetheart? For me? We need to be there to help Neil with Courtney . . . and Jared . . . We just don't know what we're going to find when we get there."

He left her standing there, stunned, unable to absorb the blow. It tumbled through her like a storm.

She loved Helene. So much. Family . . . that's what she'd been. It didn't matter that they weren't related by blood. Helene had been there in every memory that counted.

But it was the thought of Jared being taken from her life

that pushed Aly's back up against the wall, her chest heaving when the grief finally struck.

"No," she whispered. "Please, no."

"Today we gather to celebrate the life of Helene Rose Holt."

A deep, mournful sob broke in the row directly in front of Aly as the minister began to speak. Jared's father, Neil, sat hunched over as he wept, and Neil's father placed a hand on his slumped back. The older man's words were indistinct as he whispered something in his son's ear. Neil Holt shook harder and wept more.

Aly sucked in a breath, unable to hold back the tears falling from her eyes. Her throat felt so tight and her chest so empty. She'd been crying for days, and she didn't know if she was ever going to stop.

Beside her, her mother squeezed her hand so tightly it hurt, as if the pain emanating from Neil Holt was her own burden, too.

Aly squeezed her back. None of this felt real to her. How could it be? It seemed impossible that someone could so suddenly be ripped away without warning. It seemed savage and cruel.

A gust of cold air stirred the surface of the ground and rustled through the barren trees. Branches creaked as they bowed, whining, as if they felt the void, too.

In front of her to the right, Courtney blinked down on Aly with her bright blue eyes. Her grandmother held her on her lap, Courtney's arms wrapped around the old woman's neck as she peered back at the gathered crowd, the nine-year-old little girl looking more stunned and confused than anything else.

On the other side of Aly, Christopher sat with his elbows on his knees, his face hidden in his hands. Most of the week he'd remained stoic, outwardly unaffected by the horror that had befallen their families. But Aly heard him crying at night, as if he couldn't hold his own misery in anymore. He just wasn't capable of showing anyone the way he really felt. Seeing him like that had scared her.

But it was Jared who terrified her.

Aly's bleary eyes settled on the back of Jared's head where he sat to the left of his father. He was unmoving. Still as stone.

As if he weren't really there. His body was, but he wasn't.

They'd waited to have the funeral until the day after he was discharged from the hospital. He'd been there for nearly a week recovering from broken ribs and a punctured lung. The doctors said he'd been lucky.

Aly stared at the back of his blond head of hair. It appeared stark white under the glaring winter sky, strands of it thrashing in the sharp gusts of wind that cut across the joyless ground, the relentless stirring at complete odds with the boy who sat comatose.

Lifeless.

Aly's heart hurt. It'd been hurting for days, but seeing him like this was killing her. Only once had her mom allowed her to go with her to the hospital to visit him. The entire time Jared had pretended to be asleep, as if he didn't know they were there. But Aly knew . . . She'd seen the flicker of his lids and the awareness in the twitch of his fingers.

What she'd expected today, she didn't know. Crying, she guessed. That she would witness him mourn the way he should because Aly couldn't imagine anything more horrible than losing your mother. She wanted to reach out, to touch him and tell him it was okay and that no one would blame him for grieving.

She wanted to tell him it wasn't his fault.

But he just sat there, staring directly ahead as if he had some sort of detached fascination with the large spray of red roses blanketing the top of the white casket. Around it, pictures were arranged on easels: a picture of Helene as a little girl, one in her cap and gown, dancing with Neil on her wedding day, her face filled with absolute joy as she held her newborn baby boy, the last a recent family picture of the four of them. But Jared's attention never strayed.

Maybe it was wrong that Aly noticed, that she was so aware of every move he made.

Helene's sister, Cindy, rose and slowly approached the podium that had been set up to the left of the casket. Cindy sniffled and dabbed under her eyes with a tissue. "If you're here today it's because you had the great honor of knowing my little sister, Helene. I'm sure you'd all agree with me that she was the one of the kindest, most genuine people you'd ever meet." A low murmur of agreement rippled through the crowd. "She couldn't walk in a room without making everyone else smile just because her joy was so infectious."

She wet her lips, then continued. "My sister was the definition of warmth. Beautiful. Unforgettable. She cared so deeply for everyone. But her family was the most important thing in her world." Cindy looked directly upon the front row. "Neil, Jared, Courtney . . . she loved you all so very much. I don't want you to ever forget that. I'm going to keep those memories of her close to my heart, and I hope you're able to do the same." She covered her mouth with her hand, her eyes pressed tight. She could barely continue to speak. "Thank you, everyone, for being here, for celebrating my sister's life. No doubt she is watching over us now, thankful each of you is here."

She stepped down and the minister took her place. He led them in a prayer. A somber and final "Amen" rolled over the gathering.

The casket was slowly lowered into the ground.

Aly's mom whimpered.

This time Aly was the first to squeeze her mother's hand. Her mom was hurting, and she wanted her to know that she understood. Helene had been her best friend, as close to her as a sister. Aly would never forget the way Helene's warm laughter had constantly filled their house, the lilt of her quiet but strong voice, the way her kind eyes had watched and loved and encouraged.

Aly was going to miss her, too.

Once the coffin was fully lowered, the minister made an announcement that all could come forward to the grave to give their final respects. Afterward they were all invited to a reception taking place at the Moore home.

Jared's grandfather helped Neil to stand, stayed at his side as he lumbered over the hard ground. He took a single, long-stemmed rose from a basket and dropped it into his wife's grave. For a few minutes, he just stood there, staring, lost in the bleakness of finality, of what could never be taken back, never recovered, never regained.

She tried to hold it in, but a soft sob escaped from Aly's throat. She caught a glimpse of Neil's face when he turned around. The man had forever worn an affable smile, and now Aly wondered if he'd ever smile again.

The rest of the front row stood to pay their respects, all except for Jared, who didn't so much as flinch. People cried as they approached the grave. Each one dropped a rose to the top of Helene's casket and said a last good-bye.

Aly followed her mother and father out, took her own rose, and tossed the flower into Helene's open grave. With her eyes shut tight, she murmured toward the ground, though she was speaking toward the heavens. "I'll miss you so much, Helene." Wiping her eyes, she stood aside and watched as the sea of black made its way by the grave that would permanently mark Helene's death.

The entire crowd made their pass, before they scattered out to gather in groups where people wept and hugged and comforted each other.

Aly couldn't help noticing those who whispered, ones who cast sidelong glances speculating about the boy who sat utterly alone, staring blankly ahead at the spot where his mother's casket had rested before she'd been lowered into the ground. Anger twisted through Aly's gut, and she wanted to lash out at them, to tell them to stop judging because they didn't come close to understanding who Jared was. None of them knew the kindness of the boy who had always thought of everyone, the one who loved his mother and who was so obviously destroyed.

Breaking from the circle of her family, Aly made her way back to the basket of single, long-stemmed roses, taking one in her hand. The few that remained had been at the bottom of the pile, the wilted, red petals crushed. Cautiously, she made her way over to Jared, searching for some sort of recognition in his eyes. Still there was nothing. Aly gently laid the rose on his lap and whispered, "I'm so sorry, Jared."

His hair fluttered in the breeze, and Jared just stared.

Two months had passed since the accident. Everything had changed.

Aly was in her room with her door shut, sitting cross-legged on her bed with her sketch pad on her lap. The small lamp on her nightstand softly glowed against the walls of her room. Furiously her pencil brushed across the thick, textured paper. Shadows sprang to life, her worry inscribed on the page.

So many nights she spent awake worrying for Jared, completely powerless, while she watched him fade away. How badly she wished for some way to help him, to make him see that he was only hurting himself more, and that Helene would never want this for him.

Rumors had begun to surface, trickling all the way from the high school to the middle school. They terrified Aly more than anything because she saw their truth. She saw it in his eyes every time the two of them passed, even when he didn't seem to even know she was there. It was like he saw right through her, like he was absent. Gone.

Helene was gone and now Jared was, too.

Aly stilled her pencil when she heard the soft knock at her door. "Come in."

Her mother popped her head in. "Are you still up? It's past eleven, and you have school in the morning."

Aly glanced at her pad. "Sorry, Mom . . . I just . . ."

Softly, her mother smiled. "I know, sweetheart." Karen came the rest of the way in. Sitting at the edge of her bed, she ran a gentle hand through Aly's hair. "Are you doing okay?"

"I think so." Gazing up at her mom, she asked, "Are you?"

Aly's mother pursed her lips, then offered a small, reassuring nod. "Some days. It's getting better." Then she placed a kiss on Aly's forehead. "Get some rest. It's late."

"Okay."

Karen crossed to the door and looked back at her daughter. "I love you, Aly."

"Love you, too, Mom."

The next day, Aly rushed out into the bright morning sun with her backpack slung over her shoulder. If she missed her bus, she'd have to walk to school, and that was about the last thing she felt like doing since she'd spent half the night awake. Even when her mom told her to get some rest, none would come. She felt agitated, like she could feel something building— something bad. It wasn't a premonition. It was just plain obvious.

Aly came to a stop when she saw the boy she couldn't get off her mind walking ahead of her on the opposite sidewalk toward the main street. Spring had come, the morning air crisp but warm, but still Jared wore a heavy black leather jacket, his attention focused entirely on his boots as they ate up the ground in his long stride.

She rushed across the street, closing the space between them. "Jared, wait."

He didn't even acknowledge her.

She called out to him again, "Hey, Jared, wait up."

He finally hesitated before he turned around, rushing a nervous hand through his hair. He bounced anxiously as he looked at her. Through her, really. "Aly . . . ," he managed to say.

Aly frowned, unable to look away from his pupils, which had all but disappeared, his light blue eyes too wide, frozen ice.

He glanced away, and he raked his hand through his hair again. "Hey," he mumbled into the distance.

Aly fidgeted. "How are you?" She cringed. What the hell was she thinking, asking something so dumb? How did she think he was?

Jared turned back to her, just blinked, looking everywhere but at her face.

"So, uh, we miss you at the house," Aly ventured, feeling more like an idiot, completely out of her element. But weren't they all? None of this was *their* element. Everything was wrecked, and all of them had been left on foreign ground. "Why don't you come around anymore? I know Christopher would like to see you."

She would like to see him.

She needed to see him.

Jared twitched. "I've just been busy," he said at the same moment he looked behind him, back toward the busy street. "Listen, I've got to go. I'll see you around."

Aly's heart sank. She stood watching the boy who consumed her walk away from her, his head hanging toward the ground as he gripped the hair at the back of his head.

Aly closed her eyes, wishing for a way to make things better, even though she knew there was absolutely nothing she could do.

When she opened them, he was gone.

Aly frowned when she saw her dad's car parked in the driveway after she got off from school that day. He never made it home before five.

Aly cracked open the door. The second she did, she knew something was off, could feel the tension in the air. Their house had been so much like that lately—off—emotions rising, then waning, heartbreak, then glimpses of joy, slipping back into overwhelming sadness. They'd diagnosed her mom with grief-related depression, had written her some prescriptions to help her get through the time they said would pass. There'd been some days when she never got out of bed, but like her mom had said last night, she was getting better.

Lately Aly never knew what kind of day it was going to be when she walked through the door.

Now she tiptoed inside. Today she wasn't met with the deluge of sadness. Instead she found anger.

From the foyer, Aly listened to her dad yelling accusations. "They found heroin *and* stolen pills in his locker, Christopher . . . You're telling me you knew nothing about this?"

Dread seized Aly, her heart feeling like it was going to falter while it pounded at the same time.

No.

Aly eased closer, hid herself up against the wall so she could peer inside at what was happening in the kitchen where Christopher sat on a stool at the bar and their father stood looming over him.

"Dad, I promise you," Christopher said, his voice low and pleading. "I haven't been doing any of that stuff. Yeah, I drink some and I've gotten high a few times, but I haven't been *using*. And it's not like Jared wants anything to do with me now, anyway."

Christopher's confession did nothing to calm their father. Instead he roared, "I can't believe you, Christopher. After all the trust we put in you? Go to your room. You're grounded . . . indefinitely."

"Dad—"

"Go."

Christopher's chair screeched against the tiled floor, and he stormed down the hall to his room. The slam of his door rattled through the house.

"Don't you think you're being a little harsh on him, Dave?" Karen looked up when she spoke. Aly could see she'd been crying again. "He's sixteen . . . and the last two months have been really tough on everyone. You need to be a little more understanding."

"What I don't understand, Karen, is how Jared could do this to his dad. After everything? Does he have any idea the hell he's already caused his family? And now he's doing something like this? My God, Karen, the kid had enough drugs in there to get him on intent to sell. He'd better thank his lucky stars he only got expelled and they're charging him with possession."

"He's hurting, Dave."

"That's bullshit, Karen. That boy doesn't care about anyone but himself, and I don't want my kids anywhere near him. I won't stand aside and let him take my family down, too."

Aly's mom started crying again. "Dave, please."

Her dad pressed his palms to his wife's cheeks and tilted her face up to him. "I'm just protecting my family, Karen . . . what's most important to me. Don't ask me to compromise that."

Aly slid to the floor. She'd already known . . . had seen it so clearly this morning. She wasn't surprised. It didn't mean she wasn't terrified for him, that he wasn't hurt and scared and broken.

Because she knew that's exactly what Jared was.

TWENTY-TWO

Jared

Buzzing filled the confines of the small room, the vibration of the gun an oppressive weight. I struggled for air. A slow blaze lit along the surface of my skin, the burn of the needle branding my chest. I was fucking gritting my teeth, my hands clenched into the tightest fists, my heart racing.

I always knew she'd be another mark. Another scar. Another sin to add to the insurmountable others.

"You doin' okay, man?" The tattoo artist pulled away from the job, looking up at me in twisted concern, like maybe I was the biggest pussy to ever step through his door.

The guy had me pegged. I was in pain. But not the kind of pain he was faulting me for. This hurt in the fucking darkest place of my spirit, where the obscene consorted with the vile.

"Yep. Perfect," I forced out, my nails digging into the palms of my hands.

The guy wiped up some of the blood and ink with a paper towel, then leaned in close to color more. "Just about finished here."

I nodded, but was unable to say anything while I submitted to the abuse the memories of her face inflicted on my already defeated mind. It was already November. More than two months had passed since I left her begging my name, since I fully laid it all to waste, since I swung the final blow.

The greatest lie I'd ever told had been told to Aly.

Yeah, I'd walked away, but there wasn't a chance in this godforsaken world that I could forget about her.

That girl was unforgettable.

Fucking perfect. Too bright to fully see.

So I'd done my best at blocking her out. The days had blurred and bled, slowed and sped in an unending spiral of city lights and drugs and alcohol. I'd filled my body with just about anything I could find, searching for something to take away the ache she had left behind. But there was no high that could reach the bottom of this low. Nothing came close to touching it. Nothing dimmed or dulled it. Nothing could erase it. It was like this cancer that ate and fed, rotted and decayed.

Memories of her had only intensified the void that her touch had somehow managed to fill. Even if it were only for a time, she had, and maybe that's what stung the most. I'd been foolish enough to think I'd treasure those memories, as if I'd find some sort of comfort in them once I was gone. Now I'd give anything to take them away. Because I couldn't fucking stand knowing she might be hurting like me.

There wasn't a second that went by that I didn't think of her, that I didn't regret the fact that I had skimmed and touched and taken, not a second that passed that I wasn't wishing that I could take a little bit more.

Yeah, I was one sadistic masochist.

"This looks really cool. Wasn't sure this was going to blend in with that other tat, but it came out good."

I said nothing, just tensed and ground my teeth while he seared her to me.

When the guy finished, he cleaned and covered it. "You're all set. Take that off and wash it in a couple of hours."

"Yeah, I got it."

I paid him, left a hefty tip because I figured he deserved one after having to deal with my squirming ass the entire time I'd sat in his chair.

A chime jingled overhead as I stepped out onto the sidewalk. Night lay low against the backdrop of the lurid street.

Vegas, baby.

Dark laughter rumbled deep in my throat as I shoved my fists in the pockets of my jeans. People flocked here to seek its pleasures, to indulge and gratify. But this . . . this was what they didn't want to see, what they didn't want to acknowledge, the seedy and the slum, the addiction and poverty that abounded on the outer streets, tucked just out of sight.

Why the fuck I'd come here, I didn't know. I'd intended to return to Jersey, but I ended up in the shittiest motel on Fremont Street. It was like I couldn't physically force myself to go that far, couldn't stand the thought of placing so much distance between us that it would seem as if our worlds didn't even meet.

I scoffed.

They never had.

All of it had been *the* fantasy. All of it *the* girl. As if I could have ever been enough. As if I could ever *stay*.

The only reality that remained was the spoils of what I'd taken.

I strode down the sidewalk, ducking my head between my

hunched shoulders, doing my best to avoid all the stares, the taunts, and the pleas. It was impossible. Voices swarmed, filled my ears, fueling this foreboding that fried every last one of my nerves. I was on the fucking edge. I knew it.

If there was any way to end it, I would. But fate was never my friend. No doubt, it'd intervene and once again condemn me to live out this life.

I just didn't know how to endure as I paid out this debt.

I headed down the wrong street I'd been down every night. When I got here, it'd taken me about an hour to figure this shit out. All I'd had to do was look for the right dead end.

Tonight, Keith was exactly where I knew I would find him.

I bought a bag, balled the poison up in my fist, and crammed it back down deep in my pocket, fucking hating myself more than I ever had.

The easy way out.

I *knew* I didn't get the easy way out. I'd accepted that the day they sent me away. There was no escape from this truth. Even if I touched on oblivion, reality always came back. Still I tried. I fucking tried because I couldn't do anything but run from the pictures of Aly's face that constantly assaulted my mind. The sick part was how badly I wanted to hang on to them, too, the way she'd made me actually *feel*, as if I were almost alive.

I jogged across the street toward the dump that I called home. The red VACANCY sign flashed near the front of the destitute lot, like this eternal beacon for the damned, because I couldn't imagine a soul saved in this infernal place.

Hell.

No question, that's where I'd found myself.

I let myself into the isolation of the motel room. I flipped the light switch. A dull bulb blinked to life in the corner of the room, illuminating the hollow space.

Never before had I felt so alone.

Wandering in, I let the door latch shut behind me, rubbing a hand down my face and over my jaw.

I looked around.

God, I missed her more than I had any right to.

Slowly, I crossed the room. Springs squeaked as I sat down on the edge of the worn-out bed. Grabbing the half-empty bottle of Jack from the floor by the neck, I unscrewed the cap and lifted it to my lips. Welcomed the burn. Wanted it. I lifted it again and again, swallowing down the fuel that fed the fire that continuously raged.

How much time passed while I sat there, I didn't know. Time no longer mattered. Numbness crawled out along my limbs, not enough to erase, just enough to distort, to cloud the fucking unbearable ache that had bound itself to my heart and mind.

My head spun and the bag burned in my pocket.

Climbing to my feet, I stumbled toward the dingy porcelain sink mounted against the far wall. I pulled my shirt over my head and worked loose the bandage from my chest. Heavily, I leaned on the sink, staring at myself in the mirror, unable to look away from the eyes staring back.

Sickness seethed in the pit of my stomach, stretching out, clawing at my insides, which seemed to be fighting for a way out of this body, like they, too, wished for an escape. I pulled the bag from my pocket. Sweat beaded up on my forehead, hatred pouring free.

I clenched my hand around it, knowing it wasn't the drug, but Aly that had a hold on me.

Motherfucking trigger.

It burned against my flesh, and I squeezed it tighter, felt the anxiety wind me tight. Every damned day, it was this way. I was like this fucking disaster because I didn't want anything but to be free, but there was no freedom for the condemned.

And I hated.

I hated.

I hated.

I slammed my fist into the mirror, shattering it into a million pieces. "Fuck!" I roared, the sound bouncing off the walls.

I don't want this.

The mirror rained down, shards of glass splintering as they fell, crashing down into the sink, pinging as they skittered across the floor. The skin on my knuckles gave, splaying wide. Blood seeped forward. And I could feel it, the snap as I finally slipped over the edge I'd been teetering on for so long. My fists met the wall and remnants of the mirror again and again as if I could beat this need out of me. The bag was crushed so tightly in my hand it was as if the force alone would cause it to disintegrate. Evaporate. Cease to exist.

Or maybe I would.

There was no pain, just the fury that had taken me whole for the last six years.

And I was panting, reeling, gasping.

Fucking lost.

"Shit." I clutched my head in my bloodied hands and the bag fell to the floor, my eyes frantic as they darted around the confines of the suffocating room. That feeling of confinement only escalated the anxiety that gripped me tight, provoking the rage inside. I choked, couldn't breathe.

I couldn't do this anymore.

Snatching my shirt from the floor, I dragged it back over my head, fumbled around for my keys, and ran out into the night. Tonight the darkness was thick, no moon in the sky, just the echoes of distant revelry. My bike gleamed like this flagrant symbol of escape just outside my door. I kicked it over and flew from the lot, pegged the throttle as I took the bike to the road.

The cool fall air beat furiously at my face, the rumble of my bike vibrating in my ears. I sped through the streets, lost myself in the frenzy, gave in to the need to escape even when I knew I never could. I had no idea where I was going because I had no place to go. This . . . this was my fate because I had no right to be in this world.

The lights thinned out around me as I consumed the road, and the city grew dim as I left it behind. I hit the open desert, the glare of my headlight splaying out across the pavement. My hand was fucking shaking as I pinned the throttle as far as it would go.

I hated.

God, I hated.

I forced it faster, this rage inside me spurring me forward, pressing me harder. There was nothing for me in this city.

Nothing for me anywhere.

That emotion brimmed to the edges of me, heavy and thick, my chest tight with that fucking rock that would forever be lodged just at the base of my throat. I leaned into the curves and welcomed the air that pelted and whipped, the chill that stung, welcomed the anger and the hate and the anxiety that were my constant companions.

They were the only steady I knew. The only things I could count on.

I shouted into the driving wind, cast my fury at the nothingness because that was exactly what I was.

Ahead, the road curved to the left. Sharper than I thought. I took it hard, and I felt the quiver of the bike. I fought against the wobble of the handlebars, fought to conquer the shot of instability that rolled through the length of the bike. I righted it and struggled to focus on the blurring road. I blinked hard, trying to clear the fog from my mind.

An abrupt right came up fast. So fast.

"Fuck" fell silently from my mouth, maybe as a plea as I flew into the turn. I leaned and braked hard, everything shaking before I felt the back tire begin to skid. Then the front wheel caught.

And I was flying.

Weightless.

A long time ago I'd lost control. I'd lost it the moment I'd given in to carelessness, when I'd taken the most important thing in this world and set it aside while I strove for the trivial.

Darkness surrounded me, gutted me, wrapped me inside out. And it was quiet. So fucking quiet, nothing but my mother's face filling up the bleakness that devastated my heart and mind. For a moment, I thought maybe I could feel her running her fingers through my hair, like she'd always done when I was a little boy, thought I could hear her soft, gentle voice whispering in my ear, thought I saw her looking at me like I was the light . . . when in reality she'd been mine.

I missed her. God, I missed her so much and it hurt and I wanted her to know it was the greatest mistake I'd ever made.

She shifted and faded, giving way to the girl. And Aly was looking at me exactly the same way, like maybe I was her light in the same way she'd unwittingly become mine.

My eyes went wide as I felt the ground rush up.

It was Aly.

Aly.

Aleena.

And for the first time since the day I turned sixteen, I didn't want to die.

TWENTY-THREE

Aleena

Loving someone is one of the biggest chances we ever take. Maybe the most unfair part of it is that it's rarely a conscious decision we've made. It's something that blossoms slow or hits us hard, something that stirs and builds gradually, or something that shocks us with its sudden intensity. And sometimes it's something that's been a part of us our entire lives.

But almost always, it's inevitable.

Even if I had been given the choice, I would always choose to love him. Even if he'd produced my greatest pain, he'd also given me my greatest joy.

I'd surrounded myself with his little notes that were spread out on my bed, the words that had come straight from his heart, words I would forever cherish. So many of them spoke of his shame, words that made it clear he would never believe himself worthy of the love that endlessly flowed from me. Some were just plain sweet. Those spoke of that boy who had once smiled so freely, one who just couldn't recognize the joy that was hidden inside him.

In all of them was Jared. In all of them me. In all of them—us. What we'd created, the honesty of what we'd shared.

I hugged my knees to my chest as I studied his gifts. I rocked myself, searching for comfort when none could be found. I missed him. I missed him so much that some days I thought I would die, while others I forged through because I knew I had to go on.

I had to be strong because there was no other option.

But today I felt weak.

Heightened emotions grew thick in my throat, and I held myself tighter as tears slipped down my face.

Jared had changed me. Changed who I was and the direction of my life.

Almost three months had passed since he went away. Thanksgiving was just a week away. Not a single word had reached me, not a single indication of where he'd gone, not one assurance that he was okay.

Like he'd promised, he'd walked away and forgotten about me.

And it killed me because I would *never* forget him. Couldn't because he'd permanently etched himself to me, left a part of himself forever within me. For so many years I'd loved him, but when he'd gone this time, he'd taken part of me captive, too, a piece that could never be retrieved because it would always belong to him.

I looked down through bleary eyes over the words he'd revealed to me.

On some level, I guessed we'd always belong to each other.

Classes had started and were passing in a blur, and I was

still working at the café. Really, I was just drifting through the days.

I worried about him constantly, because I knew how deep his sorrow went, how he was consumed by grief and guilt. I didn't want him out there suffering alone.

But it was what he'd chosen and it was the risk I'd taken, and now I was suffering alone, too.

Christopher was still the only one in my family to know about Jared and what he'd meant to me. As far as my mother knew, Jared had really just been passing through, and he'd stayed a few days and then gone on his way. When she'd asked what was wrong with me since he'd left, I'd lied to her and used Gabe's name, said we'd broken up, the words rancid as they'd been forced from my tongue. Saying it had felt like some sort of mortal betrayal because Gabe could never come close to making me feel the way Jared did. But by the same token, admitting what had happened between Jared and me felt like it would be an even greater betrayal. I *knew* Jared had some sort of messed-up idea that he was protecting me by keeping us a secret. But I knew there was no hiding this forever. I just wasn't ready to tell her yet.

Things had changed between Christopher and me as well. For the better. Of course after I'd moved in with Christopher, we'd gotten really close. But now we seemed to realize we didn't need to hide anything from each other. He'd become my greatest supporter. I supposed it was because even after everything, Christopher truly cared about Jared, too, that he really understood.

One day I would have to find Jared . . . tell him . . . finally reveal it all. But it was really difficult to track someone down who didn't want to be found.

I gathered up his notes and tucked them back into their keepsake box. Then I put the box next to my sketch pads because, like them, they'd become my treasure. And I finally fell into the fitful rest that I had called sleep since he left.

The next morning, I headed to the café at six for the breakfast shift. It'd been hard getting out of bed, the weakness I'd felt last night only following me into today. It was crazy because I would think it would get easier, but it only grew harder every day.

I have to be strong, I reminded myself as I wrapped my apron snuggly around my waist, tying the long straps off in the front. I set to work. It was Saturday, and the place was packed, the hours seemingly longer than my shift was supposed to last. I felt frazzled, completely frayed at the edges as I rushed around the restaurant floor, struggling to keep up with the demand while my body was bending with the strain. Flashes of blond kept infiltrating my mind, flickers of his face, my skin tingling with the vestiges of his touch.

I dropped my head as I refilled a cup of coffee in the kitchen. How could I go on like this? His absence cut me so deeply that it physically hurt. This sorrow rattled me all the way to my bones.

Clara eased up behind me, squeezing my shoulder as she contemplated me with blatant worry. "How are you doing, sweetie?"

The first time she saw me after Jared had left, she'd clued in immediately. She said there was no mistaking heartbreak like the one I wore like a visible badge. There was no hiding it. Funny how she'd warned me that she'd been there before and she didn't want to see me go through the same. But the same was exactly where I ended up.

I bit at my bottom lip, my eyebrows drawing together as I forced myself to nod. "It's been a rough day, but I think I'm okay."

I wasn't. Not at all. But I had to believe one day I would be.

"You know you can just ask if you need something. Someone to talk to or whatever you need."

Meaningfully, I smiled at her. "Yeah, I do. Thank you, Clara."

"Hey, us girls have to stick together, right?"

The rest of my Saturday shift dragged. I couldn't wait for the day to be over.

Finally, after three, Karina told me I could cut out.

I plodded out to my car and slumped into the driver's seat. I just sat there, staring at the blank wall of the restaurant my car faced, my sight blurry with the tears that I was constantly fighting, as if they'd just become a permanent part of me. I felt so worn, so frail, like I would crack from the smallest blow. Above all of that, I felt alone. I knew it'd never been Jared's intention, but this huge piece of me felt abandoned. It throbbed and ached, begging to be filled.

Wiping my eyes, I started my car and pulled out onto the street. Instead of heading toward home, I turned toward my parents' house because I couldn't stand the thought of being by myself in the desolate apartment, wasn't ready to fully give myself over to the memories of Jared inhabiting that place.

I parked in their driveway and climbed from the car. The neighborhood was quiet and the air was warm, although the scorching summer had finally passed. Swallowing deeply, I pushed myself forward, wondering if stepping through my parents' door would be the final blow, because I didn't know how to go on like this anymore.

I was splintering.

Breaking.

Now it was just a matter of holding the pieces together.

I knocked once and pushed the door open. "Mom?" I called as I poked my head inside.

"Aly?" She wasn't surprised this time. She sounded almost relieved.

I edged in just as Mom rounded the corner, coming to meet me. She took one look at my face and hers fell. "Oh, Aly." She quickened as she approached, never hesitating to pull me into her arms. "Come here, sweetheart."

Her warmth rushed over me, and I buried my face in her neck, could do nothing but let myself go. My pain bubbled up and escaped as these racking sobs, loud and uncontainable. Part of me had an uncontrollable instinct to hide this from her, because I'd hidden *him* for so long, but I couldn't hold it in any longer.

"Shh . . . ," she murmured, running her hand through my hair as she slowly rocked me. "Shh."

Her comfort only made me cry harder. "Mom." In her name was the torment I felt, a plea for her to somehow tell me that this would all be okay. And she knew none of it, had no idea what I was really going through. But I needed her.

"Why don't we go in the family room and sit down and talk?" she offered.

I nodded and she shifted her hold to my waist, supporting me as she led us to the couch. She lowered us to sitting, refusing to let me go. She tucked me close and I curled into her side. She held on to me like she'd done when I was a little girl. For a long while she rocked me and let me weep into her shirt as she emitted these soft whispers of encouragement, promising me it *would* be okay. I just didn't know how it could ever be. I was so scared. So scared of doing this alone.

"Is this about Gabe?" she finally asked.

Tears ran down and streaked my face, as if expelling them would somehow purge a part of this pain. My mouth opened wide as the confession bled free. "No, Mom, it was never about Gabe." I squeezed my eyes closed, feeling something tearing loose inside me.

A small, sympathetic breath seeped from her nose, and she caressed her hand down my back. "I didn't think so."

I guess she always did know when I was lying.

"Are Dad and Aug here?" I asked because I really didn't think I could handle having an audience for this.

"No, sweetie, it's just the two of us. Your dad drove out with him to one of his day training camps. You can tell me whatever you need to."

I wasn't ashamed. Still there were some things I just wasn't ready to say. But it was time I finally said his name.

I rolled a little so my head was on her shoulder, looking out the windows over the backyard where it was all peace and tranquility, contrasting the disorder in my heart. I shook as I filled my lungs with air. "It was Jared, Mom."

It was always Jared.

The air between us shifted from this soft sympathy to a stunning sadness. Just his name was enough to clench my heart.

Her voice was rough but knowing. "He hadn't just been at your apartment for a few days, had he?"

Slowly, I shook my head, wetting my lips as I looked up at my mom in admission. "No."

Mom's eyes filled with awareness, her words full of meaning. "So he's the one."

He was the one. The only one.

I rested my head back on her shoulder. "I love him so much. I think I have since I was a little girl . . . but I never imagined anything could feel like this."

Silence took us over while we sat together and let the truth sink in.

"Are you upset?" I finally asked.

"Am I upset that you fell in love with Jared or am I upset that you kept it from me?"

I winced, sensing her frustration, the disappointment, but there was no condemnation.

Finally she sighed. "Of course I'm not mad, Aly. I just don't understand why you felt the need to keep it from me. For God's sake, didn't you and Christopher think I'd want to know that Jared was back in town? I worried about him for *years*, and it turns out he'd been hiding out at your apartment?"

She looked at me seriously. "That day when I stopped by . . . it was so obvious that there was something going on between you two . . . or at least that you both wanted there to be. But then you lied to me about that other boy." She shrugged in something that seemed like defeat. "I don't get it. When was I ever the mom you couldn't confide in?"

"I'm sorry, Mom . . . but don't you remember what it was like after Jared was sent away? It was like no one was allowed to mention him. Dad was so angry with him. Do you think Christopher and I didn't realize he blamed Jared for finally driving Neil completely away? And neither of us knew how long Jared was going to stay. In the beginning, it really was just supposed to be for a few days while he looked for his own place. And then he just stayed."

No doubt, because of me.

That place inside me quivered and swelled, crying out, because without him, I was so empty. It was his mark, the imprint he'd left behind.

I gulped around the heaviness in my chest before I continued. "Everything changed when he showed up at our apartment. It was like this crush I always had on him instantly became something so intensely real."

A part of me realized that it'd become real the night when he was sent away, when I'd understood true heartbreak for the first time in my life at the age of fourteen. But maybe it took the two of us coming face-to-face as adults that brought it to fruition. Maybe it took our completion to shatter us wholely.

"He became my world, Mom. Living without him has been the hardest thing I've ever had to do."

"I don't know if I even want to know how long you were hiding this from me." Fidgeting, she inclined her head, making it clear that she really did want to know.

"He was there for three months."

I was always hiding things from her. And I still was because I didn't know how to voice it.

"God, Aly." She slowly shook her head, sadness coloring her words. "And I have to guess he left pretty quickly after I found him there?"

"Yeah, it all fell apart that night. He blames himself for all of it. He doesn't believe he's allowed happiness, so he destroys it the second he feels a flicker of it."

I had felt him sabotaging us that night. He *ruined* us, just because he believed he was supposed to. "All it took was me telling him I loved him, and he was gone." I figured I'd spare Mom all the details of that night because, in the end, that was all it really came down to. Jared didn't believe he deserved to be loved.

Mom's face pinched as she released a regretful sigh. "I'm so sorry, Aly, sorry that you're going through this. Sorry for ever once giving you and Christopher the impression that I didn't care about Jared or that we should forget about him. I did try to get him help. I saw him unraveling, but every time I tried to intervene, there was nothing I could do to stop it. I tried to convince Neil to get himself and Jared into therapy, but he was so wrapped up in his grief he couldn't see anything else. Neil gave up on himself . . . gave up on life. Without Helene, he didn't think he had anything."

Mom closed her eyes as if shielding herself from that pain. Neil was never the same after he lost Helene. Our family had lost him, too.

"That was the most helpless I've felt in my life . . . watching Jared destroying himself over an accident that any one of us could have caused," Mom continued, sucking in her bottom lip as she got lost in thought. She released a ragged breath. "All these years I worried for him, praying he was safe. I tried several times to get in contact with him after he'd been released, but I could never find him. I guess probably because he didn't want to be found. All I could do was hope he'd gone somewhere where he'd be able to find some peace, even if he couldn't be here. When I saw him at your apartment, it was about the greatest relief I could have imagined."

Mom cringed when she looked down at me. "But I was scared for him, too, Aly. One look at him told me he was still haunted . . . broken. All those marks covering his body, screaming out about how miserable he was inside. The fear in his eyes when he saw me standing there." Her mouth trembled, and she let her attention travel the room as if she were gathering herself. Then she turned a soft smile on me. "But there was a light in his eyes that had been missing after the accident." Mom hooked her finger under my trembling chin. "It was you, Aly. Do you think I didn't catch the way he was looking at you? Like maybe you were going to save him? Like you were the only thing that mattered in that room? And you were looking at him the same way, too."

"I miss him so much," I whispered.

"There was always something special between the two of you." She held my gaze for a long time, before she patted my knee. "Hang on a second. I want to show you something."

Mom got off the couch, wandered down the hall, and returned a couple of minutes later. She sat back down beside me, handing me the picture she held in her hand. Of course it immediately brought tears back to my eyes because over the last three months I really hadn't stopped crying, these emotions wringing me out. But this . . . this warmed and soothed and broke me a little more.

There was no mistaking the little boy, the stark white hair and beaming blue eyes. He was sitting on the couch, Helene right beside him as she helped him support the baby propped on his lap.

Softly, I trailed my fingers over the picture.

"From the minute I brought you home, you were always *his* baby. He would run in ahead of Helene, calling for you. He could barely talk, but there was no mistaking him saying your name." A wistful smile kissed her mouth. "God . . . he was just the cutest little thing, Aly. He was always looking out for you, making sure you were never left behind."

A small sob worked its way up my throat. I pressed my fist to my mouth, trying to hold it in.

Because he had . . . he had left me behind. He forgot me,

leaving me completely alone. It hurt so much. And I was trying so hard to see myself on the other side of it, to be strong because I knew there would be a time when I would treasure what he'd given me. There'd be a time when I was no longer afraid and I'd smile when I saw him in glimmers of what he'd injected into my life.

Tremors rolled through the length of my body, shaking me to my core because all I wanted was for him to be a part of it.

Mom reached out to touch the memory of her friend's face. Her voice dropped in slow encouragement. "You know, she always said the two of you would end up together. She'd watch you playing together and then give me this look that said *I told you so.*" Warm laughter trickled from her mouth, something that sounded so hopeful and so very sad. "You don't know how happy it would make her to know you love her son the way she always hoped you would . . . how happy it makes me to know you've found someone to love this way."

Her assertion burned me deep inside. "Mom, how can you say that? He's *gone.*" I emphasized the word because I realized then that was what I really needed to accept.

Sorrow squeezed my spirit.

He was gone.

Mom cupped my cheek. "Hearts have a way of finding their way home."

Tuesday evening I drove the short distance back to the apartment after my classes ended for the day. Sunlight barely clung to the sky. Golds blazed at the horizon and danced with the waning blue. Through the windshield, I lifted my face to it, hit with the intense urge to curl up on my bed with my sketch pad, to free my hand and see his face.

All I wanted was to see his face.

I wound around the lot and parked in my spot. Sucking in a deep breath, I got my bag and stepped from the car. I felt drained. Fatigued. I always felt a little bit off, like this overall sickness burdened my body. My feet were heavy as I crossed the lot, heavier as I studied them, coaxing them to take the next step. I took them one at a time, holding on to the railing for support.

All the breath left me when I lifted my head, and I was engulfed in fear and panic and an almost terrifying explosion of relief.

Because the only eyes I wanted to see were watching me from where he sat on the top step, his forearms resting on his knees, his intense ice blue eyes staring down at me.

"Jared."

TWENTY-FOUR

Jared

God, seeing her had to be about the best feeling I'd ever experienced. With just the suggestion of her face, dizzying waves of relief slammed into me, filling up that hollowed-out void.

Aly.

Slanting a nervous hand through my hair, I did my best to sit still while I stared down at the green eyes that had locked on me. Strands of the darkest hair swirled all around her, stirred up by the cool breeze that had fallen with the descending night. Frozen midstep, she clung to the railing like maybe she feared she would fall, like the world had just dropped out from beneath her feet.

I guess mine had the moment I opened my eyes to find her hovering over me that first night I'd slept on her couch.

God knew she was the only one who'd managed to change it.

A somber smile pulled at my mouth while something profoundly heavy pulled at my heart.

The girl was so beautiful. Breathtaking.

Air seemed impossible to find, my pulse all thready and harsh. Every cell in my body was screaming at me to get up, to take her in my arms, to kiss her and hold her and make sure she was real because I'd spent so many nights dreaming about her that I wasn't entirely sure what real was anymore.

Cautiously, I climbed to my feet. A tumult of thoughts fired through my mind while somehow I remained at a complete loss for words. I had no idea how she'd react to me being here, had no clue what she was thinking, couldn't tell if she was happy or relieved or angry because she just looked fucking sad.

I wanted to wipe that sadness from her face and erase it from her heart because there was no question I was the one who'd written it there. The most selfish part of me coming back was I still didn't know if I knew how. The only thing I knew was I could no longer stay away. It just wasn't possible when she was the only thing I could see.

"Aly," I finally managed to whisper, her name the sum of all the tumult coursing through me. She was all that mattered.

Five steps down, she stood there, unmoving, before her head slowly began to shake, her lips trembling as tears broke loose. Her eyes squeezed shut. She dropped her face, her free hand in a fist as she spoke toward the concrete steps. "You came back."

Her voice ached with uncertainty and loss, swam with turmoil, echoed the broken girl I'd left standing in the middle of the lot screaming my name.

And it stung. This girl had been hurting just as badly as me.

But what had I expected? That she was fine? That there'd been a second's chance that she'd moved on like I promised her she would?

I mean, damn it, there'd been no denying what I felt in her touch.

And there was no denying now how I hurt her.

Lines creased between my eyes. "How could I not?" My hand fluttered in her direction, wishing I could make every fucking inch of space separating us disappear. "I lied to you, Aly. That night . . ." I swallowed hard as my attention shot to the place where I'd left her behind before I angled it back on her. "I left knowing I could *never* forget you, but praying somehow you could forget me. And I know I shouldn't be here. I know I should give you a chance to forget, but, Aly . . . I miss you."

I missed her. God, I missed her.

Aly looked up at me through the hair shielding her face, the face that was all twisted in grief, soaked with tears and the scars I'd carved in her spirit.

"Aly—"

Harshly, she shook her head, a quick command for silence. She didn't look away from me as she slowly started up the steps. She edged to the left, and I turned to let her by. An overwhelming fear of rejection punched me in the gut when I realized I was too late.

Until she glanced up at me as she passed, her eyes imploring. *Please.*

On the landing, Aly fumbled with her keys and unlocked the door, left it open in invitation as she went inside. She didn't stop when she dumped that huge-ass purse from her shoulder and onto the floor, the act rushing me with all these memories of the days I'd spent waiting for her to walk through that door. *Shit.* Could I be more of a fool? Because here I was, asking for the same thing I'd been asking for before, seeking out her comfort when I knew it could never be something I would deserve. What the hell did I think had changed? But something had . . . I felt it deep . . . whatever had struck me that night on the deserted road in Nevada, the night I realized I wanted to live. That I had something to live for.

Because I wanted to live for her.

I wanted it. I wanted to *be* with her. And I didn't fucking want to hide it anymore.

I hesitated at the threshold before I stepped through. Inside, the apartment was the same, but somehow it felt vacant, like I'd missed too much of what had happened behind this door in the months I'd been away.

Quietly, I latched it shut.

Aly didn't spare me a glance as she disappeared into her room. I trailed a ways behind, not knowing what to expect. At the doorway, I paused. Twilight encroached on the room, natural light fading as the last was sucked into the night. Shadows danced and played, taunted and teased. So much had been shared between us here, things that changed lives and hearts and realities.

Aly stood at the foot of her bed, facing the window, her arms crossed over her chest, hugging herself, like she was struggling to keep herself from falling to her knees. Her shoulders jerked, and I knew she was crying as she tried to hold herself together.

Roughly, I scrubbed my palms over my face because I realized I wanted that to be me—I wanted to be the man who was strong enough to lift her up when she fell. But I was weak, fucking inept, and I didn't know how to make myself right when everything inside me was wrong.

Still I wanted to try. I was determined to try.

Apparently her door had long since been repaired, but not

the damage I'd done. I clicked it shut behind me. I plodded across the floor and turned her dressing table chair out to face the room. I settled on it, my elbows finding my knees, my entire frame hunched over in submission.

A dense silence blanketed the room.

"Aly, tell me what you're thinking," I finally begged. The words sounded like gravel as they scraped up my throat. "If you want me to go, just say it, and I'll walk out that door, and I promise you, this time you'll never see me again." Maybe I was too late. Maybe she had moved on. God, I couldn't fucking bear the thought, the thought of someone else touching her, the idea of someone else loving my girl. That same old insanity rose in me. I squeezed my eyes shut, trying to temper it, to block it out, because I had no right to claim her. But damn if I didn't want to.

I felt her moving toward me, and my lids fluttered open, my face pinched as I lifted my gaze to take her in. Warily she approached with her head hung low, her movements all slow and unsure.

"You think I don't want you here?" Hurt overwhelmed her expression. "Did you not believe what I told you, Jared? Or did you think what happened between us was just a game to me? I meant every single word. I *gave* myself to you." She beat her fist out in front of her, each strike pounding the air with emphasis, before she drew it up to the valley between her breasts, just over her heart. "I haven't been able to sleep in three months . . . *three months* . . . because all I could do was worry about you."

Her bottom lip trembled, and she sucked it between her teeth. "Look at you. God, Jared, you break my heart. What happened to you?" She reached out and ran the back of her hand along the fading bruises on my cheek and fluttered her fingertips over the puckered skin extending out right above my left ear. My hair had grown long enough to barely cover the rest of the scar that snaked around to the back of my head.

I'd been *lucky.* That's what they said. How many times had I heard it before? This time when I woke up in the ICU, the doctor had granted me no pleasantries. Point-blank, he'd told me, "You should be dead." And he'd looked at me like maybe he thought I deserved to be.

"*I* happened." I sat up straighter, lifting my chin so I could meet her eye, because I had no defense. "It's always *me.* I'm a fucking mess, Aly, but without you, I'm a disaster. I . . ." I winced, cutting my attention to the shadows on her floor, before I gathered enough courage to look back up at her. "You make me better. I don't even know what I'm doing here, but those three months I spent with you were the best of my life. You made me feel things I've never felt before."

Made me feel things I never thought I could feel, things I thought I wasn't allowed to feel, things that hinted at joy and swam thick with affection. And I was feeling them now, all these emotions swarming me, a tug-of-war of confusion and need.

Aly's exhale was palpable as it rushed across my face, her movements tentative as she inched forward, her legs knocking into my knees. Maybe there was something reminiscent of the first night when she'd pushed us over the edge, that intense desperation that had been present when she asked me to stay. But tonight, nothing in her intentions seemed seductive like they'd been then. If anything, she looked scared.

Fuck. I couldn't get my leg to stop bouncing as she slowly crawled onto my lap, straddling me, her warmth covering me whole.

It took about all I had not to crush her to me.

Fingertips gentled along my jaw, and she inclined her head to the side. "You can't understand how much I missed you," she whispered through the torment that wouldn't seem to let her go.

But she was wrong. It might be the only thing I could understand.

Shaking, I took her face in my hands, the tips of my fingers weaving in her hair. She reached up to cover them with hers.

"Jared," she whispered. Tears streaked down her face, hot and fast.

"I'm so sorry," I promised. "And I know I can't take back these months I've been gone, but I want to try . . . I want to try to make this work. God, Aly, please tell me you want the same thing."

Aly choked, and again, she whimpered my name.

Frantic, I searched her eyes, feeling the pain that radiated from the surface of her skin. Fear coiled, and again I was thinking maybe I was too late, I'd done too much damage, and she was getting ready to push me away.

But she was holding on to me like she was going to hold on to me forever.

I wet my lips, shaking. "Baby . . . tell me what's wrong."

Aly stared down on me with overwhelming dread as she pulled my hands from her face. For a few painful seconds, she clutched them between us. She lowered them and flattened them across her belly. The heat of her palms held my hands there, pressing, pressing, *telling*. Everything in the movement was severe, pleading, her cheeks soaked with the tears that wouldn't quit leaking from her eyes.

All the muscles in my body stiffened. My mind raced through every scenario because there was no possible way to accept her meaning.

But she wasn't clarifying, wasn't taking it back.

"No," stumbled from my mouth as I edged back in the chair, needing space, my head shaking.

Her fingers dug into the backs of my hands as she pressed them more firmly against her stomach. "Yes." It was a declaration.

"No, Aly, no."

Panic spread slowly just beneath the surface of my skin. Every cell in my body lit in an excruciating blaze, like dominoes tipped one by one, catching fire.

"How?" How could I have done this?

She slanted her face away, then jerked it back to me. "I don't know. I . . . I messed up."

She messed up? Silent, mocking laughter pounded me in the chest.

It was me who messed up. I *always* did.

The walls closed in and the room spun. I nudged her from my lap.

Aly reeled back when I set her on her feet. "Jared, please talk to me."

But I was the one who was reeling. Floundering. Standing, I fisted my hands in my hair as I began to pace her room. How could I have let this happen?

I don't get to have this.

"Don't do this, Jared. I know what you're thinking, and you're wrong."

"I have to . . . I have to go." I headed for her door. I just needed some air. Because I couldn't fucking breathe.

"Don't you dare leave me, Jared. Please . . . don't do this to me." Her words were cracked and rushed. From behind, she grabbed me by the shirt, desperate as she pulled me back. "I won't let you do this to me . . . I won't let you do this to *us*."

I wheeled around, taking her by the wrists, binding her

hands between us as I brought us chest to chest. Wide, startled eyes stared up at me, her perfect mouth parted in shock.

"Do you think I could? Fuck . . . Aly . . ."

Didn't she get it?

I swallowed, overwrought, as I looked at the girl who I'd done so wrong. I didn't know how to be okay with this because I'd never been more scared of anything in my life. I'd taken life, and I had no right to give it. But there was no staying away from the only one who had ever touched my heart.

I increased my hold. "I . . . please just give me some time."

Aly drew her lips into a thin line, her brow knit as she studied me, as if she wanted to resist. Instead she nodded quickly and took a single step back. "Okay." She swallowed and nodded again. "But before you walk away, I need you to know I love you, Jared."

I knew it. Believed it.

And I'd give anything to know how to love her back, the way she should be loved, wholly and without all the bullshit holding me down. I wanted to be enough. My spirit writhed. How could I ever be?

When I turned and walked out the door, Aly moaned as if in pain, but she didn't try to stop me.

I barreled downstairs. Night had completely taken hold. I hopped on the piece-of-shit bike I had bought to get here. I turned it over and the engine churned to life. I rolled it out, trying to see through the anxiety that seized me, constricting my lungs, jackhammering my heart. Everything about this was wrong . . . so wrong.

Stopping at the gate, I rammed the heels of my hands into my eyes, a loud groan loosed into the air. An unknown emotion welled thick, urgent at the base of my throat as it fought for release. I widened my eyes, striving to clear my vision as I turned out onto the blurry street.

I knew where I was headed.

Because I was drawn.

Traffic was heavy, the streets clogged. I wanted to scream. Raking a hand through my hair, I mumbled incoherencies, not sure I could hold it together. When I finally got across town, I slid the bike into the left-hand turn lane. The blinker flashed, and I wavered. I had a stranglehold on the handlebars when I crossed over the spot where I had taken it all, where she'd bled and I'd never wept. That unspent emotion clashed with the anger, fighting, struggling to break free.

A quarter of a mile down the street, I pulled off onto the shoulder. Dust billowed as I braked, a storm of energy rising around me. I stumbled from the bike. The old neighborhood was eerily quiet, lights glowing from windows, trees whispering in the breeze. Panting, I scoured the field that sat deserted across the street. I sucked in a steeling breath and ran across the street. Shoving the toe of my boot in the chain-link fence, I climbed it and swung my legs over as I jumped down on the other side.

Tall, grassy weeds grew high in the center of the field. I wandered out to the middle and fell to my hands and knees. Memories ran amok, a chaos that came too close and coursed too free. Aly as a little girl . . . my mother calling my name. Both pulled at me, a war between what I needed and this debt I would never be able to fully pay. Had I really deceived myself into believing if I came back here I could finally escape it? But I'd come on this impulse, an instinct that spurred me forward, promising things would be different.

Yeah. They were different, all right.

I wheezed for air.

I rose onto my knees, my hands pressed to the side of my head, trying to make sense of the million different emotions that were fighting inside my heart and mind.

"Mom," I called out to her, wishing she could hear. Praying she could. "I'm sorry . . . I'm so sorry. I tried. I fucking tried, and no matter what I do, I can't make this right. I want to make this right."

I pitched forward, clutching my stomach, knowing that I was absolutely going to lose it. Her face flickered before me, her voice so soft.

"Mom," I mumbled quietly, "please tell me what I'm supposed to do."

I just didn't fucking know anymore.

Hunched over, I buried my face in my hands. And I knew I couldn't go on like this any longer. Something had to give. I'd tried, and I fucking failed. I was tired of failing. Tired of hurting people I cared about.

In this place, Aly's presence consumed me. Impressions of the little girl who'd grown to possess me ran rampant, rushed along the hard ground, and drifted in the air.

TWENTY-FIVE

May 2006

Jared closed his eyes as he slumped back on his bed. Warmth shocked through his system, a moment's euphoria, a moment's relief. He floated, lifted, and fell. For just a little while, it didn't hurt so bad.

But it never lasted.

He curled on his side, holding his stomach, trying to deflect the surge of feeling that came storming back. Fire coursed through his veins, a foreign voice shrieking from the hollowed-out hole where his soul had once been. Jared opened his mouth and forced his face into the pillow. A silent scream ripped from this throat.

He couldn't do this anymore.

Jared sat up. He swayed. He steadied himself and tore a hand through his too long hair as he frantically looked around the haze of his room. He had to get it together and figure this shit out. He kept thinking he'd fill himself so full with poison that he'd sleep, that he'd fall and never wake. But it was never good enough, and he always was thrown back into this everlasting hell.

Jared yanked open the bottom drawer of his desk and shoved the few precious tokens of what had been into his backpack, unsure why he couldn't leave them behind, topped it with the cheap bottle of whiskey he'd snatched from his dad's cabinet. He buried his stash in the front pocket under a crumpled-up shirt he grabbed from the floor.

Not like it fucking mattered. He wouldn't be getting caught this time. He'd see it through. He'd pay, and never again would he have the chance to destroy the good.

Slinging his backpack over his shoulder, Jared went to his window and parted the drapes. With his pulse pounding in his ears, he slowly slid it open. He cringed when it squeaked. He was supposed to be grounded. That was his father's solution. *Grounding*. Jared had been arrested and expelled from school, and apparently that had been a just punishment.

Jared scoffed, his grip tightening on the frame of the window. God, his dad was clueless. Did he really think grounding him for a month and sending him to a new school was going to fix things? Really, he knew his dad didn't want to deal with him or his shit.

Jared couldn't blame him.

He'd ruined his life.

Night after night, Jared had lain and listened to his father weep, the sound resonating through the barren place that had once been their home. Courtney was gone. Two weeks after the funeral, she'd been sent to their grandparents' because their father had lost the capacity to care for anything or anyone. It was only supposed to be temporary. Jared's gut told him it was not. He just hoped she'd escaped this all, that his sister had been spared.

Jared's father was only another life he had taken.

Jared quietly inched toward his door, inclined his ear to it and listened for his father. Anxiety crawled up his spine. He couldn't afford to mess this up. A distant TV droned from the living room. The rest of the house echoed the cavernous void. Jared crossed his room to his window and pushed at the frame of the screen until it bent and gave. Holding his breath, he slipped over the sill and out into the night.

Crouched down, he ran across the yard, panting when he hit the garage wall of the Ramirezes' two houses down. Jared peered through the small window. No lights shone, and their car was gone. For years he'd mowed their lawn, and just as many times he'd sat in their kitchen drinking from a glass of lemonade when Mrs. Ramirez would call him in to take a break from the sun. He also knew what they kept in the den.

Jared raked his hand through his hair as he pressed up against the wall, searching for courage. But there was no courage. There was only pain and the throbbing call of the debt he knew he had to pay.

Jared shoved off the wall, dropped his backpack to the ground, and jerked the shirt from the front pocket. He wrapped it haphazardly around his hand, pinching his eyes closed as he sucked in the stifling air. He slammed his fist into the small, square garage window.

Glass shattered. It crashed as it fell to the concrete floor.

"Shit," he hissed quietly, jerking around to peer into the distant darkness. From down the street, a dog barked, but no one even seemed to stir or notice his presence.

Jared turned back to his task, wincing as he unwound the bloodied shirt from his hand. He softly groaned as he did his best to ignore the stinging ache. He didn't have time to be distracted.

Jared knocked the rest of the jagged pieces of window glass free with this elbow. The few remaining clattered to the floor. He gathered his bag from the ground and tossed it inside. Grunting, he wedged himself through the narrow hole.

Inside, the garage was dark. Only the dimmest moonlight spilled in through the window that had given him entry. He plucked his bag from the floor and slung it over his shoulder, making his way inside the house. A dull overhead light illuminated the kitchen, and Jared quickly crossed through and down the hall.

He knew exactly where he was going.

He flicked on the light in the den. Two worn recliners faced an old television set, and family pictures lined the walls. Jared trained his attention on his goal because he couldn't look at all those faces smiling, all that family and joy. Not when he'd destroyed his.

Against the far wall was an antique gun cabinet. The solid wood was polished and detailed, the glass panes etched. Housed inside were Mr. Ramirez's guns, two rifles, a shotgun, and a large handgun. He'd shown Jared once, told him the story behind each one.

Fear slicked like ice just under Jared's skin, and his heart beat erratically as he stared at them. It didn't matter that he was scared. His mom had been scared, too. He'd seen it. Felt it.

Jared inched forward and turned the old rustic lock. It clicked and gave way, the doors yielding to the call. Jared took the handgun from its case. It was so heavy and cold. He swallowed hard before he rummaged around and found the right bullets, held his breath as he loaded it. He shoved it in the front pocket of his backpack.

Jared was heading back through the kitchen when he heard the garage whine shut and the slam of a car door. He froze. He clutched his bag to his chest, his eyes darting around the room, looking for an escape.

Five seconds later, the door he'd come in through opened. Joe Ramirez gasped, his feet faltering below him.

"Jared?" he said more in shock than in question. He blinked away his stupor. "What are you doing in here?"

Jared fumbled in the front pocket of his backpack and brought out the gun. He pointed it at him.

What am I doing . . . what am I doing . . . what am I doing? Jared chanted in his head. Sickness swirled in his gut, pressure building in his head.

"Come, now, Jared. Give me the gun." The old man watched him with outright sympathy and a twinge of fear. "I know you don't want to do this. I *know* you."

Harshly, Jared shook his head, unwilling to listen to what Joe said, the gun trembling as he held it out in front of him. "Just . . . just sit down in that chair." Jared's tongue darted out to wet his dry, cracked lips, that void in his veins screaming out to be filled.

"Jared . . ." Joe took a step forward, a placating hand stretched out in front of him as if it could do something to mollify the anxiety twisting Jared in two.

"Sit!" Jared shouted, his own voice something he didn't recognize.

Joe nodded slowly and shuffled over to the kitchen chair with his hands held up in surrender. He sat down, eyeing Jared with the pity he hated. The man's movements were deliberate as he clasped his hands on his lap. "You don't have to do this, Jared."

But he did. He had to, even though involving someone else was never supposed to be a part of it. Jared hated scaring this man who'd only ever been kind to him. He'd just been left without a choice.

Keeping the gun pointed in Joe's direction, Jared frantically ransacked the drawers in the kitchen, leaving them hanging wide open when he didn't find what he was looking for. He groaned in relief when he finally did. The large drawer was crammed full of junk, pens and coupons and random crap. And a small twine of rope.

Jared crossed to the man and edged behind the chair. "Give me your hands."

Joe hesitated.

"Do it!" Jared yelled, nudging him in the side with the barrel of the gun.

The old man gave in and dropped his arms to his sides. Jared crouched down low and balanced the gun on his thighs. His breaths came all shallow and severe as he began to wrap the rope around Joe's wrists, securing them tight at the base of the chair.

"Jared, please don't do this," he begged.

Sweat beaded on Jared's upper lip. He swiped the back of his hand over it. He blinked hard, trying to clear the fog clouding his mind. He cinched the rope and Joe yelped.

Shit.

"I'm not going to hurt you," Jared promised through his agony, fucking hating every second of what he was doing. But there was nothing else he could do.

Jared loosened the binding so at least it wouldn't rub.

"You know that's not what I'm concerned about," Joe said.

Humorless laughter freed itself from Jared's blackened spirit, from the deepest recess where his corruption lay. "You don't need to worry about me, old man. I'm going exactly where I'm supposed to be."

Standing, Jared dug the car keys from Joe's pocket and fled into the garage. He smacked his palm against the garage door opener. The door slowly lifted just as Jared slid into the driver's seat of the oversized four-door sedan. He tossed his backpack to the passenger's seat and tucked the gun underneath it.

Nausea slammed him the second he was behind the wheel. His hands were shaking uncontrollably as he floundered with the keys. Finally he managed to slip the key into the ignition. He turned it over, threw it in reverse, and gunned the accelerator. He backed out onto the street, shifted into gear. The car swerved as he rammed on the gas.

He just had to get out of this neighborhood. Away from the memories. Away from everything that mattered.

He didn't want to do this here.

But those memories chased him, tormented him as he aimlessly roamed the streets. Where the fuck was he supposed to go? Scrubbing his hand over his face, Jared tried to wake himself up, to focus, to see through the permanent daze that had taken him hostage.

For hours he drove as the anxiety ratcheted high, lifted, and spun. Paranoia was setting in. Soon they'd come looking for him, and he had to get this done. His eyes traveled the streets, searching for a place to hide, but nothing felt right. A choked cry locked in his throat when he realized he was circling back around to the neighborhood. Fucking drawn. Hysterical laughter rocketed from his mouth. Was this some kind of cruel, sick joke?

He avoided the intersection because he just couldn't go there. He made a U-turn and then a quick right onto the street bordering the neighborhood. Jared cut left across the street. The car bounced and jerked as he forced it up over the curb, the tires spinning until they found traction on the dirt. The field was vacant, dark. Tall grasses grew up through the middle. The headlights sliced over the field, illuminating the place that had always meant so much to him, where he'd spent his days playing back when he was a child, when things were good and joy wasn't a vague impression of the past.

He'd loved it here. Now he'd destroy it, like he destroyed everything.

Out in the middle of the field, he killed the engine. It ticked and the fan hummed. Jared flipped off the headlights.

For a few minutes— or maybe hours— he sat in the dark, shaking, rocking.

Thrashing through the anxiety, he groped for the overhead light. A faint glow crept into the car. He just needed one hit and then he could do this. Jared dug in his bag, drained half the bottle of whiskey to get him to the place where he could get up the nerve, swallowed down five pills when that wasn't enough.

He hated this. Hated it.

The spoon and the needle and the bag.

But it was all he had.

He found his lighter and balled up the tiny piece of cotton between his fingers. Jared swam. His head was spinning, his mind reeling. And everything was so heavy and so light. Warm.

Jared sagged against the seat, limp, and for a few seconds, he let it go.

But it never lasted long, and he was just so tired . . . but his mind wouldn't stop working. He could hear his mom crying, fucking begging in the bowels of his brain.

He grabbed the gun from under his bag and rammed it in his mouth. His teeth scraped metal, the sound grinding in his ears and grating through his bones. Sweat coated his forehead, slipped down the back of his neck.

I can do this.

His finger trembled on the trigger.

It hurt. It hurt. And he was so scared.

Jared jerked the gun from his mouth and slammed his head back on the headrest. "Fuck," he cried.

He lifted it to his temple, forcing his finger back on the trigger. He squeezed his eyes shut, begging for her. "Mom . . . I'm so sorry . . . I'm so sorry." His hand was shaking. Shaking.

Jared couldn't fucking stop shaking.

Another handful of pills, the rest of the bottle—numbness and fire and helplessness—it sloshed on his shirt as he drained the last.

He could do this.

But he wanted to see her face one more time.

Numbness weighed him down as he rooted through his bag. He swayed to the left. Shit. Maybe he'd taken too much. But it was okay . . . it was okay . . . he could do it. He could do it for her.

He finally found his book in his backpack. Words filled the entirety of the worn journal, his hate and his shame. Snapshots of a perfect life were stowed between the vile pages. He thumbed through to the front, where he kept her picture and lifted it to find the tenderness glowing on her face.

He'd never see her again.

Lifting his lighter, he flicked it and watched as the picture caught fire. She melted before him, disappeared, just like she'd done when he stole her life.

He was just so fucking tired. Tired of it all. Sleep flitted at the edges of his consciousness. He rammed his forehead on the steering wheel, palming the butt of the gun.

He could do this.

First, he wanted to watch it burn. He set the gun on his lap, flicked his lighter, and let the flame leap and dance along the bottom of the journal. He held it in his hand, felt the heat on his face. Felt nothing. Felt it all.

Flames engulfed the cab and he was drowning.

Falling.

Suffocating.

The bullet wasn't necessary after all.

He whispered, "I'm sorry . . . I'm so sorry."

Maybe now he'd make it right.

Someone was screaming, the voice piercing through his surrender. Jared just wanted to sleep. Hands searched the fire. Dragging. Pulling. Begging.

Air.

Fists pounded on his chest.

Everything burned, his lungs and his skin.

Don't leave me. Please don't leave me. I love you. Jared, stay. Please. Stay.

Vomit pooled and gushed from his mouth.

The voice pled, promising him that it would be *okay*.

Sirens blared and she was gone.

Blackness closed in.

And Jared knew it would never be.

TWENTY-SIX

Jared

Oh, shit.

I hunched over, gripping my stomach. I tripped over the emotion cutting me thin. Realization slammed into me, spinning as this comfort and confusion and inundating warmth. I was pretty sure my heart would beat right out of my chest.

It was her.

I lifted my face to the cool night sky as the memory that had been locked up somewhere in my mind burst free.

It was her.

The world spun as my reality shifted. For years, I'd cursed this fate, hating the life sentence I'd been given. I'd always thought I'd lived as a punishment. An upheaval of questions pitched through my brain, all these voices shouting at me, because I was no longer sure surviving that night had been a penalty.

Nothing made any sense . . . except that it was *her*.

Aly.

I sprinted back across the lot and jumped the fence. Three seconds later, I had my bike on the street.

Hours had passed, time lost in the period that my truth was found. Night had grown deep, and the traffic had long since cleared. I raced because I couldn't fucking stand the distance I'd wedged between us.

I was done hurting her.

When I'd woken up in the hospital all those years ago, I was so pissed off knowing I had failed. The nurse had told me I was *lucky* that I somehow got out of that car when I did. I hadn't been lucky. I'd known then that fate had intervened. But not in the way I ever imagined.

It was her.

I flew down the streets, my nerves ratcheting higher with every mile I put under me. When I finally got to the complex, it was quiet as I eased my bike through the gate and parked in the spot that I somehow thought of as my own. I bounded up the stairs and produced the key Christopher had trusted me with so many months ago. Fumbling, I slipped it into the lock. I didn't bother to knock. One way or another, I had to get to her.

For a fleeting second, I wondered what Christopher would do if we came face-to-face on the other side. Dude would probably kill me if he found me showing my face back around here. I'd take it as it came because hiding was no longer an option.

I burst into the darkened, silent apartment. Christopher's door sat wide open, like it'd been so many times before. Undoubtedly, the guy was on the prowl.

Aly'd been left alone, again.

Frustrated air puffed from my nose. I didn't want her to be alone anymore.

Light seeped from beneath her door. I paused in front of it, fucking shaking, because the truth was, I was scared. I was so good at destroying, but clueless when it came to mending the disaster I'd left in my wake. I rapped one knuckle on her door, my heart beating all rough when I placed my hand on the knob. I didn't wait for an answer. I turned it and let it slowly swing open.

And I just stood there in the doorway, staring at the girl staring back at me. Faint light crept up the walls from the lamp on her dressing table. Her head was cocked up in shock as she sat on the edge of her bed facing out, sitting cross-legged with a large sketch pad balanced on her lap.

Affection rushed through me and I was fisting my hands, trying to keep this insanity under control. Defining Aly had always been impossible. Sexy as all hell, innocent and sweet, keen and unbelievably naive.

This girl was my perfection. Months ago, that'd been my first thought when I looked up from the couch to find her standing there. Never before had someone had such a physical effect on me. I mean, damn, it'd felt just like I'd been struck. I should have known then she hadn't just impacted me with a shot of lust. The desire and need she'd driven me half-mad with had been so much greater than that.

It'd been truth.

Was I scared of everything my returning stood for?

Yeah.

Because *this* was real.

Not some fucked-up fantasy like I'd convinced myself to believe.

Slowly Aly slid the pad from her lap and onto the bed. She blinked, green eyes acute as she watched me with uncertainty. "Jared."

With the sound of my name on her lips, I broke. In two long strides, I crossed the room and dropped to my knees in front of her.

I was giving in. I was ready for her.

A soundless gasp parted her mouth when I took her face in my hands. Her knees jutted out just over the bed, digging into my sides like a reluctant embrace. Her hair tumbled down my arms in a wave that I wanted to get lost in as I looked up at her. I ran my thumbs under her eyes, capturing the tears that fell.

I struggled to pull a breath into the well of my lungs, and my tongue darted out to wet my lips. I tilted my head to the side, caught in her unwavering gaze. Devotion poured from her. Even after all the shit I'd put her through.

"You saved me," I whispered, drawing her left hand to my mouth. I kissed along the scar where my life had made its mark. I ran my nose along it, then pressed my face into her palm because I just needed to feel.

God, I needed to feel.

It was warmth and good and the girl. And fuck . . . if it wasn't everything.

Aly started trembling as awareness took hold. Slowly she unwound her legs, and I moved back a fraction so she could drape them along my sides.

"How did you know?" I asked.

I felt her pulse accelerate, and she hesitated. "Jared . . . I . . ." She blinked through something that looked like fear.

"Baby, talk to me," I softly prodded.

She released a weighted breath and slipped both her hands

over the tops of mine, which were rested on her thighs. I
squeezed her in reassurance. "I never told anyone about that
night . . . maybe because it'd impacted me too much, I don't
know. I mean, I'd tried to tell my mom, but I guess I was just
scared." She kind of shrugged. "That whole week after you got
expelled from school, I'd been . . ." She frowned. ". . . unsettled.
Everything was so messed up. Your family was wrecked and
mine was coming apart at the hinges. I felt like I was losing
every single person I cared about."

I went rigid. *I destroy everything I touch.*

In silent encouragement, Aly reached out and smoothed her
thumb up the line that dented my brow, like she knew exactly
what I was thinking, like she *knew* me. She didn't stop talking
as she did. "There was this knot building in my gut." She shivered. "I kept getting this overwhelming feeling that something
really bad was going to happen. That night, I couldn't sleep.
Mom had finally made me turn off my light a little after eleven
since I had school in the morning, but I had a little flashlight
that I used so I could draw at night."

Aly drew back and inclined her chin to where her sketch pad
sat wide open at her side. She traced her fingers along the lines
she'd forged on the page.

My heart stuttered with the image looking back at me.

The drawing was beautiful, just like the girl, only because
it'd been rendered by her hand. But it was my face on the page,
all hard planes and angles, my arms and chest exposed, her own
interpretation of my sins swirled and shaded across my skin.
And my eyes . . . she recognized so much in me that I couldn't
see.

"People, Jared . . . that's what I keep in my books. Only the
ones I love." She ran her thumb from the bottom page of the pad

to the top, lifting them one by one to expose them, image after image of me.

Again I was reeling, because, fuck, it was just overwhelming. This girl who had leveled my walls, the only one who'd understood, the one who saw right though all my bullshit, had always *seen* me.

She turned back to me, her voice softening with caution. "After your mom died, I couldn't draw her anymore. It was like there was this block that wouldn't let me see. It broke my heart because I wanted to remember her. I guess I thought it would somehow keep her alive, but it wouldn't come... until that night." Aly drew in a shaky breath. "But it was all wrong, Jared. I could *feel* it. It was like I was compelled to draw her face, but she was crying out, and I knew she was crying for you. And I kept drawing and drawing and the same thing kept coming out until I'd worked myself into a complete panic. I had to check to make sure you were okay. I snuck out and ran across to your house. You were supposed to be grounded, so I figured I'd just peek in your window to check on you. But I found it open, and your room was empty."

Aly squinted, as if she were back in that moment. "God... this fear overtook me." She focused back on me. "Right then, I knew something was wrong. I snuck back in my room, but I couldn't sit still. I ended up grabbing my sketch pad and thinking I'd go draw in the fort. As soon as I wedged myself through the hole in the fence, I saw Mr. Ramirez's car. I *knew* it was you. I just started running. I had no idea what was happening, but I knew I had to get to you. I didn't even stop to think before I tore the door open. And there were flames." Aly sucked in her trembling lip. "You weren't moving. I thought you were dead, Jared, and nothing had ever hurt me as much as that. I was screaming at you to wake up, and I dragged you out. Then that gun dropped out onto the ground with you . . . and all that *stuff* that'd been on your lap." The words were hoarse, like she didn't want to acknowledge it.

"And I knew . . ." She cupped my face. "I knew how broken you were and it broke me, too. I pounded on your chest because I didn't know what else to do. You started throwing up, and that was when I heard a cop car stop on the street and shine its light into the field. It turned out they were already looking for you. I was a coward, Jared. . . . I ran because I was scared and I didn't know how to process what I saw. I hid in the dark in the back of the field, watching them work over you . . . watched them take you away. I'm so sorry I left you there. I'll always regret that."

"You're sorry? Fuck, Aly . . . *I'm* sorry." And fucking *thankful.* I had realized that on that deserted road in Vegas. "You saved me. You lived with that while I wasn't living at all."

"All these months I wanted to tell you, but I was scared it would drive you away. Once you came back, I saw how much you resented the fact that you lived." She dropped her gaze and wrung her fingers. "I tried so hard to keep you, but I lost you anyway."

I edged up closer to her and held her by the jaw, my voice cracking. "I'm here. Baby, I'm here."

Aly grimaced a smile, holding on to my wrists like she was clinging to life. "It was always you, Jared. Always. I can't remember a day in my life when I didn't love you."

I tucked a lock of her hair behind her ear, then slid my palms down to cup her neck.

A faint blush seeped across her cheeks, and she dropped her face and chewed on her lip. "You were my first crush." She sobered, her voice strained as sincere green eyes slanted up to me.

"And my only love." Her throat bobbed as she swallowed, almost painfully. "I've been waiting for you my whole life."

Her words penetrated my blackened soul. And I fucking got it, this innocent girl who I'd *taken*.

She'd always been mine.

I inclined my head up to capture her attention, to make sure she understood. "I'm so fucked-up, Aly, and I'm always going be. I warned you that you can't fix me, and you can't. I'm never going to outlive or outrun this shit."

All that I had left were pieces, and even those were broken. But those pieces belonged to her, and just maybe we could find a way to make a life from them.

"I wasn't lying when I said you make me better. You make me want to be better. Truth is, I can't outrun you, either, Aly. I can't be without you anymore. The last three months I spent without you have been the darkest I've ever had."

Slowly I ran my hands down the delicate skin of her shoulders. Goose bumps lifted in their wake. I trailed them all the way down, squeezing her hands, then brought my palms to rest flat on her stomach. My throat tightened and I forced down my fear.

"But I can't even begin to imagine what you've been going through without me here."

Aly closed her eyes, tears slipping free. "I needed you."

"It makes me sick that I left you." Emotion pulsed in my chest, in the deepest places of my spirit, a tumble of confusion and apprehension of what I'd never thought should be vying to be freed. "I'm terrified of this, Aly. I don't know how to do this."

Hopeful, subdued laughter fell softly from her mouth. Her teeth tugged at her bottom lip as she dropped her gaze to my hands, and she traced her fingers over the numbers marring my knuckles. "Do you think I'm not? I have no idea how to do this, either. But I know I want to do it with you."

Sliding my hands up the outside of her thighs to her hips, I tugged her to the edge of the bed, because I needed her near. I brought her flush, and she wrapped her legs around my waist. Those little sleep shorts pressed into my stomach, and I dug my fingers into the supple flesh.

"Aly," I mumbled through a groan, my face buried in her chest. I raised my head to place a gentle kiss under her jaw, breathing her in, the life and the good. "I missed you." I ached. It'd been too long since I was lost in her, too long without her touch.

Soft fingers played in my hair, traveled down to my neck and back up again. Chills crawled down my spine. Need coiled and spun with adoration. Fuck, I was in so deep. But now I knew it was the only place I wanted to be.

Easing off the floor, I climbed onto the bed, dragging her up to the middle of it with me. Aly clung to me, legs and arms and body and soul. She ran her nose along the sensitive skin behind my ear. "I missed you," she murmured, "so much."

I laid her down and sat back to take her in, my hands gripping her knees. Those long legs were bent, her back bowed. Her hair was all a mess, billowing out around that face that had become the only thing I could see.

"You are so beautiful, Aly."

Perfect.

I raked a hand through my hair in an attempt to get myself under control because I was dying to consume her. Maybe the way she consumed me.

Wholly.

I forced myself to go slow as I crawled between her legs,

propping myself on my hands and knees. I looked directly down on the girl.

Aly's mouth parted.

Holding myself suspended with one hand, I held one side of her face, my thumb caressing along her flushed skin. "What do you see in me?"

For a moment she just looked at me, intensity pouring from her, before she drew me down to bring us chest to chest. Her breath came as a whisper across my ear. "I see beauty and pain. Joy and sorrow. I see the good and I see the bad . . . and I love it all."

I sucked in a rattled breath.

I dipped down and covered her mouth with mine. Months of pent-up desire rushed from my chest and pooled in my stomach. Twisted in the tightest knot. Her tongue was all tentative, soft and slow, tangling with mine as she whispered out these little words that I felt rather than heard, utterings of love and fear that came straight from her heart. I sucked her top lip into my mouth, turned to the bottom, dove in again. And I was singed. Burned.

Hers.

Without breaking our kiss, I found the hem of her shirt with my hands. I slowly inched it up, my palms flat as they traveled her curves. I pulled back enough to lift it over her head.

A pensive smile curved her mouth as Aly tugged my shirt free. Hungry eyes roamed over me, as if she'd missed every inch of my body as much as I missed hers.

Aly lost her breath when she found the mark covering my heart. Fingertips flitted over my skin. She tipped her chin up to me, her voice rough. "Is this me?"

"Yes," I murmured, "I never could forget you, Aly. Never.

You haunted me just as much as the rest of the sins lining my body." I held her hand closer, over the knowing green eyes that would forever watch over me from their spot on my chest. But now I realized she wasn't there because she was sin. She was there because she saved me.

This was the mark her life had left on mine.

Leaning back, I edged her shorts and panties from her hips, slipped them down her legs. My gaze traveled her length, every inch of this girl like a dream. I palmed her knees, pressed them apart. This time it was my turn to lose my breath. Every cell in my body strained. "Fuck," I wheezed. "You're so gorgeous, Aly,"

This slow blush started at her stomach, traveled up her chest, kissed her cheeks. "I love you, Jared. With all of me. I am yours."

My blood pumped hard and joy leaped up in me.

Real joy. Not a hint or suggestion.

This joy was real. Overwhelming. Something tangible that Aly had shown me was still possible to feel.

My eyes locked on hers as I slowly leaned down. I feathered a kiss just above her pelvic bone where our child grew. Another mark my life had made when I'd believed I wasn't living at all. Wisps of anxiety curled, twisting with my spirit. I didn't know if I could ever be enough. But God, I was going to try.

I climbed over her, looked down at the girl who changed everything. The one who'd given me another chance at life.

Soft fingers caressed my face, green eyes intense. "Stay," she whispered.

I wound my arm under her back and brought it up to hold her head. The other trailed from her shoulder and down the length of her arm. I wove my fingers with hers and brought her knuckles to my mouth. I brushed my lips over them. Our flesh so different, the pure and the impure. Yet now I knew we fit.

"I'm not going anywhere."

Emotion rumbled thick in my chest, pushing and pulsing. I swallowed hard, my chest so fucking tight as I let myself finally *feel*, feel what I'd been fighting since I walked through Aly's apartment door six months ago.

"I love you, Aly." The words shook, but rang with truth. Our truth.

I never believed I'd get to have *this*. But somehow I'd found myself with it.

It scared the hell out of me, but I was done running.

I wound a single finger through a lock of her inky hair. A bond. It felt like home.

It was time I built another one.

Photo by Ali Megan Photography

A. L. Jackson is the *New York Times* bestselling author of *Take This Regret* and *Lost to You*, as well as other contemporary romance titles, including *Pulled* and *When We Collide*.

She first found a love for writing during her days as a young mother and college student. She filled the journals she carried with short stories and poems used as an emotional outlet for the difficulties and joys she found in day-to-day life.

Years later, she shared a short story she'd been working on with her two closest friends, and with their encouragement, this story became her first full-length novel. A. L. now spends her days writing in southern Arizona, where she lives with her husband and three children. Her favorite pastime is spending time with the ones she loves.

Dear Reader,

Thank you so much for reading *Come to Me Quietly*.

Come to Me Quietly has been such an amazing journey for me as an author. It's typical of what I write in that it's an emotional, love-filled journey of two people with a past coming together. But Jared is unlike any character I've ever written before. He is passionate. Angry. Self-destructive.

Jared wasn't originally supposed to be a character in *Come to Me Quietly*. He was the lead in a paranormal romance I began writing more than three years ago. But as I started writing that story, there was just something about Jared that stuck out to me. He was different. Special. And he just kept screaming at me that he belonged in a different story from the one that I had initially planned for him.

So that paranormal romance was shelved, and I began to plot out the story Jared wanted to be in. I so clearly saw this broken man who had so much love and passion buried beneath the pain he held inside him. I saw his burden and shame. I saw his eyes and I saw his anger.

And I saw this young woman, Aleena Moore, who was the only one deep enough to touch it.

Their story became *Come to Me Quietly.*

Through the process of writing this story, I absolutely fell in love with both of these characters. Jared and Aleena have had such a profound effect on me as a person and an author. They grew and became a permanent part of my heart and mind.

I'm absolutely thrilled that the story of their lives will be continued in my next novel, *Come to Me Softly*, because their story has really only just begun.

In *Come to Me Softly*, Jared and Aly will be able to explore their passion freely for the first time because their love is no longer a secret.

I've already seen what it will be like for them, waking up together each day. . . .

Aly stood at the kitchen counter, pouring a glass of orange juice. Locks of nearly black hair were all ratted and a mess, her bedhead about the cutest fucking thing I'd ever seen. Of course, the girl was wearing those shorts, exposing the length of those long legs that drove me out of my mind.

Shit.

One glimpse of her, and my body was already begging.
After I'd had her all night.
I inched up behind her and pressed myself flat to her back. I grasped the counter, her sweet little body pinned. My nose dove through the waves that spilled over her shoulders to the sweet spot just below

her ear. I inhaled the delicious coconut and the good and the girl.
"Fucking gorgeous," I whispered, because she really fucking was.

I could almost feel her blush, the heat rising from her skin as she
bit at her bottom lip to suppress her grin.

That thing that felt like joy lit in my chest, reminding me that I
really fucking was happy.

"Ahh . . . are you kidding me?" The obnoxious voice that could
only belong to Christopher broke through our moment. "Do I really
have to wake up to this bullshit every morning? That is my little sister,
you know." It was all tease, but I didn't miss the lingering remnant of
his distrust.

I just pulled my girl closer and tossed him a smirk. Fucker de-
served it. "Get used to it, man, 'cause I'm not going anywhere."

But even though I know that in the next book, Jared will have
returned to Aly, I also know he still has his demons and still
keeps them locked up tight. It is Aly who holds the key. She's the
one who makes him feel, the one who makes him realize he has to
face his past if he's to live a normal life. Face his family, really face
himself. But that past is one filled with shame and regret.

This is something he will struggle with in the new book. . . .

I stood outside the shitty, run-down house, shaking. Fucking
shaking.

What was I supposed to say when he answered the door? I guess
the better question was, what would he say to me? Chances were, he'd
tell me to go to straight to hell. Exactly where I deserved to be.

Warily, I raked a hand through my hair and glanced back at the
street, where Aly sat in the driver's seat of her car. The girl. Her face
was all soft and perfect and reminded me why I was doing this in the
first place. I had to do this for her. Had to do this for them.

Swallowing down the lump wedged in my throat, I turned back and forced myself to ring the doorbell.

In *Come to Me Softly*, Aleena is and will always be his rock, the only one who can hold the shattered pieces together. And Aleena and the baby will be what drives Jared to the places he'd always most feared.

I can see how she loves him in the next book. . . .

I wrapped myself around his back, my cheek pressed into his spine and my hands fastened around his stomach.

Jared released a weighted sigh. For the longest time, silence overtook us. We swam in it. Tension thickened in the crisp fall air.

I knew he was hurt. Those words had cut him deep. I'd wanted to shield him from them, protect him, but this was just another obstacle we had to face. All I could do was support him, hold him the way I was now, my touch a promise that I didn't believe the insinuations that had been spewed.

Finally, he spoke, the words a strained groan. "Fuck, Aly." Harshly, he shook his head. It seemed in surrender. "I knew I shouldn't have come here. I don't belong here. Your dad is right." He slumped farther forward in a blatant attempt to move away. "Every fucking word of it . . . he's right."

His pain pushed into my spirit, and I wound my arms tighter around him, unwilling to allow him to drive that distance between us. My voice came as a whisper as I begged at his back, "No, he's not. He doesn't know you, not the way I do. He's just surprised." I blinked into the darkness, trying to make sense of what had just gone down inside. "Shocked," I added. "There's a big difference."

Even though my voice lowered, my tone strengthened. "And even if he really believed what he said, it doesn't change anything." I hugged him closer, my cheek pressed flat against his shoulder blade. "Do you remember what I told you the night you came back? I love all of it, Jared. I love all of you. And what I think is what's important—not what he or anyone else thinks. It's just you and me. Nothing else matters."

Hesitation stilled him before he turned around to stand between my legs. His strong hand spread out against my still-flat belly, where our child grew. Blue eyes flamed as they locked on mine. "Just you and me and this."

Everything softened, the tension, the worry, the shame that had seethed through his veins.

It was Jared's own promise. An oath.

We wouldn't let any of this stand in our way.

"Just you and me and this," I promised back.

His gentle gaze slipped all over my face. A caress. "I love you, Aly Moore. You know that, don't you?"

I cupped his face. His fire burned my skin, the connection we shared greater than anything that should be possible. My head listed to the side, lost in his desperate expression. "Of course I know that."

I had known it long before he knew it himself.

In *Come to Me Softly*, Jared will finally be ready to face his past head-on.

When jealousy and secrets and dishonest intentions threaten Aly and their baby, Jared will be ready to stand up and become the man he has always wanted to be—even if he destroys himself along the way.

In the new book, you'll see Jared protect what is important to him. . . .

"What did he say to you?" Rage coiled in the pit of my stomach, bled free as a hiss from my mouth as I stormed the room.

Aly flinched, blinked, twisted her fingers in her hands. She choked over the words. "He didn't say anything. He was just standing there. Waiting. He knew where I was going, Jared. What does he want?"

It didn't matter what the fuck he wanted. I wasn't about to let him have it. No one would touch her. I'd die first.

I invite you to come visit my Web site at www.aljackson author.com to get an early peek at *Come to Me Softly.*

And look for the whole story when the book is published in the summer of 2014.

Thank you again for investing your time in me and my characters. I hope that you have enjoyed meeting them as much as I have and that you'll continue to join me as the hearts and lives of Jared and Aly are shaped in *Come to Me Softly.*

All the best,
A. L. Jackson